ALSO BY JUDITH A. BARRETT

Grid Down Survival Series

Maggie Sloan Thriller Series

Riley Malloy Thriller Series

Donut Lady Cozy Mystery Series

To Carol
You keep reading;
I'll keep writing!

# Danger in the Clouds

## Grid Down Survival

## Book 1

Judith A. Barrett

Judith A. Barrett

DANGER IN THE CLOUDS

GRID DOWN SURVIVAL SERIES, BOOK 1

Published in the United States of America by Wobbly Creek, LLC

2019 Florida

wobblycreek.com



Edited by Judith Euen Davis

Cover by Wobbly Creek, LLC·

ISBN 978-1-7322989-5-8

## CHAPTER ONE

While Major Dave Elliott rocked on the back porch of his old farmhouse and gazed at the blue sky, a feeling of dread washed over him. He frowned as he leaned to scratch his dog's ears. "Sometimes the loneliness drags me down, Shadow. I'm sure glad my son and his family will visit us next month. It's been too long."

The ringing phone interrupted their afternoon break. The retired Florida Highway Patrol officer stretched before he rose from his comfortable position and strode inside. His eyes widened. *Why would my son's law partner call me?*

"Major Elliott, I have sad news about Ted and Merilee. They were involved in a multi-vehicle crash on the interstate near their home and were killed, but thankfully, your granddaughter has only minor injuries. Ted was a close friend; I can't tell you how sorry I am."

Major frowned and shook his head, so he could focus on the lawyer's next words.

"You're the guardian for your seventeen-year-old granddaughter. I assume you know she has autism. I must tell you Aimee Louise is a brilliant, delightful young woman."

After he hung up, Major shuddered. *The one call no parent wants to receive.*

"How are we going to do this, Shadow? What do a couple of bachelors like us know about teenage girls?"

The young German shepherd leaned against Major's leg and laid his head on Major's knee.

"The last time I saw Aimee Louise, she was six years old. And Trish—" Major's voice cracked, and he rubbed his forehead. "Trish was still alive. Ted and his family visited us for two weeks that summer. Trish loved little Aimee Louise. They were something to see—the two of them were inseparable. Trish and I were excited when Ted called us about their next visit, but Trish died. After that—Ted said he couldn't—"

Major cleared his throat and scratched his dog's ears. "We need to get a room ready for Aimee Louise."

Shadow followed Major as he trudged up the stairs to the second story of his three-bedroom farmhouse. When Major opened the door to Ted's old bedroom, he sneezed. "Been a long time since we were in here. Let's open the windows and air out the room."

Major stripped the two single beds and carried the bedding downstairs then slumped against the washer. "This is all wrong. Trish should be doing this, and Ted should be coming here." He tossed the sheets into the machine and sobbed.

At day's end, Major collapsed onto his chair on the back porch, and Shadow flopped next to him. The sun lingered on the horizon, and the sky changed from pink to orange. When the darkness crept in, Major hesitated as he walked into the house. *How many new state trooper recruits did I train in my career? Hundreds, but I'm not ready for this.*

* * *

Major stood near the gate when Aimee Louise's plane landed. He strained to see her as each person came through the door from the plane, then he saw her. *I'd recognize those blue eyes anywhere.* Her eyes widened, and she froze in the doorway. *All the people crammed into the small Florida terminal have overwhelmed her.* The stream of passengers behind her jostled and bumped into her, and she covered her ears and clutched her backpack to her chest for protection, then she reached the wall.

Major pushed his way past the crowd as they rushed to the terminal then called out in his booming voice, "Aimee Louise."

Her voice was weak, but he heard her. "Pops?"

Major wore an olive drab T-shirt, faded blue jeans, and scuffed work boots and reached her in three strides. "I'm glad you're safe and here," he said.

While they waited for her luggage at the baggage claim, Major said, "Aimee Louise, did you know your blue eyes are the same color as Gram's? You're tall and lean like your dad, and your mama's hair was dark brown, almost black, like yours. I would have known you anywhere."

Aimee Louise gazed over his head. "You too, Pops. I would have known you anywhere."

As they walked to the truck, Aimee Louise said, "Florida is hot. I can feel the heat through my boots." Major nodded as she pulled up her sweatshirt hood to protect her neck from the hot sun.

"I found a close parking spot," Major said. "Today's warmer than usual for this time of year—must feel really warm to you. I hope you like dogs because Shadow couldn't wait to meet you. You aren't allergic or anything, are you?"

"Can't I get shots if I'm allergic?" She pulled and twisted her sweatshirt neckband. "I like dogs, but pets weren't allowed in the apartment."

Major lifted her suitcases into the bed of the white truck before he unlocked the doors. "I'd forgotten about the apartment rules. I left the engine on to run the air-conditioning for Shadow."

When Aimee Louise opened the passenger door, the gush of cold air and the strong dog odor startled her. She put out her hand for Shadow to smell, like Dad showed her. Shadow sniffed her hand, her arm, and her ear, and he sneaked in a tiny lick on her neck. Aimee Louise giggled because it tickled. After Shadow shifted to make room for her, she climbed into the truck. "I like dog smell," she said.

Shadow moved closer to Aimee Louise and put his head on her lap; She rubbed his ears and stroked his neck.

Major maneuvered through the airport parking lot and pointed at the Mickleton Airport sign. "This is our closest airport. It'll take us a little over an hour to get home. The farm is near the town of Plainview."

Aimee Louise stared at the passing fields and sides of the roads. "It's all sand. How could anything grow in sand?"

"It's not easy, but there are some crops that thrive here," Major said.

When they reached the outskirts of Plainview, Aimee Louise searched the horizon for tall buildings.

"This town is small. It looks like the entire town could fit into our subdivision in Cincinnati," she said.

Major chuckled. "I suspect you're right."

She gawked at the grocery store, the library, the Sheriff's Office, and the few shops. Major pointed out the hospital and, down the road from the hospital, Pete's Diner.

"The diner is where everybody goes for breakfast, coffee, and local news," he said.

Major returned to the middle of town and then continued to a county road. The road was asphalt, but it was narrow and didn't have much of a shoulder.

Aimee Louise tensed in preparation for a crash. "Is this road safe?"

She gripped the armrest with her right hand and wrapped her left arm around Shadow's neck. Shadow leaned on her, and she took a breath, exhaled, and relaxed.

After six miles, Major turned onto a gravel drive, the tires crunching as the truck bumped along. "In two miles, we'll turn onto a dirt road," he said.

After Major slowed his truck then turned, Aimee Louise said, "This isn't exactly a dirt road. It's a sand road with patches of whiter sand."

"This soft white sand is called sugar sand. Tires sink in and spin because they can't get traction," Major said. "I carry boards and a shovel in the back of the truck in case we get stuck."

"I'd call it snow sand because it looks like fluffy snow surrounded by brown sand," Aimee Louise said.

When they arrived at the two-story farmhouse with a metal roof and a spacious porch, her eyes widened. "Pops, where are the rest of the houses?"

Major chuckled. "Houses aren't as close in the country as they are in the city, are they? Our farm has lots of land around it."

A wooden fence surrounded the farm across the front, then on the side, wire fencing went into the woods. A wide metal gate was open at the driveway. The yard in front of the house was sand and grass, mostly sand, and beyond the yard were tall trees and trees with thick branches.

"Pops, this is almost looks like a campground. I always liked to go camping with Dad and Mama."

Major parked in a sandy spot next to the farmhouse. "This is a Florida cracker house—it was originally a square house, like an old-fashioned cracker box. I added rooms on the sides, a second floor, and the wraparound porch."

Major and Shadow escorted Aimee Louise inside. Major held his breath when she inhaled the distinctive pungency of the old farmhouse. *What would this house smell like to a young girl who has lived in a city apartment all her life?*

"Pops, Mama liked the apartment to smell like flowers. Dad said when he got his man cave it needed to have man odor. Now I know what he meant: doggy smell and no flowers."

Major smiled as he pointed to the left. "This is the living room, but I call it my computer room. On the other side of the hall is my bedroom."

Aimee Louise followed the hall to the family room and breathed in the smell of the fireplace, and Major frowned. *Does she hate the lingering odor of coals and creosote on the firebox?*

"Pops, can I lay the fire? I always cleaned out the ashes and set up the kindling and firewood at home."

"I think that would be great. It will be nice to share some of the chores around here."

The long, wooden dining table served as a divider between the family room and the big kitchen. "I thought stoves were supposed to be electric; your stove is huge and looks like an antique."

Major chuckled. "It's a gas stove. I have a large propane tank behind the house. Gram always loved her gas stove, and when your mama came to visit, she loved to cook on it too. Your dad always talked about building a house out in the country, and your mama would always remind him that she needed a big oversized gas stove with two ovens."

The kitchen door led outside to a substantial back porch lined with five wooden rocking chairs. Aimee Louise picked the middle one and rocked.

"Is this where you sit to watch the sunset? Now I know why Mama said she wanted a porch with rocking chairs."

"Ready to see the upstairs?" Major asked.

Aimee Louise patted the wide arm of the chair and rose to go inside. "I'll be back, chair."

They climbed the stairs to the second-floor bedrooms and bathroom, and Shadow followed Aimee Louise. Major pointed to a spacious bedroom on the left.

"This was your dad's room. It isn't fancy, but we can paint the walls or change whatever you like, or you can have the other bedroom. It's smaller, but we can fix it up for you. Whatever you want. We can do it." Major furrowed his brow as he watched Aimee Louise.

Aimee Louise looked around the room. She sat at the old wooden desk and ran her fingers over an airplane carved into the desktop.

"Did Dad carve this when he was a kid? It looks like the plane that brought me here." Aimee Louise peered over Major's head. "Dad left me an airplane, didn't he? Thank you, Dad."

A braided rug in the middle of the wooden floor dominated the room. Aimee Louise knelt to rub the dark floorboards. "Smooth and silky."

She lay down on the twin bed next to the window and put her face into the worn, handmade quilt and inhaled its aroma. "The quilt smells like *comfy*, and I love that it is so soft and different shades of blue."

Major stood in the doorway. "My mother made the quilt for your dad when he was only five or six years old. She said it was a Cloud Nine pattern. We can get you a new bedspread for the bed if you like."

"Dad said you made the twin beds; they looked like they belonged in an old Western movie."

Aimee Louise reached up and ran her fingers along the smooth wagon wheel curve of the wood headboard. The low footboard and sideboards were barn planks. She rolled over and peered through the bare window. The blue sky with puffy clouds welcomed her.

"I don't need any changes because this room is perfect for me; it's mine."

"Your mama told me once that when you couldn't find the right words in all your thoughts, you would say I'm good or I'm fine."

"I'm good," Aimee Louise said.

Major chuckled and waited while Aimee Louise explored the room. Shadow lay on the rug and watched her as she put her plush rabbit on the bed.

"Soft Bunny has been with me for as long as I can remember," she said.

"Gram gave you Soft Bunny when you were three," Major said softly.

Aimee Louise hugged her rabbit. "Gram gave you to me; I always knew you were special."

Major followed her and Shadow to the porch as they dashed down the stairs.

When he reached the porch, he asked, "Like a tour of the farm?"

They started with the well and pump behind the house.

"Our water comes from an underground spring. If the town water system broke down, we'd still have water."

"Can water from the ground be safe?"

Major said, "Our water is as safe as city water, maybe safer. Our water doesn't go through miles of underground pipes."

"I need to read about well water," Aimee Louise said.

"I think that's smart. The tall trees around the house," he swept his arm in a wide arc, "are longleaf pines, and the trees with spreading branches are oaks."

When they reached the chicken coops, Pops said, "Three might seem like a lot of coops, but it takes a while for older chickens to adjust to younger chickens. We have three different ages of chickens—older hens, teenagers, and babies. Two of the coops have roosters. No roosters in the baby coop unless one of the babies is a rooster. We won't know until one crows."

Major opened the door to one of the coops. Aimee Louise peeked in. Her nose twitched, and she sneezed at the smell of the straw in the nest boxes, the pine shavings on the floor, and the poop in the bins under the roosts. Major smiled. *At least the smell didn't make her sick to her stomach.*

The chickens cooed and clucked while they scratched in the leaves.

"I like chickens; it sounds like they are speaking their own language," Aimee Louise said. "Do you suppose I can learn to understand them?"

"Pawwwp," the chickens said, and Aimee Louise laughed.

"Are they talking to me or about me?" Major asked.

"I'll have to think about it," she said.

As they walked past the barn, Major said, "I'd like to get some goats someday."

When they reached the equipment shed, Aimee Louise climbed up onto the tractor and wrapped her hands around the metal steering wheel.

"I want to drive the tractor someday."

"We can certainly make that happen. The farm is big, but most of it is woods—oak trees, pine trees, and underbrush. A lot of wildlife live here. Your Gram wanted a place with wildlife. National Forest surrounds most of the farm."

Aimee Louise scanned the area. "This is where old-time pioneers walked."

"You're right." He waved toward the west. "That way is the power-line easement. It runs parallel to our property line, and beyond the easement is another state road. The house we passed when we turned onto the dirt road is the Gastons'. They're our nearest neighbors."

When Shadow stood next to Aimee Louise, she reached down and scratched his ears.

"There aren't any houses nearby, and that's a little scary, but I'm safe with you and Shadow," Aimee Louise said.

"You certainly are, and I'm glad you know that."

Toward the end of the day, Major prepared supper. "Would you like to set the table?" He pointed. "The plates are in that cupboard, and silverware is in this drawer."

After they ate, Major asked, "Ready for some rocking chair time?"

The three of them settled down on the back porch as the sky turned from pink and orange to the muted gray of dusk.

Major rocked in his chair. "Hear the cicadas? This light breeze keeps the mosquitos away. Air's still muggy, though."

Aimee Louise matched his rocking pace. "Mama said I don't do well with conversations, but I talk a lot about things I like or know really well."

Major chuckled. "I'm not all that great at conversations either. I talk about Shadow, the farm, and the weather; just like you said: things I like and know really well."

Aimee Louise gazed over his head. "Dad would want me to tell you about clouds. You have a strong cloud."

She leaned back in her rocking chair and took a deep breath while Major waited. She rocked forward and gazed at Shadow.

"I don't see people's faces—no eyes, no noses, and no mouths. When people say a dog is smiling, I see the dog's teeth and its tongue hanging out, so when I was in second grade, I guessed people would smile like dogs do. You know, show their teeth and hang out their tongues. I tried it once, but it felt weird; my friend said it was a good silly face, but it wasn't a smile."

Major nodded as he slowed his rocking.

"Because of the autism, my brain isn't wired like other people's. Mama said I have a gift. People have clouds, and I see them. The clouds kind of hide their faces. There are different kinds of clouds. Happy, strong, caring." Aimee Louise sighed.

Shadow rested his chin on her knee, and she scratched his ears. "People don't always act like their clouds. I've seen sad clouds on people who were laughing and saying happy things. I used to be confused, but I learned the clouds are true and not fake because Mama said people can fake talk."

Aimee Louise rocked in her chair and gazed at the sky. "I can see farther in Florida. There are no tall buildings in the way."

Major cleared his throat. "I think your mama was right—your clouds are a gift. Thank you for telling me about them."

"I like to hear about Shadow and the farm."

"Good. Then I'll talk about Shadow and the farm when I feel like talking, and you can talk about whatever you want when you feel like talking."

Aimee Louise nodded.

Major continued, "It might take me a while to understand the clouds, but that's okay. We've got time."

After the mosquitos chased them into the house, the electricity suddenly went off, and it was dark.

"Are you okay, Aimee Louise? Give me a minute, and I'll light a lantern. I keep one on the fireplace mantle, so I can find it easily."

"I'm good."

After Major lit the lantern, he said, "We don't lose our electricity very often, but I'd like to be more prepared than I am. Maybe you can help me with that. I've been meaning to set up the well with solar, but I just haven't done it yet. I do have a large fuel tank for the tractors and my farm truck to get around the property and for my generators in case we lose electricity for an extended period, but there are a lot of other things that I could do that I just haven't done."

"We lost our electricity for three days once at the apartment during a bad snow storm. We had our fireplace for heat, but Mama didn't really know how to cook on a fireplace. The elevator didn't work, so Dad used the stairs when he went to the store to get food, but when he came home, he told us the shelves were empty. Mama and I stayed in the apartment. After the lights came back on, Mama told him she didn't want to do that again, and that's when they talked about building a house in the country."

"Your dad told me he really liked his job, but he didn't care for living in the city."

"Pops, Dad always told me that I would like living on a farm, but I'm worried about school." Aimee Louise pulled at her shirt neckband.

The lights flickered then came on a little before bedtime, and Major extinguished the lantern.

"What if the electricity doesn't come back on for a long time?" Aimee Louise asked.

"Hadn't thought about that in a long time; your gram was the best planner I ever knew; I guess we need to plan more like she would."

## CHAPTER TWO

Major woke early the next morning and fretted about Aimee Louise and school while he fried bacon for their breakfast. When Aimee Louise bounded down the stairs and into the kitchen, she was dressed in her jeans and her blue sweatshirt; she stopped to scratch Shadow.

"Pops, I can see the sun come up from my bedroom window. I like the Florida sunrise; My first morning in Florida officially began when the daylight popped out of the darkness."

"I've got eggs with yolks that are as golden as the sun. One or two eggs?'

"Two, please."

They ate breakfast in silence, and Major smiled. *Trish never liked a lot of chatter during meals either.*

After breakfast, Major said, "There's a school bus that you can take to school that would come here if we asked, or you could catch it at the Gastons' house, but this morning, Shadow and I will take you to school then pick you up. We can talk about the school bus later."

* * *

When she entered the school, Aimee Louise focused on the tiled floor and her feet in her effort to avoid touching anyone and to shut out the overpowering odor of teenage bodies and the roar of unintelligible conversations as she maneuvered her way to her English class. She paused to maneuver around a cluster of girls who had gathered in the hallway and blocked the classroom doorway. One of the girls grabbed Aimee Louise's arm as she sidled past them. "Hey, new girl. Why don't you talk to anyone? Do ya hate school or something?"

Aimee Louise flinched at the rough touch and jerked her arm away before she continued to her desk.

One of the other girls said, "Cheryl, you gonna let her walk away like that?"

After Aimee Louise hung her backpack on the back of her chair and sat, Cheryl marched to Aimee Louise's desk. "Well, I know I hate school, and I can't stand to get up in the morning while it's still dark, and I'm not too stuck-up to talk to people."

Cheryl slammed her books on Aimee Louise's desk and planted her hands on the desktop. When she leaned over Aimee Louise, her group murmured in admiration.

"I like mornings," Aimee Louise said. "The sun pushes away the dark."

Cheryl sneered. "Did you hear that, ladies? New girl talks. She likes mornings. And the sun." She leaned closer to Aimee Louise's face.

*Interesting, her breath smells like chocolaty cereal, bubblegum toothpaste, and cigarette smoke. Angry cloud with an edge of sadness.*

"Well, *Sunny*, no one else is a morning person here. Anyone? Morning person?"

Her group shook their heads. The rest of the class ignored her.

"We'll call you *Sunny*. Sunny Sunshine. Yep, that's it. New girl is Sunny." Cheryl smirked as her group laughed.

Aimee Louise examined the small band of girls. *Some clouds are angry, some are lonely, others are frightened.*

When the teacher came into the classroom, Cheryl's followers scrambled to their seats.

"Something I need to know about?" the teacher glanced at the fleeing girls and Cheryl, who snatched up her books from Aimee Louise's desk.

"We were getting better acquainted with our new friend, Sunny." Cheryl strolled to her seat. "Tried to make her feel welcome."

The teacher narrowed her eyes and tapped her finger on the open book on her desk. "I'm sure you did; let's focus on English."

* * *

Major and Shadow went to Pete's Diner after they dropped off Aimee Louise.

While Major sat at the counter and sipped his coffee with Shadow at his feet, Pete asked, "How are you doing so far?"

"I don't know; I'm worried about Aimee Louise and school."

Pete refilled Major's cup and poured one for himself. "Adjusting to a new school is tough enough, but high school is particularly brutal. You have any spies that can keep an eye on her? I have a feeling her guardian angel will be working overtime today and wouldn't mind the extra help."

Major nodded. "That's a good idea. I've got a couple of kindhearted souls in mind."

* * *

The following week, the math teacher asked, "Sunny, can you explain how to solve question four?"

Aimee Louise had her elbows on the desk, her head down, and her hands over her ears to shut out the ongoing classroom whispers so she could focus on question four.

The teacher stepped closer to Aimee Louise and raised her voice as she tapped on her desk. "I asked you a question, Sunny. Can you explain how to solve question four?"

Aimee Louise thought about the different ways to answer question four: three ways—six, if each step had to be explained. *Which one do I pick? Is there a right answer?* Aimee Louise frowned as she inhaled then glanced at the floor. *Teacher smells like coffee with a whiff of body odor, and her right shoe shows heavy scuff marks on the toe.*

"Okay, I guess you can't. Cheryl, can you answer?"

Cheryl said, "Well, I started with—"

Aimee Louise cleared her throat. "My name is Aimee Louise."

"Excuse me, Sunny," the teacher said. "You had your turn to speak. Now it's Cheryl's turn."

Aimee Louise nodded. *New rule. No talking at school.*

"It's okay, Sunny." Cheryl turned her head toward her friends and snorted. "I'll help you later if you like."

The teacher frowned. "That's enough, Cheryl. Back to question four."

On the way to the next class, three girls came up behind Aimee Louise and pushed her into a wall. One of them said, "Oh, sorry. Dark pushed Sunny." They giggled as they scurried past her.

Aimee Louise picked up her books that she had dropped then gazed at the girls who disappeared into the hallway crowd. *The three-banded armadillo rolls itself up as protection against predators. I can be three-banded.*

Aimee Louise heard stealthy footsteps behind her. When a hand reached toward her, Aimee Louise instinctively pulled her elbow against her ribs as she sidestepped to see who it was. Cheryl sneered as she slammed herself into a locker and slid to the ground.

"New girl pushed me," she wailed. Two teachers rushed to the fallen girl, and the math teacher said, "Come with me, Sunny. We're going to the office."

While she waited outside the assistant principal's office at the end of the week, a school aide sat next to her. "Aimee Louise, I don't think your new plan to wait until no one was in the hallways before you go to class worked. That's what you've been doing, isn't it? Cheryl and her friends are laughing that you've been a regular in detention. Are they targeting you? I'll give your grandfather a call, but you'll need to talk to him."

Aimee Louise glanced at the school aide. *Kindness cloud*

"Again, Sunny?" The assistant principal shook her head. "Detention."

That evening Major said, "A friend of mine who works at the school called me about your detentions and told me the school has a bullying problem. Is school a problem for you?"

Aimee Louise thought about being pushed and being blamed for pushing, being late for class, the noise and crowds, angry teachers, no friends, and getting lost in the maze of hallways. "Yes."

"I'll take you to school tomorrow and talk to the principal."

* * *

The next morning, Shadow trotted to the truck behind Aimee Louise.

"Sorry, boy," Major said. "You'll need to stay home today. I'm going to drop Aimee Louise off at school before I drop by to see Pete at the diner; he said he wants my opinion on something."

Shadow returned to the shade of the porch and flopped down.

After Major accompanied Aimee Louise to her first class, he strode to the principal's office.

"You here about Aimee Louise, Major?" The principal motioned toward the visitor's chair in his office. "I hear she's been quite a problem; I'll bet she's been a handful at home too."

Major stepped into the office but remained standing; he narrowed his eyes, and his voice was cold. "She's having trouble getting used to this larger school. Maybe we can come up with some ideas to help her adjust."

"Let me see what's going on." The principal stepped to the file cabinet and pulled out a folder. He glanced through the papers and frowned. "Major, I didn't realize she's had six detentions this week for arriving late to class. I wonder if she's getting lost. We'll get her a map to help her find her routes. Do you think that will help?"

The principal pointed to a page in her folder. "One of the teachers mentioned that Aimee Louise waits until everyone clears the room and hallway before she leaves for her next class. She's obviously trying to avoid the rush out of the classroom and the crush in the halls.

Pops frowned. "She waits until everyone leaves? My experience as a cop indicates that's a behavior to avoid being bullied. You have anything like that going on around here?"

The principal's face reddened. "Of course not. We don't allow bullying in our school at all. We received a grant this year because of the success of our anti-bullying program."

Pops crossed his arms and scowled. "Let me know immediately if she's assigned to detention again, and you might want to be sure you're using your grant wisely. If you need a professional assessment of the compliance of your program to the grant requirements, I know some good people. There's no shame in improvement."

When Major parked at Pete's Diner, he saw his neighbor, Russell Gaston, head to the diner door. Russell wore a white, short-sleeved shirt and tie. Russell had spent his boyhood in Plainview and returned four years ago as the Operations Manager for Southeastern Electric.

Major shook his head and smiled. *Only Russell runs errands in office attire. Even as a kid, he always wanted to dress nice. Only four-year-old I ever knew that always wore a suit to church.*

Major walked in as Russell was hailed from the circular booth unofficially reserved for the locals who met at Pete's. "Hey there, Russell. Haven't seen you in a while. Join us. We were talking about the psycho county commissioners. Heard the latest?"

Pete motioned for Major to sit at the far end of the counter away from the booth. "Major, I've got something I'd like for you to look at. Be right back."

He picked up the coffee Pete had poured for him and leaned against the counter while he scanned the room as Russell made his way to the booth in the back of the diner.

The old men scooted around to make room for Russell. As he slid in, he leaned down and the vapor from the hot coffee steamed up his glasses.

"One of us now. Blind leading the blind." The farmer next to Russell elbowed him with a grin, and Russell chuckled.

The man across from Russell slurped his coffee. "They made big reversals in the county zoning and land taxation. Huge loss of revenue for the county and doesn't benefit anybody but a new out-of-state land developer."

"Town council gave the same yahoos incentives to build an apartment complex.The council bought into the phony claim it's good for the town because it means more jobs," another man said, "but the jobs are mostly construction—temporary. And I heard yesterday they'll bring in their own people for the work."

The farmer scooted the cream pitcher over to Russell. "Yep, and I heard they got a big government loan. I wonder who they'll find to rent all those fancy apartments. We about to have a population explosion I didn't know about?"

"Been meaning to ask you, Russell." The man across from him set his empty cup close to the edge of the table for a refill. "I read some big city out west had a huge power failure, and thousands of people were without power for four days. Could that happen here?"

"It could, but it's unlikely," Russell said. "Our smaller power systems are easier to manage, and if ours had a failure, we could connect with one of our other smaller systems for power until ours was repaired or whatever was needed."

The farmer next to Russell nodded. "That must be why my brother's farm north of here was out of power for only thirty minutes while the big city north of him was out for seven hours."

While the old men continued their conversation, Pete returned and handed Major a paper with a land listing. "I've got an option to buy this property. What do you think?"

Major read the description. "Hunting land? Looks like a good piece of property. Nice that it backs onto the national forest. Might want to check a flood map with the creek so close, but that's the only thing I can think of."

Russell excused himself and rushed out of the diner.

"He was always in a hurry even when he was a kid," the farmer said. The rest of the men nodded.

"I need to head home too," Major said. "Hope that property works out for you, Pete."

* * *

That evening, Major asked, "Did things improve at school?"

Aimee Louise thought about no more pushing, teachers not so angry, still noisy, and still no friends.

*Went from one hundred percent to fifty percent awful.*

"Yes."

## CHAPTER THREE

Russell rushed into his house, unlocked his desk drawer, and flipped through the papers he'd mailed to a company at his stepbrother's request: names, addresses, home phone numbers, and spouse names of the county commissioners and members of the town council.

He researched the company on his computer and discovered it was a paper entity—no history. A search of the officers referred to the company, nothing else. He called his stepbrother, but Lee didn't answer, and his voicemail was full. Russell's stomach churned.

*I should have been more suspicious. Lee was always getting into trouble, but he never dragged me in before now. Why would I need to give anyone public record information? And I sent it to them and signed it—like I was a part of whatever this is. Wonder if I should talk to the sheriff?*

His wife interrupted him at sunset. "You've been working on your computer all day. Come to the table. Dinner's ready."

"Just a few—"

"Russell, we'd enjoy your company."

He tore himself away from his computer and bolted down his food then returned to his office and closed the door.

Margo tapped on the door, and Russell glanced at the clock as the door opened. *Almost ten.*

"The children are ready for bed. Can you say goodnight?"

He rubbed his eyes and stretched. "Yes. I need to tell my little Floridians goodnight."

Margo chuckled. "Would you believe we've been here four years? I was so worried about a small town in Florida accepting us, and now our Michigan-born children complain when it's cold."

Russell closed his laptop, kissed his wife as he hurried past her, and bounded up the stairs.

* * *

Two weeks later, Russell's office phone rang, and the caller ID showed *Private Caller.* "Gaston," a distorted voice said, "the Board needs your cooperation. You need to keep this quiet. We have your brother. We don't want to hurt him. We just need your help with a few things."

The next day, Russell got a box in the mail with Lee's old baseball glove in it. The thumb of the glove had been roughly cut away, and an included note read: *Memento for you.* Russell shuddered.

The person with the distorted voice called again. "Did you get the box? Thought you'd appreciate a little preview. The Board needs schematics."

Russell cleared his throat. "You know you can get the schematics on the internet or any Electrical Engineering 101 textbook."

"We need it from you. Don't make me repeat myself."

When Russell went to bed, he stared at the ceiling. After two hours of shifting from his left side to his right and back again, he eased out of bed then paused and listened to his wife's breathing. *Still asleep.* He tiptoed downstairs and sat in his recliner in the dark family room.

*Whatever happens, my priority is my family.*

He sent the schematics to the email address the voice had given him. *If I talk to the sheriff about a hypothetical situation, how do I phrase it?* He made a pot of coffee then sat in his chair and sipped coffee the rest of the night.

The next morning, he strolled into the Sheriff's Office. "Can we talk privately, Sheriff?"

"Sure thing, Russell. Let's go into my inner office."

While the sheriff closed the door behind them, Russell scanned the office. *Wait. These people are smart. What if they bugged the Sheriff's Office?*

The sheriff sat at his cluttered desk and cleared a section to set down his coffee cup. "Do you want some coffee? What's on your mind?"

"I've had my day's quota of coffee. The town spring festival is in a couple of months. Wanted your opinion on my staff doing some demonstrations to get kids interested in science." Russell chuckled. "I know it's not ever been done before."

The sheriff laughed. "You're right. It hasn't been done before, and there's a certain reluctance to new things around here. I think it's a great idea, so you have my support. I suggest the best person for you to talk to would be Pete, at the diner. He'll help you, and I'll help however I can. Let me know."

Russell was disheartened but not surprised when the next call issued a warning.

"Careful what you say to the sheriff, Gaston. We're everywhere."

Subsequent calls demanded confidential files and passwords. Russell's step slowed, and he slumped at his desk.*The escalating level of these threats against my wife and children is dragging me down.*

After two weeks of sleepless nights, Russell gazed in the mirror as he brushed his teeth. "Face it. This is not going to end well. Whoever this board is, I know too much."

"How'd you sleep last night?" Margo asked while she cooked breakfast.

Russell cleared his throat. "Oh, you know. I was a little restless. There are a lot of things going on at work, but I'm fine."

Her back stiffened.

*She doesn't believe me.*

The next night he walked to the road and around the house to clear his head. *I need to do something. Anything would be better than nothing, which is what I do when I sit in my chair all night and worry.*

He powered up his computer and documented everything they had asked him to provide. Over the next few weeks, he contacted his peers in the industry and not only uncovered the collection of additional related data but also traced the destination for the information.

*It feels good to put my research and analytical skills to work.*

He pressed on at an almost maniacal pace, consumed by the compulsion to untangle the sinister web and its implications.

After three weeks, he leaned back in his chair and stared at his computer. "I wouldn't believe it myself if I didn't have this paper trail to back up all my findings. I might not live to see it, but you're going down, Board."

He copied everything from his laptop to two thumb drives, wiped his computer, sold it, and bought a new laptop.

Late the next night, Russell sat in his home office. The glow of the computer screen was the only light in the room. He inserted the thumb drive and read through all his documents, even though he had them memorized. He wiped away the sweat dripping down his face, but he couldn't wipe away the dread. His hand trembled.

*Indisputable. But when I think about the people who are involved, where can I turn? Maybe Major? No, I'd bring him and his family into this circle of terror. These people are too high up, and they're everywhere.*

He slammed his fist on his desk.

*It's like I walked into a room and turned on a light, and the cockroaches didn't even bother to run. State and federal government agencies, law enforcement, judges—all are involved. I'm a dead man. All I can do is save my family.*

Russell placed his head on his arms and sobbed.

The next morning, Russell met with one of his most trusted childhood friends. "I have a USB flash drive I need to be kept safe for a while. It's highly confidential, and I know you understand confidentiality. I'm taking my family on a short vacation. See you when we return."

Russell called his stepbrother again and was surprised when Lee answered.

"Lee, we need to talk."

"Sure. Anytime. Got some work stuff going on right now, though. Can I get back to you? Say hello to your wife for me."

Lee hung up. Russell called back. No answer.

*God, help me save my family.*

## CHAPTER FOUR

Margo Gaston knocked on the Teagues' front door and bit her lip as she waited for Jolene to answer. *Might as well answer the door, Jolene; I'm not going away.*

Margo held her breath then exhaled when she heard movement inside the house. Without opening the door, Jolene said, "Now's not a good time, Margo. I'm not really dressed for visitors, and the house is a mess."

"That's okay; I'm your friend, not the white glove home inspector, so you don't have to worry about a little dust and clutter. I'm wearing my old jeans not a skirt, so I'm definitely not dressed to be a visitor."

"I don't know..."

"It's cold out here; can I come in to argue with you, please?" Margo asked. *Wonder if I stepped over a line there.*

Jolene cough was wet as she cracked open the door. "Margo, I never knew before what a pest you are; come on in."

Jolene stumbled to the sofa then sunk into her seat. "Wore myself out getting to the door."

"I stopped at the bakery and bought vanilla scones. Shall I make some coffee?" Margo asked.

"I don't suppose you'll take no for an answer, so suit yourself."

Margo smiled as she hurried to the kitchen then her brow furrowed at the dirty dishes on the table and piled in the sink.

"I'll get the coffee going then straighten up in here a little while it perks."

"Fine," Jolene mumbled.

Margo found the garbage sacks under the sink and quickly scraped the food on the plates into a sack then rinsed the dishes, loaded the dishwasher, and started the machine. She found a bottle of cleaning spray in the pantry; she sprayed and wiped down the counters and the table before the coffee was ready. She pulled out two coffee cups and two small plates from the cupboard that were relatively clean and rinsed them out.

"Coffee's ready. What do you like in your coffee?"

"Plain is fine," Jolene said.

Margo carried the coffee and plates into the living room; she cleared dirty clothes from a chair then set Jolene's cup on top of magazines on the table in front of the sofa.

"I'd forgotten what a steamroller you are." Jolene's smile was weak.

Margo chuckled. "It's my best skill."

When Margo picked up the bakery sack, Jolene said, "I can't eat anything."

Margo put the two scones on the plates and broke one scone in half. "Maybe after you've had a little coffee you can try a bite."

Jolene picked up her cup with two hands and held it close to her chest. "I've been so cold lately; this feels good."

"How long have you been sick?" Margo sipped her coffee then pinched off a bite of her scone. "Mmm, this is good."

"I'm not really sick; I'm just so tired all the time. Marty says I need to take my vitamins."

Margo waved her hand. "Ha, he's a husband and a doctor; what does he know?"

Another coughing spell interrupted Jolene's chuckle. When she caught her breath, her mouth twitched a smile. "That's a funny thing for a pharmacist to say."

"It's true; it's like the old saying about the cobbler's children and shoes. Marty's an outstanding emergency department doctor; an internal medicine specialist is more experienced at diagnosing ongoing medical problems. I love the new doctor here; she's been practicing women's health medicine for fifteen years and always takes the time to listen to me. Let me know when you have an appointment; I'll be happy to drive you."

Jolene rolled her eyes as she pinched a piece of her scone then put it into her mouth. "Mmm. It is good. You're so subtle."

"Subtle steamroller." Margo smiled. "I like it."

After Jolene ate almost half her scone and drank her coffee, she put her head on her pillow, and Margo pulled her blanket over her.

"I'll just rest my eyes for a bit," Jolene mumbled.

Margo finished her scone and coffee then gathered up the dirty clothes in the living room and the towels from the downstairs bathroom and tossed them into the washer. After she started the machine, she swept and mopped the kitchen then cleared and dusted the coffee table and stacked the magazines on a bookcase. When the washer finished, she threw the clothes into the dryer then swept the living room.

She put her trash sack and the one from under the sink by the front door then put a fresh trash sack into the trashcan.

Margo sighed as she gazed at the sleeping Jolene. *You're so sick, honey. I wish I could do more.*

When Jolene woke later that afternoon, her eyes welled up then the tears ran down her cheek. *Margo is such a good friend. It's so relaxing with the clutter gone.* Jolene made her way to the kitchen and smiled. *Even the kitchen is sparkling; I think I'll have a sandwich and take a shower.*

* * *

The next morning, Jolene woke before Rosalie was awake. She quickly dressed in her blue church dress then gazed down and frowned at her once formfitting dress that hung from her bony shoulders. *I didn't realize how much weight I've lost.*

She pulled out a pot and the box of oatmeal then smiled as she heard Rosalie creeping down the stairs.

"Mom, you're wearing your favorite dress. Are we going somewhere?"

Jolene turned and smiled at her sixteen-year-old daughter. "Well, I don't know, honey; do you plan to stand around all day or get dressed for church? Oatmeal's almost ready."

"Mom, Your smile is the most beautiful smile in the world."

Rosalie dashed upstairs; when she returned to the kitchen, Jolene laughed.

"You're wearing your red dress. That's my favorite of all your dresses. Let's eat."

While they ate breakfast, Jolene said, "Rosalie, you are my 'mini-me' with your bright red hair and green eyes, and we're both short and slender. You know my friends used to call you J.J. for Jolene Junior."

"I didn't know that. When did your friends call me J.J.?"

"When you were three. You were as sassy then as you are now. You got it from me."

After they arrived at the church, they sat near the front in their favorite pew. Jolene put her arm around Rosalie and pulled her close. Rosalie closed her eyes and inhaled then whispered, "Mom, I love your sweet fragrance of vanilla and raspberries."

The service began with a hymn, and Jolene sang alto in harmony with Rosalie's clear soprano voice. Jolene smiled at the scuffling noises of the older women behind them that were jostling one another to be close enough to hear Rosalie sing.

The choir director joined Rosalie and Jolene after the service. "I was tickled by the competition in the pews to sit close to the two of you. Did you notice? Rosalie, what do you think about singing in the choir? Or maybe a solo at Christmas? I'd love for you to sing 'Do You Hear What I Hear?' It's perfect for you."

Jolene said, "Oh, no. Rosalie needs to focus on her—"

Jolene gazed at Rosalie and cleared her throat. "Could certainly be a possibility. It's up to Rosalie, of course."

Rosalie's face lit up, and the choir director beamed as she squeezed Rosalie's hand. "Sounds wonderful. We'll talk more, Rosalie."

The choir director hugged Jolene and whispered, "Let me know how I can help."

When they got home, Jolene said, "Thank you for going to church with me. It was wonderful to sing with you again, but I wore myself out."

The next day, Jolene woke when Rosalie came into the house after school.

Jolene rubbed her forehead when Rosalie asked, "Can I tell you what happened today at school?"

"I'm really sorry, honey. Today's not a good day for me." Jolene rolled over to hide her tears of pain.

Before Rosalie went upstairs for bed that evening, she sat on the sofa next to Jolene.

"Mom, nights are the worst for me because I'm alone upstairs, and you're alone down here."

*I wish I was strong enough to do something for my daughter.* "I'm so sorry, honey. Maybe I'll be better soon."

Jolene held Rosalie and hummed an old lullaby she used to sing to her baby daughter, and Rosalie relaxed. After Jolene ended the tune, Rosalie said, "Thanks, Mom; that helped."

A little after midnight, the scrape of a door key downstairs woke Jolene. *Marty comes home in the middle of the night then leaves before anyone else gets up. I wonder if he's slipped back into his old habits. I need to protect Rosalie.*

* * *

Jolene woke early the next morning when Marty tapped his fingers on the kitchen counter while the coffee maker gurgled. She tried to rise when she heard Rosalie scramble down the stairs, but she was too weak.

Rosalie cleared her throat. "You know, Dad, sometimes I don't see you for weeks. Where do you sleep when you don't come home?"

Marty snapped at her. "It's not your business, but when the night shift runs over, I grab a nap at the hospital before my next shift."

Rosalie continued, "It is my business. I'm worried about Mom."

Marty opened a cabinet door, slammed it, and opened another. "Is something wrong? Is she sick?"

"She must be sick; I know she's more than tired," Rosalie said.

"Doesn't sound like much to me. She gets tired if she doesn't take her vitamins. Well, I have to run; I'm late. Tell her I said to be sure to take her vitamins."

When Rosalie raised her voice, Jolene pushed herself to a sitting position and fought the nausea.

"You need to be here," Rosalie shouted. "You need to check her yourself."

Mary banged his cup on the counter and growled, "You're not a doctor. Gotta run."

"I never said I was—"

Marty slammed the door as he left, and the coffee maker beeped to signal the end of the brewing cycle.

When Jolene heard Rosalie sobbing, she called out in a weak voice, "Rosalie."

Rosalie stumbled into the living room and dropped onto the sofa next to Jolene, who wrapped her frail arms around her daughter, and they sobbed together.

"I'm so sorry, honey; this is so awful for you."

Rosalie sniffed. "I just don't know how to help."

"I understand. Neither one of us can fix your dad because he has his own problems that only he can fix. We know I need more than vitamins. I'll work on that, and I'll work on making things better for you. Go to school and work hard. I'll rest this morning, so I'll have some energy this afternoon. I just need to be stronger."

Jolene hugged Rosalie, then Rosalie grabbed her backpack and left.

* * *

As she ran to school, Rosalie tried to dodge the young boy on his bicycle as he careened down a driveway, but the bike's front wheel struck her knee. After the handlebars slammed into Rosalie's ribs, the force of the bike knocked her across the sidewalk onto the curb.

She lay on the ground, trying to catch her breath. *Ugh. Kicked to the curb. Not funny.*

The bicycle flipped toward the lawn and dumped the boy onto the wet grass. The boy removed his superhero helmet. He was red-faced, and tears streaked down his cheeks.

He rubbed his elbow and sniffled. "I couldn't stop."

Rosalie splinted her ribs with her hands as she got up. "I know. Don't worry, Champ. It's okay."

The boy's mother ran to Rosalie. "Is that blood on your jeans? I can call your parents. What's your number?"

"I'm fine. Got a little bump on my knee," Rosalie said. "I'll be okay."

"If you're sure." The mother turned to her son. "You need to come inside, Logan. We have to change your clothes. You've got grass stains on your new pants."

Rosalie waited until the boy and his mother went inside before she limped away. She broke out in a sweat in her efforts to avoid putting any weight on her right knee without further aggravating the pain in her left hip from landing on the concrete. To ease the pain in her ribs, she bent her arm and held it tight against her chest.

*Breathe. Take it slow and easy.*

When Rosalie reached school, a small group of girls stood near the front steps.

"What's wrong with you?" Cheryl said. "Trying to get out of a math test? You write with your hand, not with your foot."

The group howled with laughter, and Rosalie glared as she struggled up the steps to school. "Ha ha, very funny."

Later, when Rosalie hobbled to the cafeteria down an almost-empty hallway, her focus was on the throb of her swollen knee, the pain in her hip, and the ache in her ribs.

A sudden push to her back threw her off-balance, and she collapsed onto the hard tile floor. Rosalie looked up in time to see a group of girls scatter. She remained on the floor and closed her eyes as she worked on breathing through the pain.

*Where's a kid careening on his bicycle when you really need one? Coulda bowled them all down for me, Logan.*

Someone sat down on the floor next to her. "I am Aimee Louise. What do you know about armadillos?"

Rosalie opened her eyes. Everybody in school knew Aimee Louise didn't talk. Rosalie squinted to examine Aimee Louise's face and switched her gaze back to the floor.

She matched Aimee Louise's intonation. "I am Rosalie. I would like to hear about armadillos."

"Well, Friend, only one kind of armadillo can roll up into a ball to protect itself from predators."

*I can't believe Aimee Louise talked to me. She called me Friend. I wonder if she can't remember names. I don't care; I have a friend.*

Rosalie listened while Aimee Louise said, "The secret of the three-banded armadillo is that its defense against predators is to roll into a ball, so the predator can't find anything to seize onto. Predators don't know what to do if they can't find anything to grab."

Rosalie nodded. *It'll work. Never give a predator anything to grab. Absolutely brilliant.*

* * *

When it was time for Rosalie to be home from school, Jolene padded to the bathroom, washed her face, and brushed her hair. After she changed her shirt, she returned to the sofa and sighed. *I have to keep pushing myself for Rosalie.*

Rosalie grinned when she came into the living room. "Mom, can I tell you what happened today? I have a new friend; she's Major Elliott's granddaughter."

"Come sit with me, and tell me all about her." Jolene patted the sofa next to her.

"A kid knocked me down with his bicycle on the way to school. I'm fine, but I was limping when I reached school."

Jolene shook her head as Rosalie told her about the girls who ambushed her then Aimee Louise's story about three banded armadillos.

"Everybody at school says that Aimee Louise is autistic, and maybe she is, but she's also brilliant. She has a hard time with loud noises, so we took our lunch outside. She loves to run too, so we run after we eat."

"I'm glad you have a friend at school, honey."

* * *

The next day, Jolene woke when her phone rang. *Why is the school calling me?* Panic rose in her chest. *I hope nothing has happened to Rosalie.*

"Mrs. Teague, I'm calling on behalf of the staff because we're concerned about Rosalie. She and Major Elliott's granddaughter are outside on the playground eating lunch, and it's raining."

Jolene glanced out the window. "You're right; it's raining. She has always been very interested in the weather, so I'm not surprised because she left this morning with her raincoat. It wasn't forecasted, you know. She's been my most accurate source of weather since she was five. Has someone stolen her raincoat? She told me about the girls who have been bullying her at school. I had assumed you'd have that under control by now."

"Bullying is not allowed at our school, Mrs. Teague. You need to tell Rosalie that she isn't allowed to take her lunch outside. She must eat in the cafeteria with everyone else."

"What's wrong with being outside during her lunch break?"

"It is raining very hard; some of us are concerned about her well-being."

"Well, look into that bullying and ask the principal to call me to discuss Rosalie's well-being."

The caller hung up, and Jolene shook her head. *Busybodies are everywhere.*

* * *

A week later, Jolene heard Rosalie come in the back door and drop her backpack. Rosalie came into the living room with two glasses of water and handed one to Jolene.

Rosalie sat next to Jolene. "Mom, Aimee Louise wants me to go home with her and meet her dog."

Jolene sighed as she set the glass on the nearby table and shook her head. "I'm really glad you have a friend at school, but you know our rule: you're not allowed to go to other people's houses. Besides, Major Elliott lives out in the country; it's just too far away, and I'd worry about you. You need to focus on your schoolwork."

Rosalie snorted. "There's nothing wrong with my schoolwork or my grades, and you know it. I don't understand why I'm being punished. Oh, forget it." Rosalie grabbed her glass from the table and stomped toward the kitchen then stopped and returned.

She softened her tone as she sat on the sofa at her mother's feet. "If you want company, I'll go with you to the doctor. Schedule an appointment or tell me who you want to see, and I'll make the appointment."

Jolene sat up, gazed at Rosalie, and a single tear slid down her face. "Thank you. I'll think about it. No, I'll do it. I'll call today."

"You won't forget?"

"I won't. I promise. Love you, sweet girl."

Rosalie's eyes twinkled, and she grinned. "I guess I better get to that dreadful mountain of homework the hard-hearted teachers assigned."

Jolene's eyes widened then she chuckled. "Oh, I get it, funny girl."

## CHAPTER FIVE

Margo packed the cooler then packed a box with food that didn't need refrigeration; she snorted in disgust at what was in the box. *This is all the junk food that Russell bought. My only contribution is the bag of apples.*

She checked the list she'd made. *I don't know whether Russell wants the children to have flashlights. He made it very clear that we need to have a low profile.*

She set a case of bottled water on top of the box of food then set out three changes of clothes to go into the children's backpacks.

After she changed from her slacks and blouse to jeans and her blue flannel shirt, she rolled three days of clothes for her and for Russell, put their clothes into their backpacks, and added a hairbrush, toothpaste, and the family's toothbrushes to hers. *I hate not knowing what I'm doing because I didn't have enough time to plan.*

She carried the backpacks to the kitchen and dropped them on the counter. *Russell and I have always talked about pulling together what Russell called go-bags in case we had to evacuate, but we never got beyond just talk. It was never a priority.*

Margo walked to the mailbox at the end of their driveway to wait for the children to come home from school. She peered at the sky and spotted a red-shouldered hawk as it rode the thermals and searched for an unwary rabbit or field mouse. *Is that what's happening? Is the predator circling us while he watches for his opportunity to dive down and pick us off one by one?*

Margo strode back to the house as she chided herself. *I never wait for them at the gate. They'll think something's wrong for sure.*

When Annie, Josh, and Aimee Louise ran to the porch, Margo cleared her throat then said in a flat tone, "There you are." *That was a puny attempt at being cheerful. Get a grip.*

"I lost track of time," she said in a livelier tone of voice, "but I'm glad you're home. Hurry inside, and I'll fix a snack."

Margo frowned as she gazed to the west at the darkening clouds. *Bad omen; we don't need this.* "It'll rain soon. Never know, might be a bad storm."

When Annie and Josh didn't move but stood on the porch and stared at her, Margo herded them toward the house.

Annie grabbed her backpack as it slipped off her shoulder. "What's going on, Mom?"

Margo noticed Aimee Louise was watching her closely. *She thinks something's wrong too.* "Aimee Louise, you're welcome to stay for a snack if you want, but I'm not sure when the rain is going to start. You might want to leave right away."

Aimee Louise said, "I'm fine." She and Shadow ran toward the woods and the shortcut to their farm.

Margo watched Aimee Louise and Shadow until they were out of sight before she closed the door. *Was that a man or a shadow on the edge of the woods?*

Josh stood in the foyer. "Whoa. No lights."

"Let's play a game." Margo said. "Let's pretend our electricity doesn't work and talk about what we'd do without it."

"Mom, is something wrong?" Annie frowned.

Margo narrowed her eyes at a shadow in the woods that moved. "Don't be silly, Annie. What could be wrong?"

"Mom, your voice sounds weird." Annie asked.

Margo stared out the window until she noticed that Annie jerked her head to see if someone was behind her.

"Well, Josh. What do you think we'd do?" Margo asked.

Josh pursed his lips and stroked his chin with his thumb and finger. His face broke into a grin. "We'd turn on our power boosters for lights and teleport hot pizza for supper."

"I like your teleport idea; but for today, Dad said it was important we stay inside and don't turn on any lights or anything electrical until he gets home." Mom sighed. "No lights. No candles. No television."

"Why?" Annie pressed her lips together and narrowed her eyes.

"He didn't say. He said it was important, and he'd tell us when he got home."

As the house darkened, Annie pouted at the table as she sat with her arms crossed, and Josh drummed his fingers on the table.

When Annie clenched her teeth, Margo said, "That's enough, Josh."

Josh slid out of his chair to hide under the kitchen table. "I'll just be here."

Margo bit her lip when Annie turned her chair, so she couldn't see her brother.

When it was close to twilight, Margo served the sandwiches that she had packed into a cooler.

Annie shook her head. "Mom, this is different; you always cook dinner, even on a camping trip."

Margo heard a quiet scrape at the back door, and hurried to see who it was; she exhaled when Russell came inside.

"What are you doing home so early, Dad?" Josh asked.

Russell absently patted Josh's shoulder.

"Nice job, Margo. The house looks like no one is home, which is what I hoped. I have three weeks' vacation approved, and I sent the school an email, so we're all set. We need to leave right away. Were you able to pack what we would need for at least three or four days? What about Aimee Louise?" He glanced around. "Is she here?"

"No, Aimee Louise didn't stay. As far as the packing, I'm sure I've forgotten something, but yes, I've got everything packed in two suitcases and the two boxes. And I packed the kids' backpacks."

"Good. Now, kids, we'll be gone for a while. Go to your rooms and get something to take with you. A toy, a game, something you like to sleep with, but nothing electronic. Think camping in the woods. Let's hurry. We need to leave right away."

Annie and Josh raced up the stairs. Josh returned first with his sketchbook and Margo's stuffed brown dog. He set the stuffed brown dog on the table, and Margo ran her fingers along the precise, neat stitches Annie made when she was five after she cut brown dog open for what Annie she declared as emergency surgery. Russell told her that the precise stitches were professionally done. A tear slid down Margo's cheek. *Of all his toys he might have picked to take, he rescued my brown dog. He knows something's wrong.*

Annie hugged her blue lion as she made her way down the staircase.

Margo smiled at poor blue lion. *I felt awful when I pulled him out of the dryer and his fluffy mane had melted into a blue blob. But he's still very much loved.*

"Blue Lion is still fierce, isn't he, honey?" Margo asked.

The family slipped out the back door and didn't talk or make any noise. Margo noticed that Annie watched her dad lock the door and check that it was secure.

* * *

Howie crouched in the woods behind a thicket near the Gaston house. The Boss gave him a cushy gig—keep a close eye on Russell Gaston. He didn't mind the woods except he worried about bears. He had stopped at the hardware store in town for bear spray, but the woman at the hardware store told him bear spray was useless, and instead, sold him bug repellent for the no-see-ums, tiny gnats. Howie had never heard of them, but after an hour in the woods, he sprayed himself and his clothes like she told him. *Good advice, lady. Thanks.*

The kids came home, and the girl and the dog ran off. He knew their routine. *Strange. The missus hasn't turned on any house lights, even with the sky dark with storm clouds.*

As dusk set in, there were still no lights on at the house. The town lights glowed in the distance. *Something's about to happen. Better call The Boss.*

"Boss, it's Howie. My neighbors are at home, but I don't see any lights on."

"If they leave, follow our procedure and check to be sure their house is secure. Stay in touch with them and me."

"Got it."

Howie moved to a spot where he could see the front and back doors and watched Gaston coast to the back door with his car lights off. After a short time, the family climbed into the car, and Gaston drove away, leaving his lights off until he got to the paved road.

"No worries, Mr. G. I'll follow the GPS tracker I installed on your car and catch up with you later." He patted his pocket. *This dealer key to unlock Gaston's car doors will come in handy.*

He strolled to the house and picked the lock to the front door. When he was inside, he was careful not to disturb anything except the new laptop computer. He carried out the laptop as he left the same way he entered.

When he turned onto the highway, he frowned. *I don't remember hearing the front door latch when I left.*

He pulled to the side of the road to turn back. *Naw. It's okay.*

## CHAPTER SIX

At breakfast, Major stroked his chin and contemplated his chicken coops. *I can expand one side of the north coop to make a maternity wing with a wire wall where the other chickens can see the baby chicks but not hurt them.*

"Friend can't come see me," Aimee Louise said.

Major was startled. "What? Why is that?"

*Aimee Louise never talks at breakfast. I thought it was another Aimee Louise rule.*

Aimee Louise rose from the table and cleared her dishes. "Her mama is sick."

"I'll check with Rosalie's aunt Josie. She'll know what's going on," he said.

A few days later, Major came across Josie in the grocery store. "Josie, Aimee Louise invited Rosalie to spend a day or weekend with us at the farm, but she says Rosalie can't because Jolene is sick. Is there something we can do to help?"

Josie picked up the dinosaur her toddler had thrown on the floor. She swiped it across her pants leg and handed it back. Major stared at her.

"Fourth kid." Josie laughed. The boy tossed his dinosaur a second time, and Josie caught it midair.

"Well done, Josie." Major laughed with her. "I'd forgotten how challenging little guys are."

"I don't know what to do about Jolene." Josie frowned. "She won't even talk to me anymore, not that she ever has. What if I set up a meeting with my brother? I know he takes his lunch break at the hospital cafeteria. I'll schedule something and get back to you."

Major nodded. "That would work."

Josie called Major the same afternoon.

"I didn't expect to hear from you for a week or so," he said. "Kind of a surprise."

Josie's words tumbled out. "Here's the deal. Marty says Rosalie can visit Aimee Louise any time, including overnight and even weekends. I suggested he should add the stipulation that Rosalie has to leave a note to let them know she's at your farm, but Marty said that wasn't necessary."

She took a breath. "This next part might sound strange, but Rosalie can't have company at their house. Marty says people make Jolene nervous. I have never understood Jolene, and I certainly don't understand her sudden aversion to people because she was always the most popular girl in school, but that's what Marty said. Anyway, the girls will have to spend their time together at your house. I told Marty it was fine. It is, right? He said he'd talk to Rosalie in the morning."

*That's a relief. Those two girls don't need adult supervision as much as they need an adult presence and someone to be responsible for their welfare.*

"Yes, it's fine with me. I'll check with Aimee Louise, but I suspect she'll be excited."

At supper that evening, Major said, "Rosalie's aunt Josie called me. Rosalie can visit the farm and stay here on weekends. Rosalie's mom doesn't feel well, so you girls can spend all your time together here."

Aimee Louise flapped her hands then crossed her arms to hide her hands. "I can't wait to tell her."

"Her dad will tell her in the morning. You can talk to her at school tomorrow, and the two of you can plan whatever you like. I'll plan on three at the dinner table."

That afternoon, Major and Shadow sat on the front porch to watch for the girls. "Who's more excited, boy? You or me?"

Shadow ran to the road and returned with Aimee Louise and Rosalie.

Major grinned. "Welcome, Rosalie. What's the plan for today?"

"Thank you. Aimee Louise and I would like to learn about chickens," Rosalie said. "And we'll do our homework this evening. I'm a year younger than Aimee Louise, and we don't have any classes together, but we can still help each other study."

Aimee Louise said, "I can show her my room."

"Sounds good. Rosalie can put her things there. Meet me at the coops when you're ready, and we'll take care of the chicken chores."

As the girls headed to the stairs, Major heard Aimee Louise say, "It can be your room too."

After the girls raced to the coop, Major showed them how to let the chickens out of their runs. "It's easier to clean when the chickens aren't underfoot. They get to be wild, free-ranging chickens, and we can get our work done much faster without chicken supervision although Ruthie likes to be picked up, rocked, and sung to."

"Do all the chickens have names?" Rosalie asked.

"Yes," said Major. "Does that sound strange?"

Rosalie smiled. "No, it's good."

Major showed them how he removed chicken poop by using a kitty litter scoop to sift through the sand in the bins under the roosts.

"It's amazing; these chickens are housebroken," Rosalie said.

Major chuckled. "When the chickens poop at night, the bins under the roosts catch the poop. They spend most of their days outside and poop outside. I guess it does look like they are housebroken."

Rosalie dumped the chickens' drinking water into the butterfly garden and scrubbed the containers. Major showed her how to examine them for algae.

"It isn't algae," Rosalie said. "It's green slime."

Aimee Louise sniffed the container. "Stinky green slime."

"The hanging food containers are low on food, but you'll find a lot of feed in the pans under them," Major said. "I check the pans to be sure the food isn't moldy and pour it back into their food containers or toss it to them as a treat. They're sloppy when they eat."

Rosalie climbed into the coop to look. "There's food on the floor too. They must flip through their food looking for the good stuff on the bottom."

Major went to the barn and returned with a fifty-pound sack of chicken feed in his utility wagon. "See where Shadow's positioned? He's on guard where he can watch his people and his chickens."

Rosalie sang while she worked, and Aimee Louise hummed along. Several of the chickens crowded around the girls and joined in with clucks and coos.

"The chickens like your songs," Major chuckled. "I never knew they needed tunes out here."

After Major returned to the barn to put away the utility wagon, his phone rang, and he frowned as he answered. *Has Marty changed his mind?*

"I convinced Jolene to see a doctor," Marty said. "She saw a medical specialist in the city who admitted her to the hospital for some tests. She might be in for a while. Do you suppose Rosie could stay full-time at the farm? I'd worry about her being by herself at night when I get caught up at the hospital. If you don't think it's a good idea, I'm sure my sister can make room for her."

"It's fine with me. The two girls are pretty much inseparable, and Shadow and I enjoy the company. Have you talked to Rosalie?"

"No, she'll be fine; just tell her for me, okay? Thanks."

"No. She needs to hear from you. She's right outside. I'll call her in so you can talk to her."

Marty hung up.

Major scowled at the phone. *What's going on with you, Marty?*

He leaned out the back door. "Aimee Louise, Rosalie, can you come inside for a quick meeting?"

The girls and Shadow ran inside.

"How about some iced tea?" Major filled three glasses with ice, and Aimee Louise poured the tea.

The girls grabbed their glasses and flopped onto the sofa. Major took a seat in his recliner and leaned forward.

"Rosalie, your dad called. Your mom's been admitted to the hospital for some tests."

"I knew it; I knew she was sick because she hasn't been herself in ages." Rosalie set her glass down. "Will she be okay? What did dad say?"

"I guess there are a lot of tests to do because he said she would be in the hospital for a while."

"That's good, right? They're going to be thorough." Rosalie rubbed her forehead. "I've been worried for a long time."

Aimee Louise stared at Major. "Will Rosalie stay with us?"

"As far as I'm concerned, that's an excellent idea. What do you think, Rosalie?"

"Dad works all the time, and it isn't fun to be alone. I'm not lonely here." She reached down and patted Shadow's back. "I'd like it, but do you think it would be okay with Dad?"

"I'm sure it is because he knows where you are and that you're safe, but we could give him a call if you want to talk to him about it."

"I never call him at work. I'm sure he's worried about Mom and knows he doesn't have to worry about me because I'm here."

* * *

A week later, Major sat on the back porch and leaned back to watch the sunset. *Farm life agrees with us. Rosalie sings cheerful, funny songs. Aimee Louise's collars and sleeves have lost their stretched-out look. Shadow guards his girls, and I don't have time to be melancholy.*

The girls and Shadow ran from the coops up to the back porch.

"Pops," Rosalie said, "could we start a photo diary of the wildlife around the farm?"

"Excellent idea. I've wanted game cameras for a long time, and I can't think of a better excuse than wildlife photos. You two can swap out the memory cards in the cameras."

"We can do that," Aimee Louise said.

Rosalie grinned. "Right up our alley."

Major sat with the girls at the dining table and drew a rough outline of the farm, with the farmhouse in the middle then pointed to his drawing. "This is where I thought we could place the cameras. We could put one camera west of the farmhouse, near the power-line easement. The second one, south of the farmhouse. There are signs of a well-used deer trail there. Deer highway, almost. The third one we can place east of the farmhouse in the pasture near the intersection of the gravel road and the dirt road. Of course, we can move any of them later."

Rosalie pointed at the intersection. "We saw an area in the pasture where the grass was mashed down like a bedding site. It's not too close to the roads, and it's close to trees where we could put the camera."

"We'll do it," Major said. "I'll take the tractor. Won't take us long to install the cameras. I could hitch up the trailer if you'd like to ride. Or would you rather run?"

"Run," Aimee Louise said.

After they installed the last camera, Major smiled as Aimee Louise, Rosalie, and Shadow raced back to the farmhouse. *No way could I keep up with them; glad I have sense enough not to try.*

* * *

Two days later, Aimee Louise said, "Time for a run."

Rosalie nodded. "We need to check the cameras."

Aimee Louise grabbed three bottles of water and handed one to Rosalie. "For your backpack."

Rosalie slipped on her backpack. "What's the third bottle for?"

"Shadow." Shadow's ears perked up.

Before he went to the computer room to work, Major walked to the back door with them. "See you later."

After he reviewed his farm expenses, Major searched and found a blog on preparing for hurricanes. *This would be a good list for us to follow before hurricane season.*

When the girls returned, Rosalie said, "We have the cards; we saw raccoon tracks and maybe deer tracks. I took a picture, so you could see. We found an area of flattened grass near the east camera that we want to measure next time."

Major nodded. "Sounds like a bedding site. It will be interesting to watch."

While they ate that evening, Rosalie said, "Pops, we thought there were bears in northern Florida, but we haven't seen any."

"The Florida black bears are shy and hide in the dense brush. In April, which is next month," Major shook his head, "time's sure going by fast, mama bears will be out with their cubs. If you come across a bear, the best thing to do is to back away and don't startle the bear or draw attention to yourself. Their chase instinct is triggered when an animal or human runs. You don't want a bear to chase you because black bears can sprint up to thirty miles an hour. Oh, and don't get between a mama bear and her baby."

That evening, Aimee Louise popped each card into the slot on the computer, and Rosalie and Major sat on either side of her.

"No bears," Aimee Louise said.

Rosalie scooted her chair closer. "What a beautiful doe. Oh, look, two smaller deer."

"They look like yearlings," Major said. "Still hanging around with their mother."

Rosalie pointed to the computer screen. "There's Carl. He's the only coyote I've seen with that notch on an ear. Wonder how he got it? Maybe a dog? We haven't seen any dogs, except for Shadow."

"The property is fenced on all sides. If we saw another dog, I'd say it was time to check for a hole in the fence somewhere," Major said.

"Shadow patrols the farm; he'd know if another dog was close," Rosalie said.

"Shadow knows," Aimee Louise said.

Major chuckled. "In the old days, people had no television, no cell phones, and no internet. It was before my time, but I remember my dad talked about it."

"No internet? No cell phones?" The pitch of Rosalie's voice rose almost an octave.

Major laughed. "Hard to believe, right? None at all, so for entertainment, people listened to stories on the radio, and one of the shows was called *The Shadow*. It always began with 'Who knows what evil lurks in the hearts of men?'" Major shifted to a deep, haunting voice. "The Shadow knows."

"Pops, we would love to hear radio stories," Rosalie said.

He rose to change seats with Aimee Louise. "Okay, radio stories. I'll find something for us to listen to. It'll be perfect evening entertainment."

* * *

The next morning before school, Rosalie said, "Pops, I've designed a tracking system for the animals, and Aimee Louise can develop a computer database system if we can use your computer. Would that be okay?"

"Sounds good to me, and we can talk to the county extension agent. It might be something she could support as a school project."

"We can start today." Aimee Louise rose and cleared the table.

Rosalie rinsed and placed the dishes in the dishwasher.

"Gotta run," Rosalie said. "Thanks, Pops. A school project we can work on together sounds great."

After the girls left, Major gazed at the horizon. "A project for the two of them. I like the sound of that. Something normal for a family to do, and those two girls deserve some normalcy, right, Shadow?"

## CHAPTER SEVEN

After doing the evening dishes, the girls joined Major and Shadow on the back porch.

"Are we under a water restriction?" Rosalie asked as she and Aimee Louise flopped into their rocking chairs.

"Where'd you hear about that?" Major said.

"People in the grocery store," Rosalie said.

"Lots of worried clouds," Aimee Louise added.

Major nodded. "I'm not surprised because the town is under a water restriction, and people can't water their lawns or wash cars. The whole county and much of the state is under a burn ban. No open fires, no fireworks. The fire hazard level's severe right now. We aren't under the town restriction because we don't use the town water, but wildfires are a worry for everybody when it's so dry."

The phone rang in the computer room; when Major answered, the girls could hear his conversation.

"That close? That's not good…An old one…On my way."

Rosalie said, "Sounds important."

When he walked out to the porch, Rosalie asked, "Worried?"

"Strong with determined and something, maybe duty or service. Dad had that too sometimes; edges of worried," Aimee Louise said.

"Talking about me?" Major asked.

"Yes," Rosalie said.

Major reached inside and removed a ring of keys from the key rack. "There's a wildfire, and Mr. Samuel's horse farm in the next county is in the path of the fire. I'll take the truck and our old horse trailer to see if I can help move horses before the fire gets any closer. I'm not sure how long I'll be gone."

"I'll make coffee," Aimee Louise said.

"I'll grab an apple from the fridge and some brownies from the freezer for you, Pops, and carrots for the horses," Rosalie said. "We made a double batch of Gram Trish's brownie recipe this week and froze the extras."

The aroma of the fresh coffee swirled through the air. Aimee Louise poured the steaming brew into a thermos, and Rosalie packed the water and snacks into a small ice chest.

Major came inside after he hitched up the trailer. "Coffee smells great. Thanks for packing drinks and energy food. Look after each other and Shadow."

The night sky was clear as Major headed south toward the glow in the distance, and the full moon shone with a reddish-orange tinge.

After he'd been on the road for an hour, he reached the horse farm and shook his head. *Looks like chaos; everybody needs to slow down.*

Major waved at a Florida state trooper that he had worked for him before he retired. "What's the game plan, Rich?"

Rich snorted. "Not sure because it seems to have fallen apart. I thought I'd work that smaller horse barn away from all the yelling."

"Care for a partner?" Major asked.

The two men moved their trucks and trailers to the smaller barn then went inside the barn.

"Can you take two horses? I can take three," Rich said.

"Sounds good. Let's load yours first after we calm these beauties down a bit." Major zipped up his jacket. *This night air is chilly.*

As the two men approached the first horse, Rich said, "I was sorry to hear about Ted and his wife. I understand your granddaughter is living with you now. Are you feeling older or younger?"

Major chuckled. "Pretty much both at the same time, but for the first time in years, I feel alive. Her friend's mother is very ill, so her friend is staying with us too. That reminds me, the girls gave me carrots for the horses. If we have any balkers, maybe we can try bribery."

While they loaded the horses into their trailers, the farm owner gave them directions to the farm that was going to be the safe haven for the horses. They drove to the new destination and unloaded the horses then returned.

After they parked, Major shook his head. "Seems worse than it was when we were here earlier."

"I know; feels like an accident waiting to happen. Be safe, Come find me when you're ready to load, and I'll help."

While Major helped load a skittish horse, his phone rang, and he stepped away to answer.

Rosalie said, "I have you on speakerphone, so Aimee Louise can hear too. We're getting ready for bed and we see fire glow in the southeast, and I smelled smoke."

"Thanks for letting me know. The progress here is slower than I expected. The horses are jittery, and it's hard to get them into the trailers. The carrots help a lot. Keep your cell phones charged and next to your beds. I'll be home as quick as I can."

At midnight, Rich found Major helping with another nervous horse.

"The wind has shifted and is coming from the east. There's more smoke in the air, and the horses can smell it." Rich said, "Let's get our trailers loaded and get out of here."

On their way to their trucks, Major said, "We're blocked in; we have to help those three drivers load up before we'll be able to move."

A little before two, Major and Rich finished loading their trailers. The horse owner ran to their trucks. "We just got word the fire jumped the fire break and is threatening farms around Plainview."

Major's eyes widened. "I have to warn the girls." He pulled out his phone and sent both of them the same text: "Get out. Fire too close."

"I have to call the house; you go ahead, Rich. I'll catch up."

While his house phone rang, Major muttered, "Wake up; wake up."

When Aimee Louise answered, he said, "I sent a text, but I'm calling to be sure you got it. You, Rosalie, and Shadow need to go to Plainview. Your safety is more important than anything in the house. Take the house key to Rosalie's house in town and go there. I wish I could leave here and pick you up, but the fire jumped the fire break and shifted. It's between us now. Let me talk to Rosalie, and I'll tell her the same thing. I love you."

When Rosalie came on the phone, he repeated what he told Aimee Louise then added, "You don't have any time to do anything except get out of there."

"Right behind you, Major," Rich shouted. "Lead the way."

As Major made his way across the fields toward the road, he watched all the trucks with trailers turn right at the paved road. Major narrowed his eyes at the long line as the trucks crept along the highway.

He called Rich. "I'm going left. There are too many trucks going right. One flat could be a disaster."

"I'm with you."

"It'll take us about an hour and a half going left."

"Or three hours if we join the crawling caravan that turned right."

When they were forty-five minutes from the destination farm, Major called Rich. "There's a truck with no taillights ahead blocking our lane."

"What do you want me to do?"

"Back me up."

"I've got my pistol and my deer rifle. Before you get out of your truck, call me then drop your phone in your top pocket. I'll make my way to your rear bumper."

*Rich was always sharp even as a rookie.*

Major left his headlights on as he climbed out of his truck.

As Major strolled toward the dark truck, he said, "I see two men; I'm going to step off the pavement to get a view of the passenger's side. The bright moon is really helpful."

Major slowed his pace. "Two more men on the passenger side; they're crouched down. My money's on an ambush. I'm going to go slow. Go to the passenger's side of my truck; don't cross in front on my headlights."

Major stopped, and called out. "Hello, there. Are you broken down?"

"First, I ran out of gas then ran the battery down," a man said.

"I've got a buddy in the next town who will give you a tow to the closest gas station. Want me to give him a call? Do you have your family with you?"

"No, just me and my buddy; we work odd jobs, mostly farming. We don't really have any money for a tow. How far is it to the next town? Do you have any gas? We've got money to pay for gas."

"The two men on passenger's side are creeping toward the back of their truck," Rich said. "I called my buddies that are on duty tonight. They'll be here in two minutes."

"About five miles. I've already called the state police because you don't have any taillights. That's really dangerous on these backroads at night."

"What about gas?"

"No gas, sorry. I've been evacuating horses all night to get them out of the path of a big wild fire that's headed this way. Don't you smell it?"

"I thought it was somebody's fireplace. A wild fire?"

"Yep; they're really unpredictable. You don't want to get caught in a wild fire because there's no way to outrun it; wild fire travels like ninety miles an hour and it leaps through the trees."

"Hey, boss, want I should try to crank the engine again?"

"Yeah. Maybe some of that gas has trickled through the system. Get it going and let's get out of here."

When the engine started, the man who had been talking ran to jump into the driver's seat as the other man climbed out, but before he reached the truck, two state troopers roared toward them.

Rich had moved to the passenger's side. "Hold it right there." His command voice was clear, and Major moved to the passenger's side.

"Backing you up," Major said.

In a few minutes, Rich said, "We're released, Major."

Before they left, Major's phone rang. "Major, this is Pete. We heard you went to help evacuate the horses. I thought you'd like to know the roads are clear here. The fire missed us this time."

Major climbed into his truck, then he and Rich resumed their trip.

As they neared the destination farm, Major led the way in, and a man met him at the gate. "You're the first here; go right over to that first barn, and someone will unload for you. You've had a long night."

While Major and Rich watched the farm hands unload the horses, Rich said, "Major, I'm not sure I knew what a slick negotiator you are. You had me ready to run jump in my truck and get out of there."

"I was grateful you were with me. My neck prickled when I saw the truck with no lights in the middle of the road with no one with a flashlight to warn us about their truck. It's been quite a while since I've seen or heard of a road ambush."

"I know; I'm not sure I've heard of any either. Their careers as highway robbers are over for a long time," Rich said. "My trailer's unloaded. I'm going home to my sleeping kids and my worried wife. Thanks again for working with me tonight. Don't tell my wife, but it was fun."

Major chuckled. "It was that. I've got to get to my girls."

The two men shook hands, and Rich climbed into his truck and left.

As Major climbed into his truck, his phone rang.

"Major Elliot, this is the Plainview Hospital. Aimee Louise, Rosalie, and Shadow are here with us in the emergency visitors' area. They aren't here as patients. The girls and Shadow saved a family from a house fire. The baby suffered smoke inhalation and will be admitted, but she'll be fine with treatment. The girls and Shadow are heroes."

"I'll be there as fast as I can."

"Be safe, Major. The girls and Shadow are safe here."

After he hung up, Major shook his head then climbed into his truck and called Aimee Louise as he sped to Plainview.

"I'm on my way to pick you up." Pops said. "The road is clear now. I got a call—the fire missed the farm. I'll be there as fast as I can."

Major burst into the waiting room and rushed to Aimee Louise and Rosalie. He knelt in front of them and gathered them into his arms. "I can't tell you how proud I am of you two. You know you saved that family and their home. You are heroes."

"Shadow," Aimee Louise said.

"Shadow led us to the house. Aimee Louise put the fire out."

"Rosalie has a loud voice," Aimee Louise said.

"Sounds like the three of you are a great team." Major chuckled. "Let's go home."

On the way, Rosalie said, "Pops, something bothered me. The baby's room filled with smoke from the fires on the porch, but the mom said the smoke alarm didn't go off until she opened the bedroom door. How is that possible?"

"Good catch, Rosalie. It's not likely, but an open window, a disconnected smoke detector in the baby's room, and a tight seal on the bedroom door—it's possible."

"I get it, thanks," Rosalie said.

Aimee Louise asked, "Are the horses okay?"

"Yes, they are. It was a challenge to get them into the horse trailers because they were so panicked by the fire. It took a lot of extra time to calm them, keep ourselves calm, and coax the horses into the trailers, but we got them all moved to a safe location."

"I have another question," Rosalie said.

"Okay."

"Can we sleep in tomorrow?"

Major laughed. "You have my permission, but I'll bet we're all up at our usual early time to say good morning to the day."

* * *

After the girls trudged upstairs, Major strolled to the back porch, and Shadow followed him. *The night air still has the lingering odor of smoke.*

Major bent down to stroke Shadow's back. "When I heard about the girls being in the path of the fire, it took me back to the time a hurricane was bearing down our area, and I reported to duty and left Trish at home with a six-year-old. I needed to help the community, but my family needed me too. I felt so guilty about Trish and Ted being alone. I knew she was a strong, capable woman, but it was my job to take care of my family."

He stepped off the porch and paced. "If I hadn't gone to help move horses, at least three horses if not more, would have died in the fire. I can't shake the guilt that I wasn't here to take care of the girls."

He gazed at the moon. *Fact is—I saved horses, and the girls saved a family. Time to move on.*

* * *

When Major rose early the next morning, he smelled fresh coffee.

"Good morning, Pops," Rosalie said as Aimee Louise handed him a cup of coffee.

He inhaled the aroma that swirled from his cup. "Good morning; it's a new day with new challenges and adventures."

He sipped his coffee and chuckled. "That's the end of my pre-coffee, profoundly philosophical thoughts."

## CHAPTER EIGHT

When people asked what he did, The Boss answered, "I'm in the supply chain and logistics business. I manage local and imported products, and I'm a big supporter of local small businesses."

He didn't bother to mention his sole goal was maximum profit, and legality was not a concern. *None of their business.*

When he got a call from a trusted former partner about a business proposition, he listened. "The Board will contact you with a rare and profitable opportunity. I've got the West Coast, and they want you to manage the East Coast."

The Boss knew about the Board. They were a nationwide organization and had operated illegally without scrutiny for years because of their tight affiliation with high-level political and law enforcement leaders; nobody challenged them.

A week after the heads-up call, a representative of the Board phoned The Boss to present their plan for the two-phase project. The Boss listened to the mechanical, distorted voice. Because he was bilingual and fascinated by accents and regional dialects, he could pinpoint the speaker's country and region with ease if he heard the undisguised voice, but he didn't care. He cared about money.

"We need information," the voice said. "If you are interested, we can guarantee you a safe window to move your merchandise, and you keep one hundred percent of the profit. We have Phase One and Phase Two. Phase One is a test for Phase Two. Both phases will provide you maximum profits with no risk."

The Boss checked around, and everyone confirmed what his gut told him: "The Board delivers."

"I don't get it," The Boss said in a conversation with his most trusted colleague. "What's in it for The Board?"

"Don't ask questions," the colleague said, "and you'll live longer, but the only thing bigger than our lucrative businesses is to take over the government."

"Got it," he said. "Above our pay grade."

The Boss assembled five teams for Phase One. He needed the assurance the team members would not bond with each other but would remain loyal to him.

He met with Max and Alejandro, designated as Team Three, at a coffee shop to give them their instructions.

He claimed a seat at a table where he could see the door and sipped his coffee. "This will be the only time I'll meet with you, Team Three. You'll be picked up and delivered to your assignment and receive instructions from your drop-off handler or your driver. You'll be paid in cash at the end of each assignment. It's critical you follow my orders without hesitation or question."

Max squirmed in the undersized wrought iron café chair. "Me and Pedro won't let you down, Boss. Right, Pedro?"

Alejandro looked at The Boss and said, "*Sí, Jefe.*"

The Boss sauntered to his car. *Team Three will be my most reliable team. No possibility of bonding between those two.*

* * *

Max shifted his backpack to ease the stiffness in his shoulders. *This gig is boring.* He preferred more excitement, more body contact, and more pain for somebody else. He was a bouncer at his last job. Damn good one too.

*I'd still be there except for the skinny frat boy showing off for his friends. Thought he'd push me. Called me an ignorant, stupid gorilla. Screamed in my face. Who knew college boys were so delicate? Musta been a bleeder.*

A ten-mile, cross-country hike at night with a forty-pound pack in the company of a moron was not Max's idea of a good time. Max stumbled over the uneven terrain, tripped on vines, and occasionally wandered into spider webs. *Hate spider webs, but I'm walking in front. Pedro can bring up the rear in case a bobcat attacks.*

Max didn't care what his companion's name was. If he answered to Pedro, it was good enough for Max. When Pedro called The Boss *Heffie*, Max was sure Pedro and The Boss were old friends. He knew enough Spanish to know jalapeño was spelled with a *j* but pronounced with an *h* sound, so he figured *Heffie's* real name was Jeff.

Max plodded along. *Always the same, week after week. We're dropped off, get directions, hike, and get picked up. I never understand the directions. No street signs. No buildings. Nothing. Pedro does. Thought I had a frat boy for a partner. Might not be so bad after all.*

Pedro grunted behind Max, and Max turned left into the brush. *Amazing little dude. Always knows which way to go.*

Max was glad they hadn't been working the night of the big fire, although he overheard his driver tell another driver that The Boss was angry about the missed opportunity. *Whatever that meant.*

* * *

Alejandro hiked behind the big stupid man, Gordo. The big man once asked him why he called him *Gordo*, and Alejandro told him it meant "Big Man." Alejandro didn't care why Gordo called him *Pedro*.

Alejandro chuckled to himself. *Gordo flinches at every sound. He hears wild animals in every rustle. If we see a bear, I'll yell Run! And let the bear chase Gordo while I back away.*

Alejandro had walked his whole life. The backpack was cumbersome at first, but he was soon used to it. The walk was easy, and he liked the generous pay. *If Gordo slips up, I'll slit his throat and leave him in the woods for the local pumas.* He carried a second, smaller pack to get used to the added weight in case he had to take over Gordo's backpack.

"Hey, Pedro. Why ya carry a second pack?"

"Supplies."

Gordo snorted. "Yeah, tacos."

Alejandro put his head down to hide his smile.

My fat city guy Gordo has a lot to learn.

* * *

The Boss kept a close watch on the progress of every team and every detail of his plan. The backpacks included GPS trackers. *Good data. Technology is great.*

He ran an analysis of planned versus actual for each stage of the project. So far, his plan was tight. He eliminated Team Two when their driver reported the two men talked quietly to each other on the way to a nightly assignment.

*Can't afford any mavericks. No loose ends.*

## CHAPTER NINE

Major, Aimee Louise, and Rosalie reviewed their game camera photos from the last three nights. Aimee Louise moved closer to the computer screen to look. "Two men?"

"Can't believe it." Major frowned. "This is from what, two nights ago? Two men with rifles slung over their shoulders and large packs. Which camera is this again?"

Rosalie pointed at the bottom of the screen. "West camera. The time stamp is ten pm, and they're headed south."

He flipped to the next photo. "Going north early the next morning at four thirty."

After Major pulled up a satellite view of the power lines, he searched south. "The power lines go to the regional substation a little over four miles away."

When he switched the screen back to the men, Aimee Louise stared at him. "Pops, your protector cloud swirls from your chest then rises up and obliterates your shoulders and head. It's a strong cloud."

Major leaned back and met her gaze. "Sometimes I think I'll never understand your clouds, then suddenly you give me a brief but very clear insight."

He turned back to his screen. "Have either of you ever seen these men before?"

Rosalie examined the screen. "No, Pops, I'm pretty sure I haven't."

"Well, that one," Major said and pointed to the one with his rifle on his left side, "may be left-handed."

"Left-handed like me; I need to see something," Aimee Louise said.

Major relinquished the chair in front of the computer. Aimee Louise skillfully zoomed in on the man's left hand. "Man at the feed store. Dragon on his left hand. Danger cloud."

Rosalie scooted closer to the screen. "I can see the dragon. The head is on his thumb, the body wraps around the back of his hand, and the tail goes down his pointer finger. That's awesome."

Major sat back and frowned. "We were at the feed store on Monday. I thought you said, 'danger dragon,' but I wasn't sure, so I decided I didn't hear you right. Do you remember anything else?"

Aimee Louise recited a license plate number.

He shook his head. "I forget you see things other people don't see or don't bother to notice. I'll ask the sheriff to check the license number. You know, we need a code word we can use to let each other know we have a problem. What do you think?"

Aimee Louise said, "Uncle Dan."

Major rubbed his head. "Uncle Dan? Did I miss something?"

"*Dan*-for Danger. Uncle Dan."

"That makes sense. What do you think, Rosalie?"

"I have a way to remember *Uncle Dan*." She sang, "Uncle Dan, he's the man. He's there on the double in the middle of the trouble. And we all scoot, we all skedaddle, up the river with canoe and a paddle."

Major chuckled. "Well, I won't forget Uncle Dan. I'll go into town tomorrow and show this to the sheriff. It's probably nothing, but I'd like to get his opinion."

* * *

Major and Shadow dropped the girls off at school and headed to the sheriff's office. Major smiled at the memory of his first meeting with Jack eighteen years ago when Jack was a newly graduated deputy.

"Shadow, I bought him his first cup of on-duty coffee at Pete's Diner and told him he'd be a damn good sheriff someday. The only time we ever disagreed was when I retired from the state police, and the sheriff still called me *Major*. I told him I was a farmer. I'll never forget what he said, 'You'll always be Major in this town.'" He shook his head. "I guess I'm officially old, boy. All soft and sentimental."

Major and Shadow stepped into the sheriff's office, where Shadow was an honored guest.

The admin giggled when Shadow pranced over to her. "Sit, Shadow?" Shadow thumped his tail against her desk, sat, and received his dog-treat reward.

Major joined the sheriff at the coffee pot. "Sheriff, my girls have game cameras to take pictures for their wildlife project, and I've got a few pictures of two men near my property along the power lines late at night and early in the morning. I can't imagine what they were doing. I don't recognize them, but one of them was at the farm store this week. Here's the truck's license plate number."

The sheriff frowned as he looked at the photos. "They're obviously not hunters. I'll run the plate and see what we get. Want blueberry pie with that coffee? Molly made it and told me to share." The sheriff patted his middle-aged spread.

"I never turn down a piece of pie, especially homemade by Molly," Major said.

They talked about the drought while the sheriff's admin put the plate number through a search then handed the sheriff a page from the printer. "Here's your information."

The sheriff said, "The license is for a red pickup owned by Richard James in the next county. Have you met him? I know him pretty well. He's a rancher and has a big operation. It makes sense one of his hired hands would be at the farm store, but I don't know why anyone would go for a stroll at night like that, though. While they technically trespassed on the utility easement, I'm not sure what to investigate, unless you have some ideas."

The two men strolled to Major's truck, and Shadow followed.

"No," Major said. "Just wanted to touch base with you. Glad to know there's nothing to worry about. With the two girls at the farm, I'm probably a little overprotective."

"I wouldn't expect anything different from you," the sheriff said. "I might investigate a few things myself. Maybe give Mr. James a call."

## CHAPTER TEN

When Pedro and Gordo arrived at their drop-off point, The Boss emerged from a car and waved them over.

*I bet Gordo did something stupid. I hope I get a new partner.* Pedro glanced at the big man. Gordo's shoulders slumped, and his head hung down.

"There's a game camera on your primary route to the target," The Boss said. "I need for you to find it and disable it. I have a couple of tools for you to use."

He handed Pedro a device that looked like a tool to find wall studs in a house. "This is a camera detector. Expect the camera to be at a level between your chest and knees. It'll be on the first part of your hike. The finder will light up when it senses a camera pointed at the path."

The device he handed to Gordo looked like a laser pointer. "When you find the camera, hold this in front of it and press the button for thirty seconds. It'll fry the circuitry and zap the memory. Don't touch or damage the camera. Got it?"

The men nodded.

"Okay. Do this right. Find the camera. Here's a cell. Text the usual number with a picture of the camera and return here immediately. Your car will pick you up."

Pedro worried about what was on the camera and how *El Jefe* found out about it, but he didn't say anything. He narrowed his eyes at Gordo, whose demeanor resembled *un perro grande peludo*, a big shaggy dog, caught with the master's chewed-up slippers. Pedro scowled to erase the smile about to erupt across his face.

Either Gordo did something or he's used to being blamed. *Pobre tipo. Poor guy. I'll bet the cat did it.* Pedro coughed into the crook of his arm.

The two men began their hike. Pedro pointed the detector at the path while Gordo took the lead, as usual.

After several miles, Pedro hissed. "Gordo, stop. The light went on. The camera is around here."

Gordo looked for the camera. "Got it. It's here."

"Don't touch it."

Gordo took out the disabling device and pointed it at the camera. "I'm not stupid."

*I don't think you are, Gordo.*

"Okay. I've got the timer set."

When the timer beeped, Pedro said, "And stop."

Gordo squinted at the camera. "It doesn't look any different to me. Take the picture and send the text. Let's get out of here."

"Done. Let's go."

The two men returned to the pickup point before the car returned.

Pedro smirked when he saw the car on the road. "We beat them back. We made good time."

Gordo nodded. "We're a good team."

The next night, Team Three was scheduled for another walk to the target. When they arrived at the drop-off point, their handler gave them a cell phone, bulletproof vests, and thick envelopes. "Open 'em up. Need to be sure it's all there for you."

When they looked inside, they saw fifty- and one-hundred-dollar bills. Pedro grimaced. *We always receive our pay after we return from the target, never in advance, and our backpacks are heavier this time.*

Another car pulled up. The Boss got out and approached the two men. Pedro's ears tingled. He glanced at Gordo. Gordo frowned, and his mouth tightened.

*Gordo senses it too. Something's off. Almost feels like an ambush.*

"Listen carefully," The Boss said. "Walk to your target, place your backpacks as close to the target as possible, and take a picture. Text the picture to the number saved on the phone. It's here." He pointed to the only number saved in Contacts.

"After you send the text, grab your backpacks and return. Got it?"

The two men nodded.

"This time," *El Jefe* continued, "the goal is speed. Get there, set the backpacks down, take the picture, and send the text. Fast. The second you send the text, grab your backpacks and get back here. Make it fast. Not a second wasted. I need to see how fast you can be with the extra weight. Think of this as a race."

Pedro and Gordo stuffed the envelopes inside their shirts, put on the bulletproof vests, and grabbed their backpacks and rifles. Gordo set a fast pace.

"You doing okay, Pedro?"

"This is a good pace, Gordo. We can keep it up all the way there."

When the men arrived at their destination, they set down the backpacks. Pedro aimed the cell phone to take the picture.

He lowered the phone. "I don't like this. Something's not right."

"What?" Gordo said. "What are you thinking? Because a bad feeling's been with me the whole way."

"Why were we paid so much money in advance? Why bulletproof vests? To distract us? What's up with doing it all fast? Is it so we won't stop and think?"

Gordo ran his hand over his face. "You're right. We're being set up. I can feel it. Whatta we do?"

Pedro scanned the area. "We'll follow instructions, but we won't be close to the target when we send the text. There's a rise over there.

We can send the text from the other side of the hill with some distance and dirt between us and the backpacks, like a bunker."

Gordo nodded. "Sounds paranoid. Let's do it."

"Picture's taken. Drop the vests, the rifles, and the money here with the backpacks. Let's go."

Gordo raised his eyebrows. "Everything?"

"Yes. Everything they gave us."

The two men ran to the hill and dove into a small ravine.

"Here's hoping nothing happens. Get your head down," Pedro said as they hunkered down. He pressed Send and tossed the cell phone over the hill like a hand grenade.

The sound of the explosion at the electrical substation reverberated for miles. A ball of fire lit up the sky.

The Boss watched the GPS trackers on the backpacks, bulletproof vests, envelopes, rifles, and cell phone blink off. He smiled. *Clean. No loose ends.*

* * *

It was almost instantaneous: the boom, the flash in the sky, the lights going out. Major dashed outside with Aimee Louise, Rosalie, and Shadow close on his heels. Major narrowed his eyes, and the girls gasped at the sight of the ball of fire high over the trees. Shadow barked and moved to a position between the girls and the far-off blaze. A tower of fire lit up the sky.

Rosalie inhaled and bit her lip. "Are we going to be okay?"

"I'm guessing we won't have electricity for a while, but we'll be fine," Major said. "For tonight, let's get our flashlights, check the chickens, and eat ice cream before it melts."

Aimee Louise stopped pulling at her shirt cuff to smooth the hackles between Shadow's shoulders.

"Pops," Rosalie said, "you are one smart man."

Aimee Louise gazed at the fireball. "We are three-banded."

## CHAPTER ELEVEN

Major woke in the middle of the night. *I need a plan.* He put on a light jacket then he and Shadow went out back for a security walk. After he and Shadow walked around the house, they strolled to the front gate then walked along the fence line to the woods. Major picked up his pace as he strode to the chicken coop then back around the house. When he reached the front, he sat on the porch and rocked as he waited for the sun to rise. *We can be safe and self-sustaining in case of an emergency or disaster.*

He smiled as he heard the girls stir upstairs then tiptoe down the stairs.

"What are you doing up so early?" he asked when they joined him on the porch.

"I couldn't sleep," Aimee Louise said.

"I thought it was time to watch for sunrise because Aimee Louise was awake," Rosalie said. "Why are you up so early?"

"I woke up in the middle of the night and thought about water, food, sanitation, and electricity, and came up with a plan," Major said. "We'll be fine."

Aimee Louise sat on the porch next to Shadow, who put his head on her knee. Rosalie sat on the other side of Shadow, and he stretched to touch her leg with a back paw.

Major continued. "I'd like to go into town for supplies we're low on, and the earlier, the better."

"I can pull together a work list," Rosalie said.

"We have to watch the sun come up."

Major leaned back in his rocker. "You're right, Aimee Louise. We need to remember what's important. First, sunrise."

The three of them gazed at the horizon. Shadow relaxed between the two girls.

"Good morning, sun," Aimee Louise said as the sun rose.

After they went inside, Major cooked breakfast while Aimee Louise fed Shadow and set silverware and napkins on the table, and Rosalie sat at the dining table and wrote in her notebook. Aimee Louise glanced over Rosalie's shoulder. "Add fill buckets for washing."

Major set three plates of blueberry pancakes on the table, and they all dug in.

After breakfast, Rosalie pointed at her notebook. "Want to look over our chore list? Basically, we have our chicken chores, clean up the kitchen dishes, sweep, and feed Shadow."

"When I get back from town, I can pitch in with the chores, then we can set up the generators. Back to your list, think of things we need to do before dark, like fill the lanterns with kerosene, and I need to order more propane for our tank while I'm in town. Here are the lists I pulled together for the feed store and the drug store. Do you see anything I missed?"

Rosalie said, "Feminine products."

"Added," he said. "Before I leave, I just remembered my amateur radio license is current, and I still have my old transceiver and charger. Be good to hear what's going on around us. I think I know where I put them."

He found a box marked *Electronics* on the top shelf in his closet and carried it to the dining table. "Do I smell coffee?" Major asked.

"It's almost ready," Rosalie said. "You didn't look like yourself this morning without a coffee cup in your hand."

"You're right. Didn't feel like myself either." When he opened the box, he moaned. "This is a tangled, jumbled mess."

"Let me look." Aimee Louise reached past a few cables and cords and deftly pulled out the transceiver and the charger.

"How did you do that?" Rosalie asked.

"I looked for what I want, not at what I don't want."

"Looked like magic to me," Major said. "We'll charge the batteries for the radio this evening when we have the generators for power. I better get outta here before another distraction jumps into my head."

Aimee Louise said, "I can set up the radio."

Major filled a cup with steaming coffee for the road, and Rosalie poured the remainder into his thermos.

* * *

When he drove into town, Major noticed that plastic sacks covered the gas station's pump handles. *One less worry for me—truck's tank is full, and gasoline's stored at the farm for the generators.*

His first stop was the feed store.

The manager leaned against the front door. "Good morning, Major. You got cash? I can make change out of my coffee can. It doesn't need electricity."

Major chuckled. "Sometimes the old ways are the best, aren't they? I've got cash, and chicken feed and dog food are at the top of my list."

Next was the drug store where the front door was propped open. Like other small-town drug stores, Plainview Drug and Sundries had a pharmacy and items like food, cleaning supplies, toys, paper products, and candy.

He dropped his small flashlight into his pocket and walked in with a sack of empty medicine bottles. The sun streamed through the windows and provided light for the front of the store, but the back remained dark.

A twenty-year-old leaned against the checkout counter. Her smock strained against her ample midsection.

"You open?" he asked.

She popped her gum. "Sure. Nobody's at the pharmacy, though."

*Scratch prescriptions.*

He found everything else on his list and paid cash.

When he climbed into his truck, he noticed the grocery store's parking lot overflowed into the road. He turned the other way.

The sheriff's office was his next stop. The sheriff nodded when he saw Major but continued the meeting with his deputies and several of the local ham radio operators. Major turned to leave, but the sheriff called after him. "Major, don't leave town until we've talked."

The deputies and hams laughed, and Major raised his eyebrows.

The sheriff laughed too. "No, no. You aren't under arrest."

"I'll see you after your meeting." Major smiled.

He drove to the library and chuckled when he went inside. "Not everyone remembers the old card checkout system. You all have the smoothest operation in town." The librarians beamed.

When he left with his books, the sheriff waited near his truck. "Major, I have a favor to ask. I'll be on duty around the clock until this electrical thing's over, and I'd like to bring my family and dog out to the farm."

"We've got plenty of room. They're more than welcome."

The sheriff's tense face relaxed. "Thanks. It won't take us long to finish packing up. And here's a spare department radio and solar charger. It'd be helpful if you'd keep an eye on your end of the county. I have no idea what to expect."

## CHAPTER TWELVE

Russell Gaston glanced back at his children sleeping in the back seat. He'd developed facial tics, and his hands dripped with sweat. *Why did Lee say he couldn't help? I've always been there for him.*

Russell's instincts told him that someone was following them, but even after taking sharp turns and hiding the car in the woods, he hadn't seen anyone. His mouth was dry, and his throat was tight when he tried to swallow.

"Margo, we need the children to be safe. I want to send you and the kids to the sheriff."

Margo clenched her hands and lifted her chin in defiance. "No. I stay with you, and they are babies."

"I'm sorry I got us in this position, Margo, but you and our children will be safer away from me. I know the sheriff will protect you. Let's take a break at the next rest stop. You and I can talk while the kids run off some energy."

As they strolled past the picnic area, Russell said, "Margo, I stepped into a trap."

He explained his research and the entanglement of blackmail and extortion.

"That's horrible; I'm so sorry." She hugged him. "There must be something we can do; I need time to think." They clung to each other and cried.

That afternoon, Russell parked near an abandoned church, and the children ran to examine the old cemetery.

"Okay," Margo said after the children were out of hearing distance, "I agree it's the best to send the children to the sheriff, but I absolutely refuse to leave your side."

"I won't have it," Russell said.

Margo's smile was weak. "You're a wonderful man, and I love you. I have to be by your side."

Russell called the children then headed back toward Plainview.

When they were three miles from town, Russell pulled over. "I have a challenge for you," Russell said. "This road goes straight to town and to the sheriff's office. Your challenge is to get to the sheriff's office without anyone seeing you."

Margo added, "You have to stay together, and remember, hide if you hear a car."

"Strange game," Annie said. "Will you meet us at the sheriff's office?"

"That's exactly what we plan to do." Russell squeezed Margo's hand as tears slipped down her cheeks.

Josh climbed out behind Annie. "Don't cry, Mom. We'll win."

Annie closed the car door, and they stood on the roadside.

Russell turned to his wife. "Please, Margo. I need you to go with the children. If you're with them, I'll know you'll keep them safe. It's important to me. Go."

"No, I won't leave you; don't make it harder. The children will be safe with the sheriff, and we need to leave now or tell them to get back in the car." Her voice cracked. "Let's go."

Russell put the car in gear, glanced in his rearview mirror, and waited until Annie and Josh stepped off the road into the brush, where they couldn't be seen. He grabbed Margo's hand and drove away. Margo turned her face and sobbed.

Later, Russell pulled into a convenience store southwest of Plainview. "I'll park here in the shade away from the building. We can go inside and refill our water jug."

When they returned to their car, Russell froze. *A car parked next to us.* "Wait a second, Margo."

He stepped closer. *Car's empty.* "Okay. Just being cautious."

He scanned the parking lot while he unlocked the car. The two of them slid inside and closed their doors.

A man's voice came from the shadows in the back of the car. "Keep looking forward, or I'll kill the missus. You too, missus. You move, and I'll kill your husband."

Margo flinched. Russell caught a glimpse of a gun barrel close to her head. His pistol was locked in the console next to him. *Might as well be at home in a locked drawer. I'll keep my eyes open for any opportunity to escape or…or what?*

Russell smelled the man's sour sweat and almost gagged. The man reeked with an overtone of slight sweetness. *Smells like an overweight man, a diabetic, maybe. Margo would know.* He looked down and saw her hands were shaking.

"Stay calm. Nothing fancy," the man said. "Drive toward town. I'll tell you when to pull over."

Russell pulled onto the state road to Plainview. His hands clutched the steering wheel, and his knuckles were white. He glanced at Margo. Her face was pale, and tears slipped down her cheeks. He moved his left hand down to the bottom of the steering wheel and signed *I love you* in American Sign Language.

The man said, "Slow down. Pull off the road on the right in about a quarter mile. I'll tell you when."

Russell took his right hand off the steering wheel and reached for Margo's hand. She took his hand, closed her eyes, and kept her breathing even.

"Here. Pull off the road and drive down into the ravine. I'll tell you when to stop. Don't try anything funny."

Russell drove the car into the ravine and tapped the brake to slow the forward motion.

The man said, "Stop here. Turn off the engine. Keep looking straight ahead. Hand me your wallets. And your jewelry. Where are the kids?"

"They're safe with my stepbrother," Russell said.

They handed their wallets to the man and didn't look back. They removed their watches. Margo passed back her engagement ring. Russell saw her drop her wedding ring and her mother's ring on her lap. He did the same with his wedding ring.

He said, "I'm sorry."

Margo glanced at him. "I love you. You are my hero."

"They're safe," he said. Margo nodded. "Let my wife go. Her name is Margo. She won't try to look back. She didn't have anything to do with this."

"I'm getting out of the car. Look straight ahead for five minutes."

* * *

Howie put on rubber gloves and poured liquid from a small vial onto a square of gauze. He swiped the gauze across the backs of their necks. The moment the gauze touched their skin, they died.

He stepped out, locked the doors, and dug a small hole. He dropped the gauze and vial into the hole and tossed the gloves on top. He kicked in dirt and walked back to his car as the sun set. *Easy. Now make sure they didn't drop the kids off. I'll tell The Boss about the stepbrother.*

## CHAPTER THIRTEEN

The sheriff's wife, Molly, their seven-year-old twins, Brett and Sara, and their dog, Penny, arrived at the farm later that afternoon. Molly and Major unloaded the car, and the kids pitched in.

"Major," Molly said, "show us where you want us to sleep, and we'll get our things put away. This explosion has knocked me off-kilter. I don't feel very organized."

"Mommy likes to have a plan," Sara said, grinning, and her hazel-green eyes sparkled.

Molly laughed and tossed her curly, dark-blonde hair. "You're right about that, Sara."

"I feel better with a plan too. Spare bedroom's upstairs. Let's see if it works for you."

Sara and Brett raced up the stairs. Brett's long legs took them two at a time. Sara chased after him, but her short legs couldn't quite keep up with Brett.

Molly was out of breath by the time she got to the bedroom. *Doc says I need to lose thirty pounds. Guess now's the time to start.*

After Major joined them, he said, "The room isn't expansive, but the bed's comfortable. Do you think this will work?"

"This is great, thank you. I expected to sleep on a sofa, and there's plenty of room here for the two cots I brought for the twins." After Molly and the twins set up the cots, they went downstairs in search of Major.

Major and Aimee Louise sorted through items in the kitchen and put them into the pantry or cabinets. Rosalie sat at the dining table and recorded the locations on her inventory list.

He looked up. "Here they are. Let's take a break."

Molly and the twins sat together on the leather sofa, and Aimee Louise and Rosalie sank into the frayed blue-and-red plaid sofa. Shadow flopped down near his girls, and Penny sat on Molly's feet.

Major leaned back in his soft chair. "Welcome, Molly, Sara, and Brett. First thing I want you to know is that you are safe, and we're glad you're here. We don't know when the electricity will come back on, but we've got food and beds, and the house will keep us safe and dry. Two rules: one, stay close to the house; two, when Molly or I call *Inside*, run as fast as you can. No questions. Remember, run. Molly, your thoughts?"

"Sounds good to me," Molly said. "I'd like to add if anyone is worried about something or has questions, feel free to talk to Pops or me. There's lots of us and lots of work to do, so we'll need to look after each other and pitch in. Maybe we can organize the work. Major, I like to cook; is it okay if I take over the meal planning and cooking?"

"I would appreciate it. We'd survive on my cooking, but it's not my best skill." Major chuckled.

Rosalie held up her hand. "I have a question. What should we call Mrs. Starr? Molly doesn't sound right."

"Whatever you like is fine with me," Molly said. "What would you suggest?"

"You could call her Mom Starr," Sara said.

"Nope," Brett said, "sounds too much like *Monster*." Brett put out his arms and shuffled stiff-legged around the room.

Molly laughed. "Good point."

Aimee Louise said, "Aunt Molly."

"Yes," Molly said. "Perfect. I like it. We're family."

Major rose. "If nobody needs me for anything, I need to secure my farm equipment and get the generators hooked up. Molly, the girls have whistles. It's our emergency signal."

"Might be something we should get too," Molly said.

She peered into the refrigerator. "Is there paper and a pen I could use? I want to draw up meal plans for the next couple of days."

Rosalie dashed to the computer room and returned with notepaper and a pencil. "Here you are, Aunt Molly. I love lists."

"Oh, good. Maybe you can look at my meal plans to see if I missed anything. I want to eat up what might spoil first."

* * *

An hour later, Major strode into the kitchen. "Wow, Molly. Do I smell meatloaf and biscuits in the oven? Reminds me of when I was a kid and came in from a hard day at work in the fields. I told my dad I knew what heaven smelled like, and he agreed. Salad looks good too. You have magical culinary skills."

Molly's cheeks turned a light pink. "Thanks, Major. I used the refrigerated ingredients first. Aimee Louise set up a handwashing station next to the sink, and the twins made name tags for the hand towels. Food's about to go on the table."

After everyone took their seats, Major looked at the eager faces and bowed his head, and everyone followed his example. "Bless this food and bless this family."

"Amen," Molly said. "Everyone serve yourself but eat what you take. If you aren't sure how much you can eat, take a little, and you can have seconds later. We want to be sure everyone gets enough to eat without any wasted food."

"My dad had a rule." Major buttered a biscuit. "He said always leave a little for the next person. He said his brother had a different rule—eat it all up so you don't have to put away the leftovers."

Brett grinned. "Was his brother's name Brett?"

Major laughed. "Coulda been."

Molly held her breath while the twins took their time and considered how much food to put on their plates. *I would have dished up a little more for Sara and a little less for Brett, but they have a better idea of how much they can eat.*

"Before everyone gets up from the table," Major said. "Let's review."

"Stay close to the house," Brett said.

"If Mommy or Pops says go inside, run. No questions," Sara said. "Oh, and if Pops hears a whistle, he runs to the house."

"Good job," Molly said. "I think if any of us is outside, and we hear a whistle, we all run to the house. Right, Pops?"

"Yes. Well done, Sara and Brett."

"Anybody think of any more questions?" Major asked. Sara opened her mouth and then pursed her lips. He smiled and nodded encouragement.

"I was just wondering." She frowned and gazed at the table. "Will it be dark upstairs? Like when we go to bed?"

"Excellent question, Sara. Yes, it will, but I bought two rechargeable flashlights with cranks on them today—one for each bedroom. They're in the pantry."

Rosalie jumped up and returned to the table with the two flashlights.

Major turned the crank on one of them. "Charge the batteries by turning the crank. When they're charged, we have light."

"That is awesome," Brett said. "Mommy, I need to save up my money for a crank flashlight."

"Sounds smart, son. We'll put it on your list."

The twins helped Rosalie clear the dishes while Aimee Louise went outside to start the generators.

"We feed Penny at home," Sara said. "Can we feed Shadow too?"

"I'll help you," Rosalie said.

"Molly, can we talk on the porch?" Major asked.

Molly sank on a rocker and sighed. "I've got weary bones. Love this breeze. I understand now why the old Florida cracker houses always had big wide porches. Don't sit downwind of me. We get showers tonight, right?"

"Yes, showers before we turn off the generators. Otherwise, I'd have to hold my breath to take my shirt off tonight," Major said.

"Funny, and true for me too."

"The sheriff gave me a radio and a solar charger to stay in touch with him. I have my old amateur radio. We can listen to keep up with the news."

Molly closed her eyes and rocked. "Good, it'll help us not feel so isolated. From a safety standpoint, I locked our shotgun and ammunition in the hall closet with the trigger lock on the shotgun. Do you have a better idea?"

Major and Molly talked about security, safety, and potential threats.

"I don't want to scare the children, but I want them to be safe," he said. "Why don't I talk to the older girls and you talk to the twins about being aware of their surroundings?"

Molly found the twins near the chicken coops. "Time to go inside. We can talk on our way. I need for you to think about your safety. If something doesn't feel right, run to the house."

Sara said, "Are we under a watch, Mommy?"

Molly turned to look at her daughter. "Maybe. What does that mean?"

"Well, Rosalie said a weather watch is when conditions are right for a storm. A warning is when the storm is headed your way."

Molly's eyes widened. "Good analogy. Yes, we're under a watch. So, let's get cleaned up for the night and brush our teeth. After you put on your pajamas, we'll go to the family room, and you can pick a game for us to play before bedtime. We'll use the kerosene lanterns when it gets dark. It'll be like frontier days."

* * *

While Molly and Rosalie organized baths, Major, Aimee Louise, and the dogs walked the house's perimeter. The sun was low on the horizon, and the air had cooled; the haunting call of a barred owl drifted from the woods.

"A Native American legend says a hooting barred owl warns of death, but the Greeks said a barred owl flying over a battlefield meant victory," Major said.

"What do you think, Pops?" Aimee Louise asked.

"I think stories are great, and I want the barred owl to stick around and eat the mice and snakes."

Aimee Louise gazed at the sky. "I never saw stars at our apartment, but Dad talked to me about stars when we went camping. What was he like when he was a kid?"

"Your dad was a hard worker and threw himself into whatever he was doing. He worked hard, played hard, and loved to be outside. When he was eight, he set a tent up in the backyard and slept there most nights of his summer vacation. Your gram tried to talk him into coming inside when it rained, but he told her he'd been wet before and he'd be wet again." Major chuckled.

"Dad used to say that all the time when we went camping," Aimee Louise said.

"Gram put her foot down when a big storm hit, though, and made him sleep inside. He still slept on the floor in his sleeping bag in his room. When your dad was twelve, he got a bigger tent because he'd grown so much, and he slept most of his summers in his tent until he left for college."

"Do you have the tents?" Aimee Louise asked.

Major stopped and scratched his head. "I don't know if I do or not. I thought your dad took the big one with him to college, but

I'm not positive. We can look through the storage room sometime. Sounds like a great activity for a rainy day."

Aimee Louise said, "I like to be outside."

"While we're out here, look at the house. With the lanterns lit, the house shouts *occupied.* The trees give plenty of cover for anyone who wants to watch the house, but there's no cover for anyone to sneak up close to the house. You'll notice that Shadow guards the perimeter."

"Shadow runs a circle around us when we stop on a run," Aimee Louise said.

"We're lucky because he taught himself to guard." Major said. "Maybe it's because of the chickens. I told him not to scare the chickens, or he couldn't go outside when they free-ranged."

Aimee Louise and Major strolled to the trees and returned to the house.

*Dad gave me his love of the outdoors. Thanks, Dad.*

* * *

When Major came into the house the next morning after a perimeter check with Shadow alongside. Aimee Louise and Rosalie were helping Molly with breakfast, and Sara and Brett were setting the table.

"You're just in time, Major." Molly smiled. "We're ready to serve up breakfast. Since we don't know how long our outage will be, we're still eating what was in the refrigerator first."

After everyone was seated, Major dipped a biscuit into his runny, golden-orange yolk. "This is a feast—eggs, biscuits, sausage, and jam."

"These eggs are wonderful. Good job, chickens," Molly said. "We won't have to worry about breakfast around here."

Brett's mouth was full, muffling his words. "I like refrigerator food. Sausage is yummy."

Molly said, "Don't—oh, never mind."

Aimee Louise said, "Pops, we want to check the cameras."

Rosalie nodded. Her mouth was full too.

Major worked to get his last bite of egg on his fork. "I'd like to know what's out there, but I don't know about the two of you going so far from the house alone. What if the three of us go? Molly, are you okay if we're back in thirty or forty minutes?"

"Sure, we can weed the garden, and Penny will guard us."

"Before we leave, I'd like to check the ham radio for news," he said.

While everyone else cleared the table, Major showed Aimee Louise how to check the fuel levels, and she started up the generators.

Rosalie joined Aimee Louise and Major at the ham radio, and Aimee Louise made a few adjustments to improve reception. While Rosalie took notes, Molly stood in the doorway to listen.

When the radio quieted, Major said, "Rosalie, you have our summary?"

She nodded. "Quite a few folks said they didn't have electricity. The hams wanted to determine how widespread the outage was, but I think it's too soon to gather much information."

"I think so too. Molly, we're ready to check the cameras. If you get the feeling we've been gone too long, bring the kids inside, lock up, and call the sheriff. I hate to leave you, but I want to see what the cameras have picked up."

"We'll be fine. If I get a case of the nerves, we'll come inside."

After they left the house, Major said, "We'll walk together. After we get close to the cameras, you can run."

The girls encouraged Major to go faster because they wanted to run. He broke into a brief jog. *These two could run actual circles around me.*

"The trees look like burnt matches." Aimee Louise pointed.

"Yeah, and there some that were tossed aside by a giant." Rosalie frowned. "I caught a whiff of smoke."

"No surprise. We'll have a lingering smell of smoke for a while," Major said. "It was a huge fire."

When they reached the first camera, he leaned against the tree to catch his breath. "Go ahead. I'll exchange the camera cards."

Major smiled as Aimee Louise, Rosalie, and Shadow raced away to the next two cameras. *Three unbridled mustangs released into the wild.*

They checked all the cameras and returned to the farmhouse after being gone only twenty-five minutes.

"I don't see anyone. Stay behind me," Major said.

Shadow ran to the house and scratched at the door. When Sara opened it and waved, Penny ran outside.

"You can run to the house," Major said.

Aimee Louise and Rosalie raced to the house. When Major arrived, Molly was on her cell phone. She handed the phone to him. "The sheriff needs to talk to you."

"Major, I have two more to come to the farm. We have the Gaston children, but we don't know where their parents are. Molly can explain."

"That's disturbing, but we can make room," Major said before they hung up.

"What do we know, Molly?"

"The sheriff didn't know much, but from what Annie and Josh told him, the family left home after dark a few weeks ago," Molly said. "Annie said it was a vacation to visit their uncle Lee, but when their dad called him, their plans changed. The kids said their dad told their mother Uncle Lee sounded funny."

Major frowned. "I think I know when they left. Aimee Louise came home after school one day and said Annie's mother had a panic cloud. I wasn't clear on what she meant, but I understand more about clouds now."

"The kids said they moved around," Molly continued. "Josh said they went to a big city for a few days. After the city, they camped in the woods in their car, according to Josh, not in a tent. I'm not sure what happened, but Russell drove the children about three miles outside of town yesterday, and after the kids got out of the car, he told them to stay near the road and walk to the sheriff's office. He handed them their jackets and their backpacks that contained their clothes and snacks."

"By themselves?" he asked.

"Yes. They left the kids on the roadside and drove off." Molly's voice cracked. "Russell and Margo would never leave their children, and certainly not alone on the side of a road, unless something dreadful was about to happen."

Molly dropped to sit on the old sofa. "The kids said it was a challenge game. If they heard a car, they were supposed to hide, and if no one saw them before they got to the sheriff's office, they won. Josh said when their mother cried, he told her not to be sad because they would win the game."

Major shook his head. "This is so out of character for Russell and Margo. Did the kids know who they were supposed to hide from?"

"I don't think so, but someone must have been looking for them because Annie said they heard a car drive up and down the road. They stayed out of sight and hid in a ditch until it got dark before they ran to town. They spent the night in the old shed behind the sheriff's office because they didn't see any lights on anywhere in town. They knocked on the office door at daybreak, and one of the deputies heard them."

When tears slipped down Molly's cheeks, Sara slid next to her and patted her hand. Molly smiled at her daughter.

"The sheriff said the children suffered from bug bites and were cold and hungry, but after the deputies cleaned and treated their bites, and the kids warmed up and ate, they seemed fine. He'll stop by our house to pick up our rollaway bed and another cot before he brings them to the farm. When he goes back to the office, he'll stop at their house."

"Maybe he can pick up some of their clothes while he's there," Major said.

"Family is growing," Aimee Louise said.

"We read it's good strategy to be part of a group when something bad happens," Rosalie said.

"Well, we are turning into quite a group," Major agreed.

"That's the truth," Molly said. "What do we do about sleeping arrangements?"

"If you're okay with the two younger girls in your room, I have room for two cots for the boys in my room. No change for the two older girls seems important."

"I was thinking along the same lines," Molly said.

"Aimee Louise, I need a cot from upstairs," Major said. "Could you get it? I'll shift my bed for the two cots."

Aimee Louise headed upstairs.

"Rosalie, what about two more chairs at the dining table?" Molly asked.

"On it."

* * *

On the way to Major's farm, the sheriff asked Annie and Josh, "Do your folks own any rifles or pistols?"

Annie said, "Dad keeps his deer rifle on the top shelf in his closet and a pistol locked in his desk drawer in the computer room. His ammunition is locked in a box, but I'm not sure where that is."

"That's all he has," Josh said. "He told me he always wanted a shotgun too, but Mom said no. He told me he always listens to Mom, and I should too."

"Your dad is the smartest man I know," the sheriff said.

The sheriff pulled into Major's driveway only thirty minutes after he talked to Molly; everyone was waiting on the porch. When

Annie and Josh stepped out of the car, Molly gasped at how exhausted they looked.

"Let's go inside," Molly said, "and have a snack of crackers and milk."

The house was quiet for the next ten minutes except for the sounds of munching and slurping.

Brett finished his snack and scooted his chair back. "Josh, I'm glad you're here. I was tired of being the only boy." The boys fist-bumped.

"Annie, I'm happy you're here," Sara said. "Aimee Louise and Rosalie are friends, and now I have a friend too."

Annie beamed.

"Where does Shadow sleep?" Josh asked.

"Shadow sleeps near the front door. He stays on guard," Major said.

"We used to have a dog, but he got old. We don't have a dog anymore. I miss him. I like dogs," Annie said.

"Me too," Josh agreed. He scratched Penny's ears, and she flopped over so he could rub her tummy, and Josh grinned.

Sheriff put his arm around Molly, and she accompanied him to his car.

* * *

As the sheriff drove down the long driveway to the Gaston house, his eyes narrowed at the open front door. He checked in on his radio. "House check. Stand by for backup."

The sheriff approached the house with care. When he stepped inside, leaves littered the entryway. *No signs of any intruders.*

He scoured the master bedroom and reached up on the shelf in the closet. *Rifle's right where Annie said it would be.*

When he checked Russell's home office, the top of the desk was bare, with no computer or even a pen, and the desk drawer was unlocked and empty.

*House is neat. Undisturbed. No signs of forced entry.*

He found two oversized laundry baskets and filled them with clothes for the children. He loaded the baskets and the rifle into his cruiser and returned to the house for one last check. After he closed and locked the front door, he tried to open it. *Locked tight.*

He picked up his radio mic and reported in. "Stand down. Nothing found." He sat in his car and examined the house's exterior.

*Could have left in such a rush they didn't secure the door.*

The sheriff frowned. "Well, that's a little far-fetched in light of Russell's connection with the electric company, the explosion at the substation, and the strange way Russell left his children by themselves on the road. I have absolutely no plausible explanation."

The sheriff drummed his fingers on the steering wheel. *All I have is an uneasy feeling about the Gastons.*

## CHAPTER FOURTEEN

When Molly tiptoed downstairs not long after sunrise, Major and Shadow were already on the front porch. She perked a pot of coffee and carried two steaming cups outside. Penny clicked along behind her.

"Major, yesterday the sheriff said the explosion caused a surge in the entire regional electrical system. What does it mean for us?"

Molly scooted her chair around to face him, and Penny flopped down next to her.

"We may be without electricity for several weeks, but it's too early to tell. I listened to the ham radio this morning. The hams talked about a built-in safety net that halted what could have been a domino effect and a much wider outage. One bit of good news is the hospital in Plainview may get power earlier than other areas." Major returned her gaze. "We'll be okay. Are you worried?"

"A little."

"I understand, but I'm grateful all the kids are here with us."

"You're right. We're all safe here. Thank you for that." Molly gazed at the horizon. "If there's no word from their parents, I'd like for Annie and Josh to go home with us when the electricity comes back on. The girls are welcome too."

"Sounds fine, but as far as my girls are concerned, we'll stay together."

Rosalie came out of the house. She wore a red flannel shirt and jeans, and her flaming red hair was in a ponytail. "Hey, you're up early."

"Good morning, Rosalie," Molly said. "Anybody else awake?"

Rosalie sat on the porch next to Shadow, and he placed a paw on her leg.

"Nobody but me and Aimee Louise."

Aimee Louise joined them on the porch. She sat next to Shadow, who flopped his head on her lap and sighed.

"Molly, what if the girls and I cook breakfast this morning?" Major said. "We make magnificent blueberry pancakes and eggs, and I spotted blueberries in the freezer."

"Okay." Molly laughed. "I'll start the generator for the refrigerator and freezer. I've watched Aimee Louise, and I'm ready for cross-training. Before everybody finishes breakfast, I can get the well and water-heater generator going too."

"I might take a turn on the laundry today," Major said.

Aimee Louise said, "Rosalie and I can chop down a tree for firewood."

"Well—" started Molly.

"Good idea," Major interrupted. "Let's cook breakfast. We'll let Molly and the kids clean up. If you help me with the laundry, I'll teach you to use a chainsaw."

Rosalie sang, "It's upside-down day on the farm. All the animals turn on their charm."

The younger kids appeared. Annie jumped in to add verses to the song.

"The cow goes cluck, and the chicken says moo," Annie sang. "The owl says woof, and the dog calls whoo."

The boys leaped from foot to foot, hunched over with bowed legs, swung their arms, scratched their ribs, and scrunched their faces.

"Oo-oo ee-ee."

Sara rolled her eyes. "Boys."

Molly chuckled. "What a great way to start the day."

Sara and Brett set the table, and the hungry group took their places, eager for pancakes and eggs.

"Guess I need more practice in serving a crowd." Major mixed a second batch of pancake batter.

Josh waved his fork and dripped syrup down his arm. "Anytime you need somebody to eat pancakes, Pops, you let me know." Penny eased closer to Josh.

After breakfast, Major and the two girls hung damp laundry on the clothesline. When they were finished, he stood back and watched the clothes flapping in the wind. "I'd forgotten how satisfying the fresh smell of clothes dried outdoors is. Let's grab our backpacks and hook up the small trailer to the tractor. If we can find two medium-sized trees, you can each fell a tree."

"Can I drive the tractor?" Rosalie asked.

"You can drive the tractor to the trailer, and then I'll drive. My old bones need a rest day."

While Rosalie rushed to the tractor, Major and Aimee Louise gathered backpacks, chainsaws, and equipment, and then loaded everything into the trailer.

"You two get the safety awareness award for the day. Glad to see you wore your work boots," he said.

"Pops," Aimee Louise said, "We want to stay with you."

Major didn't realize the girls had heard the discussion, but he was glad Aimee Louise expressed her wishes. "I know, Aimee Louise. We will always stay together."

When Rosalie returned with the tractor, Major helped her hook up the trailer.

Molly stepped out of the house. "Major, if you take your cell phone, I'll keep mine on until you get back."

"Will do. You girls can ride in the trailer, run alongside, or alternate. Whatever you feel like."

"We'll run," Aimee Louise said. Shadow ran with the girls.

*Glad I was smart enough to claim the driver's seat.*

Major examined a stand of trees on the west side of the farm property. The girls and Shadow circled back and joined him. Rosalie shaded her eyes with an arm to look at the trees too.

He pointed to a group and said, "Let's go over there. Those trees are medium-sized and have a clear target direction to fall."

When he climbed on the tractor, he looked around. "Where's Aimee Louise?"

"I don't know. I don't see Shadow, either," Rosalie said.

"They've gone to look at trees. I'll call Shadow."

Major clapped his hands to call Shadow.

"Pops, Shadow wouldn't leave Aimee Louise." Rosalie pulled out her safety whistle and blew it. "Wait, listen." Rosalie pointed toward the trees. "It came from there."

She blew her whistle again. The responding shrill tweet was a little louder and a little clearer. Rosalie blew her whistle and listened.

Major said, "There they are."

Both Aimee Louise and Shadow panted as they ran up.

"Where were you? Where did you go?" he asked.

"Pops…" Aimee Louise gasped for breath then bent over and put her hands on her knees. "Pops, people in a car."

"What? What people? What do you mean, in a car?"

Rosalie stared at Aimee Louise then guided her to the trailer. "Here, sit down, Aimee Louise. You and Shadow ran hard."

"People in a car, Pops," Aimee Louise said. "Gray, and no clouds."

"Is the car gray?"

"No, the people are gray and don't have clouds."

Major's skin crawled, and his stomach churned with a sour feeling about what Aimee Louise may have found. Rosalie handed Aimee Louise a bottle of water, placed Shadow's travel bowl on the back of the trailer, and poured water for him.

Major hurried to start the tractor engine. "You all can ride in the trailer. If you point, Aimee Louise, Rosalie can direct me."

"We go straight ahead in the direction we saw Aimee Louise and Shadow," Rosalie said. A few minutes later she added, "Pops, turn toward the right, two o'clock."

As Major made the turn, he was pleased Rosalie remembered they used clock positions to pinpoint direction to indicate animals or droppings.

Rosalie said, "Stop, Pops. We walk from here."

Major realized they were a half mile from the state road. *Could the car be on the road?*

"Down there, Pops." Aimee Louise pointed.

He only saw the car in the ravine because Aimee Louise showed him where to look. He saw no obvious body damage to the car that would indicate it had crashed.

"You girls wait here," Major said. He couldn't shake off the dread. A slight, icy-cold breeze brushed the back of his neck. *Looks like Russell's car.*

When he reached the car, he saw the two bodies—one in the driver's seat and the other in the passenger's seat. Their seatbelts were still on, and they held hands. *Aimee Louise was right.* Their skin was gray. Now he understood why she said "no clouds." They were lifeless. Major tried all the doors. *Locked.*

He called the sheriff on his cell phone. "Sheriff, we've found the Gastons. They're in their locked car in a ravine close to the state road, about two miles north of Red Springs. Both appear deceased. The car doesn't look like it crashed."

Major answered the sheriff's questions as he headed back to the tractor.

"Girls, I'll call Molly. I need you and Shadow to go back to the house. You can drive the tractor and trailer. Drive slow and be safe. Molly will call me when you get there. I'll either walk home or get a ride with the sheriff; he's on his way here. If you have any problems with the tractor, leave it and run home. We can always get it later."

"You drive, Aimee Louise." Rosalie and Shadow climbed into the trailer and sat near the tractor before Aimee Louise drove away.

Major called Molly. "Aimee Louise and Shadow found Russell's car. The Gastons are inside the car, and they are…deceased. The sheriff's on his way. Let me know the second you see the girls; they are on their way back with the tractor and Shadow."

Major had grabbed a bottle of water and his backpack off the trailer before the girls left. He sat near the road in the shade of an oak tree and gulped a long drink then poured water into his hand and splashed his face with the cool water. *I didn't realize how thirsty I was. What a shock seeing the Gastons. It'll be rough for Annie and Josh.*

He covered his face with his hands, sighed, and lifted his face to the sky. "God, this will be hard. Sure could use a little help."

His phone beeped. It was a text from Molly. "Girls here. All ok." His shoulders relaxed. He didn't realize how tense he was.

When he saw the sheriff's car, he stepped closer to the road and waved. The sheriff parked and stepped out of his car.

"This way, Sheriff." Major led the way toward the ravine.

"State troopers are on the way and should be here soon," the sheriff said as they maneuvered the ravine incline to the car. "They'll begin the investigation, and the feds will take over. After the state guys arrive, I'll take you back to the farm. The investigators will want to talk to Aimee Louise and you. They understand Aimee Louise's communication style, but they are still interested in her perspective."

The sheriff tried all the doors. "Russell and Margo. Can't believe it," he said.

The two men returned to the road before the state troopers arrived. The troopers stared at Major in awe and took notes while he told them how they found the car. After they clarified a few points, the sheriff showed them where the car was.

When the sheriff returned, he said, "I'll give you a ride to the farm. I talked to Molly. She'll tell Annie and Josh their parents passed away. I'll tell my children. Will you tell your girls?"

"Of course," Major said. "I'll text Molly and let her know we're on our way."

After Major and the sheriff arrived at the farm, Molly said, "Annie. Josh. Let's go to the back porch and talk."

"What's going on, Aunt Molly? You look upset," Annie said.

The three of them sat on the back porch.

"I have very bad news," Molly said. "Worse than bad. Sad news."

Annie frowned and crossed her arms. Josh cocked his head and crossed his arms.

"It's about Mom and Dad, isn't it?" Annie asked.

"Yes."

"I don't want to hear it." Annie jumped up and covered her ears.

"Your mom and dad died," Molly said. "Their car was on the side of the road in a ditch. They didn't crash. Sheriff doesn't know how they died, but they died."

"No!" Annie screamed.

"You're wrong." Josh growled and grabbed his sister's hand. They faced Molly and glowered.

"I'm sorry," Molly said. "This is terrible news."

Annie turned her back on Molly and snatched her hand away from Josh.

When Molly grabbed Annie and Josh into a hug, the two children broke into sobs. Molly clutched them tightly while tears rolled down her face.

"It isn't fair; we shouldn't have left them," Annie said.

"Whatever happened, they wanted you to be safe. They protected you because they love you so much. And it isn't fair that they died," Molly spoke softly through her own tears.

"I should have stayed with Dad because Mom would be okay now," Josh said.

"Your mom and dad wanted you to stay together and look after each other. You were safe because you stayed together that night, right? Just like they wanted you to do. They knew they could count on you."

"What happens to us next? We can't stay at our house by ourselves," Annie said.

"You'll stay with me and the sheriff, and Sara, Brett, and Penny. We'll all be safe together. Are you interested in a walk? We can walk and talk. Or just walk."

The three of them strolled to the woods. The sheriff and the two younger children joined them on their walk.

Aimee Louise and Rosalie helped Major with the chores while Molly and the sheriff stayed with the younger children.

"Breakfast is the last time anyone has eaten. I'll grill chicken," Major said.

"I'll scrub potatoes and put them in the oven and open a jar of green beans," Aimee Louise said.

"I can set the table and help with the chicken," Rosalie added.

Molly, Sheriff, and the children returned to the house.

After everyone had taken a seat at the table, Major said, "Our hearts are heavy. Give us strength and peace."

"Amen," the sheriff said.

After the meal was over, everyone rocked or sat on the back porch and watched the sunset.

"Annie and Josh, would you like to talk?" Molly asked.

"No." Annie slumped against Rosalie; Rosalie reached for Annie's hand, and their fingers intertwined.

"Did you know Mom?" Annie asked.

Molly smiled. "I knew your mom very well. She volunteered at the school, and we worked on a lot of projects together. Did you know she was a pharmacist before she and your dad were married? She was smart and organized. Whenever the school had a difficult project, everybody would say, 'We need Mrs. Gaston on this one.'"

Annie said with a small smile, "Dad said nobody was smarter than Mom."

Molly nodded. "She led the project to have recess at school every day. The administration and the school board claimed the pressure to perform on the statewide tests didn't allow for time away from the classroom. They said they'd compromise with ten minutes of recess two or three days a week, but not every day. Your mom was persuasive and persistent. She was the force behind the twenty minutes of free time outside every day at school. She was awesome."

Tears gathered in Annie's eyes and escaped down her face. "Mom was awesome." She swiped at her face.

Josh sniffled and asked, "What about Dad? Did you know Dad?" He edged close to the sheriff's chair.

"I knew your dad when he was little and lived in Plainview," Major said. "His father was proud of him. He used to tell me how serious your dad was about school. He told me one time when your dad was in third grade, your dad wanted to wear a tie to school so the teachers would know he was serious. Your grandfather talked him out of it, but you could tell how proud he was of his son. Your dad was the smartest kid in school."

The sheriff added, "The people who clean the sheriff's office for me used to work for your dad. They said before your dad took over, the previous managers knew nothing about what it was like to work in the field. Your dad did, and everyone respected him for it. He was smart, serious about his job, and serious about their safety. They said he was a hard worker, a great boss, and an amazing man."

Josh shifted closer to the sheriff, who wrapped an arm around the boy's shoulders. Tears slid down Josh's face.

Sara moved next to Annie and put her small hand in Annie's other hand.

"Sorry, Annie," she said in a tiny voice.

Annie nodded, and more tears spilled down her face. Molly wiped away her tears.

Aimee Louise moved close to Major. He put his hand on her shoulder.

The farm family sat in silence and watched the sun go down. Molly escorted the sheriff to his car. Major and Aimee Louise started up the generator for the well and water heater for baths.

"Bath time. Younger girls first, then boys," Molly said after the sheriff left.

After the four children bathed, Molly took a quick shower and turned the bathroom over to the older girls. All six of the children and Molly came to the family room scrubbed, clean, and wearing their pajamas, robes, and slippers.

Major greeted them with cups and a pot of hot chocolate on the table. "I liked hot chocolate when I was a kid."

After the hot chocolate, everyone said goodnight, and Major took a final walk around the house and checked on the chickens. When he returned, all the children were in bed, and Molly waited for him to lock up.

"Molly, let's look for some curtains or material tomorrow in the storage closet. The lanterns shine like beacons."

"I agree. I'm sure we can find something. Good night and thank you for being here for all of us."

* * *

At the end of the week, the sheriff arrived at the farm and headed straight to Major in the barn. "I wanted to talk to you before anyone noticed I was here. The investigators found Russell's pistol locked in his center console. I'm convinced they were ambushed, and Russell had no time to react. He would have protected Margo if he had a chance. However, their wedding rings were in their laps, and Margo had a second ring in her lap. I'll bet it belonged to the family. I'm sure they left the rings for their children. I'll talk to Molly. We may put them away for Annie and Josh for a while."

Major loaded chicken feed into the utility wagon and shook his head. "I'm so sorry Russell and Margo are gone. Such a tragedy."

The sheriff nodded. "I talked to Pastor John. He planned a memorial service. He doesn't have a date set yet. After the coroner completes the autopsies, their ashes will be buried in the church memorial garden."

"Thanks. Good to know."

"How's it going here?" Sheriff asked as he strolled along with Major, who pulled the wagon to the chicken coops.

Major stopped and gazed at the sheriff. "Six months ago I was a lonely man. Today I'm scrambling to stay ahead of three women and four children. I come to the barn for quiet."

The sheriff chuckled. "On another note, we got word the larger towns have electricity, and we are next. Things in Plainview have been a nice surprise after the initial chaos. One church provides breakfast, and another church hosts a meal in the late afternoon. They never know where they will get food, but it appears. Do you have spare eggs you could donate?"

Major lifted the sack of feed into the metal storage bin and turned toward the house. "I sure do. We've got plenty of eggs. We'll see what else we can find. I'd always heard when times get bad, neighbors turn against neighbors. Sounds like our community drew closer together."

"There have been a few incidents, but overall, I'm proud of how our town is doing." The sheriff stopped and scanned the surrounding area. "You have a clear buffer between the house and trees all the way around. Any blind sides?"

"There are windows on all four sides, upstairs and down, but I haven't looked for any blind spots. Need to check sometime."

Sara spotted the sheriff. "It's Daddy." Everyone ran to greet him, including the dogs. Molly was the last to reach the sheriff.

She puffed and put her hands on her hips to catch her breath. "Darn kids run fast around here."

"Hello, Old Woman. I've missed you."

"You're older," Molly said, "and I missed you more." She wrapped her arms around his neck and kissed him.

"Eww," Brett and Josh said in unison.

"Does anybody mind if we send our eggs to town so other folks can have eggs?" Major asked. "We can have oatmeal for a few days."

"It would be a nice change," Molly said.

"I like oatmeal," Rosalie said, "but I could never make it as good as Mom."

"You're in luck," Molly said. "Your mom and I both took home economics in high school. We weren't in the same class, but the same teacher taught us. Your mom told me one time my oatmeal was as good as hers."

Rosalie cocked her head and said, "Really, Aunt Molly?"

"Yep. You can judge."

"We can make you a blue ribbon if you win, Mommy," said Sara. "Or a red one if you come in second. Rosalie is the judge, right?"

"A breakfast contest. Best idea ever," said the sheriff and winked at Molly.

Molly said in a soft voice, "Sometimes, this is not the farm. This is the zoo. And you fit right in."

Major smiled, and the sheriff's shoulders shook as he laughed. The kids looked at the sheriff to see what the joke was. He pointed at Molly, who glared at him.

"Let's load the sheriff's car," Major said. "Aimee Louise and Rosalie, gather the eggs in the kitchen and check the nests. We'll send all we've got. The rest of you kids come with me. I'll need help to carry things to the car. Brett, would you take the utility wagon back to the barn?"

Brett ran to the coops and soon returned from the barn.

The farm family pitched in and carried rice and dried beans to the sheriff's car. Major pulled out a frozen chicken from the freezer.

"Major, I can't thank you enough," the sheriff said.

"It's from all of us," Major said.

* * *

The next morning, Major and Molly sat on the porch before daylight with coffee.

"How are you doing, Major?" Molly asked.

"I'm fine," Major said.

Molly nodded. "Let me rephrase that, how are you doing, Major?"

Major chuckled. "Before Aimee Louise came here, I was lonely and not very motivated to do anything about it. I thought I was happy with my quiet, uncomplicated life until it suddenly exploded into chaos, responsibility, and noise; I'm truly happy but still adjusting; I've found a little time alone in the barn moving tools around or just staring at them helps. What about you?"

"I'm fine." Molly snickered. "I always prided myself on being organized and on my ability to arrange my life so there were no surprises. When the two children went to school, Penny and I enjoyed our quiet routines. I understand what you mean about life suddenly exploding into chaos and noise. When it becomes almost more than I can bear, I take a yodel break, which is what I call it. I walk into the woods and yodel; to the untrained ear, it might sound like a scream. It's very therapeutic."

When the rumble of feet coming down the stairs broke into their discussion, Molly smiled. "Let the chaos begin: it's showtime for the breakfast contest."

When they went inside, everyone was in the kitchen and dressed. Molly smoothed down the front of the fiery-orange apron with red chili peppers that she wore. "It's my lucky apron because it belonged to Gram."

Rosalie set the table with a green tablecloth and cloth napkins with shamrocks. Annie and Sara made place cards for each person. The boys moved the place cards around.

"It's a better contest if we sit in different places," Josh said.

"All contests have to have an element of surprise," Brett added.

"That makes sense," Sara said. "I may be sorry I said that."

Major relaxed in his chair in the family room, drank his coffee, and stayed out of the way. "Let me know if I can help, Molly. Right now, I'm basking in the energy."

"I've got this," Molly said. "Might want to find your seat soon, though."

Everyone found a seat at the table. Shadow took his place at the back door, and Penny took her place next to Josh.

"Rosalie, you say the blessing," Brett said.

"Thank you for this family. Thank you for oatmeal."

"Amen," said Brett and Josh.

Molly dished up oatmeal, and Aimee Louise served Rosalie first. Rosalie put a little sugar and milk on her oatmeal. Josh put a lot of sugar and some raisins on his. He called it "Bugs and Lumps." Brett fixed "Bugs and Lumps" too. Annie and Sara made their oatmeal like Rosalie. Major sprinkled a little brown sugar on his. Aimee Louise and Molly waited.

Rosalie took a bite. "Mmmm. This tastes creamy—not too thick and not too thin."

"What's the verdict?" Annie asked.

Rosalie waved her spoon with a dramatic flourish. "One more bite."

After her second bite, Rosalie said, "I have a rhyme: It's as good as oatmeal can possibly be. It tastes exactly like Mom's to me."

Everyone clapped, and the girls presented Molly with the blue ribbon.

"Good job, Molly. Let's eat," Major said.

After breakfast, everyone was busy with morning chores when the sheriff called Major on the radio.

"Ask Molly to turn on her cell," the sheriff said.

When her cell rang, Molly stepped outside. Before long, Molly came back in.

"Parts of the town have electricity. We can pack up. We'll go home this afternoon or tomorrow morning at the latest."

The children jumped, danced, and high-fived.

"Annie and Josh said they'd go home with us," Molly said. "The sheriff called their uncle Lee, who agreed it would be better for them to at least finish out the school year here. In fact, he said they would be better off with a family. He has no children at home anymore. All grown."

"It'll be quiet after you leave. We'll be sad to see you go," Rosalie said.

"You can visit anytime you like, you know," Molly said. "You can stay as long or as short as you want."

Aimee Louise was silent for a few minutes. "I'm good, Aunt Molly."

"Yes, you are, dear. Yes, you are." Molly helped everyone to pack.

"Major, I'll take the sheets and towels home with me so I can wash and dry them in my machines," she said. "Bring me your laundry until you get electricity. It's the least I can do for all you've done for us."

"It'd be a time-saver, that's for sure. Thanks, will do."

When Molly and the children turned toward the dirt road to Plainview, Major said, "Let's get our chores caught up for today. Molly has supper for us in the oven. After dishes and showers, let's check the photos from our game cameras."

That evening, Major strung an extension cord from a generator through the computer room window. Aimee Louise plugged in the computer and turned it on. When the screen lit up, Rosalie called out, "It works, Pops. Come on in."

Aimee Louise inserted the first card and scrolled through the pictures.

Major scooted a little closer to the computer. "Not as many animals as before the explosion."

"But Carl's still around. See his notched ear?" Rosalie pointed to the screen.

Aimee Louise inserted the second card. "This one's from the east side of the property, near the roads."

"Only four pictures," Rosalie said, "but aren't those three raccoons the ones we always see there?"

"I think you're right," Major said.

"And the last one is from the west pasture," Aimee Louise said.

The screen went black, and a message appeared: "SD card is not accessible. The file or directory is corrupted or unreadable."

Aimee Louise ejected the card and reinserted it with the same results. "Let me work with this a bit," she said. "I'll let you know when it works."

A half hour later, Aimee Louise stepped into the family room. "I turned off the computer. I can't get the card to read."

"I'll turn off the generators." Major headed out the door. "If you'd like to read tonight, get your mini-headlamps. I'll build a fire in the fireplace, unless you want to, Aimee Louise, and we can relax for a bit before bed."

"I'd like to build the fire. I want to check the west pasture camera tomorrow," Aimee Louise said.

He stopped and turned around. "What do you expect to find?"

"Something," she answered.

## CHAPTER FIFTEEN

After morning chores, Aimee Louise asked, "Is it okay to check the west pasture camera?"

"That would be fine; I'll go along as security, then we can pull lunch together after we get back," Major said.

Aimee Louise and Rosalie threw on their backpacks. Shadow whirled around and tore across the yard.

Major hurried to start up the tractor.

"Shadow just challenged us to a race," Rosalie said.

When the two girls dashed after Shadow, Major followed. *This is something the girls wanted to do themselves.*

When they arrived at the west pasture, Rosalie said, "Let's take some pictures." She stood with her elbows bent and fists up as she flexed her biceps for the camera, and Major covered his mouth by rubbing his nose to hide his smile.

Aimee Louise stood next to Rosalie and said, "Here, Shadow."

After she and Shadow posed for the camera, she asked, "Pops, is it okay if we take the camera back with us?"

Major tilted his head. *Don't know why, but I guess we'll find out why later.*

"I don't see why not."

"I'll take it down." Rosalie unhooked the strap and stashed the camera in her backpack.

When they were in sight of the farmhouse, Major said, "I'll get the generator going and put the tractor away later."

Aimee Louise ran inside; when the generator went on, she turned on the computer, and Major joined them. After Rosalie handed Aimee Louise the card, she placed it in the slot.

"No pictures found," Aimee Louise said. She ejected the card and inserted it with a firm push to be sure the card was well seated.

"Now we know; it's the camera not the card," Major said. "I have a camera I'd planned to install near the chicken coops, but we can put it in the west pasture instead."

"Do you think the explosion damaged the camera?" Rosalie asked.

He frowned. "I don't know what to think. Ready to pull lunch together?"

"We'll get it started if you want to put the tractor away," Rosalie said.

After lunch, they loaded the truck with books to return to the library and the morning's eggs for Molly. On their way to town, Rosalie sang, and Aimee Louise hummed along in harmony.

"Is it okay if I drop you off at the library with the books?" Major asked. "I want to go by the sheriff's office. You can check out more books if you like. I'll meet you at Molly's with the eggs."

The two girls and the dog hopped out of the truck.

"Well, I guess Shadow's with you." Major grinned.

When Major strolled into the sheriff's office, the sheriff looked up from his paperwork. "You here to rescue me, Major? I wouldn't mind going for a walk."

As they strolled around the block, the sheriff asked, "What's going on?"

"Not much, which is good; the girls and I checked the game camera in the west pasture, and it seems to be damaged. It's odd because even though it's the camera closest to the explosion, the grass and trees close to it are fine. What about you?"

"The realization of the potential seriousness of the outage must have set in because people are suddenly on edge. Our domestic violence calls tripled last night, we've spent most of the morning breaking up fist fights in the grocery store, and we were inundated with calls last night about stalkers that turn out to be a neighbor walking a dog; today there's a petition going around for a curfew for dogs. What worries me is what would it be like if we had an outage that lasted longer than a few days."

"Trish was always telling me that it was important to be self-sustaining, but I never really saw the need. I'm going to pull out some of her old checklists and look them over. It was different when it was just me; now, I've got the girls."

"I know what you're saying," Sheriff said. "Let me know when you find those lists; I need to be thinking along the same lines as Trish too."

When they returned to his office, the sheriff said, "Thanks for the break."

Major climbed into his truck and headed toward Molly's. *If I can't find Trish's list, that blog checklist will work.*

Major strolled to the Starrs' side door and called out. "Anybody home? I've got some eggs here."

"Come on in. We're in here, snack time—cheese and crackers. Join us, and thank you for the eggs," Molly said.

While he ate, Aimee Louise said, "Pops, if we had a second computer, I could install a Wi-Fi network."

"If Aimee Louise and I share a computer, it will be much easier to finish our homework in the evenings," Rosalie said. "We can do our animal research and not worry whether you have work to do. You won't have to worry if we need the computer when you update your farm records."

Major rubbed his chin. "Could we get Wi-Fi to take care of three computers? Wouldn't each computer need a printer?"

"Yes, but no need for three printers," said Aimee Louise.

"Aimee Louise could set up Wi-Fi for three computers and a shared printer. That's easy for her. But we can share a computer," Rosalie said.

"I understand, but I'd rather get two computers, so you don't have to share. What do we do? Do we go to the computer store here and see what they have?"

"That would be the best place to start," Aimee Louise said.

After hugs and goodbyes, Major, the girls, and Shadow left for the computer store.

* * *

Major listened while Aimee Louise and the store clerk talked. Rosalie and Shadow stood on either side of Aimee Louise. Rosalie faced the front door, and Shadow scanned the store.

*Interesting. Never noticed Rosalie and Shadow guarding Aimee Louise like that before.* He raised his eyebrows as he watched them. *And I've never seen Aimee Louise so animated except when she's talking to Rosalie or Shadow.*

After a lengthy discussion with Aimee Louise, the store clerk walked over.

"Major Elliott? Aimee Louise and I have a pretty good idea of what you need as far as two additional computers and a network with Wi-Fi, but we don't have the computers here, and we don't have any routers. I do have cabling, but Aimee Louise wants to get the hardware first. Smart. I suggest you order the computers online and go to the electronics store in Mickleton for the rest of the equipment. Aimee Louise can tell them what she has in mind. She could get everything online, but it makes more sense for her to talk to a techie for her first network. Oh, and we had a big box of promo flash drives, but the company went out of business. I've checked them—no viruses or malware. I gave Aimee Louise a sack of them."

Major's eyes widened. "Thanks for your help. Good suggestion."

On the way home, Aimee Louise wrote in a notebook while Rosalie watched.

"Looks like a good plan for the Wi-Fi network. I can help price the computers and hardware," Rosalie said.

"This is out of my league, but I can listen and learn," Major said. "Aimee Louise, you are awesome. I was so impressed and proud as I listened to you. I knew you were smart, like your dad."

"Say thank you. That's all you need to say," Rosalie said.

"Thank you, Pops. I love you."

*Another Aimee Louise first.*

"I love you too, kiddo," he said.

"Hey," said Rosalie. "I love you two. T-W-O."

"I love you, Friend."

"Me too. Make it T-W-O, Rosalie," Major said.

After a comfortable silence, he asked, "Where did you think we'd put the computers? Do we need to get two more desks?"

"Aimee Louise specified laptops. We won't need computer desks," Rosalie said. "We can sit at the dining table when we do homework and in the family room when we do research."

"When do we order the computers?" Major asked.

Rosalie tapped Aimee Louise's notebook. "Aimee Louise wants to be sure my computer has the muscle I'll need."

"I need to understand her educational goals," Aimee Louise added.

"Sounds good," Major said. *I know what muscle is. I don't know what a computer muscle is. And educational goals? I'll learn a lot from these two.*

When they got home, he said, "Let's check the generators and get some firewood from the woodshed. How do blueberry pancakes and bacon sound for supper tonight? I'll cook."

"I love blueberry pancakes and bacon," Rosalie said. "Maybe I like all the food on the farm."

* * *

The next morning, Major asked, "What do you think about a road trip this afternoon? We'll go to the computer store in Mickleton, and you can talk to them about network equipment. Have you decided on the laptops and software? We could order now if you know what you want."

Rosalie handed him a sheet of paper. "We pulled this price list together for you, so you'd know what Aimee Louise thought."

Major looked over the list and raised his eyebrows. *Computers are much cheaper than ten years ago, and software is more expensive than it used to be, but overall the bottom line is less than I expected.* "Well done. Let's get this order in. Watch over my shoulder."

After chores and lunch, Major turned on his phone before they left to see if there were any messages and read his one text from Molly. "School on Monday."

"Girls," he said, "school starts back up on Monday. Today is Thursday. We have a four-day weekend ahead of us."

"I'm sad and happy," Aimee Louise said.

"I know. Me too," Rosalie said. "I've had a lot of fun, and I've learned so much on the farm, but I don't want to get behind in school."

On their way to the city, Rosalie said, "I'd like to explore the possibilities of whether animal movements and behavior forecast the weather."

"Where would you start?" Aimee Louise asked.

"Maybe find a study or white paper I could use as a model," Rosalie said.

"Explains why you got the book on weather forecasting," Aimee Louise said. "Was it any help?"

"Yes. It focused on weather systems, which was a big help. I think if I can track weather systems, I can correlate animal behavior to the different systems."

Major's heart swelled as he merged his truck into the busy interstate traffic. *My two talented, intelligent young women.*

Aimee Louise clutched her plan for the Wi-Fi network as they entered the electronics store. The store was busier than Major expected.

The young woman behind the counter was as tall as Aimee Louise. She had deep dimples on her round face and appeared to be five years older. Her coffee-brown skin complemented her turquoise store shirt with the bright red logo. She asked, "Is there anything I can help you with?"

Aimee Louise handed her the list and said, "I am Aimee Louise."

"Hello, Aimee Louise. I am Jennifer," she said, mirroring Aimee Louise's speech pattern.

"Do you have any recommendations for our plan?"

Jennifer and Aimee Louise talked about the plan while Rosalie listened. Shadow stayed close.

"How many computers do you want on your Wi-Fi?" Jennifer asked.

"Three," Aimee Louise answered. "And one printer."

"One desktop and two laptops?" Jennifer said.

"Right," Aimee Louise said.

"This is what I think." She pointed to the list, where she had crossed out a few things and added other notes.

Major wandered around to look at equipment. Rosalie found a rack of books. She examined the titles and read the back covers. Shadow stayed with Aimee Louise.

When Major sauntered close to a middle-aged man, the man nodded toward Aimee Louise. "Is that your daughter?"

"Granddaughter." He smiled.

"She is brilliant. You're a smart man to step back and let her take off with the project on her own."

"Thank you, but I'm not sure what choice I have. I don't think I could add any value to the conversation."

The man laughed. "I know what you mean. Jennifer is my daughter. I dropped by to pick her up for lunch. I always like to watch her work. I don't often understand what she says, but I'm proud of her."

Aimee Louise walked over to Major. "Uncle Dan."

He pursed his lips and glanced at the store wall clock. "That's right, we're supposed to meet Uncle Dan for lunch. If you'll get Rosalie, we need to scoot."

Aimee Louise stood next to Rosalie at the bookrack. "Uncle Dan."

"Right," Rosalie said. "I'm with you."

The three of them left the electronics store, and the girls climbed into the truck. Major scanned the area before he opened the driver's door.

As they drove away, he asked, "Uncle Dan?"

Aimee Louise nodded. "A man with a danger cloud walked in. He looked around, but our backs were to him. Jennifer said he made her nervous because he didn't act like a typical customer. She left with her father too; they have a word they use for trouble."

"Let's find a diner and get a good burger," Major said. "It's past lunchtime, and we need some brain food." He glanced at his rearview mirror. *Don't think we were followed, but I'm rusty. Less suspicious if I drive straight to the restaurant. Don't want to look like I'm trying to shake a tail.*

After the girls selected a table, Major settled into a chair that faced the front door. Aimee Louise and Rosalie decided to share a burger, and when their order arrived, Rosalie's eyes widened. "Good choice on our part. This burger could feed three people."

The girls ordered chocolate shakes, and Major asked for coffee. He ordered fries with his burger, and even though the girls nibbled on them too, there were leftover fries at the end of their meal.

"Dessert?" the waiter asked. He grinned at the groans. "Okay, then. Next time."

Major sipped his coffee. "When do we go back to the electronics store?"

"Jennifer said go here for what we need." Aimee Louise pulled out a slip of paper from her pocket.

"Good," he said. "I was wondering how long we should wait before we went back."

* * *

When they parked at the small computer store, Rosalie said, "I'll wait in the truck. I want to take notes on my ideas for the weather project."

Aimee Louise gave her list to the computer clerk, then as Major paid, he and Aimee Louise received the same text from Rosalie: "Dan."

Major picked up their packages, then they strolled out of the store. Major glanced at Rosalie, and she tilted her head to the left. He followed Aimee Louise to the passenger side. After Aimee Louise and the packages were in the truck, Major put his hand up to adjust his cap and moved to the driver's side then eased out of the parking spot.

"What did you see, Rosalie?" Major asked.

"It was the man at the electronics store." Rosalie shuddered.

"Write down what you remember about him, and add what Aimee Louise said. I'll talk to the sheriff tomorrow. Let's go home."

* * *

Howie hurried into the convenience store then waited in line to pay for his gum and a bottle of water. *So far, gum's working since I quit smoking nine days ago.*

The checkout line stalled with three people in front of him. He shuffled his feet and clenched his hands to keep from grabbing the customer at the register and shaking her. *Shut up and pay! Nobody cares about your sick husband.* His face felt hot, and he swiped at his damp forehead.

The young woman who stood in front of him held onto the sweatshirt hood of a small girl. She glanced at him and clutched the child's hand as she returned the gallon of milk to the cooler and carefully circumvented Howie with her head down before she walked out.

*Settle down. Never good when people notice.* He breathed in then exhaled.

*This place would be a snap. Only one clerk. Low counter. No view of the register from the outside. Their surveillance camera looks ancient. I'll bet it's not even hooked up to anything. Easy hit.*

When he returned to his car, he made his call.

"Hey, Boss. It's me, Howie. I checked out three of those electronics stores. I'm at the last one now. It looks like a small operation, and I didn't see a delivery door in the back. The first store on the list is your best bet. It's in a strip mall with a nail place on one side and an insurance agent on the other. It's in the middle of the string of stores, and behind them is a self-storage place. The electronics store looked like they have some sophisticated surveillance equipment, and they have sensors for shoplifters, but I found easy access in the back. You'll never guess who I saw in the first store: that farmer and his two nosy kids."

Howie listened. "Naw, they didn't even notice me. One of the girls had a list. Maybe for a school project or something, but they didn't buy anything. Must be pricing stuff."

When The Boss yelled, Howie moved the phone away from his ear. "I'm sure they didn't see me. The farmer was talking to an old man, and the girls were busy with the store clerk."

After another tirade, Howie continued, "To be sure, I followed them, and they went straight to a restaurant. I sat for a while, and they didn't come out."

Howie fielded another question. "No, they didn't see me follow them."

*Sure am sorry I said anything, but it'd be big trouble if The Boss found out later.* Howie bit his lip. *Still haven't told The Boss about the stepbrother, but nobody can rat me out on that.*

"Okay, I won't go into this last store. Yes, I'll leave. Right away. Yes, I'll let you know if anything else comes up."

After he disconnected, Howie looked at his phone. He almost expected The Boss to reach out and grab him by the throat, and he shuddered. *The Boss sure can get worked up.*

## CHAPTER SIXTEEN

Major turned onto the road to the Gaston house, and Shadow ran toward the truck. Aimee Louise and Rosalie wiggled in their seats.

"It's Shadow," Aimee Louise said. Shadow yipped a greeting.

He stopped the truck. "Do you want Shadow to ride with us?"

"Oh, no," Aimee Louise said as she and Rosalie jumped out of the truck. "We'll run."

*No surprise there.*

Major pulled into his driveway and frowned when he saw a car parked by the house. His muscles tensed, and his mind leaped to protection for his girls. He unlocked the truck console, removed his holstered pistol, and stuck it into his belt. He parked his truck between him and the waiting man.

Major stepped out of the truck, assumed a relaxed pose, and examined the gaunt man as he strode quickly over with his hand out. Major frowned.

*Marty's lost a lot of weight, and he's got face sores and scabs. Not good.*

"Major, it's good to see you," Marty said.

Major narrowed his eyes. "Well, this is a surprise. Rosalie and Aimee Louise will be here soon. They're running home from the road with Shadow."

Marty turned, shaded his eyes with his arm, and peered toward the farmhouse. "How's everything? I want to apologize for not coming out sooner. Time gets away from me. Is there anything Rosie needs I can get her or help you with?"

"No, nothing I can think of. The girls are always busy, but she'll be glad you're here."

"Hi, Rosie." Marty waved. "How's my girl?"

Rosalie ran to her dad, and he stopped her approach with his hand on her shoulder.

"I'm fine," she said. "How's Mom?"

Aimee Louise stepped close to Rosalie.

Marty dropped his hand. "Rosie, she isn't doing well. The doctors discovered she has advanced cancer. It may be what caused her to be so tired all the time. I can take you to visit her if you like."

"Cancer? Are they sure?" Rosalie stepped back and blinked. "Yes, I want to see Mom, and I'd like to come back here if it's okay with Pops."

She glanced at Pops, who nodded. Aimee Louise chewed on her collar and watched Marty.

Rosalie said, "When can we leave? Do we go now?"

"I'll pick you up in the morning," Marty said.

Major squinted and examined Marty's face. *I'm not crazy about the idea, but maybe Aimee Louise and I could follow them.*

"Okay, Dad. I love you, but I have so much to do on the farm."

Marty patted Rosalie's shoulder. "I understand. Love you too. I'll be here first thing in the morning."

He hurried to his car and drove away in a trail of dust.

"I am sorry about your Mom," Aimee Louise said.

"Thank you. Me too."

As the three of them carried the boxes of network equipment into the house, the lights came on.

Major said, "Can you believe it? Electricity's on."

The girls squealed, and Shadow barked. Rosalie jumped and danced, and Aimee Louise spun in circles.

*Kind of feel like dancing and spinning myself.*

He grinned. "I'll disconnect the generators, roll up the extension cords, and pull a pot roast out of the freezer for the slow cooker tomorrow. And do laundry."

"After we unbox the equipment," Rosalie said, "I want a shower."

* * *

The next morning, Major got up before dawn. He sat on the front porch with his coffee and Shadow. *I understand why Aimee Louise loves the sunrise so much. Peaceful.* The door creaked as it opened behind him.

Aimee Louise said, "I like to watch the sun come up."

"So do I," he agreed. "I've learned to enjoy each fresh, new day. I'm glad we're together on the farm."

Major and Aimee Louise sat back in their chairs in quiet companionship and watched the sky turn from dark to pale gray to light blue with streaks of pink.

"Good morning, sun. Pops, I miss Mama and Dad, but you and Rosalie are my family too. And Shadow."

Shadow's ears perked up, and he moved closer and leaned on Aimee Louise.

"That's a dog hug, you know."

"Yes." Aimee Louise hugged Shadow. "Can I ask you something, Pops?"

"Go ahead. Anything."

"Where are Mama and Dad buried?"

"In the memorial garden at the church in Plainview. Pastor John led a short burial service and will conduct the memorial service when you're ready."

"I'm glad Mama and Dad had a special service, but I'm not ready to say goodbye."

*I never made the connection. She sees the service as a final goodbye.* Major nodded. "I think I understand. We can wait until you're ready."

Rosalie appeared in the doorway and yawned. "When's breakfast?"

"As soon as I get up out of my chair," Major said. "I need to do a few things in Mickleton today, Rosalie. What if Aimee Louise and I follow you and your dad to the hospital? Then you could ride home with us after you visit your mother."

"I'd like that. You'll talk to Dad?"

"Yes, I will."

Rosalie sat on the porch. "I'm worried about Mom. We didn't hear anything until Dad showed up yesterday and said she had advanced cancer."

Aimee Louise slipped her hand into her sweatshirt sleeve and patted Rosalie's hand.

"Thanks, Aimee Louise."

Major smiled. *Another breakthrough for Aimee Louise.*

Later in the morning, a heavy truck rumbled down the road; Major and Shadow hurried to open the gate for the propane truck.

When the man got out of his truck, Major shook his hand. "I wasn't sure when you'd get here."

"I wasn't either. There's talk that the main office wants to shut us down, so we're getting to as many customers as we can until we're told to leave our keys in the office. Dang fool time to get all spooked, if you ask me; they seem to be running scared, but I don't know why. Some of the guys think some conglomerate or such is buying them out. After I leave you, I'm going to fill my mama's tank then my own before I go back to the office to see if I'm fired. I turned my cell phone off yesterday."

"All the best to you and yours."

"Thanks, Major; you too."

Major and Shadow went into the house, so the man could work. Not long after the propane truck left, Rosalie packed sandwiches for lunch while Aimee Louise washed apples, and Major tossed the pot roast, potatoes, and carrots into the slow cooker. When Marty drove up, Major walked out to greet him while the girls grabbed their backpacks.

Marty opened his car door. "Well, let's hit the road, Rosie. Her doctor said mornings are best for Jolene."

Major and Aimee Louise jumped into the white truck with their backpacks. Shadow trotted to his sentry spot in the sun and flopped down.

On the road to the hospital, Major said, "When we get back, we can do the chicken chores. After that, you can work on the network, and I have some fence repairs to do."

Aimee Louise nodded and watched for cattle, goats, and horses in the open fields. She read signs and watched the clouds. "Seven cows in that field. Pops, what is it we need to do in Mickleton?"

"I haven't quite figured it out. We can shop or go for a hike. There's a state park near the hospital."

"So what are those things you needed to do in Mickleton?"

"Make sure Rosalie is safe."

"I don't like her dad's cloud." She picked at her sweatshirt sleeve. "It's not exactly an Uncle Dan cloud. It's more like a hide-something cloud. Or sick, but not like sick and get well. It's hard to find the words, but it isn't good."

"Must be why I wanted to go to Mickleton. It's hard for me to find the words too. I do have a couple of things I'd like to have on hand. Let's go by the farm store then we can wait in the hospital parking lot."

When they reached the farm store, Major said, "I don't have any spare tires for the tractor, and it wouldn't hurt to pick up a little chicken feed while we're here. Can you think of anything else?"

"We're getting low on Shadow's dog food and treats," Aimee Louise said.

"I'll grab a flat on our way in," Major said.

When they arrived at the farm store, Major found a long cart and headed to the chicken feed and dog food aisle. Aimee Louise stopped at the clothing that was near the front and picked out leather gloves for her and Rosalie then joined Major.

"Good idea; wouldn't hurt for me to have a spare too."

Major pushed the loaded-down cart to the tires, and Aimee Louise picked up treats for Shadow and antiseptic for animal wounds.

When she joined Major, he said, "I found the right size, but I'm going to need a cart."

"I'll grab one," Aimee Louise said.

When she returned with the cart, Major loaded the tires. While Aimee Louise stood in line with their two carts, Major picked out gloves and a packet of sockets that were on sale.

After they'd checked out and pushed their carts to the truck, Major loaded the large items into the bed of the truck then glanced at the other nearby stores. "There's a thrift shop. Your gram loved to go into thrift shops. She occasionally bought a few things, but she just loved to browse."

"I've never been in a thrift shop," Aimee Louise said.

"Would you like to see what's there?" Major asked.

"No, the aisles might be too close together."

Major nodded. *I don't understand, but that's okay.*

"Ready to sit in the hospital parking lot?" he asked.

"Yes. My friend might be waiting."

After Major parked, Aimee Louise pointed. "She came out of the visitors' doors." Aimee Louise waved, and Rosalie ran to the truck.

Marty motioned for Major to join him as Rosalie climbed into the truck. Major narrowed his eyes as Marty fidgeted and scratched his face. "I won't be long, girls."

As soon as Major was close, Marty said, "Jolene was much worse than last week. Her doctor doesn't expect…"

Marty stopped and looked away. "Sorry. Her doctor said she may not make it through the night."

"I'm sorry, Marty. Does Rosalie know?"

"I didn't exactly tell her, but she knew it was the last time she'd spend any time with Jolene. Rosie wanted to stay with her mother until the end. Jolene made me promise I wouldn't let her do that. This is all hard." Marty lowered his head.

"What can I do?" Major asked. "Did you want to take Rosalie home with you?"

"No, she wants to stay at the farm. I couldn't go home right now either. I'll stay with Jolene tonight and tomorrow, and I need to work. I've been offered a new position. Would you be Rosie's temporary guardian? I may need to travel out of the country; my health insurance covers her, and I'll take out an annuity toward her living expenses." Marty took a deep breath. He ran his hands over his cheeks and turned his head.

*Marty won't look me in the eye anymore. What's with him? Seems off. Dramatic.*

"Rosalie can stay with us as long as she likes," Major said. "And I could be her guardian if it's what's best for her. I don't need any money, though. Want to talk to her before you leave?"

"No, we said our goodbyes. I'll get back to Jolene."

"Well, I won't slow you down. Our prayers are with you."

Marty headed toward his car. Major frowned but remembered the hours before and after Trish died, and his heart ached as he walked to the truck.

On the way home, Major pulled over at a rest stop, and the three of them ate their sandwiches in silence at a picnic table. They continued their melancholy ride to the farm.

"Rosalie, if you want to take a break and skip chickens, Aimee Louise and I can handle it," Major said.

"No, Pops. I want to help with the chickens."

After the girls finished their chores, Aimee Louise ran to the computer room to work on the network with Rosalie and Shadow right behind her.

Major worked on fences until dusk.

When he walked into the house, the aroma of the pot roast overwhelmed his senses, and his stomach growled.

"Did you purr, old fella?"

Aimee Louise sat on the floor near the computer desk, where she wrapped the extra wire into a neat figure eight.

"Pops, Aimee Louise has everything at a point where she's ready for the laptops, and they'll arrive next week," Rosalie said. "She's amazing."

"Yes, she is," Major agreed.

"She's right here," Aimee Louise said. "Hey, I said something funny."

"You did," Rosalie said. "Well done."

"I'm ready for pot roast and need to make gravy. Someone want to pull together a salad?" Major asked.

"I'd like to, but I don't know," Rosalie said.

"I am so sorry," Major said.

"I've got this," Aimee Louise said.

During dinner, all three sneaked pieces of pot roast to Shadow.

"I'm so glad I got to be with Mom and sing with her. She knew how sick she was. She told me…" Rosalie bit her lip. "Mom said I needed to be safe and stay with you…and some other things." Tears slid down Rosalie's face. She tried to brush them away with her sleeve, but they were relentless.

Aimee Louise shook her head. "I am sorry."

"I know you understand. I'd like to listen to music and read tonight; be together because we're family."

"That's what we'll do," said Major. "Sounds good to me."

The house phone rang. It startled them because it had been so long since they'd heard it.

Major answered it. "I don't think so. Yes, I'll ask."

He covered the phone with his hand.

"The memorial service for the Gastons is scheduled for next Saturday. Pastor John said Annie and Josh want Rosalie to sing. I said I didn't think so, but it's up to you, Rosalie."

"I'd like to, for Annie and Josh, but I need a little time to think about it. Is that okay?"

"I'll tell Pastor John."

After he hung up the phone, Major said, "Pastor John wants to know if we'll come to church on Sunday. Rosalie, he asked if you'd like to sing with the choir. I said maybe."

"Aimee Louise, will you be in the choir, too, and hum with me if I sing?"

"Do I get to wear a choir robe?"

Rosalie nodded. "Pops, we'll do it if we can wear choir robes."

Major sighed. Pastor John had tried to get him into church for years. He'd laugh if he'd known all it took was a couple of choir robes.

Major turned on the radio. "It's nice to have tunes again. I'll lay a fire. You two can read, and I'll catch up on some computer work."

"Can I help with the fire?" Aimee Louise asked.

"Of course. Your dad always liked to lay the kindling and firewood in the fireplace too," he said.

After a relaxing evening with no more interruptions, the girls took showers and said good night. Major and Shadow stepped outside to check around the house.

"Rough day," Major told Shadow, "but our family is strong."

* * *

After breakfast, Shadow growled and let out a single bark. Major hurried to the door and saw Marty's car turn at the farm gate. "Rosalie, your dad's here."

Aimee Louise moved closer to Rosalie, and the two stood shoulder-to-shoulder as Marty came in the door.

When Marty sat on the leather sofa, Rosalie and Aimee Louise sat on the old blue-and-red plaid sofa across from him. Major and Shadow stood in the doorway.

Marty looked down and ran his hand through his hair. "Rosie, Mom died early this morning. I liked your idea to stay; I'm glad I was with her."

"Thanks, Dad." Rosalie bit her lip and crossed her arms. Aimee Louise moved closer to her.

Marty rose and shook his head. "I'm sorry, Rosie."

"We'll be at church tomorrow. We might sing in the choir. Would you like to come?" Rosalie asked, her voice breaking.

"I don't know, Rosie." He left with his head down.

"Your cloud is sad," Aimee Louise said.

"Yes. I'm sad." Tears ran down her face. "Mom was sick too long and died too early. It's not fair."

Aimee Louise sat in silence while Rosalie sobbed. Major brought Rosalie tissues and sat on her other side.

Rosalie took a big breath and exhaled. "Mom liked to be outside before she got sick. Let's go outside, Aimee Louise."

Major said, "There go two strong women."

Shadow yipped his agreement.

## CHAPTER SEVENTEEN

After lunch, a delivery truck on the dirt road appeared to be chased by a plume of dust.

"Can we run meet the truck, Pops?" Rosalie asked.

"No, not this time. I have to sign for the computers."

Aimee Louise asked in a sad voice, "You don't want to run with us?"

"Great joke," Rosalie said. "No offense, Pops."

"Well done; you two have me pegged." He smiled and walked to the door.

After Major signed the delivery slip, the girls carried the equipment inside and opened boxes.

Major stood for a few minutes. "I've got some things to do. Call me if you need my help. Ha. Now I made a joke."

He stood on the back porch and gazed at the horizon. *When we checked the camera two days before the explosion, all the pictures were wildlife. The camera failed sometime after that. I need to check the explosion site.*

Major stood at the computer-room door. "I'm headed out to the west pasture."

When he got to the kitchen, he realized no one acknowledged him. He turned around and knocked on the doorjamb. "Hey. West pasture on the tractor. Won't be long."

Rosalie waved without looking up. "Okay, Pops. We'll be right here." She sat on the floor with Shadow while Aimee Louise set up the laptops.

"You staying to guard your girls?" Shadow looked at him and wagged his bushy tail.

Major fired up the tractor. *I need to think about an ATV or better yet a utility ATV, whatever they're called. I wonder if I can find any ATV safety classes the girls could take. I'll talk to the sheriff.*

Major stopped the tractor near the west camera location and spotted several well-traveled trails. He walked a few yards and examined the divergent paths. Two of them narrowed and swerved at different places into the large patch of saw palmetto trees with thick trunks and three- to six-foot-wide fan blades. The silvery-green edges of the short palms sported sharp spines.

*No way to push through these thickets with oversized backpacks.*

One path stayed close to the power lines and veered away only to avoid obstacles like the swatches of uncleared brush. Major rushed back to his tractor. He drove along the easement and stayed within sight of the trail.

He came to a section of fence with access to the easement. He drove through the opening and noticed signs of motorized traffic. He examined the different styles of tire tracks made by numerous vehicles. His stomach tightened. *Never realized we had this much activity so close to the farm.*

Major reached the edge of the explosion burn. He scouted the scorched perimeter and discovered a substantial rise about thirty yards from the substation. The side away from the substation didn't show any signs of the aftermath.

*That's where I'd be if I expected an explosion.*

As he walked toward the substation, he kicked something that was hard and buried in the debris. He stirred through the ashes and debris with his foot and unearthed a melted mass of plastic—a cell phone?

*This is odd. I'll take it to the sheriff.*

He stuck it in his pocket. When he was within sight of the farmhouse, the two girls ran to meet him.

"Pops, the sheriff called. He's on his way here," Aimee Louise said.

"Jennifer from the electronics store called too," Rosalie added. "Someone robbed the store last night, and their security cameras were fried. Do you think it was the danger cloud guy? She told the police about him, and they might want to talk to us."

"More camera problems? Interesting. I'll tell the sheriff what Jennifer said. Any requests for supper? I've got chicken thawed. How about BBQ chicken and baked potatoes?"

"We'll make a salad, and one of Gram's salad dressings," Aimee Louise said.

"Our computers are all set up," Rosalie said. "Next, we'll plan what we'll wear to church tomorrow."

Major mumbled as he went out the door. "Yeah, church tomorrow."

"Did he have a grumpy cloud, Friend?" Rosalie asked.

"He did." The girls giggled.

Major yelled from the front yard. "I heard that."

The giggles turned to laughter, and he smiled.

The sheriff pulled up to the house and reached into his back seat. "Major, Molly sent me with a stack of folded sheets for you."

After Major took the laundry inside, they walked to the barn. "Sheriff, something's up. I don't know what it is, but it feels like a storm in the distance." He handed the sheriff a brown paper bag. "Here's the cell phone I found."

"I feel it too, Major." The sheriff looked in the sack. "This was definitely at ground zero, wasn't it?"

Major nodded. "Just happened to stumble over it. I jotted down a few thoughts, and these are Rosalie's notes."

The sheriff looked at the notes. "Couple of things jumped out at me. One is the explosion happened right after the men walked past the west pasture game camera, and the camera failed about the same time. There's the whole mystery around the Gastons. I talked to Annie and Josh, and the family left the house by the back door. Annie was positive her dad secured the front door."

Major's face tightened. "Aimee Louise is the reason I wanted to talk to you here. She sees things the rest of us miss. What if whoever's behind all this figures that out and decides she's a threat?"

The sheriff frowned. "Her communication style may help protect her, you know. She's not one to strike up a casual conversation."

Major glanced down at his hands, grabbed the old red rag from his back pocket, and wiped the grease off his fingers. "Hadn't thought of that, thanks."

"I'll send the cell phone to the state office for inspection and tests. You keep the notes because I have a nagging feeling my office isn't as secure as I thought."

"I don't like to think that might be true," Major said, "but I agree it's better to be safe."

As they walked back to the sheriff's car, Major said, "I'll have the camera checked at the electronic repair shop in town."

"Good idea. Let me know what the shop finds. Another thing you might want to consider is a security system. Maybe one that alerts you if someone's near the house."

"Shadow does a pretty good job of it, but I'll look into options. No, I'll have my in-house electronics guru research it."

* * *

Major woke just after midnight when he heard a sound he didn't recognize. He sat on the side of his bed. *Maybe it was a dream.* He rose and dressed then he and Shadow went out to the back porch, and he listened for night sounds. *Everything is quiet.* He went back inside and heard it. *Sobbing.* He walked to the bottom of the stairs and whispered, "Come downstairs if you want to talk."

The sobbing stopped; he returned to the family room then opened the back door, stepped out to the porch, and gazed at the stars. *I'm out of my league here.*

"Pops?" Rosalie asked.

Major turned, and Rosalie and Aimee Louise stood together in the family room.

"I was crying, and Aimee Louise hummed my favorite song. I'm sorry I woke you up."

"Don't be sorry. How about some hot chocolate?"

After Major set two cups of hot chocolate on the table, Rosalie asked, "Would it be okay if we take the hot chocolate upstairs?"

"Of course," Major said.

As they carried their hot chocolate upstairs, Aimee Louise whispered, "Better now?"

Rosalie whispered, "Yes, thanks to you and Pops."

Major exhaled and scratched Shadow's ear. "I didn't always understand Trish, and I certainly don't understand what just happened here, but I think I accidently did something right."

Major returned to bed and yawned.

He woke before dawn and dressed for breakfast. He made a pot of coffee then he and Shadow walked around the house for their early morning perimeter check. When they returned, he put a large cast iron skillet on the stove and dropped bacon into the skillet to fry.

He smiled when he heard Rosalie ask, "Is it time to get up?"

"That's bacon," Aimee Louise said, and the two girls dashed down the stairs.

Major grinned as they raced into the kitchen. "Oh, you're up early. Get dressed, and we'll have a farm breakfast for my two choir girls."

It didn't take long for the girls to dress. Aimee Louise wore her dark blue pants with a blue-and-white striped shirt. Rosalie wore her black pants with a pale pink shirt. While they ate, the girls chattered about their new computers and the wildlife database.

Rosalie became quiet. "I wish Mom could hear us sing in the choir. Mom liked animals and would have loved our wildlife project. She shouldn't have been so sick." Tears slid down her face.

"I understand. When you write up your report, you can include a dedication page," Major said. "In fact, both of you can."

While the girls cleaned the kitchen and washed dishes, he dressed for church in dark jeans and a long-sleeved blue shirt.

Rosalie said, "You look nice, Pops."

"Thanks. Let's load up."

Shadow walked them to the porch and flopped down with a huff when Major said, "Stay."

* * *

Major selected a seat close to the front so he could see his girls while Rosalie and Aimee Louise dashed to the choir room to find robes. When the church service began, Marty slipped into the pew next to him. Marty had shaved and wore a gray suit, white shirt, and blue tie.

"Peer pressure?" Major leaned over and whispered.

"No. Girl pressure. You too?" Marty whispered back.

"Yep."

When Rosalie spotted Major and her dad, she smiled and waved. Major smiled and returned her wave, and Marty nodded.

Marty bowed his head and closed his eyes when the choir sang.

Major glanced at Marty then listened to Rosalie's bright, beautiful voice and Aimee Louise's accompaniment.

*I wish Trish and Ted could hear them.*

After church, Major and Marty shook hands with the beaming pastor.

Major smiled. "Don't even say it."

"Hey," Pastor John said, "I'm just here for the entertainment." The three men laughed.

"Marty, would you like to come out to the farm for lunch?" Major asked.

"I don't think so. I need to stay in town because my sister offered to clean the house. I'll pack most of Jolene's things away for Rosie to look at when she feels like it. I might be by later."

"Come for supper. I know Rosalie would love it," Major said.

"I can do that."

"We'll see you around six."

Rosalie and Aimee Louise joined them. Marty said, "You have beautiful voices. I'll see you tonight at the farm, by the way. I'm invited to supper."

Major noticed Aimee Louise pulling on her collar. Rosalie hugged her dad, and the girls ran to the truck.

* * *

On the way home, Major asked, "What are your plans for today?"

"Could we fell some trees after the chicken chores?" Aimee Louise asked.

"I'd like to drive the tractor with the trailer," Rosalie said. "I need the practice."

"Sounds like we've got a full day ahead of us. How about ham and sweet potatoes for supper? We can toss them into the oven before we go out for firewood."

"Sounds great to me," Rosalie said.

When they were ready to leave, Rosalie drove the tractor to the trailer, and Major talked her through hitching the trailer to the tractor.

"Well done," he said, and Rosalie grinned.

After a quick lesson on backing, she moved forward then backed it into a spot they designated as a parking spot.

Aimee Louise gathered the chainsaws and equipment. While Rosalie practiced her tractor skills, Major and Aimee Louise reviewed the care of the chainsaws. He coached Aimee Louise as she started the chainsaw and cut a downed tree limb into fireplace-length logs.

Major pointed at a nearby tree. "Let's say we're cutting down this tree. We do a walk around before we pick the direction we want the tree to fall. These are our three cuts." He picked up a stick and indicated the locations and angles of the cuts. "You can walk me through it when we find your tree."

Major and Aimee Louise joined Rosalie.

After they joined Rosalie, Major said, "Rosalie, drive the tractor, and Aimee Louise, take down a tree. I'll ride in the trailer behind Rosalie."

"Shadow and I will run," Aimee Louise said.

Rosalie grinned as she concentrated on driving the tractor and changing gears while Aimee Louise and Shadow stayed within sight of the tractor and trailer. They ran ahead, circled back to the tractor, chased it for a while, and sped forward.

Aimee Louise took down her first tree and cut it into logs. The girls carried and loaded the wood onto the trailer with Major's help. Rosalie backed the tractor and turned it around to drive home. Aimee Louise and Shadow jumped onto the trailer with Major.

On the way to the farm, Aimee Louise said, "I'll help unload the trailer and stack wood."

"No rush to unload. Firewood needs to sit and season," Major said. "I'll get busy with supper, and the two of you can work on your project, if you like."

"Slideshow?" Aimee Louise asked.

"Sounds good," Rosalie yelled back.

When they arrived at the farmhouse, Major said, "I'll cover the wood with tarps. It looks like we might get a little weather from the west tonight."

The girls ran inside as he parked the trailer near the shed and threw a sizeable brown tarp over the wood. When he went into the house, Rosalie and Aimee Louise had completed their wildlife slideshow presentation with music.

After Marty arrived, Major sliced the ham, and the girls set the table.

Marty leaned against the refrigerator. "I hope it hasn't been too much for you to have Rosie here."

"Not at all," Marty said. "The girls have been good for each other, and we all keep busy."

Rosalie nodded. Major dished up the food into serving bowls, and Aimee Louise and Rosalie set the bowls on the table before the four of them sat down to eat.

"The best thing for me today was the two of you singing at church," Major said.

"The best thing for me was driving the tractor with the trailer," Rosalie said.

"I am a lumber friend," Aimee Louise said.

Everyone turned to look at her. She took a sip of milk and smiled.

Rosalie laughed. "I get it. You aren't the sheriff. You aren't a lumber*jack*. You are a lumber friend."

Major put the words together and laughed as much at himself for being so slow on the uptake as he was at the Aimee Louise joke. Marty furrowed his brow as he forced a smile.

Major narrowed his eyes. *He doesn't get it. I don't think Marty laughs much these days.*

"The best thing for me today," Marty said, "is to be here with you, Rosie." His head dropped, and he turned away.

Major sighed louder than he meant to. *I'm tired of the drama, Marty.*

After the girls rinsed and stacked dishes and put away the leftovers, they showed Marty their slideshow while Major secured the tarp around the wood, unhooked the trailer, and closed the chicken coops with Shadow's supervision. When the rain began, Major and Shadow dashed into the house.

"We've got a little storm on the way. It won't last long," Major said. "Anybody interested in some popcorn and a radio show?"

"Yes," the girls said.

"Sounds good to me," added Marty.

After the storm passed, it was close to nine.

"I need to get back to the house in town. I've got a few more things I'd like to get done tonight," Marty said as he left.

* * *

After breakfast the next morning, Major said, "Looks like more rain today. We've already got a little wind and a few sprinkles. I'll take you to school, and I'll pick you up afterwards."

"We're fine," Aimee Louise said.

"We've been wet before; we'll be wet again," Rosalie added.

"True, but I've already called your bus driver, so he knows he doesn't have to come out of town today."

"Okay, Pops," Aimee Louise said. "But we like to run."

*My plan to keep a close eye on them is not going to be as easy as I thought.*

* * *

After Major dropped off the girls, he went to the library. "I don't know exactly what I'm looking for, but do you have any books that have practical advice on living off-grid?"

"We certainly do. Are you interested in fiction or nonfiction?" the librarian asked.

Major furrowed his brow. "Fiction with practical advice?"

The librarian tittered. "You'd be surprised. I'll show you a couple that I like then we'll find you some nonfiction books."

Major thumbed through the two books the librarian recommended. "I could sit down and read these right now."

She nodded. "That's exactly what I did. One of our avid readers returned them and told me she learned quite a bit about off-grid in addition to meeting some wonderful characters, except she said, 'new friends.' I understood completely because that's how I feel when I get into a good book."

Major walked out of the library with an armload of books. *The girls will have to help me read these, or I'll be renewing them at least two more times.*

After Major left the library, he stopped by Pete's Diner, and Pete had his coffee poured and on the counter when he walked inside.

"Did you get that property you were looking at?" Major sipped his coffee.

"Sure did. My son put a mobile home on it, so we can have our version of a hunting cabin. He's already had a well dug and septic is lined up for today. We're on a list for electrical power, but we couldn't get a firm date, so he's putting in solar for the well and has solar panels and batteries to install this weekend. He's a CPA, so he's enjoying this manual labor work. He told me he's the only CPA in the county with calluses that aren't from pushing a pencil." Pete chuckled as he refilled Major's cup.

"Solar sounds smart," Major said.

"I was skeptical until we had that little outage; I don't know about anybody else, but that was a wakeup call for me."

"I know what you're saying."

After Major returned to the farmhouse, he and Shadow walked the fence line and found two breaks. "Always something, isn't there, Shadow?"

When it was time to pick up Aimee Louise and Rosalie at school, Major strode to his truck and chuckled at Shadow who was guarding the driver's door. "Not going to let me go into town without you this time, are you? Okay, let's get the girls."

Major opened the back door of his truck, and Shadow leapt inside.

Major and Shadow stood on the school steps to wait for the girls.

On the way home, Rosalie said, "We were trying to decide why those guys blew up the substation, and Aimee Louise said it had to be a cover-up for another crime, but it would have to be something pretty big for all the trouble and cost to be worthwhile."

"Drugs was the most obvious," Aimee Louise added.

Major's eyes widened. *Is anybody else even thinking about this?* "That's logical."

"That's what I thought. Aimee Louise said the outage was a classic distraction tactic."

Major frowned. "Everyone including law enforcement focused on the outage. If a criminal gang wanted to move a lot of drugs, that would be the ideal time."

Rosalie nodded. "Aimee Louise said they'd have plenty of time to prepare because they were the ones who scheduled the outage."

"A sudden increase in deaths caused by overdoses in large cities would be an indicator," Aimee Louise said.

"We can research that," Rosalie added.

Major blinked to focus on his driving. *I want to tell them to leave it alone but that would be useless. I'm lucky they're comfortable telling me what they're thinking.*

When they were home, Major asked, "What's your plan for the rest of the afternoon?"

"Chicken chores, a quick run, and supper then homework," Rosalie said.

"Need any help with the chicken chores?" Major asked. "I'm smart enough not to ask if you need any help with your homework."

Rosalie giggled. "Pops is joking in a nice way. He's saying we won't need his help with our homework because it's easy for us."

Aimee Louise nodded. "Thank you."

As they headed out the back door on their way to the coops, Rosalie asked, "You still didn't get it, did you?"

"Nope," Aimee Louise said.

"That's okay," Rosalie said.

"Yes, I'm good," Aimee Louise said, and the two girls giggled as they raced to the coops with Shadow behind them.

I *don't get it. Why was that funny?* Major shook his head.

## CHAPTER EIGHTEEN

The next morning, Major and Shadow walked the perimeter of the property that surrounded the farmhouse. "I don't know what I expect to see, Shadow, but I feel like our regular presence is a deterrent for any predators: probably yours, more than mine," Major said. "What's our excuse for taking the girls to school today? We need to come up with something."

After they returned to the house, Major started his pot of coffee then took a cup out to the porch and sat in his rocking chair. After his drained his cup, he said, "Girls will be racing down the stairs soon, let's go inside."

After Aimee Louise and Rosalie raced downstairs for breakfast, Rosalie said, "Pops, if it's okay with you, we'd like for you to be our transportation to and from school again today. And we'd like to pack lunches."

Major raised his eyebrows. *Didn't think they'd suggest it; so much for worrying.* "I'd be happy to be your chauffeur. I'll give Mr. Sanders a call to let him know. I can pack your lunches."

"We can do it," Aimee Louise said. "Thank you."

Major loaded the large cooler into the back of his truck for a trip to the grocery store. After Major and Shadow dropped the girls off at school, they headed to the Sheriff's Office.

* * *

The sheriff waved the coffee pot at Major when he saw him.

"Oh yes, thanks," Major said.

Sheriff poured a cup. "I'm glad you dropped by. Marty scheduled Jolene's service for Thursday. He said he called the farmhouse earlier, but I guess you'd already left. I think he has some other things to talk to you about. He gave me his number."

Shadow trotted to the admin's desk. He did his very best doggie-sit and held up his right paw.

"High-five!" She giggled and touched Shadow's paw with her left palm. She reached into her desk drawer and rewarded Shadow with a dog treat. He munched, and she rubbed his ears.

"I'll give him a call," Major said. "Do you know of any teen or youth classes on ATV safety? I might get an off-road vehicle for the farm, but I'd feel more comfortable if the girls had formal training."

"I don't know of any right off, Major. But I think it's an excellent idea. And since you mentioned it, I know of a UTV for sale at a good price. It's a little old, but it will be easy to maintain—fewer electronics. Here's the guy's name and number if you're interested.

Did you and Molly talk about a UTV? She mentioned it'd be nice for the farm."

Major stuck the note in his shirt pocket. "Yep, we did. Molly's not a fan of running with the antelopes, which is what she calls our galloping children. I'll give him a call. Thanks."

"You won't believe this, Major, but my new cleaning crew found an electronic bug in my office and one near our admin's desk. The bugs were on our broken-down ceiling fans. I've sent them off to the State. The bugs—not the crew." The sheriff chuckled at his joke.

"At least your leak was not anyone on your staff, even if it took inside access to install the bugs in the first place," Major said. "Guy with a ladder and a name on a shirt. That's all it would take."

"You're right. I was relieved."

The admin gave Shadow one more treat before Major and Shadow left the Sheriff's Office. After he slid into the truck, Major called Marty.

"I want to tell Rosie about the service plans for Jolene myself. Could you come to my house? Today?"

"We'll be there right after school."

Major called the man about the UTV and arranged to see it in an hour. The man's farm was less than thirty minutes southwest of Plainview, near Red Springs.

"Time enough to stop by the grocery store, Shadow," he said. "We need to pick up a few things on my list."

Shadow stayed outside to guard the grocery store and greet his fans. After shopping, Major took the road to Red Springs to look at the UTV. When he arrived at the farm, he recognized Mr. Young, a man in his eighties who was a frequent customer at the diner. His wife had died thirty years before.

"Major, nice to see you," Mr. Young said as they shook hands.

"You too, sir. Where's this off-road vehicle you want to sell?"

"Mr. Young waved toward the barn. "It's there. The UTV is old, but it's in good shape."

Major walked around the machine. "Looks good."

"Jump in. Let's go for a ride. I'll show you around."

Major climbed into the driver's seat and turned the key. It cranked right up.

They drove around the farm, and Shadow ran alongside. When they returned to Mr. Young's farmhouse, Major said, "This is nice. How much do you want for it?"

Mr. Young took his red handkerchief out of his back pocket, wiped his face, cleaned his glasses, and then slid them back on. "I'll take thirty dollars for it."

"What? It's worth a lot more than that. I'll give you—"

"Wait. You've got those two little girls now, and I know you'll put this to good use. In fact, come into the barn. I've got some power tools and other things I don't use anymore. See what you could use."

Major picked out a couple of hammers, two hatchets for the girls, a hand drill, and a shovel. Mr. Young added a table saw and stand.

"Thanks for everything," Major said. "I'll be back tomorrow to pick up the UTV."

"I forgot to tell you, the UTV comes with a trailer. Hitch up the trailer and take the UTV. I'll sign the trailer and UTV over to you. You don't know how happy I am to know my old machine will be in good hands."

"We'll take good care of your things. Here's my cell phone number. Call me if you need any help. Call anytime."

"Thank you, Major. And thank you for what you've done for this community."

It was close to lunchtime by the time Major hitched up the trailer, loaded the UTV onto it, and secured the vehicle with the straps Mr. Young claimed came with the trailer.

At the diner, Major ordered a ham sandwich, coffee, and water for Shadow. Pete insisted the medium-rare steak he plated up for Shadow was meat scraps. Major sat outside at a picnic table, and he and Shadow enjoyed their lunches.

"You know, Shadow, when Aimee Louise first came to live with us, she always spent her lunchtime at school outside by herself. The school called me. When she and Rosalie became friends, the two of them always ate lunch together, most of the time outside. The school called me again. Like there's something wrong with the outdoors. Any day outside is a good day. Right, boy?"

Shadow finished his steak. He eyed Major's sandwich and licked his upper lip.

"Let's go pick up the girls. I don't want to park this rig at school, though. We can leave the truck and trailer at the town park. Can you see us in the parent pickup loop?"

Shadow grinned his doggy smile. Major finished the last bite of his sandwich.

After he eased the truck and trailer into two parking spots at the town park, Major put a harness on Shadow and attached a leash. It was for show, and Shadow didn't mind. The two of them reached the school right before the dismissal bell rang. The girls hurried out of school together. They stopped on the steps to look for the truck.

"Here," Major yelled and waved. Shadow gave a single bark. The girls ran to them.

"Where's the truck?" Rosalie asked. "Why's Shadow have on a harness? Why's he on a leash? Do we run home?"

"No running. The truck's at the park with a surprise. Shadow's on his leash so little kids will talk to him. It's his Kid Magnet."

"What's the surprise?" Rosalie bounced from foot to foot. "Did you get a new truck?"

"No, not a new truck."

"A new puppy?" Aimee Louise asked.

"No, not a new puppy."

Rosalie skipped along the sidewalk, and Aimee Louise flapped her hands in anticipation.

"I know," Rosalie said. "A baby goat."

Major laughed. "Not a baby goat."

"An RV?" Aimee Louise said with hope in her voice. "I could drive it. If you teach me."

"No, not even an RV." Major chuckled. *Sure am glad the truck isn't any farther away. I couldn't take much more of this badgering.*

When they saw the UTV, the girls squealed and ran to climb on it.

Major smiled. "You'll need lessons in safety, and I'll expect you to demonstrate safe driving skills before you can drive it. You can still drive the tractor, but there might be times when I need it."

"I think its name is Number 48," Rosalie said.

"I'm curious, Rosalie," he said. "Does everything have to have a name? Is there a reason it's Number 48?"

"Yes and yes."

Major laughed. *Walked straight into that one.*

As he started the truck, Major said, "Rosalie, your dad wants to talk to you. We'll go to his house to see him."

Rosie frowned. "Okay. But afterward, I go home, right?"

"Right."

Rosalie's eyes widened when she walked into the house. She shuddered and wrapped her arms across her chest. Major took a step closer to her.

Marty carried boxes into the living room. He wore a food-stained gray T-shirt, and his tattered khaki shorts had a rip at the pocket. He looked like he hadn't slept or shaved since the last time Major saw him. "Oh, the house. Josie was here with a cleaning crew. I've got six large boxes of Rosie and Jolene's things."

Aimee Louise moved closer to Rosalie.

"Rosie, your mother's service is Thursday afternoon at the church. I leave Saturday for my new job. Look around to see if you want me to keep any furniture or anything else. I'll put them in storage for you."

"Thursday. And you leave Saturday. Okay." Rosalie glowered and took a big breath.

She pulled a notepad and pen out of her backpack, and her lower lip trembled. "There are a few things I'd like to have. I'll put notes on them." The girls headed upstairs.

Marty said, "Major, I've talked to a lawyer, and she's drawn up papers for you to sign. Are you available tomorrow morning?"

"Sure."

"I also talked to the school. The principal excused the two girls from classes on Thursday and Friday."

Major leaned against the doorjamb. "Okay."

Marty fiddled with boxes. He moved them around, opened some, and rifled through the contents. After a few minutes, the girls returned.

"Dad, I've marked everything Mom got from her mom. If I've missed anything, would you include it?"

"Will do."

"Where are Rosalie's boxes?" Major asked. "We'll load up."

"In the kitchen." Marty waved his hand toward the back of the house.

Major, Aimee Louise, and Rosalie headed for the kitchen.

"Wait a second, Rosie," Marty said.

Major stopped and turned to Rosalie. "It's okay. We'll take the boxes out and wait for you outside."

"Pops, we won't be long." Rosalie raised an eyebrow and glanced toward Aimee Louise.

Major peered at Aimee Louise who pulled on her sweatshirt neck then glanced at Rosalie, who nodded.

*I don't know what's going on, but Aimee Louise is upset, and Rosalie wants me to stay close.*

He and Aimee Louise waited outside the door, so he could listen.

"Rosie, I'll miss you. Oh, I think I misplaced something I got for a kid at the hospital. You didn't run across anything that looked like a small toy, did you?"

"No. Nothing new. No toys. I'll miss you too. You know I'm happy with Major and Aimee Louise, right?"

"Yes, and I'm so thankful for them."

"Me too, Dad. Well, they're waiting for me. Guess I'll go."

Major and Aimee Louise stepped to the sidewalk, and Aimee Louise pulled at her sweatshirt cuffs.

"Rosalie's dad. Different cloud. Distant cloud," Aimee Louise said.

"Distant cloud. I don't think I understand."

Aimee Louise sighed. "I don't understand, either. I can't find the right word, and I don't understand the cloud. It isn't good. I don't trust him."

Major nodded. "Sorry I'm no help, but maybe *distant* is the word. I'm not sure what's up with him, but I don't trust him either."

When they were in the truck, Major asked, "You okay, Rosalie?"

"Yeah. Well, no. The house was a shock; no Mom, and everything was boxed up."

He nodded. On the drive to the farm, Rosalie was quiet as she gazed at the passing landscape.

Major turned at the driveway. "I haven't been home at all today. We've got leftovers in the refrigerator, but we need to do the chicken chores before dark, unload the truck, and unhitch the trailer."

Rosalie broke her silence. "I can start the chicken chores."

"If you feel like it," Major said. "Otherwise, I'll see to the chickens right after I unhitch the trailer."

"I feel like I was kicked out of the house," Rosalie said.

"I'm sorry," he said. "It was shocking to see the house all boxed up."

"Yes, and not a sign of Mom or me." Rosalie's voice cracked. "But I'd like to talk to the chickens."

"I can put supper in the oven and help unload the truck," Aimee Louise said.

After they finished the outside chores, Aimee Louise made a salad, and Major pulled dinner out of the oven.

"Before I forget, Rosalie's dad called the school, and the two of you are excused from school Thursday and Friday," Major said.

"I'm glad I'm part of this family," Rosalie said.

"I'm glad I'm part of this family too," Aimee Louise agreed.

Major's eyes misted. "Me too." He cleared his throat. "My turn for dishes. The two of you can work on your homework."

At the end of the evening, Rosalie said, "Pops, we looked over Gram's recipes. Some of them sound easy enough for us. We'd like to make her Greek chicken pasta tomorrow night."

"Here's the list of the ingredients." Aimee Louise pointed to the note on the table.

Major picked up the list. "I forgot about Gram's Greek chicken. It was one of my favorites. I'll pick up what you need on my way home after I drop you off at school."

"One more thing, Pops," Rosalie continued. "We also saw a canning recipe for green-chili pork stew. Do we have a pressure canner? Do you think you could help us with it sometime?"

"Yep, we have Gram's pressure canner, and I could help you with it. I helped Gram."

* * *

After Major dropped the girls off at school Wednesday morning, he headed to the diner. He noticed the sheriff's car as he pulled in for a cup of coffee.

When he walked in, the sheriff hailed him. "Hey, Major, have a sit. How did yesterday go?"

"I went out to Mr. Young's farm. I can't say I bought his UTV—it's more like he gave it to me. I couldn't talk him into more money for it."

Major scooted into the booth across from the sheriff. "Darnedest haggling session I've ever been in. Seemed like if it had gone on much longer, he'd have paid me to take it."

The sheriff chuckled. "He told me he wanted to give it to you and the girls. I wondered how it would go."

Pete waved the coffee pot, and Major nodded. "We'll make good use of it, that's for sure. Did you know Marty leaves for a new job this weekend?"

"I heard he had an offer but didn't expect him to leave right away."

Major took a sip of his steaming coffee. "I've got an appointment this morning with his lawyer to review some papers. Marty said he wanted to give me temporary custody of Rosalie. If I need to deal with the school, it will be easier, but I'm not sure I understand his reasons. I guess everyone grieves in different ways."

The sheriff lowered his voice. "I've got a couple of things to talk over with you. How about if I come out to the farm for lunch?"

"That should be fine. I don't expect to take long at the law office."

## CHAPTER NINETEEN

Major completed his shopping with a few minutes to spare before his appointment with Vanessa. Rod had been his lawyer for years, and it was a real blow to the community when Rod died of a sudden heart attack three years before. His wife and law partner, Vanessa, kept the practice open. When Major walked into the law office, Marty was already there.

Vanessa welcomed the two men into her office. Her brown hair was streaked with glittery silver around her face, and her stylish cut was shoulder length. She wore gray slacks and a bright turquoise blouse.

*Nice color shirt. Brings out the sparkle of her blue eyes.*

Major raised his eyebrows. *Where'd "sparkle" come from? Must be the girls' influence.*

Shadow nuzzled her hand as he walked in, and she scratched his ears.

*Smart boy.*

After everyone found a seat at the conference table in her office, she said, "Major, Dr. Teague would like for you to have full legal guardianship of Rosalie. He will still be responsible for her health insurance and has set up an annuity for her support."

Major narrowed his eyes at Marty. "Didn't you say *temporary* guardian?"

Marty shifted in his seat and looked out the window. "I don't know how long I'll be gone, so it was hard to come up with a time limit for temporary. Permanent is better for Rosie, and I don't have to be here to sign more papers."

Major followed Marty's gaze out the window but didn't see anything. He turned to Vanessa. "Could you explain? And what's your recommendation?"

Vanessa said, "Would you excuse us, Marty?"

Marty stepped out of the office.

Vanessa closed the door behind him. "Temporary guardianship required an end date to be specified. Marty claims he can't provide a date for renewal. If the temporary expires, and he isn't available to sign, Rosalie would be in limbo. From my discussion with Marty, I recommend permanent. Marty understands it can't be revoked once he signs it, which I see as protection for Rosalie given his fluid circumstances."

"Fluid circumstances?"

Vanessa shook her head. "Not up for discussion."

Major rose and gazed out the window. "I want Rosalie to understand before I sign."

"That's understandable. Bring her to my office after school today, and I'll explain the details and answer any questions she may have. And any questions you may have after you have time to think it over. We do still have the option of temporary guardianship; however, it is not what I would recommend."

"We'll be here after school."

Vanessa opened her office door. "Marty, we'll finalize the papers this afternoon. Major wants Rosalie to understand the implications before he signs."

Marty stood. "Thank you, Major. I'll see you tomorrow. I have another appointment this afternoon. Vanessa, will you let me know if you need me to sign different papers?"

"I will, Marty."

After Marty left, Major said, "Vanessa, I don't understand Marty. He has given up his parental rights. Do you know why?"

Vanessa pursed her lips and shook her head. "When I asked him almost the same question, he told me he wanted to do one thing right by Jolene's daughter. I thought it was a strange answer, but to take it at face value, it's what he thinks is best for Rosalie."

Major drove to the farm and tried to comprehend the abrupt change. He believed Rosalie deserved the opportunity to hear her options and choose for herself. *I don't understand Marty at all, but I guess I don't need to. What's best for Rosalie is what matters.*

The sheriff drove up as he put the last of the groceries away. Major caught himself humming one of Rosalie's songs and laughed.

"What's funny, Major?" the sheriff asked as he let himself in.

"I think I've got the hang of living again. I've got a full larder, a full freezer, and a couple of girls who bring me joy."

The sheriff nodded. "What did the lawyer say?"

"Now this is crazy. Marty asked me earlier to be Rosalie's temporary guardian but for some reason had the lawyer draw up papers for permanent legal guardianship. Vanessa recommends permanent because we won't be relying on Marty to renew a temporary guardianship. I'm fine with it, but the girls and I will go to the office after school so Vanessa can explain to Rosalie. I want her to know she has a choice."

"Permanent seems a little extreme to me." The sheriff frowned. "Not anything I'd ever want as a parent, but that's irrelevant, I suppose. Makes sense for Rosalie to have a choice."

He dropped the sack he carried onto the kitchen table. "Because I invited myself to lunch, I stopped at the diner and picked up a couple of barbecues and some potato salad. How about some coffee? As far as the investigation goes, we've got more questions than answers, but I wanted to talk on a more personal level."

Major set up the coffee pot and turned on the burner. When the coffee perked, he poured two cups. "The girls eat lunch outside every day at school. Let's go out to the porch."

"Works for me," the sheriff said.

Major shook his head. "You know the girls got a detention one time when they ate outside. I was pretty steamed when I found out about it."

The sheriff sat in a rocker. "Well, write me up."

The men dug into their lunches.

Major picked up a napkin to wipe his face. "Good choice. Love the barbecue. Wonder if all diners make fresh potato salad every day?"

"Don't care to find out. Pete's is the best. You know, this outage opened my eyes to a few things. The electric company laid off most of their employees. Huge impact on our local merchants. A few of the women who were laid off began a cleaning service. They found the bugs in my building."

The sheriff stood up, stretched his back, and looked toward the barn. He stared down at his coffee cup.

"More coffee?" Major asked, and the sheriff nodded. Major went inside and came out with the pot. He refilled both cups.

The sheriff said, "Now all the electric companies are nervous and beefing up security at their substations. They're focused on the next explosion. Seems short-sighted."

"What do you think?" Major asked.

"Several things. Overall, my family and I were not prepared for an electrical outage more than a few hours long. You don't know how much I appreciate that you took in my family after the explosion."

"Molly was a huge help. She has a knack for organization I frankly don't have. And her cooking is superior," Major said. "Maybe we can start with a list of what we'd need for the long term. I know I want to expand the garden, and the girls have already talked to me about canning."

The sheriff nodded. "Couple of other things. We're in the process of adopting Annie and Josh. The bank turned their house over to us. If we need to move out of town, the house is available, but I'd rather my family stay with you if I have to stay in town."

"Fine with me, and congratulations," Major said. "I'm sure you all feel like a family already."

"We do." The sheriff stepped off the porch and scanned the area around the house. "I met with the city council and asked them what they learned from the outage. They told me it was over, and everything was back to normal. I asked what they saw as problems, and they said the electric company took too long to turn the electricity back on. Like companies could flip on a magic switch. Their other complaint was the governor didn't declare the county a disaster area the next day. I asked them how they planned to ensure the city provided enough safe city water for those who relied on it."

"I'm almost afraid to ask, but what was their answer?"

"It was like I was talking to the walls. One of the council members complained about the meals the churches served. I couldn't listen anymore, so I left in the middle of his rant. I can only hope I sowed a seed of sanity and they'll think about it."

Major chuckled. "I could guess who complained about the food, but I bet there were a couple who listened."

"You're right. The local pastors have formed an informal group to see what the churches might do to help the community in case of another emergency."

"We have brownies in our freezer. Want one?"

Major didn't wait for an answer. He returned with two frozen brownies wrapped in plastic wrap and tossed one to the sheriff.

The sheriff unwrapped his and took a bite. "I never turn down a brownie. Trish's recipe, I'll bet." He stopped to take another bite. "I talked to the sheriffs in counties near us. We've ordered more solar chargers for our radio batteries. We want to keep communications open between our offices."

The sheriff finished his brownie and sighed. "I'm sorry. I didn't mean to dump it all on you. Like I said, it shook me up. Or maybe it shook me awake."

"Sheriff, this is what keeps me up at night. It would ease my mind to work out a plan."

"Can we get together on Sunday after church? We'll provide the food. If we come here, the kids can run around with the dogs."

Major gathered up their trash and dropped it into the sack from the diner. "Good. I'll get my thoughts on paper."

"I better get back. Thank you, Major. For everything."

Major had over an hour before it was time to pick up the girls at school. He refilled the chickens' food and water in case the visit with the lawyer went longer than expected. Trish's Greek chicken pasta didn't take long to prepare. The thought of it made his mouth water. Before he left the farm, he gathered a load of dark clothes and tossed them into the washer.

*It's funny, one of the things that's always in the back of my mind now is washing clothes as soon as I have enough to start a load.* He chuckled and headed to his truck. He reached to start the engine and stared at his scarred, arthritic hands. *I'm an old man. Can I do this? Can I protect a large family? Can I keep everyone safe?*

He cranked the engine. *Yes, I can.*

* * *

"Don't we look like a couple of pros in this parent pickup loop, Shadow?" Major asked.

When the girls climbed into the truck, he said, "We'll stop by the law office before we go home. The lawyer has papers for permanent custody. Rosalie, the choice is yours, but whether you decide on temporary or permanent guardianship, you'll live at the farm. I asked the lawyer to explain it to you and Aimee Louise."

Rosalie said, "Okay, as long as I stay at the farm. Mom said that was important. We'll still make Gram's Greek chicken pasta for supper, right?"

"Oh yes," Major said. "I shopped this morning, and we have all the ingredients."

The lawyer wanted to talk to Rosalie alone but agreed that Aimee Louise could come in when Rosalie insisted. Major heard Aimee Louise whisper to Rosalie, "Confident cloud. It's good."

Major and Shadow waited on the porch outside. He jotted down notes for Sunday's meeting. Shadow sniffed the surrounding grass and flowers, marked a few spots, and flopped down next to Major.

He worked head-down on his list until Vanessa stepped out after almost an hour. "Major, would you come in? The Friends would like to talk to you."

Major noticed she called the girls "the Friends." *Always thought Vanessa was sharp, but this is impressive.*

He also was aware Vanessa wore a silky pale-gray blouse. *Her shirt tugs at her chest when she breathes. When she moves, I can't help but stare at her curves.* Major's mouth was a little dry.

Rosalie spoke first. "Ms. Vanessa says Aimee Louise and I will be sisters. We decided that was good. And we'd stay friends. She also said you would always be Pops, no matter what."

"Okay." *I know this is leading up to something.*

"Family is the most important thing to me, and you and Aimee Louise are my family. And Shadow. Aimee Louise and I agree with Ms. Vanessa. Permanent guardianship is the best way to ensure we stay a family."

"I think that's smart. I didn't look at it from the family standpoint, but if Ms. Vanessa advises permanent guardianship is the best way to keep the family together, then I agree too."

"Thank you, everyone," Vanessa said. "Major, I need your signature, and I'll give you copies of all the papers. Your packet includes the insurance information and card for Rosalie and the annuity payment information for you. The annuity will come as a check in the mail on the first of every month. If you prefer an electronic deposit, I've included the information on how to set it up. I will always have copies, too, of all the papers and would represent Rosalie if anyone challenges the guardianship."

"For your information," Vanessa continued, "I've completed my obligation to Marty. Rosalie has retained me as her lawyer. There is one other thing. Rosalie can legally change her name. She requested to assume the last name of Elliott because she is part of the family. This is not an adoption. It's a legal name change. Do you have any objections? Would you like to discuss them with me in private?"

Major was surprised at first, but he realized he shouldn't have been. *The girls always worked through all the options.* "No objections, but I do wonder why, though, and doesn't Marty have to approve?"

"No, he doesn't," Vanessa said. "He signed the papers for you to have legal guardianship. The approval comes from you as the legal guardian. Rosalie and I confirmed it with the judge. We called him, and he talked to Rosalie. As far as why, you can ask my client. We called Josie, and she had no objections. I also called Marty as a courtesy, and he had no objections. We've covered every base. The packet will include, then, the name change. I will send a directive to the health insurance company, and they will issue a corrected insurance card."

*I don't think I'd want to take on these three. They are quite a team.*

"You said Josie didn't have any objections. Did she say why? Why isn't she fighting for custody of her niece?"

"She and I talked about that. She said Rosalie never had the opportunity to have friends or even be a kid. She already has a houseful of children and wouldn't be the parent Rosalie needs. She told me Rosalie belongs with you and Aimee Louise."

"Sounds like there are no objections at all; let's sign papers," Major said.

After Vanessa gave him the packet of papers, she hugged the girls, shook hands with Major, and gave Shadow a face rub.

*I must be old. I'm jealous of a dog. I want a face rub too.*

He frowned, shook his head, and tried to shake off his irritation.

"Second thoughts, Major?" Vanessa frowned. He heard the concern in her voice.

"No, not at all. Guess I need to pinch myself."

"I understand." Vanessa smiled. "You are a lucky man. You have a wonderful family."

"Thank you." He stumbled as he went out the door. "Oops, sorry."

He was red-faced as he strode to the truck. *I apologized to a door threshold.*

On the way home, Major said, "Rosalie, Ms. Vanessa said she was your lawyer on retainer. Doesn't it require payment in advance?"

"I had five dollars. It was my emergency grocery money. Ms. Vanessa said it was how much her retainer was. I think she gave me a kid discount."

"You know, I never thought about that. Let's put some cash in your backpacks for you two to have on hand for emergencies. I have another question. Is it okay if I ask about the name change?"

"Mom told me when she was sick…" Rosalie cleared her throat, and Shadow nuzzled her ear. "Mom said I needed to be with my family on the farm. When I told the judge what Mom said, we talked more about the farm and Mom; the judge told me I had the option to change my name. Mom would like that."

Aimee Louise said in a sing-song voice, "I gotta Friend. My sister is my Friend. We gotta Pops. Our Pops is great. My sister can sing. She sings wonderful songs. She rhymes all her words. If I knew how to rhyme, this song would go on. I don't."

Major, Rosalie, and even Shadow looked at her in surprise. When the song ended, Major laughed, and Rosalie applauded. Aimee Louise beamed. Shadow's grin said, "I love this family."

While they walked into the house, Major heard Rosalie say, "Now?"

"After homework," Aimee Louise said.

*I guess I'll wait until after homework.*

## CHAPTER TWENTY

After they finished their homework that evening, Rosalie said, "Pops, we'd like to call Jennifer on Friday. We think it might be long distance, so we wanted to ask for permission in case there's an extra charge. We're curious about the stolen equipment."

"One more thing," Aimee Louise added. "There is a storage place behind Jennifer's store, across the alley. I would like to know if anyone checked their security cameras."

Major's heart rate jumped. He wanted to forbid them from calling Jennifer. *I hadn't thought about the storage place, and I'll bet no one else did either.*

He took a breath and calmed himself. *Don't want to scare Aimee Louise with a panic cloud.*

"I'm not crazy about the idea, but I'm interested in why you want to know about the equipment."

"The explosion at the substation was a test—maybe to check the recovery time or create a distraction," Aimee Louise said. "Everybody is focused on another explosion. There is something bigger in the works, but I'm sure it will be different. We think the stolen equipment might give us a clue about the next outage."

Major raised his eyebrows, surprised that Aimee Louise's answers were so thorough. Her analysis and conclusions were similar to the sheriff's, but the sheriff didn't mention the electronics break-in and Uncle Dan as possible connections to the explosion or a future event.

"What if I talk to the sheriff tomorrow and ask him to check on the theft from the electronics store and the storage-place security cameras? I can explain we're convinced the type of stolen equipment is a clue about the next outage. I'm worried Uncle Dan might get nervous if there is a direct connection between us and a query about the break-in."

Rosalie looked at Aimee Louise, who focused on Pops.

"Aimee Louise," Rosalie asked, "what do you think?"

After considering, Aimee Louise responded, "I think Pops is worried about safety. I think it's smart to hand it off to the sheriff and safer."

He expected more argument. "Thank you. And yes, I am worried about safety."

He breathed a sigh of relief. "With everything going on, I never took the camera to the shop to see if their technicians can repair it. I'll put it in the truck to help us remember the next time we're in town."

* * *

During breakfast the next morning, Major said, "We should leave for the church right after lunch. I'd like to get the chicken chores done this morning, and I'd like to take Number 48 out to ride the fence. What do you think? We'd still have time to clean up and have lunch before we have to leave."

"I'd like that," Rosalie said.

"Me too," Aimee Louise agreed.

"Aimee Louise programmed your handheld ham radio with the frequencies of nearby repeaters. Could we take it with us to see if we can pick up anything?" Rosalie asked.

"Sounds good. Where'd you get the frequencies, Aimee Louise?"

"Local ham club website."

"I didn't even remember we had a local ham club. Maybe we should check them out sometime. See if we want to go to a meeting or something."

"Sounds good," Aimee Louise echoed.

"I'll go wherever Aimee Louise goes," Rosalie said. "After all, she sang with me in the choir."

"Hummed," Aimee Louise said. "I hummed."

"Okay, hummed. Then I'll hum at the ham club meeting."

Major chuckled. *These two are such a joy in my life.*

The three of them refilled the chickens' water and food, cleaned the poop bins in the coops, and raked the runs while the chickens free-ranged under Shadow's protection.

"I like how the chickens, even the roosters, know Shadow has their backs," Rosalie said.

Major picked up buckets for the compost. "One time I was in the garden, and Shadow let out a single bark. All the chickens flew and ran as fast as they could to their coops. I was about to ask Shadow what happened when I saw the fox at the edge of the yard. The fox ran away because he realized Shadow saw him."

"Wow," Rosalie said. "What a great Shadow story."

The four of them climbed on Number 48. Major and the girls buckled up. Shadow sat up straight in his seat. If the girls rode, he'd ride too.

"Nice clear day," Major said. "Warm, but the humidity is low."

As they rode across the pasture, Rosalie said, "The wind from no windshield is fun, but it might be smart to have another rule—no talking while riding."

Aimee Louise nodded. "Bugs."

The girls turned on the ham radio and listened for the repeaters' periodic sign-ons. When they heard one, Major pulled over.

Major identified his call sign. "Radio check."

A ham operator responded with his call sign. "Loud and clear."

Rosalie brought her notebook. She wrote down the repeater's frequency and the ham's ID.

*Wonder if we'll track hams next.*

"Pops, we need a database of who picked up our signal off which repeater, and where we were," Rosalie said. "Oh, and time of day and weather. Maybe we could use our wildlife-tracking database as a template."

"Yes," Aimee Louise said.

*Finally. I got one right.*

"Meant to tell you, the sheriff and Molly and I want to develop lists of what we would need if there were another outage, or what we needed more of," Major said. "Kind of like a debrief session on what we could do better. If you think of anything we could have used or needed more of, let me know. I'm open to ideas."

When they got back to the farmhouse, they dressed for church. Rosalie wore a red blouse with black pants, and Aimee Louise wore her bright blue blouse with navy pants.

"Mom liked bright colors. She would be happy to see us in our bright colors."

Major said, "I've got a light blue shirt and a dark green shirt. Which should I wear?"

"The dark green is close to emerald green, Mom's favorite color. And she laughed when I wore red because she said us redheads weren't supposed to wear red. Aimee Louise's bright blue is the same color as Mom's favorite dress for church."

"Then we are all appropriately dressed. Excellent," said Major. "We should eat before we go, but it can be light. There will be a lot of food, and we'll be expected to bring a ton of leftovers home."

They snacked on cheese, crackers, and apples.

"Can Shadow go with us?" Aimee Louise asked.

"I'd like it," Rosalie said.

Major shook his head. "He'd be happier to keep an eye on things while we're gone."

Shadow settled on a shady spot on the porch.

When they approached the church, Major noticed the crowded parking lot. Aimee Louise had turned pale and was taking quick, shallow breaths.

"Let's go to the park," Major said, and he drove away from the church. They sat on a park bench.

"Breathe in through your nose. Hold it. Hold it. Okay, now breathe out through your mouth. You too, Rosalie. Breathe with Aimee Louise. It will help her."

Aimee Louise slowed her breathing, and Major said, "Too many people?"

"I wasn't prepared. Sorry, Rosalie."

"Let's see if we can come up with some ideas to help," Major said.

"We can send everyone home," Rosalie said with a fierceness in her voice.

Major suggested, "We can wait until everyone is there and stand in the back."

"We can sit in front, so we don't see anyone," Rosalie said. "Would that help?"

"Might," Aimee Louise said.

"Would it help," Major asked, "if we leave the truck at the park so we won't get blocked in?"

Aimee Louise glanced at the trees and flowers. "Yes."

"We'll be with Rosalie while we celebrate her mother's life," Major said. "We're there with Rosalie. No one else."

"Right," said Aimee Louise. "Let's do this."

Rosalie had a catch in her voice. "Let's do this."

The three walked together, with Rosalie in the middle. Major opened the solid red door, and they were greeted by the timeless, familiar smell of old wooden pews and burning beeswax candles. The sunlight filtered through the stained-glass windows and rested on the faded red of the aisle carpet. Sunbeams gave the old carpet touches of fiery radiance. The low murmur of voices floated through the church with a soft rhythm of comfort and a community that grieved together.

"Do you see all the red for your mom?" Aimee Louise asked in a soft voice.

"Yes," said Rosalie.

Aimee Louise said, "In front is best."

They discovered a front row reserved for the family. Major appreciated the respectful, hushed voices and the low volume of the organ. Aimee Louise relaxed as the soft music lent a sense of reverence and peace. Right before the service began, Marty slipped in next to Major, and they all scooted over. Rosalie frowned and clutched her hands in her lap. Major draped his arm over the back of the pew and patted Rosalie's shoulder; her face and hands relaxed.

After the service concluded, a reception in the church social hall provided the opportunity for the family to receive condolences. Major and Rosalie conferred in hushed tones then he spoke with Pastor John. Rosalie said goodbye to her father, and Major guided the girls out a side door.

"We won't stay," Major said to Aimee Louise outside the church. "Rosalie and I agreed. We'll go home. She doesn't want to talk to people, and Pastor John understood. He said Aunt Molly and the sheriff would come to our house later with the kids."

Aimee Louise breathed a sigh of relief. "Thank you."

When they reached the park, Rosalie sat on a bench. "That last day…when I was with Mom."

Aimee Louise sat next to her.

"Mom asked me to forgive her." Rosalie placed her face in her hands and sobbed.

Major sat on the other side of Rosalie. He glanced at Aimee Louise. Tears trickled down her face.

Rosalie continued, "I told her I loved her, and there was nothing to forgive, but I forgave her. I asked her to forgive me. And she said she loved me and forgave me too."

Rosalie leaned on Major's shoulder and wept uncontrollably. He held her, and Aimee Louise hummed a soft tune.

After her tears subsided, Rosalie sat up. "Mom said my family would help me. Thank you."

The three sat in silence for a few moments before walking to the truck.

"I have the west pasture camera," Major said. "Okay if we drop it by the repair shop before we go home?"

Rosalie nodded.

"Can we wait in the truck while you go in?" Aimee Louise asked.

"Sure. It won't take long to drop it off. The shop can call me when it's ready."

Major parked in front of the camera store and went inside. He gave the camera to the tech behind the counter. The young man opened the camera, pointed to the interior, and handed it to Major.

The tech said, "Major, something fried the camera's circuitry, and it was deliberate. Only intense heat or a concentrated beam could have done it. I don't see any signs of damage to the camera case, but I can't fix it or recover anything."

Major came out of the store and climbed into the truck. "The tech said the camera's fried."

"Same thing Jennifer said—fried. More to tell the sheriff," Aimee Louise said.

"Yes," Major replied.

They were quiet on the ride home. When they got to the gravel road, Rosalie turned from the window and said, "I'll miss Mom."

"Yes," Aimee Louise said.

"Do you miss your mama?"

"Yes, and Dad."

"I'm going to miss Mom always," Rosalie said.

"Yes. I like to think about the happy times too, like when Mama and Dad laughed."

Major missed Trish, and he always would. But he saw how healing love could be as he listened to the girls.

"I need to change into farm clothes when we get home," Rosalie said.

Major nodded. *I did too.*

"Would it be okay if Rosalie and I took the test for the amateur radio technician's license?" Aimee Louise asked. "There's a test sponsored by the local ham club next Wednesday night, and study sessions on Monday and Tuesday nights."

"That's fine with me. Can you catch up on the schoolwork you've missed?"

"Yes," Aimee Louise said.

"We have only a little left, and we can finish today," Rosalie added.

"What else?" *I have a feeling there's more.*

"We would like to have an amateur radio base station. We'll need a tall antenna because of our distance from any repeaters," Aimee Louise said.

"Okay. After you two pass the technician's license test, we'll install an antenna and get a base transceiver."

A thought flashed through Major's head. *I am so glad they haven't developed an interest in rocket ships. Or whales.*

"Have I told you how proud I am of you? I am. I think a base radio station is an outstanding idea for the farm," Major said. "After we get home, show me what you think as far as an antenna is concerned and where you think would be best to install it."

With Aimee Louise at the keyboard, the three of them sat at Major's desktop computer and compared different antennas. Shadow whined and gave a quick yip. They looked out the window and saw the sheriff's truck turn into the driveway.

The truck pulled up, and Penny and the kids spilled out. Molly called the kids back to help carry things into the house.

When she came to the door, Molly said, "We have some food from the reception at the church. We took most of it to the domestic abuse shelter and the nursing home. I've brought almost all my canning jars, lids, and canning supplies. I love Gram Trish's setup for canning. It's much more organized than my kitchen. I'd like to do all my canning here, and, Aimee Louise and Rosalie, you can help me if you like. We didn't have time to eat at the church. Okay if we put the food on the table and eat?"

Major realized he was hungry, and the girls ate well too. After everyone helped clear dishes, the kids ran outside with the dogs. Major loaded the dishwasher, while Molly and the sheriff covered, labeled, and put the leftovers away.

"Sheriff, I have a couple of things for you," Major said. "One, Aimee Louise thinks the items stolen from the electronics store are related to a future event. Jennifer from the electronics store said their security cameras were fried. By the way, Aimee Louise believes the explosion was a test for a much larger outage. She'd like for you to investigate the stolen items and their potential use during another outage. And one more thing, Aimee Louise asked if the security cameras for the storage business behind Jennifer's store were checked. Do we even know if there were security cameras?"

The sheriff whistled low. "I don't know if anyone else thought of the storage business. I'll call first thing tomorrow morning."

"Second, I took the camera from the west pasture to the camera store. The technician told me the camera was deliberately fried. I'll give it to you. Maybe the feds can run some tests on it and learn more. I don't like this at all."

"I don't either," agreed the sheriff. "We know Aimee Louise is smart, but how does she come up with all this?"

"I don't know. Worries me."

"If you'll excuse me," Molly said, "I'll corral our crowd. We need to finish our homework before bedtime."

"You okay, Major?" the sheriff asked.

"I'm fine. I scramble to stay ahead of Aimee Louise, but I'm not very successful. She's brilliant, and Rosalie, too, but they are still young; at least they trusted me enough to tell me what they are thinking."

"Tell them I'll inquire about the stolen electronics and check into the storage business's security cameras. We'll plan on being here Sunday. Let me know if something else comes up."

* * *

While they ate breakfast Friday morning, Rosalie said, "Pops, we can't sing tomorrow. In fact, we'd rather not go, if that's okay. We talked to Annie and Josh last night, and they understand. It's too..."

"Too soon," Aimee Louise finished.

"I'll give Pastor John a call to let him know we won't be there tomorrow," Major said. "I think it's a wise decision."

"Thank you, Pops," Rosalie said.

"I've got more calls to make. I'll call the technician class instructor if you're still interested. Are you?"

"Oh yes," Rosalie said.

"I'll ask if I can sit in the class. It's been a long time since I got my license, and I wouldn't mind a refresher. I'll call the test manager to sign you up for the test next week."

"Pops," Aimee Louise said, "I have the list of everyone in the county who has an amateur radio license. It's public record. I thought you'd like to see it. I also have a list of everyone in the state too, if you are interested."

"Thanks. I'd like to see the county list first." Major looked over the list. "Now this is interesting. Mr. Young has a current license. He's an Extra—most advanced level. It might be helpful to have him look at our plans for an antenna and transceiver. Maybe he'd have some suggestions. I'll give him a call too."

While Aimee Louise and Rosalie worked outside, Major made his calls. He arranged for all three of them to sit in on the study class and for the two girls to take the technician test.

He called Mr. Young. "The girls are interested in ham radios. We have plans for a base station and hoped you'd review it with us."

"Right up my alley. Why don't you and the girls come to my farm, and I'll look over your plans."

After they arrived at Mr. Young's farm, he surprised them with a base station transceiver and an antenna then gave the girls study books for the technician test.

"I was an instructor for years, and I like to stay current," he said. He talked to them about radio basics, explained the test organization, and suggested ways to prepare for the test.

"I have some questions about the transceiver, the antenna, and the nearby repeaters," Aimee Louise said.

"Sure," Mr. Young said. "Let's sit under the tree in the shade."

Mr. Young gave Rosalie a guitar and a beginner's book. She immediately sat down and worked through the first few lessons.

Major sat on the truck's bumper and listened to Rosalie strum and Mr. Young and Aimee Louise's animated conversation. *Mr. Young is a miracle worker.*

Rosalie gave Mr. Young the brownies they had packed for him.

"I got the better end of this trade," he said. "These brownies are authentic killer brownies. They taste like the ones your grandmother Trish used to bake. She was famous for her brownies."

Rosalie grinned. "It's her recipe."

When they were ready to leave, Mr. Young gave Major several cases of canning jars.

"You're a man of surprises. I can't tell you how much all of this means to us. Thank you," Major said.

After they were home, Aimee Louise and Rosalie finished their homework and studied for the upcoming radio test. When they took a break from the books, Rosalie worked through several more of the guitar lessons, and Aimee Louise tested the reception of the transceiver.

Major worked on his supplies list. He stopped a few minutes to listen to the girls quizzing each other and to the strum of the guitar. *I could sure get used to this. But I agree with Aimee Louise, something's brewing.*

## CHAPTER TWENTY-ONE

The Boss reviewed the data he'd sent to The Board before the Phase One explosion and the data he helped gather after the explosion. *I can see how Phase One provides a view of the response capability to return to partial, then full service. Easiest money I ever made.*

He stared out his office window. *My people positioned over forty thousand kilos of drugs to move north before Phase One.* The explosion was the trigger for his massive transport organization to spring into action, and the product was on the road. The Board guaranteed the explosion and the outage would overwhelm law enforcement resources. *And they were right. The entire operation was smooth, profitable, and unhindered.*

After Howie's call, The Boss alerted his contacts at a bogus delivery company to begin Phase Two. "Drop the boxes off at the first address."

An unmarked box truck delivered five refrigerator-sized boxes to the electronics store at closing time, when it was too late to log them into the inventory system.

Four hours later, the burglary crew disabled the security system and cameras. They loaded the five large boxes, the entire stock of solar-powered chargers, and everything else they could get into their delivery truck before their allotted on-scene time of ten minutes expired. They left the back door locked and secured.

The Boss parked his car at the warehouse to wait for the burglary crew. *They're good—not quite as good as Team Three, but close. Almost sorry about Team Three, but no loose ends with Phase One was critical.*

The Boss removed his paisley tie, rolled up the sleeves of his white shirt, and helped unload the truck at the warehouse. *They need to know I'm as strong as any of them.* Plus, it gave him a firsthand opportunity to examine the delivery. The real purpose of the break-in was to pick up the boxes that were not in the store inventory. The chargers for his crews were a bonus.

He examined the large boxes that belonged to the Board. He didn't know what was in them and didn't care. He was another well-paid link in the untraceable supply chain that moved the boxes toward their destination.

*Boxes are undamaged—not a crease. I can breathe when they're picked up in two hours.*

The Boss collected passwords and other information for the Board. He didn't have any details for the second phase, but he sent his wife and family to her parents' home two states away and positioned an even larger inventory of drugs ready to move. The Board promised him four hours' notice before the second phase kicked in.

He heard a buzz of similar activity from associates in California, Texas, Chicago, and the Northeast.

One of his buddies said the real purpose of phase two was to overwhelm law enforcement with the coordinated flood of drugs into the big cities and to disrupt the power grid to cause the economy to collapse so The Board could take over the government.

*Planning is the key. I'm immune to any economic or political crash.*

* * *

Major installed the antenna where Aimee Louise and Mr. Young determined the reception for the nearest repeater was best. Aimee Louise connected the antenna to the transceiver, and Rosalie stood by to help.

Major watched for a while. "I need to go into town for some of the things on my supplies list. Number one is more gas for the generators. I've got cans to refill."

Rosalie pulled a sheet of paper out of her notebook. "Here's our list. Hope it helps."

He glanced over the list. "Oh, extra gas cans. I'll add that. Good idea. I'll get everything on your list too."

"We held a debrief session," Aimee Louise said. She stood up, dusted off her knees, and sneezed. "After we finish the installation, we'll be ready to test the antenna."

"We plan for it to be all set by the time you get back." Rosalie put her hands on her hips and surveyed the room. "And I need to dust in here."

Major found all the supplies on both lists. As a surprise, he picked up a battery pack and solar charger for the ham radio. He stopped at the grocery store for ice cream and pizza for their evening meal. On the way to this truck, he chuckled. *I'm a good shopper.*

* * *

Major, Aimee Louise, and Rosalie were up by dawn to watch the sunrise. At breakfast, Aimee Louise said, "The antenna needs a few adjustments to improve reception."

"Minor, right?" Major asked.

"Yes," Rosalie said. "The overall performance is great."

"Will you sing with the choir today?"

"Not me," Aimee Louise said. "I hum. Friend sings."

"Yes, I'm singing, and Aimee Louise is humming with the choir," Rosalie said.

"I guess I should have said, Will you hum-sing?"

The girls laughed, and Major smiled. *I'll take that as a sign my jokes are improving.*

After church, the sheriff and his family came to the farm. Molly packed fried chicken, potato salad, and homemade rolls, with peach pie for dessert.

While they ate, the sheriff asked, "How's the ham radio setup?"

Major shrugged and grinned. "Remember you asked."

Aimee Louise went into detail about the setup, tests, and range. She talked for over thirty minutes, and Rosalie interjected a few comments. Major enjoyed the surprised looks on the sheriff's and Molly's faces. They obviously had never heard Aimee Louise speak with so much enthusiasm.

After lunch, the younger children asked if they could run with Aimee Louise and Rosalie.

Before Molly said, "Don't go too far," the six of them, plus Shadow and Penny, were out the door.

Aimee Louise called back. "We won't."

The adults reviewed their lists and found only minimal duplication because the approach each took was different. They categorized the items by criticality.

"Sounds like we've got a little work to do to get our highest-priority items done," Major said.

Molly and the two older girls canned pork stew the rest of the afternoon while the younger children did chicken chores. The sheriff helped Major with fence repair around the coops and the garden.

The sheriff and his family left before dusk. Aimee Louise and Major sat at the radio, and he tested the setup by transmitting on several different frequencies.

"This is great. We got responses on almost all our frequencies. Well done," Major said.

* * *

Howie got word from The Boss about another job, and Howie swaggered into their usual coffee shop. *I tole them guys I was the best. The Boss likes my work, and The Boss don't like nothing.*

The Boss said, "I want you to find those two kids two days after the next outage. And do whatever you like." The Boss narrowed his eyes at Howie. "Tell me what you're supposed to do."

Howie swallowed. "Find the two kids. Two days after the outage. Then I can do whatever I like."

"Good. I'm counting on you to do this right."

Howie nodded. He rented a room in Plainview and waited for the outage.

## CHAPTER TWENTY-TWO

On Monday morning, Aimee Louise said, "This will be the slowest day ever."

"Slowest day in the history of the world," Rosalie said.

"I agree," Major said. "I'll spend this morning on well maintenance and the afternoon on generator maintenance. I'm not sure if anything will help the day go any faster."

After he and Shadow dropped off Aimee Louise and Rosalie at school, Major said, "Let's see how much we can get done before time to pick them up."

Later that afternoon, Major rolled the last generator back into its place in the equipment shed. "It's finally time to leave."

Major and Shadow waited in the parents' loop, and when Aimee Louise and Rosalie hopped into the truck, he asked, "How was school today?"

"It dragged all day," Rosalie said.

Major snorted. "I asked the wrong question: what did you do today?"

"Thought about radio class," Aimee Louise said.

"Me too; I'm excited," Rosalie added.

"Can't say I blame you; it is exciting that tomorrow night is the test."

When he turned onto the dirt road, Major smiled while they quizzed each other.

"What type of identification is used to identify a station on the air as Race Headquarters?" Rosalie asked.

"Tactical call sign," Aimee Louise said. "Which amateur band do you use when your station transmits 146.52 megahertz?"

"Two-meter band," Rosalie said. "What electrical component is used to protect other circuit components from current overloads?"

"Fuse." Aimee Louise gazed out her window. "We're almost home."

"Why does time go so fast when we talk about radios," Rosalie asked, "and sneaked backward when we were in school?"

"Not a test question," Aimee Louise said.

"We'll eat supper early tonight again, right, Pops?" Rosalie asked.

"Are you thinking the earlier we eat, the sooner we can leave for class?" he asked.

"Would it work?" Aimee Louise asked.

"I would normally say no, but it wouldn't hurt to try." Major chuckled.

"Homework time, then we can eat," Rosalie said.

*Mistake on my part; we may be eating supper in fifteen minutes.* Major rolled his eyes.

At four thirty, Rosalie and Aimee Louise raced into the barn where Major and Shadow were working.

"We're done," Rosalie said. "What do we need to prepare for supper?"

"I'm going simple: eggs, bacon, and toast."

"We'll get started with the bacon," Rosalie said as they raced toward the house.

Major closed his toolbox. "We better hurry, Shadow, or we'll miss supper."

The three of them arrived twenty minutes early. "Oh good. We can sit in the front row," Rosalie said. "Mr. Young said the radio classes are designed to help the students pass the technician test."

At the end of the class, Major said, "Glad I came. Good refresher."

The girls quizzed each other about the evening's major topic, radio safety, on the way home.

* * *

The next morning, Major and Shadow dropped off the girls at school. "I'm desperate, Shadow," Major said. "Let's go to the grocery store and see what's on sale. It wouldn't hurt to get a little coffee and maybe something simple for supper.

When Major came out of the grocery store, his cart was overloaded. Shadow had waited outside the store and loped along with him to the truck.

As he loaded the truck, Major said, "I never knew Tuesday was when the grocery store had their specials of the week. I picked up subs for tonight; I thought that would be the easiest and fastest. We've got time for a quick hardware stop since we're in town. We'll get back home by lunch, so I can catch up on the laundry this afternoon. I may have time to strip the beds."

* * *

At two o'clock in the afternoon, The Boss received a text: "4." *Four hours until Phase 2.*

He made the calls to move drugs and trotted to his car that he had packed two nights ago then headed north to join his family.

* * *

At three, the dismissal bell rang, and Aimee Louise and Rosalie dashed out to meet Major.

"I wish we could go take the test right now." Rosalie climbed into the truck.

"We're ready," Aimee Louise said.

"I didn't hear a word in class today because I kept thinking about my favorite topic: amateur radio." Rosalie hugged Shadow, who sat next to her.

"School time is slow," Aimee Louise said.

When Major parked his truck next to the house, Aimee Louise, Rosalie, and Shadow jumped out.

"We'll drop our backpacks then take care of the chickens," Rosalie shouted as they raced to the house.

The girls and Shadow returned before Major finished putting away the groceries he'd unloaded earlier. "I did several loads of laundry today. I stripped our beds and washed our sheets and blankets. I've made my bed; would you make your beds then fold and put away your clothes. I bought some new tools and would like to put them away in the barn."

When they got to the farm, they hurried through their afternoon chores. The girls bolted down the subs Major had picked up earlier in the day.

When they arrived at the classroom, he said, "We're early. We've got time to settle down before the class begins." The girls paced in the hallway until the coordinator appeared.

At six, the class coordinator said, "Welcome, everyone. Let's get started," and the lights shut off in the classroom. The TV screen and overhead lights went dark, and the air handler cut off.

Someone in the back said, "That's annoying. Dropped the network."

The room glowed with the light of the battery-operated laptop computers and cell phones. One of the class instructors stepped outside to talk on his handheld ham radio.

"Let's go see Aunt Molly," Major said. "Now."

As they stood, the instructor said, "Well, we're not the only ones without electricity, but no one heard an explosion. Probably a brownout. We'll start class when the lights come back on. Shouldn't be long."

After they were in the truck, Rosalie said, "Another outage, Pops?"

He nodded.

"Will we come back to class when the lights are on?" Rosalie asked.

He shook his head. "I don't think they'll be back on anytime soon."

Aimee Louise pulled at her sweatshirt sleeves.

Rosalie sang. "Shoulda paid the light bill. It was your turn. The electrical trolls need money to burn."

Major laughed, and Aimee Louise relaxed her hands.

At Molly's house, he turned to the girls before they got out of the truck. "This will be a quick stop. We'll check in to see what we can do."

Molly stood at the door. "I knew you'd come straight here. The sheriff called and said for us to go to the farm. I have some things for you to take in the truck. They're too big for my car."

She waved toward the corner of the dining room. "They're stacked over there. I've got a few more things to load. We'll be no more than ten minutes behind you."

Major and the girls loaded the truck.

"Would you mind if Penny goes with you?" Molly asked. "I'm afraid we've made her nervous with all this rushing around, and we could use the extra space for boxes."

"Do you want some or all of the kids to ride with us too?" he asked.

"No, I can use their help, and I know you want to get back to Shadow. We only have a few more things to load into the car. We won't be much longer."

By nine that night, all the cots were set up for the night at the farmhouse.

* * *

Major got up early so he could listen to the ham radio at sunrise. Molly wore jeans and a college sweatshirt and had a pot of coffee on the stove.

On his way to the radio he smiled, despite the circumstances. *That coffee pot will earn its keep.* Major switched the radio over to the battery pack, turned it on, and discovered two girls at his elbows.

"I think this morning we'll want to listen. I need more coffee. Someone want to take the driver's seat?"

"Aimee Louise does," Rosalie said.

## CHAPTER TWENTY-THREE

Aimee Louise slid into the chair vacated by Major, and Rosalie scooted her chair closer. Rosalie pulled out her notebook and pen, ready to take notes.

After he filled his cup, Major returned to the computer room and asked, "So what's the word?"

Rosalie said, "Might have been more than one outage. Is that possible? We went down at six, and it sounds like most of the East Coast, Gulf Coast, and Texas were hit at the same time. Then, two hours later, at eight our time, much of California, the West Coast, and Mountain states went down. All this is from what the hams pieced together."

He took a deep breath, shook his head, and walked out of the room, while the girls turned their attention back to the radio.

"Molly," Major said, "we need to talk to the sheriff as soon as possible. We need to prepare for the worst." He told her what Rosalie had reported.

"I'll call him. We need him here to talk."

After the sheriff arrived, the adults took their coffee to the back porch while the kids ran a loop around the house.

Molly said, "I need to run, but not with them. They are fast."

"The consensus in town is that this is another outage like the first one. They expect the electricity to be back on by the end of the week," the sheriff said. "When I mentioned it might be longer, some were angry, like it would be my fault if it didn't come back on. I suppose the good news is no one has hit panic mode yet. The stores are open, but the shelves are sparse."

"I suspect the grocery-store shelves will be empty by the end of the day," Major said. "It may be only three more days before things turn ugly."

"Pete has positioned the diner for the long run. He's gone to a limited menu with morning hours only. He started what he and the regulars call a morning barter in the parking lot. The purpose is to encourage people to show up with things they want to trade."

"Pete and 'the long run' made me think," Molly said. "What will be more difficult to do later? Can we do them in our three days?"

"Good question," agreed Major. "One thing I can think of is the generators. I don't think the engine noise will catch anyone's attention in the next three days, but it might later. We can run all the generators—the one for the well and water heater, the one for the refrigerator and freezer, and even the one for the washer and dryer."

"We need all the medicines we can get," Molly said. "Can we talk to a doc and get refills for meds and prescriptions for antibiotics?"

"I'd like to load up chicken food, dog food, vet medicines, and other farm supplies," Major said. "I need garden supplies like insecticides, rodent control, and vegetable seedlings and plants to get a jump start on my plan to extend the garden."

"Molly, I'll need a list of everyone's meds," the sheriff said.

"I've got the list," Molly said, "and I'll tell the kids our plan for the next three days. We'll get it all organized."

"You're okay with the generators, Aimee Louise?" Major asked.

"Yes."

"I'd like to learn about the generators." Annie followed Aimee Louise.

"I want to leave right now for the farm store," Major said. "I think we've got only today for any trips to town and shopping."

"I think you're right," the sheriff said. "I'll throw together a couple of sandwiches. We've got to move fast."

Molly ran into the house and returned almost as fast as she left. "Here's the list of prescriptions. And here's an old backpack with the cash I've saved for emergencies."

The sheriff raised his eyebrows and kissed Molly on the cheek. "Thanks. You're always full of surprises."

He slapped together bread and cheese and handed a sandwich and a stack of bills to Major. "Here's your sandwich and more cash. I know you've already got some, but you have the bulk of the bigger-ticket items. Let's go. We need to be back before dark. Molly, call me if there's any trouble here."

Molly stood on the front porch with her arms crossed and stared while the two men left. She shuddered. *It's real. I can't believe it, but it's real.*

* * *

A little before lunch, Molly and Aimee Louise were canning when Shadow and Penny barked warnings. Molly ran to the back door and yelled, "Inside!"

The children ran to the house. "Everyone upstairs to the back bedroom. Quick," Molly said.

Aimee Louise led the young ones upstairs to the back bedroom. Rosalie and Penny brought up the rear.

Molly stepped to the front door with a shotgun, and Shadow assumed his on-guard position next to her. Molly frowned at the road dust from a truck and camping trailer. The truck slowed for the turn at the driveway, pulled in, and stopped about halfway to the house. The driver stepped out and limped toward the house with his hands raised.

"Aunt Molly," Rosalie called down from the girls' bedroom. "It's Mr. Young. I can see him with the binoculars. It's Mr. Young!"

Molly lowered her shotgun, but Shadow stayed on guard. Mr. Young hobbled toward the house. Molly and Shadow hurried out to meet him.

"Hello, Mrs. Starr. I listened to the ham radio traffic this morning. Bad times are around the corner, and it won't be good for a lone old man. I won't be any trouble. I can stay in my camper."

Molly took his arm and helped him to the house.

He sat on the leather sofa and accepted a glass of water from Aimee Louise. "I spent this morning loading up the truck and camper with things I thought would be useful."

"I'll drive the truck and camper closer to the house," Molly said. "We'll figure out where to park them later."

Molly sat in the driver's seat of the truck and glanced at the trailer. *That's a big trailer. I've never done this before.*

She took her foot off the brake and pressed on the accelerator with a slow, deliberate touch, and the truck moved forward. "No need to go fast. Drive straight, no turns. It'll be fine. You can do it. Piece of cake. You got this. Good job." Her hands were damp with sweat. She applied the brake with firm pressure and turned off the engine. She wiped her hands on her jeans and chortled. "Piece of cake."

Molly returned to the house. "Mr. Young, I need a list of your medications."

Mr. Young pulled out his wallet and took out a small sheet of paper. Molly looked it over and texted the list to her husband. "Add for Mr. Young."

"Mr. Young," said Molly. "We're canning as much as possible today. If you're okay, I'll get back to it."

"I'm fine. Needed to catch my breath. Thanks for the water, Aimee Louise. I'll unload the camper first. There's some kitchen stuff. I've got frozen venison roasts and canning jars."

"Can we help, Mr. Young?" Josh asked.

"We're good helpers," Brett added.

"Thank you, young men. I would like that."

Mr. Young and the boys lifted the utility wagon out of the truck bed. The boys helped load the cart. With Josh pulling and Brett pushing, they moved the wagon to the back porch. Annie and Sara carried kitchen items inside to Rosalie, who organized and put things away.

After lunch, Mr. Young and the younger children unloaded the remainder of the items in the camper and truck.

"Do we need to organize how we put the items in the shed?" Mr. Young asked.

"If we group items, I'll count them, and the boys can put them into the shed by groups," Rosalie said.

* * *

The pharmacy department in the back of the drug store had a battery-operated lantern on the counter. The pharmacist was locking cabinets and glanced over his shoulder.

"I'm getting ready to shut down and leave, Sheriff. But if you need some refills, I can take care of them. I'll write everything down and then record them in the system when we get our electricity back."

"I've got a list from Molly. And I'm supposed to pick up Mr. Young's refills too."

"Give me the list, and I'll get busy. You have any shopping to do? This might take me a little extra time."

"That's my other list from Molly." The sheriff waved the paper and chuckled.

After loading up with over-the-counter medicines, the sheriff wheeled his cart to the medical equipment and supplies aisle. When he returned to the pharmacy department, the pharmacist set three sacks on the counter.

"Here you go, sheriff. I've recorded everything. I'm hoping I'm wrong, but I think we've got a hard road ahead of us." He locked the remaining cabinets and left.

When the sheriff reached the front of the store, the manager joined him. The manager was in his mid-thirties, and he wore a white shirt with the store logo and khaki pants, but his short dark hair with the cowlick gave him the look of a high school student.

His mouth was set, and his brow was furrowed. "Sheriff, the whole town is at the grocery store buying toilet paper, milk, and bread. Everybody says we'll have electricity by the end of the week, but I'm not so sure. I expected the weekly truck this morning from the distribution center, but it never came. Don't mean to pry, but your cart looks like you don't expect electricity any time soon."

He rubbed his forehead and gazed at the sheriff. "My wife wants to go to her parents' farm in Georgia. I can't decide if we should wait a week or so to see how things play out or leave now, which is what she wants to do. I loaded my car early this morning similar to what you have in your cart, except I have extra supplies for the baby. Am I paranoid? Should I wait a week or two?"

The sheriff met his gaze. "I don't have any inside information, and I'm not any more qualified than the next man to give you advice. But I sent my family to a farm last night."

The manager nodded and straightened his shoulders. "Thanks. I'm locking up now and going home. We'll settle up next time the store's open."

The sheriff stopped at the thrift store. The only person in the store was the clerk. She was perched on a stool at the counter, smoking a cigarette.

"You're my first customer of the day, sheriff." The clerk snuffed out her cigarette in an overflowing ashtray and set it under the counter. "Everyone else ran to the grocery store. I'm going to wait until tomorrow when their shelves are restocked. It's a zoo in there right now. People are crazy, you know? Anything I can help you find?"

"No, I'll just help myself. Thanks." He glanced at the sign on the counter. "Five dollars a bag for clothes?"

"Yep. Helps clear out the inventory. Clothes are the hardest thing to sell."

The sheriff filled bags with socks, underwear, shirts, sweatshirts, pants, and shoes. He guessed at sizes. *What they don't wear now, they can wear later.*

"No winter jackets?" The sheriff asked.

"Might have some in the back." She chuckled. "You're welcome to look, but it's the wrong season for coats."

The sheriff carried four sacks to the back room and filled them with cold weather gear of all sizes.

"Appreciate your business, sheriff. You donating stuff to the children's adoption agency? That's mighty nice of you. Need a receipt?"

"No, I'm fine. I'll take these sacks out and come right back for the others. Thanks."

After he returned for the rest of his purchases, he stopped before leaving. "Not sure the grocery store will restock by tomorrow. You might want to do your shopping today."

"I never took you for one of them doomsday types, Sheriff." The clerk's cackle turned into a cough, and she reached for a cigarette.

* * *

The sheriff turned at the farm driveway and parked near the back of the farmhouse. Major followed him down the driveway but drove straight to the sheds and parked the truck. The boys and Rosalie ran to the back porch from the shed, and Mr. Young followed them. Aimee Louise and Annie ran from the garden, and Molly and Sara came out of the house to the porch.

"My feet were ready for a break," Molly said as she sat in her favorite rocker. Mr. Young sat next to her with a soft groan.

"I'm glad you came to join us, Mr. Young," Major said when he reached the house.

Mr. Young stood, and the men shook hands. "Thank you, Major."

"I talked to the four deputies and suggested they relocate to the Gaston property," the sheriff said. "The two married deputies will move their families first thing in the morning. The two single deputies will join the families in a day or so. One of the deputies has a large fifth-wheel trailer. He moved it today for the single guys."

"I did my best to load down the truck with everything we might need from the feed store," Major said. "They had chicks, ducks, and rabbits for sale. I bought six rabbits and three dog kennels for temporary housing. They're in the bed of my truck right now. We'll put them in the barn for tonight, and I grabbed some books on how to raise rabbits."

"Rabbits?" Annie said. "I've always wanted to raise rabbits."

"No, you always wanted to raise goats," Josh said.

"Rabbits too." Annie growled.

"Goats." Josh ran to the shed when Annie stepped toward him.

"Major, my hunting rifles are in the camper," Mr. Young said. "They're locked up. We can move them whenever you like."

"If you all unload the vehicles and get Mr. Young's camper in place, Aimee Louise and I will work on supper. We're done canning for the day," Molly said.

The boys and Annie unloaded and hauled the smaller items from the sheriff's truck. After the children carried in what they could, Annie asked, "Pops, would it be okay if I read the books about rabbits? I'd like to help raise them."

Major frowned. "You know the rabbits are for meat, right? They won't be pets."

She nodded. "I understand. That's why I want to help raise them. I want to help feed the family."

Major raised his eyebrows and glanced at the sheriff, who nodded his approval. "Okay, Annie, you and I can raise the rabbits together. We need to build hutches. Okay with you?"

"Yes." Annie danced and bounced on her toes.

With Brett's help, Rosalie added the final leaf to the dining table and made sure the ten chairs all fit.

After they sat down to eat, Major said, "I am thankful for this family."

The crowd of hungry folk responded with a rounding chorus of "Me too!" The boys said, "Me three!" and "Me four!"

After kitchen cleanup, Molly said, "Let's get going with baths."

Major headed to the back door.

"You unloading?" The sheriff asked. "I'll come along."

As the two men strolled to the shed, the sheriff said, "The young manager from the drug store is taking his family to Georgia to stay on his in-laws' farm. The pharmacist is leaving town too."

"A rowdy group came into Pete's diner when I stopped by to see how he was doing. Four men I didn't recognize. They seemed to be looking for a fight. You probably knew Pete keeps a shotgun in the kitchen. I didn't. He looks pretty fierce when he's mad." Major shook his head.

"Awful quick for the rough element to be showing up. I'm really glad my family's here." Sheriff and Major unloaded the rest of the items and secured the sheds and barn.

After they returned to the house and walked into the kitchen, Molly asked, "Coffee? We just put on a fresh pot."

Major shook his head. Sheriff said, "Molly, it still amazes me that you can drink coffee at night. The only time I do is when I have the night shift."

Mr. Young was cutting a sizeable, partially thawed venison roast off the bone and into large pieces. "We've already planned our canning and meals for tomorrow. Molly's going to marinate the roast overnight in apple cider."

Molly wrapped the bones in foil and put them in the oven to roast for the dogs. Shadow and Penny stayed close to the kitchen. "Look at our drooling oven guards," Molly said.

* * *

*The outage happened like The Boss said.* Howie waited two days and walked from town toward the farm. He noticed the Gaston house ahead of him, but only as a point of interest, nothing more, then Howie saw them and lay down on the road.

## CHAPTER TWENTY-FOUR

After breakfast, Aimee Louise said, "Pops, we'd like to check the cameras."

"Okay. Shadow and I need to check some fence lines and pull together lumber for the rabbit hutches," he said. "We'll be around when you get back."

While they tied their shoes, Rosalie said, "I am so ready to run. Sometimes I feel like a deer. Need to run."

Aimee Louise listened to the birds, who chirped to cheer them on. She gazed across the pasture. The dew glistened and sparkled in the sunlight. *Sun glitter.*

As her feet crushed the meadow vegetation, the dew soaked her shoes and socks, and she breathed in the lingering aroma of damp wildflowers and grasses.

When they neared the dirt road, Rosalie pointed at a man lying on the road, looking hurt. He waved at them and called out with a weak voice.

Rosalie headed toward the man, but Aimee Louise grabbed her shirt and pulled her back. "Uncle Dan."

They spun around in unison and ran away from the man. He jumped up, chased them, and tried to cut them off. Aimee Louise and Rosalie changed their direction, but Uncle Dan changed course too.

A bleat that sounded almost like a child caught Aimee Louise's attention. She pointed to the left at the baby bear, and Rosalie nodded.

They headed toward the baby bear, and Uncle Dan followed. They veered closer to the woods and then took a sharp right.

A growl came out of the woods behind them. *Mama bear.*

Aimee Louise led Rosalie into the woods and stopped. The girls faded into the trees and brush, walked backward away from the growl, and didn't make a sound or any sudden moves. They froze, listened, continued their silent retreat, and blended into the shadows of the forest. The growling sounds intensified, and the crashes through the brush and woods headed toward the man and away from them. The man shouted and yelled.

*He's running, and the growling bear is in pursuit.*

The girls continued at the same slow pace.

In a quiet voice, Aimee Louise said, "No more growls or shouts."

Rosalie nodded.

"Let's go," said Aimee Louise, and they ran to the farm.

* * *

Howie ran as fast as he could, but the bear snorted and growled. *Is that hot bear breath on the back of my neck?* He was afraid to turn around to look. He heard yelling and screaming and realized it was him. He grabbed his car's door handle, but in his panic he fumbled with it. *I'm going to die in the woods. Eaten by a bear.*

He jerked the door open, fell into the car, and slammed the door on his feet. He roared in pain, but he somehow pulled his feet into the car before the bear closed the door when she rammed into it. She clawed and scratched at the door and roared at the window. Howie smelled her breath through the glass. *Jeez, who knew bear breath was sweet?*

After one last scratch and snort, she turned away.

Howie sat behind the wheel and placed his hand on his chest. *My heart is pounding; I can't breathe.* He bent over to catch his breath, and his feet throbbed with pain. He raised up and stared at the bear as she lumbered away. The smaller bear followed her. After a few deep breaths, he stopped shaking.

Howie picked up his phone and called The Boss. The phone went from ringing to a fast busy signal. Howie looked at his cell. Hung up. And called again. Fast busy.

*The Boss said to find them and do whatever I want. I found them. I want to leave. They can stay here with the bear.*

"Okay, bear," Howie said aloud, "I'm going back to the city. It's safer there than here. I'll find some of the guys."

Howie thought about all the guys who bragged that if the city ever had a big problem they'd go to the country and live off the land.

*And get chased by an angry bear? No, thank you.*

He spun his tires in his haste to speed away.

* * *

When they were close to the farm, the girls blew their whistles. Major jumped in Number 48 and roared toward them. When he got to them, they scrambled in.

Aimee Louise pulled at her sweatshirt cuffs. "Pops, it was Uncle Dan."

Rosalie brushed her hair out of her face and caught her breath. "He tried to trick us, but Aimee Louise saw his cloud, and we ran."

"He chased us," Aimee Louise said. "After we saw a baby bear, we heard a mama bear."

"We think he tried to run away from the mama bear. We walked away, backward and slow like you said," Rosalie added. "Then we ran."

"Can you tell me where?" Major asked.

"Near the dirt road close to Annie's house," Rosalie said.

"I'll drop you off at the house. Go inside right away and call the kids in too. Stay there until I get back. The sheriff and I will find Uncle Dan."

The sheriff met them at the house then he and Major grabbed their hunting rifles and sped off on Number 48.

* * *

When Aimee Louise and Rosalie went into the house, everyone stared as they waited to hear what happened.

"We don't have time to stand around," Molly said. "We've got farm work to do. Let's get busy with the canning, and I need laundry done. Mr. Young, would you stand watch?"

"Annie and I can help with canning," Rosalie said. "You want to help with canning too, Sara?"

Aimee Louise said, "Josh and Brett are strong and can help me with the laundry, and I'll keep an eye on the generators."

Mr. Young returned from his trailer with his deer rifle and saluted Molly. "Private Young on duty, ma'am."

Molly rolled her eyes and returned his salute while the children giggled. She glared and everyone scattered. Molly covered her smile with her hand as she walked to the kitchen.

* * *

It was close to noon when Major and Sheriff returned. Their faces were grim. Molly poured them coffee.

"We're ready for some lunch, Molly," the sheriff said.

While they ate, Major said, "Uncle Dan was gone. Both bears were gone. We found where he parked and where he turned his car around. Be a good idea for everyone to stay in sight of the house."

"I agree," said Molly. "This was really scary."

"Looks like you all got lots done this morning," the sheriff said. "What's the plan for this afternoon?"

"I have some lumber, fencing, and other building supplies at my house in the barn," Mr. Young said. "Maybe the deputies could build a chicken coop. And do you think one or two of the families in town might be interested in my house? I've got a small garden and an old chicken coop in good shape."

"I can pick up the lumber," Major said.

"Mr. Young, do you think Major can find everything you have in mind?" the sheriff asked. "Maybe one of the kids could go with him to help load."

"It's all in the barn. It's locked, but here's the key. What about families for the house? I thought Pastor John and his brother Chuck might want to move their families out of town sooner rather than later."

"Can I help get the lumber?" Josh asked.

Major nodded. "I'll hook up the utility trailer for the lumber. Josh and Shadow can go with me. We'll be back before dark." Josh grinned.

"Josh, let's check your backpack," Aimee Louise said. "And we need to find you some work gloves."

The sheriff said, "I have a meeting in town later this afternoon. I'll encourage people to move in with family members or move together into a neighborhood. We'll see if anyone listens. I'll talk to Pastor John and Chuck while I'm there."

"Hey, Major," the sheriff shouted as Major pulled out of the driveway, "okay with you if Annie and I build the rabbit hutch before I leave?"

"Go for it," he shouted as he drove off.

Major, Josh, and Shadow returned before nightfall. "Want to see how to unhook the trailer?" Major asked.

"Heck, yeah." Josh glanced at the house. "Hope Mom didn't hear me."

When Major and Josh walked into the house, Major said, "Josh, smell that roast? That's a man's reward for hard work, and you worked hard."

"I'm so hungry," Josh said, "I could eat a bear."

Molly laughed. "I don't know how to cook bear, but Mr. Young has a venison roast in the oven. You all might want to wash up."

Sara grabbed silverware to set the table.

Brett said, "I'll close up the coops. It's time for the chickens to be in bed on their roosts."

"I'll go with you, Brett, then we can wash up," Josh said.

After the sheriff returned from his meeting, Molly lit three candles and placed them in the middle of the table. Mr. Young and Molly dished the food into large bowls to be passed family style, and everyone took their seats.

"I am thankful for this family," Molly said.

"Amen," Mr. Young added.

"Dinner by candlelight," Sara said. "I feel fancy."

"I used the remaining lettuce, celery, and other odds and ends of vegetables from the refrigerator for our salad," Molly said. "Mr. Young steamed eggs for his deviled eggs and made the gravy to go over the rice and venison."

The kitchen was quiet while everyone ate until Major asked, "Anything on the radio?"

"Nothing new on the outage," Rosalie said. "There's talk about government help, but some said it was only talk. No details. Some of the hospitals lost their backup generator power already, but they knew how long their power would last, so the hope is the hospitals moved their patients to safety. Some of the large cities reported looting and fires. That's scary. The hams shared ideas on what to do over the next week or so. I took notes. There's a lot of shared information on the radio. We think we should be sharing too. How do we do that?"

"I have some ideas," Mr. Young said. "Major, can you and I talk later with Aimee Louise and Rosalie?"

"Sure," Major said.

"I talked to Pastor John and Chuck, and Chuck will move their families from town to Mr. Young's farm tomorrow morning," the sheriff said. "They'll pack tonight and leave as soon as possible after daylight. Pastor John wants to stay in town at least another day."

"What about your meeting?" Major asked.

The sheriff sighed. "I'd hoped more people would show up, but maybe they'll spread the word. In one neighborhood, there were four or five families who made plans to move closer to each other."

Molly passed the venison and gravy. "Seconds, anyone?"

Josh speared a piece of meat and spooned gravy over it. "I was hungry. This is good."

The sheriff smiled at Josh. "Sounded like a few families already left town, and others were ready to leave. Some loaded their cars with food, water, and supplies. Others said they'd drive straight through to their destination."

The sheriff reached for the meat platter and put a serving of the roast on his empty plate. "I checked on Vanessa and invited her to come here, or if she didn't want to do that, to stay with one of the families in town. She said she had a few loose ends to take care of first."

"That's terrible. Should I go into town and get her?" Major scooted his chair back with a loud scrape, and rose.

The sheriff looked at him quizzically. "No, Major. I'm sure she has something in mind. She's smart."

"Oh, okay." Major pulled his chair back to the table before he sat.

The sheriff peered across the table. "Any gravy left there, Josh? Annie designed a rabbit hutch, then she built it with only a little help. She has plans for two more—one for a maternity suite and the other for babies."

After dishes, Mr. Young, Major, Sheriff, Rosalie, and Aimee Louise met outside on the back porch.

Mr. Young eased into a rocker. "If the grid hadn't gone down, Aimee Louise would have passed all the test levels of the amateur radio licenses on test night, including Extra. Under the circumstances, I suggest Aimee Louise use Joan's call sign until she gets her own."

"I remember the allowance for emergency circumstances and agree with you. Aimee Louise, Rosalie, what do you think?" Major asked.

The girls were silent. Rosalie elbowed Aimee Louise.

"Thank you," Aimee Louise said.

"Remember when you talk on the radio, Aimee Louise, don't give out any personal information, especially your name, age, and the number of people who live with you," Major said. "It's okay to talk about weather conditions. As far as location, which would be helpful with the weather, northern Florida is good enough. If someone asks questions, let me or Mr. Young know."

"Pay attention to anyone who sounds like they are on the Gulf. In the spring, our severe weather tends to come from the Gulf. Listen to information from west coast Florida, Louisiana, Mississippi, and Alabama," Mr. Young added. "Listen to the east coast of Florida for hurricanes later this summer."

"Rosalie keeps track of the weather. She's our Weather Girl," Aimee Louise said.

"I like that," Rosalie said. "Weather Girl."

Rosalie smiled and sang, "I read the skies. I watch the spiders. I listen to the frogs. I count the cricket chirps. When it comes to weather predictions, I am the superhero. Yes, that's right, I'm—"

The children ran out when they heard Rosalie sing and jumped in. "Weather Girl!"

Major smiled. *I saw this one coming.*

Molly stepped outside. "Bath time. Young ones first. I think I missed something, so I expect a full report. I suppose you'll say it will be a—"

The boys shouted together, "Weather Report!" Molly turned around and shook her head.

The sheriff laughed and wiped his eyes. "She walked right into that one. Literally."

## CHAPTER TWENTY-FIVE

The next morning, the adults and the two older girls gathered on the front porch before dawn.

"Today's our last day to run the generators. Any reason to change our plans?" Major asked.

"I think we can get everything done today. Mr. Young and I will fry all the fish we have," said Molly. "Do you suppose the deputies and their families would like to eat with us?"

"After Aimee Louise and I swap out the camera memory cards, I planned to go into town. I'll invite the deputies," the sheriff said.

"We have some alternatives as far as the trailer is concerned," Molly said. "The trailer refrigerator and the water heater run off propane, but Mr. Young and I agree it would be smart to conserve our propane."

"I have an idea for showers," Mr. Young said. "The trailer water pump runs off the trailer battery, and I've hooked up a solar panel to charge it. We can take cold showers, or as an alternative, we could hook up another solar panel to heat the water. If it works, we can see how long it takes to heat up the tank."

Rosalie pushed back her chair. "Aimee Louise, radio time."

"I'll review Rosalie's inventory lists to see if we have any potential shortages," Molly said. "You'd think the first thing to be rationed would be coffee, but we have tons. We may be drinking stale coffee at some point, but we'll still have coffee."

"Scared me for a minute there, Molly. Speaking of coffee," the sheriff said, "we need to set up a twenty-four-hour watch schedule. I know Uncle Dan shook us all up. Let's talk about it this evening."

After breakfast, everyone jumped into action. Major smiled as he and Mr. Young walked out to the trailer to see what they could do.

*This crew is a well-oiled machine.*

He shook his head as Brett and Sara argued about who cleaned the chicken coops the best.

Major chuckled. "Well, most of the time."

"Most of the time?" Mr. Young asked.

"I was thinking about how well we work together when I heard the twins arguing about how to clean chicken coops."

Mr. Young laughed. "I have the advantage of not hearing too well. Kids arguing sounds like music to my ears. Sometimes the chords are a little off, but it's still music. Kind of like the chickens squawking."

Major's thoughts turned to how to heat the trailer's small hot-water tank with solar or battery power in place of the direct heat of a propane flame. *It should be easy, but the actual process is not clear.*

"What did you have in mind for the water heater?" Major asked.

"Well, let's give it a look."

* * *

While the sheriff brought Number 48 around, Aimee Louise grabbed her backpack, a couple of bottles of water, and spare memory cards for the cameras.

"Aimee Louise, would you like to drive Number 48?"

*I would like to drive Number 48. The tractor is loud, but Number 48 is louder. Can I cover my ears? Could I steer with my elbows? I wonder why Number 48 was 48. Why not 49 or 47? I need to ask Rosalie. I'll put on my hat to cover my ears.*

Aimee Louise ran inside and returned wearing her favorite hat, a pale-blue knit Laplander hat with earflaps. She took a big breath. "Let's do this."

When the sheriff and Aimee Louise returned, Aimee Louise and Rosalie pulled up the camera pictures on the computer.

The sheriff stood at the door. "What do the cameras show?"

Molly joined him and leaned her head on his shoulder.

Rosalie pointed to a picture. "Carl's still around. He's our resident coyote and has a notch on his ear. Overall, I see more animals than we did right after the explosion, but I don't know if that's seasonal or if they hid for a while. I think they hid."

"Aimee Louise, you did a good job driving Number 48," the sheriff said. "You're a safe, skilled driver. As far as I'm concerned, you can drive anytime."

"That's great news," Molly said. "What did you think, Aimee Louise?"

"I like driving Number 48." She put her hands over her ears. "Even if it is noisy."

* * *

After lunch, the sheriff stopped by the Gaston house. He honked his horn and waited at the end of the driveway. One of the deputies, Brad, came from around back and met the sheriff at the front of the house.

"We've got some lumber if you want to build a chicken coop," the sheriff said. "We can give you a rooster and a couple of hens and some supplies and feed to get you started. You might want to talk to Major about how he built his coops. They're secure from predators, and he's got a pretty good system for cleaning."

"Wow. Awesome. I don't know what to say. Thank you."

"We'd like to invite you all to the farmhouse later today. Molly plans to fry up a mess of fish, and you are invited to eat with us."

"Let's go in and let everyone know. We'll bring something. We've got some things we need to eat up too. Sheriff, we need to talk about security. We've got some ideas. You got a few minutes?"

"Sure," the sheriff replied as they walked to the house. "Then I'm headed into town to see how folks are doing."

When the sheriff drove through town, the deserted appearance saddened him. A few of the businesses were boarded up. Where he could see inside, most of the store shelves were empty and in disarray.

He saw a handwritten note on the library door and books in a bookcase outside the door. He walked up to read the sign: "Take a book. Leave a book. If you want a book you don't see, leave a note. Thank you for reading. God Bless Us All."

The sheriff shook his head. "People are amazing."

He drove to the diner, where he spied a large hand-painted sign: "Open at dawn. Closed midmorning. We have water. Bring a container. We have no food." Someone had painted "For Trade" in large letters on a board and leaned it next to the sign. The board had slips of paper tacked onto it.

The hospital's parking lot was empty. He continued to the fire station and noticed a car parked next to the building. When he pulled in, a young firefighter walked out of the station. He was the newest recruit and was still in uniform. Two men in jeans and black leather jackets flanked the young recruit. All three of them wore holstered pistols on their belts.

"Sheriff, good to see you. These are my brothers. We'll walk home first thing in the morning. We have some medical supplies in the storeroom. We were planning to secure them in the trunk of my brother's car; it's out of gas. You interested?"

"Sure."

The three young men carried out four boxes and put them in the sheriff's trunk.

After they finished, the oldest brother pulled the sheriff aside. "Sheriff, you might not want to come back to town again in a vehicle. No one else has enough gas to drive anywhere, and you stand out like a sore thumb. People will think if you have enough gasoline to drive around, then you have a lot of other stuff too, and they'll plan to help themselves."

The sheriff shook the young man's hand. "Thank you. I should have thought of it myself. I pray for safe travels for you and your brothers."

The sheriff drove to Vanessa's house and knocked on the door, but she didn't answer. He went to her office and thought he saw movement behind a window. He stepped out of his car.

Vanessa stuck her head out the door and waved at him. "Come on in."

When he got to the door, Vanessa said, "It's about time one of you came to get me. I ran out of gas when I got to town, and the office was closer than my house. I have some animals to load up and need some help. I got a call right after the electricity went off. Old friends of mine left town and wanted me to pick up their animals, so now I've got baby goats in my office. The boy is stinky."

The sheriff coughed when he stepped inside. "Whew, you weren't kidding. I can smell that rascal from here. Do you have anything at your house you'd like to take to the farm?"

"No, I've got everything here with me. I have two suitcases, three large bags of goat feed, and a large box of people food. I have a rug I can lay in the bottom of the kennel and a shower curtain we can put under the rug, so your car won't smell like mine."

On the way to the farmhouse, the sheriff said, "How do you suppose Noah tolerated it? What do you know about goats?"

"Allergies," Vanessa said. "The man suffered from allergies, so he smelled nothing. And I knew nothing about goats two days ago. I got a book from the library and know everything in the book. Or I will as soon as I read it."

The sheriff laughed. "Of course." He coughed, almost gagged, and rolled down his window. "Remind me not to breathe until we get to the farm. I hope Molly hasn't finished the laundry. Our clothes will need modern laundry facilities and perfumed soap."

* * *

Major glanced at the sheriff's car as it pulled into the driveway. *A passenger?*

After the sheriff parked, he opened the back door, and the baby goats leaped out of the car.

Major exhaled when Vanessa climbed out of the car. *What a relief to see she's okay.*

Josh was the first to come around the corner of the house. "We got baby goats!" He shouted. "Come see the baby goats."

When all the youngsters dashed to watch the kids bound around the yard, the sheriff chuckled. "No surprise these baby goats are a hit."

"Look at Shadow stand guard while Penny tries to keep the goats together," Molly said.

"There's a small pen next to the chickens where we can put them for now," Major said. "The fence is too high for them to jump. It won't take much to throw together a lean-to for shelter. I've got plenty of scrap lumber."

While the children squealed with delight and helped Penny corral the baby goats, Major approached Vanessa and held out his hand. "Welcome to the farm."

"Thank you, Major," Vanessa said as they shook hands.

*Nice handshake. Strong. Velvety hands.* Major's face warmed, and he turned away.

"Sleeping arrangements," Molly said. "Any ideas?"

"I have a double bed in storage," Major said. "We could set it up in the computer room for you and the sheriff, Molly. Vanessa could sleep in the room with the girls."

The sheriff said, "I think it would work. I like the idea of being downstairs. Molly?"

"Good idea, Major."

"You know," Vanessa said, "I'll be fine on a sofa. Or a palette on the floor."

"We would love to share our room with you, Ms. Vanessa," Annie said.

"Yes, we would," said Sara.

"It's decided then," Major said. "Unless you want to argue for a while, Ms.Vanessa, but I warn you: you'll lose. This crew is quite a force."

Vanessa threw up her hands. "Okay. No sense in wasting time."

"We've got lots to do," Molly said. "We need to finish the laundry and move a bed into the computer room. And we'll have company here for our big fish fry. So let's do this."

Aimee Louise, Rosalie, and Sara were the first to see their company arrive—Wally and his wife, Kris, along with their three-year-old and six-month-old daughters; Brad and his wife, Heather, with their two-year-old son; and the two single deputies, Jim and Stuart.

Sara ran to the front door and called inside. "They're here!"

She bounced and twirled on her toes next to Aimee Louise and Rosalie and counted. "We have twenty people at the farmhouse."

"Lots of family," Aimee Louise said.

Rosalie asked, "Too many people?"

Aimee Louise looked at Rosalie. "You have a worry cloud. No, not too many people because it's family."

Rosalie nodded.

"Oh, look. Your worry cloud is gone. You have a soft, swirly calm cloud."

"I wish I could see my soft, swirly calm cloud. It sounds nice."

"It is."

"Wonder if I could do a soft, swirly calm cloud dance?" Rosalie asked.

"I can," Sara said. She moved in a slow, flowing, almost lyrical turn and waved her arms with a motion of floating in zero gravity.

"Awesome," said Aimee Louise, and she and Rosalie applauded. Sara blushed and curtsied.

Major, the sheriff, and Molly went outside to greet their visitors. The men shook hands, and Molly cooed over the babies and toddlers. Major and Josh helped carry food to the kitchen, where Molly, Aimee Louise, and Annie arranged the food buffet style on the kitchen counter.

Molly announced to the crowd, "We're all set up—we have fried fish, French fries, Kris's slaw, Stuart's crab cakes, Mr. Young's deviled eggs, and Heather's cookies."

Major said, "Mr. Young? Would you do the honors?"

"Thank you for food, friends, and family," said Mr. Young.

"Grab a plate," Molly said. "Sara and Brett rolled silverware in napkins, and Josh and Rosalie set up the drinks."

Vanessa and Major sat together on the back porch.

"This is a real feast," Vanessa said. "We have gourmet cooks in our midst."

After everyone ate, Jim and Stuart volunteered for cleanup duty. Molly stayed to supervise and shooed everyone out of the kitchen.

"Molly," Kris said when Molly joined the group outside, "I think your children and the toddlers invented a new game. It's the run-in-circles, fall-in-the-grass, catch-each-other-and-giggle game."

Baby Sophie squealed and waved her arms, and Mr. Young laughed.

"Appeals to all ages, I see," Molly said. "I'll grab a ringside seat."

Aimee Louise and Rosalie excused themselves to listen to the radio.

"We need to talk about security." The sheriff shared the caution he'd received from the firefighter's brother.

"What do you think if we drop a couple of trees across the road near the turnoff to our house?" Brad asked.

"I think it's a good idea," Major said. "We could do it first thing in the morning."

"Do we need a warning system or code?" Wally asked as Stuart and Jim joined them.

"We have one. I'll explain clouds as best I can and *Uncle Dan*," Major said.

When Rosalie and Aimee Louise returned, Rosalie said, "The news on the radio is not good. The large cities are still burning. People who live near big cities are worried. Gangs broke into homes and robbed and hurt people. People who reported gunshots in the distance say they are closer. Some people are scared. Some people talked about neighbors who got together, and they don't sound as scared."

"Are you scared?" Major asked.

"I'm scared because it is scary, but I'm not scared because I feel safe," Rosalie said. "Does that make sense?"

"Family," Aimee Louise said.

Heather nodded. "Aimee Louise, would you give me a tour of the garden?"

"Kris, if you would like to go along, I'll watch the little ones," Molly said.

Kris and Rosalie joined Heather and Aimee Louise.

"I'll tag along too. I'm interested in the garden," Stuart said.

"Since when?" asked Jim.

Stuart rushed down the path.

"Mr. Young, can you show me your solar heater?" Jim asked. The two men left to look at the trailer.

"Ms. Vanessa, Josh and I have some questions about goats," Annie said.

"Yeah. Like how big will they get?" Josh said.

Vanessa fetched the goat book and flipped pages for reference. After a few more questions, she closed the book and said, "Let's set aside time every day for a lesson about goats. We can start with chapter one tomorrow. Maybe we can study a chapter a day."

"Good idea," Annie said.

"Yep, sounds good," Josh added.

"Thank you, Lord." Vanessa exhaled.

Major grinned. "Told you. Formidable force."

"Major, Stuart and I are interested in your chicken coop construction and security," Brad said.

"How about a tour? And we can pick out lumber, wire, and nails," Major added.

"Sounds good. Let me see if I can tear Stuart away from the girls," Brad said.

Major frowned. *Hope that was just a joke.*

At day's end, Brad and Stuart loaded lumber on Brad's truck, and the deputies and families left.

Molly said, "Time for baths." The younger children dashed upstairs.

Vanessa sat down in the family room next to Major. "This is different from what I'm used to."

Mr. Young smiled. "I know. Me too. Isn't it wonderful?"

* * *

A week later, the sheriff returned from the Gaston house in time for lunch. "Wally and Kris's baby has a high fever. Kris is exhausted. Is there something we can do to help?"

"Kris and her baby could move into the trailer," Mr. Young volunteered. "Would it be okay to power up a generator to run the air conditioner?"

"Good idea. This definitely qualifies as an emergency as far as gasoline is concerned," Major said. "I have some ideas on how to muffle the noise."

"The small generator is quieter," Aimee Louise said.

"I'd like to stay in the trailer to help with the baby," Rosalie said.

"While you pull together your things, Mr. Young, I'll organize a straighten-and-clean party for the trailer. And I'll pull together a palette for you to sleep on, Rosalie," Vanessa said.

"I think we have a plan. Sheriff?" prompted Major.

"I'll take Number 48 and talk to Kris and Wally. Hopefully, I'll come back with Kris and the baby." He returned with an exhausted mother and a sick baby.

"Oh my goodness," Molly said. "Sophie's so pale. Kris, here's a jar of applesauce we canned and a sterilized jar of boiled water to mix with the dry formula."

* * *

After three days, Rosalie, Kris, and the baby came into the house for breakfast.

"I can't thank you all enough," Kris said. "Sophie's fever broke this morning. Rosalie was a lifesaver." She hugged Rosalie. "I don't think I'd have slept at all if you hadn't been with us."

"Look at that sweet baby smile," Molly said. "I can puree some oatmeal, and we have applesauce unless she's sick of it."

"Sophie loves your applesauce," Kris said. "And a little oatmeal sounds like a great idea."

After breakfast, Kris and Sophie were ready to go home. Kris hugged Rosalie again. "Thank you so much. You made a difference for both of us."

Rosalie blushed. "You're welcome, Aunt Kris. I'm glad Sophie feels better."

* * *

The week after Kris and the baby left, Aimee and Rosalie came to the breakfast table with the radio report. "The hams from East Texas and Louisiana reported severe storms pounded their areas yesterday. Tennessee and Alabama expect rough weather today," Rosalie said. "We can expect severe weather—wind, rain, and maybe hail—tomorrow."

"Our newest structures, like the latest chicken coops, rabbit hutches, and the goat shed, haven't been through any significant storms. We need to assess how weather-hardy we think they might be," Major said. "And we'll need to put all the farm equipment into the barn before nightfall. Mr. Young, if the bad weather hits before morning, you'll need to move into the house."

"What direction will the wind come from? The west? Northwest?" Vanessa asked.

"It depends," Mr. Young said. "Sometimes these large systems to our west and north pull moisture from the south, and our storms come from the southwest. And sometimes our surface winds would be southeast. We get it from all directions."

"Well, that makes it hard," Vanessa said.

"More of a challenge, yes," Mr. Young agreed.

"We need to secure everything outside and do whatever we can in advance," said Major. "For example, give the chickens and animals extra food and water. Or if we can't, at least have the extra food ready, like for the rabbits. We'll also need to secure the animals before dark."

"We'll plan our meals for indoor cooking, and we'll need extra water inside the house," Molly added.

In the middle of the night, the sounds of the increasing wind woke Major. He stepped onto the front porch; the wind whipped around the house from the northwest. He slipped back into the house, sat in his recliner with his feet up, and listened to the wind.

Early in the morning, the low rumble of thunder woke Major.

Mr. Young came into the house. "Is that coffee I smell?"

Major stepped outside with Shadow and Penny. They walked a circuit around the chickens, barn, and sheds, and the three of them then returned to the house.

Five minutes after Major and the dogs came inside, the storm hit with strong winds and heavy rain. The sound of the wind and rain woke up the rest of the adults and Aimee Louise, who wore her Laplander hat.

"Why are the children still sleeping?" Molly paced until the sheriff wrapped his arms around her. She hid her face in his chest. "I couldn't sleep in a storm like this. The sound of the wind makes me nervous."

"Might be because it's still dark or because of the low-pressure system," Major said.

"Or both," Mr. Young added.

The thick cloud cover and driving rain obliterated the sun. Molly lit the kerosene lanterns, and the lamps brightened the kitchen and dining area for the rest of the morning.

The four younger children played a board game, while Mr. Young lay down on the sofa and soon slept with a soft snore. Molly reorganized the kitchen.

Vanessa flipped through book after book. "I'll read this one. I don't know anything about hydroponic gardening."

The sheriff sharpened all the kitchen knives.

Major stood at the back door for a while. He then wandered into the computer room to listen to the ham radio with Aimee Louise and Rosalie. The rain slowed to a light shower, and when the birds chirped to announce the end of the storm in the late afternoon, the family hurried outside to assess any damage.

"The rain gauge shows over five inches of rain," Rosalie said. "I don't think anyone expected more than two or three inches."

Sara covered her ears and said, "Listen to the chickens squawk about being cooped up all day."

Josh said to the rooster, "Tell me about it, Bud." The rooster crowed again.

"All the nest boxes are wet," Vanessa said. "Let's pull out this wet straw and dry them out."

Major brought dry straw from the barn in a wheelbarrow. Josh handed fresh straw to Vanessa and sneezed with each handful. "Still smells better than the stinky wet straw," he said.

"Annie, the rabbits didn't have any water intrusion. Your design was excellent," Major said. "But the sheds I threw together for the goats were too small, and the goats are wet."

"Annie and I can work on a new design," Mr. Young said.

"Definitely a good shakedown storm to help us understand where we need improvements," the sheriff added. "We all have new projects from the storm."

"Could have written a nice reminder note," Molly said as she carried in the wet towels Vanessa and Josh used to dry out the nest boxes. Vanessa nodded in agreement, and Major laughed.

* * *

Early one morning toward the end of the month, Major and Mr. Young relaxed on the porch with their coffee while they waited for the morning radio report.

Rosalie hurried out to the porch. "The hams called the news disturbing, and Aimee Louise and I agree. It sounds like the government, although no one is sure which agency, has set up shelters with food in large cities."

Major frowned. "That's a temporary stopgap. Do they have a long-term plan for all the people who will flood their shelters? This has been done before, and it was disastrous."

"No one mentioned any plan," Rosalie said. "They distributed flyers with locations—like sports arenas or empty warehouses—and what people can bring with them. Someone had a copy of a flyer and read it."

Molly brought the coffee pot out for refills, and Vanessa followed her.

"Can you sit where I can hear better?" Mr. Young asked.

## CHAPTER TWENTY-SIX

Rosalie grabbed one of the seat cushions stacked near the back door and dropped it on the porch close to Mr. Young. "It was difficult to take notes."

Aimee Louise brought a cushion out and sat next to Rosalie. "The person who read also commented as he went along. It got tough to follow what was actually on the flyer."

Rosalie referred to her notes. "I'll try to pick out the highlights. Things like no weapons, not even pocketknives or knitting needles. Only one bag per person and not bigger than an airplane carry-on. No electronics, including medical equipment. No canes, walkers, or wheelchairs. No animals, not even service animals. No pillows or blankets, no toys, and only one child per adult. No food or drinks. Only prescription medications, but no narcotics and only two weeks' worth of meds. There was a lot more."

"Only one child per adult, and no toys—that's insane," Molly said as she refilled cups. "What do they expect a young, single mother with a baby and a toddler to do?"

"The man who had the flyer finally said he'd read it straight through so everyone would know what was on it," Rosalie said.

"And the hams agreed on a frequency and time for discussion. Otherwise, I think we'd still be on the radio."

"I can imagine," Major said. "What an inflammatory flyer."

Rosalie set her notes down on the porch. "One of the hams said people would comply out of desperation. One guy said either they expected a lot of people and didn't have much space, or they were trying to limit the number of people because of a low food supply. A lady said the chance of theft was lower with less personal stuff."

"What do you think, Rosalie?" Vanessa asked.

"I'm glad to be here."

"It sounds awful," Mr. Young said. "I can't imagine reading a list like that and not commenting. Whoever came up with the idea of discussion on a different frequency was brilliant."

"Aimee Louise," Rosalie said.

Mr. Young nodded. "Well, then, I was right: brilliant."

* * *

When the season grew warmer, Molly and Mr. Young shifted their cooking tasks to earlier in the day to avoid the afternoon heat.

Molly sat on the back porch and shelled peas with a bucket between her knees. "Have you noticed how the garden flourished under the children's care? When the plants droop from lack of rain,

Sara and Annie pump water from the well into buckets, and Josh and Brett haul the buckets to the garden with the utility wagon."

"The garden grew from small, delicate plants to a green jungle with an explosion of vegetables. Amazing green thumbs," Mr. Young said. "You want the pods to go into the compost or to the chickens?"

Molly ran her fingers through the pods. "Let's give the chickens a treat. The vegetable rule the kids came up with—bragging rights if you don't pass on a vegetable—is genius. I can't believe how competitive this crowd is. I was afraid they would turn up their noses at vegetables. Silly me."

Mr. Young laughed. "I'm second behind Josh in the number of bragging rights cards that Sara created. BRCs are the new currency around here. Did you know we trade cards for chores? Josh and Brett developed an elaborate trading system."

Vanessa joined them on the porch and dropped into a rocker. "Getting hot. Annie and Major wanted you to know they plan to butcher rabbits this morning for supper tonight. I peeked at the garden, and we have an avalanche of tomatoes, peppers, green beans, and cucumbers. A regular garden smorgasbord. I'll organize a crew to do the picking when you're ready to can, Molly. Let me know."

Molly stood and brushed off her apron. "Thanks. I'll cook the rice, and Mr. Young will make the gravy because nobody makes gravy like he does. I'll throw together a salad if your crew picks enough for tonight."

Molly finished shelling, and Mr. Young took the pods to Sara and Brett for their chickens.

On his way back to the house, Mr. Young stopped at the garden to watch the sheriff, Aimee Louise, and Rosalie, who were working on their latest project. "Rosalie, I've been thinking about the animals you've been tracking on camera. I think I can rig a battery pack to keep your laptop charged. We still don't have internet access, but at least you can still show what you've found on your camera cards once or twice a week."

"That's great." Rosalie grinned. "Annie's been asking if we've found any wildlife babies."

After Mr. Young continued on his way to the house, the sheriff said, "As soon as we finish this drip irrigation system with water from the rain barrels, I'll run with you." *I may regret this, but I know the girls want to run.*

When they finished the irrigation project after lunch; the sheriff said, "Okay, let's go."

Aimee Louise, Rosalie, and Shadow ran ahead of him, sprinted back, and ran forward again.

At bedtime, the sheriff groaned when he pulled off his jeans. "I didn't know two sweet girls and a dog could bruise my ego, not to mention slaughter my leg muscles. We won't let them run by themselves, so I feel obligated to run with them; it's rough."

Molly handed him three ibuprofen tablets.

On the second day of the sheriff's new running routine, he stopped to catch his breath. The girls and Shadow ran back to him and stopped. When he ran, they did too. The younger children had told him about the no-talking running rule, but no one had mentioned the if-one-stops-all-stop running rule. *I love that rule.*

While the sheriff and Molly were getting ready for bed at the end of the week, he said, "I've finally learned to pace myself and need only a few stops when I run with the girls to check the cameras and the perimeter of the property."

After he climbed into bed, he kissed Molly good night then asked, "The ibuprofen is great, but would you stop calling me 'Old Sheriff?"

"Nope." Molly grinned.

* * *

Toward the end of the month, while everyone relaxed on the back porch in the evening, the sheriff stopped the slow rock of his chair and leaned forward. "I'd like to check on the deputies and the roadblock in the morning, but I'm not sure I need to take Number 48. If I leave right after breakfast and come back before lunch, I could avoid the worst of the heat."

"Run together," Aimee Louise said.

"We'd like to run with you," Rosalie said.

The sheriff raised his eyebrows. "Your call, Major."

"The girls will be safe with you, and they'll watch your back. It's an easy run for you."

"Good. That's what I thought too."

Aunt Molly chuckled. "Yes. And I'm busy tomorrow morning, so you'll have to run without me."

* * *

The next morning, the sheriff, Aimee Louise, Rosalie, and Shadow left for the Gaston house. They spotted Heather and the two toddlers working in the garden. Heather pulled weeds, and the two toddlers dug in a spot Heather called "Toddler Garden."

"This is a pleasant surprise." She stood and stretched out her back.

Wally and Stuart strolled out of the house together. Wally said, "Hi, Sheriff. Brad's at the chicken coop. We were on our way to go to the road. Jim left not long ago."

"Okay if I tag along?"

"Sure."

"Me too," Aimee Louise said.

"Aimee Louise wants to go with you," Rosalie said, "but I want to visit Aunt Kris and Sophie."

"Sheriff?" Wally asked.

"Aimee Louise, why don't you stay with Rosalie?"

"No, thank you."

The sheriff scratched his head, puzzled. "Okay, Aimee Louise. Let's go."

Aimee Louise and Shadow took off. The sheriff headed out and called back to the deputies. "We run."

Stuart turned to Wally. "When did the sheriff become a runner?"

"Don't know. They just left us in the dust."

The two deputies jogged after the sheriff and Aimee Louise.

When the sheriff and Aimee Louise were within sight of the road, they saw a woman in a yellow, ill-fitting dress stooped over a man sprawled on the pavement. Aimee Louise stepped behind the sheriff.

The woman looked up, brushed her unkempt brassy hair away from her face, waved, and shouted. "Help! We need help! He's hurt!"

Aimee Louise remained behind the sheriff. She grabbed the back of his shirt.

"Aunt Danielle," she said.

"What? Do you know her?"

Aimee Louise tugged at the sheriff's shirt.

"Aunt Danielle. Uncle Dan."

"Can you run back and tell Wally and Stuart *Uncle Dan* without her seeing you?"

Aimee Louise turned and ran. Shadow stayed with the sheriff.

The sheriff limped and stopped like he was out of breath. "What's…wrong?" he gasped.

"I don't know. I think he's hurt bad." She stood up with her left hand on her hip and her right hand behind her back.

*That's Jim. Bleeding head wound.* The sheriff bent down and picked up a large stick to use as a cane. He slowed his pace to a shuffle as he chose the placement of each step.

"Sure looks like a bad wound. What happened? Who is he?" he asked.

The woman appeared agitated; she shook her head, and her eyes were wide as she looked from side to side. "I don't know. I came along and found him; maybe he was robbed. Hurry up, would you? He needs help. Hurry!"

The sheriff moved like he was attempting to walk faster but slowed his forward pace even more. He heard the call of a cardinal to his right and a cardinal call to his left.

He was ten yards from the road when the woman pulled a gun from behind her back, pointed it at the sheriff, and aimed. At the same time, two men with pistols jumped up from behind the barrier and headed toward the sheriff. Shadow gave a low growl. The men raised their guns but froze when Shadow deepened his growl, bared his teeth, and prepared to spring.

When a shot rang out, the woman dropped to the ground. The two men aimed their guns, and one of them fell to the ground. The sheriff shot the second man. The sheriff ran to the two men while

Wally and Stuart ran to the woman and Jim. Shadow ran to Aimee Louise.

The sheriff confirmed both men were dead.

"She's dead," Wally said. "She had Jim's pistol."

Stuart said, "Jim's alive. He's conscious, but he's hurt."

The sheriff called out. "Aimee Louise!"

When Aimee Louise and Shadow reached him, the sheriff said, "I need for you to run back to the house and tell Heather we need first aid and their four-wheeler. Tell her to come to the roadblock at the road. She knows where it is."

Aimee Louise said, "One. Aunt Heather. Two. First aid. Three. UTV to the roadblock. Right?"

"Right."

Aimee Louise and Shadow ran.

Before long the sheriff and deputies heard the roar of the four-wheeler. Aimee Louise drove fast but in control. Heather held on to a first aid box and the grab bar while Shadow ran alongside.

Heather raced to join the deputies after Aimee Louise stopped. "Who's hurt?"

"It's Jim," Wally said. "He has a head wound, and we've stopped the bleeding. We think he didn't lose consciousness. He played possum after they jumped him to buy some time."

Heather kneeled beside Jim and examined him. "Jim can walk to the vehicle. He might need a little help."

Wally and Stuart helped Jim into the passenger's seat. Heather jumped into the driver's seat and left with Jim seat-belted next to her.

"Well done, Aimee Louise. Let's head back to the house. Wally and Stuart will take care of the bad guys. Is it okay if we walk?"

"Four. Water," Aimee Louise said.

She pulled bottles of water out of her backpack. She gave each man a bottle and poured water into Shadow's portable bowl.

Wally and Stuart said, "Thank you, Aimee Louise."

"You did a good job, Aimee Louise," the sheriff said. "Thank you."

After they finished their water, the sheriff, Aimee Louise, and Shadow ran.

## CHAPTER TWENTY-SEVEN

"Are you okay if Josh and I take over the goats?" Major asked Vanessa. "Annie wants to focus on her rabbits."

"I'm more than okay. That's great. I think I'm allergic to goats, especially to stinky boy goats. Want the book?" Vanessa asked. "You have Penny's help too. She wants them to stay together."

Major chuckled. "Penny hovers and herds baby goats and children all day. It's a big job."

"Seriously, I appreciate your working with Josh." Vanessa patted his arm. Her fingers lingered a bit long, and she jerked back her hand.

"Sorry," she mumbled as she rushed into the kitchen.

* * *

While Molly and Vanessa hung up the last of the laundry, Vanessa said, "Major and Josh are taking over the goats. I am so relieved. The responsibility of keeping them fed and healthy terrified me. I could never be a mother."

Molly clutched a wet towel. "I'm overwhelmed sometimes by my fears for my four children. I totally understand Penny. I want them to be in my sight at all times too, but then I wake up at night certain that everything I've done was wrong. You know who the best parent on the farm is? Mr. Young."

"You are so right. He's patient and understands what each child needs." Vanessa picked up the empty clothes basket.

"He's the perfect role model. Wonder if being hard of hearing helps?" Molly chuckled.

Vanessa followed Molly into the house, and Molly poured two glasses of tea. "Listen to the kids on the front porch. Sounds like Rosalie's teaching them a song."

Vanessa brushed away a stray tear. "These are hard times, but our days are filled with songs and laughter. I'm overcome."

"Overcome enough to take back the goats?" Molly grinned.

"Don't get me started on goats, and boy goats in particular, including that old goat, Major. He infuriates me sometimes."

Molly raised her eyebrows. "Really? Haven't you been accompanying him on his nightly security rounds?"

"Of course, I have." Vanessa snorted and carried her empty glass to the sink. "I need to keep track of what he's supposed to check. He doesn't follow a logical pattern, and it's totally exasperating. How did he survive before I showed up?"

* * *

Two weeks later, Molly, the sheriff, and Mr. Young relaxed on the back porch. "It seems to take Major much longer these days to check the animals and their pens," the sheriff said.

Molly said, "Hush."

The sheriff pouted. "What? What did I say?"

Mr. Young chuckled.

* * *

A few evenings later, when all the adults sat on the porch and the children played in the grass, Major said, "I'd like to check on Pastor John and his family. I thought I'd take Number 48."

"I think my old farm is about ten miles away cross-country," Mr. Young said. "It's twenty-five miles or so on the roads."

The sheriff scanned the perimeter from the edge of the porch. "Well, we know the roads have hazards. Cross-country sounds safer. You know the way?"

"I'll go to the power lines, head southwest, then due west. I'll cross at the state road."

Vanessa looked up from her book, uncrossed her legs, and planted her feet with a bang on the porch. "Well, I vote no; it's too dangerous, and it's certainly too dangerous to go by yourself. I'd like to know since when is a trip to check on the neighbors is an emergency. We need to save gasoline for emergencies."

Major's faced reddened. "Yeah, well. I want to go."

Vanessa raised her eyebrows and her voice. "I said, no."

Everyone, including the dogs, looked at Vanessa then Major and froze.

Aimee Louise said, "Aunt Vanessa could go too."

Everyone else remained still.

Vanessa took in a breath and exhaled. "Okay."

Major crossed his arms. "No."

Vanessa and Major glared at each other.

"Radio, Aimee Louise?" Rosalie asked, and Aimee Louise followed Rosalie to the computer room.

"Bedtime," Molly said. "Whose turn is it to shower?"

"Mr. Young," the younger children all answered at once.

Mr. Young smiled. "Can I pass my turn to the next person?"

"No, sir," Brett said, "that's only the vegetable rule, not the shower rule."

Mr. Young nodded. "Good to know."

Molly said, "Okay, let's get cleaned up before it gets much later." She scooted into the house with her entourage.

The sheriff waved his hand toward the computer room. "I'll just go, you know, to listen to the radio with the girls."

"Time for my shower." Mr. Young hurried to the trailer.

Vanessa and Major scowled at each other.

"So what's so all-fired important and urgent that you have to talk to Pastor John?" Vanessa asked.

Major rose. "Sometimes a man has private business with his pastor. I'm going in the morning."

He stormed to the back door and slammed it on his way in.

That evening, Major went on his security rounds alone.

* * *

Early the next morning, after breakfast, Major grabbed his backpack and strode to Number 48; his eyes narrowed when he saw Vanessa, who sat in the passenger's seat. Her back was stiff, and she stared straight ahead.

"You're not going." He growled.

"If you to want to leave now, you should climb in and drive," Vanessa said.

Major glared. "You're right. I don't have a reason to leave my family unprotected." He stormed to the barn.

Vanessa winced. "That didn't go as well as I planned."

* * *

At lunchtime, Major strode in the back door, glared at Vanessa, and took his plate to the back porch.

"Is Major mad at you, Aunt Vanessa?" Sara asked.

Molly shook her head. "Sara, it's not—"

Vanessa interrupted. "It's a fair question, Molly. Yes, Sara. Major is mad at me, but it's between him and me, so I need to talk to him."

"When Sara's mad at me, she punches me," Brett said. "Are you going to punch Pops, Aunt Vanessa?"

When Vanessa furrowed her brow, the sheriff said, "No, she's won't punch Major, and Aunt Vanessa said it's between the two of them, so we won't ask any more questions."

"Can I say I'm sad?" Sara asked.

"It's fine to feel sad, but the discussion stops now." Molly glared. "Isn't it time to check eggs?"

The four younger children leapt from the table and hurried out the back door.

"Thanks, Molly. I do need to talk to Major, especially since the sheriff said I can't punch him." She sighed. "He didn't take anything to drink with his lunch." Vanessa poured a tall glass of water and sauntered to the back door.

* * *

"I brought you a drink, Major." Vanessa handed him the glass and sat next to him. "I'm sorry. I get bossy when I worry about someone I care about."

Major drank half his glass of water. "Thanks. I was dry. I apologize for not talking to you first."

"It was all my fault; there's nothing for you to apologize about."

"Yes, dear." Major grinned.

Vanessa giggled and swatted his arm. "You infuriating man, and now I'm in trouble because the sheriff said I couldn't punch you. If you want to go see Pastor John in the morning, I'll worry, but I won't throw a fit."

"I should have talked to you first. I wanted to ask Pastor John if he would perform a wedding ceremony."

"What? Who's getting married?"

Major smiled and reached for her hand. "Us, if you say yes. Will you marry me?"

Vanessa stared. "You're damned right you should have talked to me first, and, of course, I'll marry you, ornery, aggravating, old man."

"You will? We'll go together. You're right about not traveling alone, bossy lady."

* * *

At breakfast the next morning, Major said, "Vanessa and I are going to see Pastor John. We'll be back by lunchtime."

"Really?" Molly raised an eyebrow. "Hmmm."

"That's great." The sheriff glared at Molly.

"We can't ask any questions, right?" Josh asked.

"Right," Vanessa said.

"Is it a secret?" Sara asked.

"You might just want to leave, Major," the sheriff said.

After Major tossed their backpacks into Number 48, he and Vanessa left the farm.

Vanessa reached over and stroked the back of his neck. "Major, want to take it back?"

"Yes," he said. "I take back the bossy lady part."

Vanessa laughed and shook her head. "You know what I mean. Really, have you changed your mind?"

"Nope," he said.

"Not sure I can handle all this sentimental, romantic stuff, you smooth talker."

The two of them laughed and giggled on the drive to Pastor John's.

When they came to the state road near Mr. Young's farm, Vanessa stayed with Number 48 while Major walked close to the highway. He sat in the brush for a while and listened.

He returned to Vanessa without a sound. "It's clear. Let's walk from here. It isn't far."

They tossed a few downed branches over Number 48, jogged across the road, and walked through the trees toward Mr. Young's farm.

"What's the best way to approach their house?" Vanessa asked.

"Why don't you stay out of sight, and I'll get within shouting distance."

"Okay. I've got your back."

When they were within sight of the house, Vanessa crouched down in the brush.

He walked a few yards closer, whistled, and then yelled, "Pastor John, it's Major!"

He waited a few minutes, walked a little closer, whistled, and yelled again. "Pastor John, it's Major!"

He whistled and yelled a third time. "Pastor John, it's Major!"

He heard a shout. "Major, it's Chuck. What's the password?"

Major groaned and yelled. "Oh, Lord, I don't know any password."

"Yep, it's you." Chuck laughed as he came from around the side of the house.

Pastor John rushed toward the house from the barn. He slowed to a walk when he saw their company was Major.

When the three men got close enough to talk, Major said, "Everything okay?"

"Yes," answered Chuck. "We were all in the back of the house. It took me a while to get to the front. I thought I heard someone call out, but I was cautious."

Pastor John exhaled. "We had an incident not long ago. A woman came to the door and asked for help. My dear sweet wife, Vicki, was suspicious and wouldn't let her in or open the door. Two men rushed out of the trees and headed toward the house. Vicki grabbed the shotgun, broke a window, and let off a few rounds. She said she meant to hit them; we found some blood later, but it didn't look like much. She scared them off, and she certainly scared us. We were out at the barn, but they disappeared before we got to the house. She was shaken and said she was a terrible pastor's wife. I told her she was awesome."

"Which she is," Chuck added.

"They sound like the same ones over close to our place," said Major. "Her instincts were right. They were thugs. They won't bother anyone else."

"Is this a social visit?" Pastor John asked.

"Yes. And no. I've got someone waiting near the trees; I'll her know it's safe." Major whistled and waved, and Vanessa stepped out of the brush.

"Hey, Vanessa," Pastor John said, "let's all go to the backyard, where we've got some chairs in the shade."

"Are you okay? Is everyone well?" Major asked. "Do you have enough to eat?"

"We're fine," Pastor John said. "Vicki and Diana have been canning. Mr. Young had planted a nice garden, and they're harvesting a bounty of vegetables. We've got a mama goat and two kids, chickens, and rabbits given to us by neighbors. How is Mr. Young?"

"We're all fine. Mr. Young and Molly are our chefs," Major said. "The kids grow every day and are smarter than all the rest of us put together."

Chuck laughed. "Isn't that how it goes?"

"We found a battery-powered ham radio and a solar charger for the battery," Pastor John said. "We listen every morning. I think I hear Aimee Louise occasionally. Do I?"

"Yes. Aimee Louise and Rosalie monitor the radio every morning and every evening," Major said. "If you ever need us, break in and let us know there's a problem at the Young farm. The girls will hear you."

Vanessa nudged Major. He cleared his throat. "Pastor John, I asked Vanessa to marry me, and she said yes. You up for a wedding?"

"Absolutely, congratulations."

Chuck shook Major's hand while Vicki and Diana hugged Vanessa. The children weren't sure what everyone was so excited about, but they jumped around and squealed.

"When?" Pastor John asked.

"Can you perform a ceremony for us next week?" Vanessa said. "We'd like for you to come to the farm, if you can. We'll pick you up so you won't be gone from your family too long."

"Sounds good. Let's decide on a day and time."

After they finalized the details, Major and Vanessa said their goodbyes and walked back to Number 48.

On the way back, Vanessa brushed the back of Major's hand with her fingers. "I'm glad you aren't still angry with me."

"You too. At least you haven't called off the wedding yet."

"Oh, you aren't getting off that easy, Bud." Vanessa giggled.

When they returned, everyone gathered to hear the news about Pastor John and Chuck and their families.

"The robbers who hurt Jim tried to get into their house," Major said. "Vicki scared them away with a shotgun. Pastor John and Chuck listen in on the ham radio in the mornings. They asked if Aimee Louise was on the radio. If they ever need help, they'll break in. Vicki is canning, and their neighbors gave them chickens and rabbits—"

Vanessa nudged him.

"Oh, right," Major said. "I asked Vanessa to marry me, and she said yes."

"What? You have a big fight and then make up with a marriage proposal?" Molly put her hands on her hips.

Vanessa laughed. "Well, when you put it that way, it does sound a little, well, unusual, but yes."

"I think it's great," the sheriff said.

Mr. Young beamed. "Congratulations."

"When is the wedding?" Molly asked.

"We'll pick up Pastor John in Number 48 early next Wednesday," Major said. "We'll have the wedding and run him back home."

"We thought we could have a celebration party Wednesday afternoon with the deputies and their families," Vanessa added. "What do you think, Molly?"

"We could have eggs in the morning, snack around lunchtime, then a feast in the late afternoon," Molly replied.

"I'll visit the deputies tomorrow to extend the invitation," the sheriff said.

"We'll be in charge of the decorations," Rosalie said.

Aimee Louise hugged Vanessa. Vanessa glanced at Major and tears welled in her eyes. Major pulled the two of them and Rosalie into a group hug.

Molly wiped away a tear. "Okay, everybody, enough mushy stuff. Let's get busy. We've got a farm to run."

* * *

After the children settled in for the night, Mr. Young asked, "Major could we take a stroll to the rabbit hutches?"

Mr. Young stopped on the way and gazed at the moon and stars that twinkled in the clear sky. "Moon's bright. Joan always loved to walk in the moonlight."

When they reached the rabbits, Mr. Young said, "Joan always wanted rabbits; she would have loved being here." He smiled. "Do you have a wedding ring?"

Major gulped. "No. I didn't think about a ring."

"I've carried Joan's wedding ring for a long time," Mr. Young said. "We never bought an engagement ring. We didn't have the money in our early years, and later Joan said she didn't need one. My kids wanted me to sell the wedding ring because it was old-fashioned, but I couldn't part with it. It would be an honor if you and Vanessa would carry our love forward into your marriage with Joan's ring."

"I don't know what to say. Thank you. I'll talk to Vanessa; I'm sure she'll agree this is an amazing, generous gift."

* * *

The next morning, Vanessa talked to Mr. Young. "If you're sure this is what you want, and the offer is still open, Major and I would love to accept your gift of Joan's ring. I'd be proud to wear it. I'd like for you to be sure, though, because you have carried it for a long time. Maybe it makes more sense for it to stay with you. Think about it, and we can talk more tonight or in the morning, if you like. Let me or Major know."

That afternoon, the sheriff and Josh ran to invite the deputies and their families to the wedding reception. When they returned, the sheriff and Josh sat at the dining table with glasses of water and a snack.

"How's Jim doing?" Molly asked.

"He's irritated at how slow his recovery is going. He's still having pain, but Heather's teaching him tai chi, and it seems to be helping. We're not supposed to know that, by the way."

Molly snickered. "You'll save that for later, won't you?"

The sheriff grinned and stopped to kiss his wife on his way out. "You know me well."

After supper, Mr. Young pressed Joan's ring into Major's hand. "I'm sure."

* * *

The following Monday, Molly and Vanessa took an afternoon break on the front porch. Molly rocked and sighed. "This past week was a whirlwind of farm work, wedding plans, and studies."

Vanessa stopped mid-rock. "You're kidding, right? The week has done nothing but drag along; a sloth in slow motion."

Molly laughed as she rose to go into the house. "Guess it's all a matter of perspective. Time for me to go chase a sloth."

After breakfast on Tuesday, Molly said, "Vanessa, when I went through the clothes the sheriff picked up at the thrift store, I found some beautiful old lace curtains folded with the jeans, of all things.

Let me show you. I think one of them would be a beautiful wedding shawl. What did you plan to wear?"

"All I brought were jeans and shirts. I do have one nice teal silk shirt to wear with my jeans. The shawl sounds like a wonderful idea. Let's look at it."

Rosalie came out of the storage room with a box. "I found these quilt pieces in the storage closet. I think I can show everyone how to make fabric flowers with rubber bands and quilt squares."

After lunch, Mr. Young said, "Do you hear the buzz, Molly? That's what excitement sounds like."

Molly peeked at the activity on the porch and motioned to Mr. Young. "Come look at the magic," she whispered. "We have elves out here making flowers."

After supper, Molly said, "Mr. Young, your buzzing has become electrified. I can feel it in the air."

"Well, I know I'll have trouble falling asleep. Good luck with your young'uns."

After everyone went to bed, Molly got up twice to go to the stairs. "Settle down. Go to sleep, girls, no more talking."

After the second time, Vanessa called out, "Yes, Aunt Molly, sorry."

Molly shook her head, and the giggles from upstairs followed her as she went back to bed. She covered her head with her pillow.

Everyone woke up early Wednesday morning and met on the porch. Aimee Louise wore her Laplander hat.

At breakfast, Josh frowned and set his fork down on his plate. "You know, no one's said anything about sleeping arrangements. Will Aunt Vanessa move into the boys' room or will Major move into the girls' room?"

Annie said, "Josh is right. Nobody's said anything about sleeping arrangements, but Mom told me that married people need their private time. Won't Major and Aunt Vanessa need private time?"

Major choked on his coffee, Vanessa blushed, and the sheriff snorted. Mr. Young appeared to look at his plate in deep concentration.

Molly glared at the sheriff and handed Major a napkin. "What good questions, and you are right about the private time. We've been so busy with our plans for the wedding and the party we forgot to think about new sleeping arrangements."

"Girls' room," Aimee Louise said.

Rosalie nodded. "I like it. There's plenty of room for Annie and Sara in our room. We'll move the rollaway and cot right after breakfast."

Sara clapped her hands. "Yay, we'll have a girls' room with no stinky boys allowed, right, Annie?"

"You're right, Sara, and we'll move our things to the girls' room," Annie said.

"That leaves us a real boys' room upstairs," spoke up Josh. "Brett and I can move my cot. You can have the bed, Brett; I'm used to my cot."

"I'm used to my cot too," Brett said. "We can move our cots after breakfast."

"Well, I guess I'd better eat fast, so I can move my things out for the boys," Vanessa said.

"Wow," exclaimed Molly. "I can't think of anything to top what you all came up with."

"One other thing," Mr. Young said. "Would you newlyweds prefer to move into the trailer? You'd have more privacy."

"Thank you, Mr. Young, but no," Major said. "I want to be in the house, close to the kids, and right by the door at night. I want to be the first line of defense."

"I agree," the sheriff said. "I sleep better at night with Major and me on the first floor with the two dogs, who can alert us. I'm happy the boys are going to be upstairs. I like their plan."

After breakfast, Molly and Mr. Young excused everyone else from kitchen duty. Major helped move the rollaway and the cots while the sheriff left to get Pastor John.

After the new sleeping arrangements were in place, Major said, "Good job, everyone. Now let's check the food and water for the chickens, rabbits, and goats and get ready for a wedding. It won't be long until the sheriff gets back with Pastor John."

When the sheriff and Pastor John arrived, Pastor John sported a clerical collar and a big grin.

The children had placed their fabric flowers and one of the lacy curtains on the grape trellis.

"Rosalie, you all did a wonderful job," Molly said. "It absolutely takes my breath away. The arch looks like a professional florist dropped by, and you've created a wonderfully romantic setting for the wedding."

Pastor John took his place at the trellis, and Major and Vanessa stood in front of him. Rosalie played the guitar, and the children sang. When Pastor John said, "Who gives this woman…" the entire farm family shouted, "We all do."

When Major said, "With this ring, I thee wed…" Mr. Young beamed as tears filled his eyes.

After Pastor John pronounced them "husband and wife," everyone applauded and cheered, then Sheriff drove Pastor John back to the Young farm.

"Okay, everyone," Molly said. "We've got a big party this afternoon. Let's get to work."

After the boys completed their chores, it took a stern sheriff voice to stop them from running to the road to watch for their guests.

"Young men, you can stand on top of my trailer and watch through the trees," Mr. Young said.

"Really?" Josh said. "Thank you, sir. We'll be very careful. Right, Brett?"

Brett nodded.

"I know you will," Mr. Young said. "And I have a pair of sentry binoculars for each of you. You'll have to be still and quiet and stand like trees in a forest. It's what sentries do."

Josh and Brett saluted and said, "Yes, sir."

The boys climbed to the trailer roof and were the most no-nonsense sentries ever seen on a farm.

"Molly, I don't know what we pay that man," the sheriff said, "but we need to double it."

Molly snorted, and the younger girls stared at her. "Excuse me; sometimes your daddy makes me snort."

Molly made tortillas, and Mr. Young made his famous deviled eggs then grilled vegetables and home-canned chicken and pork while Molly's pinto beans simmered on the stove.

When the deputies and their families came to the gate, the sentries shouted, "The troops have arrived."

The parents and children arrived in Brad's car, and Jim and Stuart came on the four-wheeler. Stuart brought his guitar and music, and Kris brought a large jug of white grape juice she called "Farm Champagne."

Heather said, "I made a double batch of cornbread and canned wild blackberry jam, so we can have Farm Wedding Cake."

"We have home-canned salsa, pickled jalapeños, and lettuce from the garden to make fajitas. I tried to make cheese with powdered milk, but the farm food critics gave it minus ten stars, so Josh fed it to the goats," Molly said.

"Molly and I planned for us to eat inside, so we won't have to fight flies," Mr. Young added.

"There's plenty of room at the dining table and family room for everyone to sit, and Mr. Young and I set up our food buffet style," Molly added.

After everyone gathered inside, Major said, "Mr. Young, would you say grace before we eat?"

Mr. Young lowered his head. "Thank you, Lord. For food, for family, for friends, for health, for love. Amen."

"Let's fix the littlest kids' plates first," said Molly. "Aimee Louise, Rosalie, do you mind eating now so you can keep an eye on the little ones while the parents eat?"

"We'd be happy to, Aunt Molly," answered Rosalie.

Annie stood next to Rosalie. "Me too. I want to help with the babies."

Molly smiled. "Vanessa and Major, would you please get in line after the babies and girls? Mr. Young, next, please, then everyone else behind Mr. Young."

The two boys jumped to stand with Mr. Young. "After you, sir," Josh said.

Mr. Young smiled. "Thank you, young man."

Vanessa motioned to Sara, "Come stand in line with me."

Sara looked at her mother; when Molly nodded her approval, Sara grinned and rushed over to Vanessa.

Wally cleared his throat, and everyone got quiet. "Today is a celebration of marriage. Give and take. Kris, I give you the opportunity to eat warm food with adults. I'll take the kids."

"Show-off," said Brad. "Wish I'd thought to say that. Me too, Heather, what he said."

The adults laughed, and Sara and Annie applauded.

"Please step in front of us," Mr. Young said, and the boys shifted back to make room for Kris and Heather.

Wally and Brad settled their toddlers in seats at the dining table, and Rosalie rocked Sophie on the porch and gave her a bottle. Aimee Louise brought Rosalie a plate, and Molly poured white grape juice for the little ones. After the little ones ate, Aimee Louise and Annie took them outside, and the rest of the children soon joined them.

The adults ate, talked, laughed, admired Vanessa's wedding ring, toasted the bride and groom, and shared stories.

Molly carried the wedding cake out to the porch and placed it on a table decorated with wildflowers gathered and arranged by Sara. Heather sliced the cornbread horizontally and smeared the bottom half with wild blackberry jam. Vanessa and Major cut the first piece of wedding cake together.

"It's traditional for the bride and groom to feed each other wedding cake," Kris said.

Major had a twinkle in his eye. "Okay, but only a tiny piece. I don't want her to sue me if I make a mess."

"You're fine," Vanessa said. "Our prenup says I won't sue you."

Major raised his eyebrows. "We have a prenup?"

Vanessa laughed. "No."

Major pinched a piece of cornbread, broke it in two, and put one piece in Vanessa's hand.

"Throw it," he said. "Toss it for the birds. It's a farm tradition to show our love by caring for others."

"Love it," Vanessa said.

They threw the cornbread together to applause, whistles, and shouts.

Kris's eyes misted. "Now that's a tradition."

Stuart brought out his guitar and Rosalie ran for hers. Stuart showed Rosalie new chords, and they played and sang while Aimee Louise hummed. The kids and Heather joined in. Jim pulled out his harmonica, and the kids romped on the grass to the songs.

Vanessa leaned her head on Major's shoulder, closed her eyes, and breathed in the sweet smell of grass crushed by little feet. "This is what heaven sounds and smells like," she whispered.

Heather brought a tambourine and showed Sara how to shake and tap it with the music. Mr. Young came back from the shed with sticks and a couple of plastic buckets for the boys to use as drums. Molly grabbed the laundry washboard and a wooden spoon and showed Annie how to use it.

"This is the most wonderful celebration imaginable," Vanessa said. "What a blessing. Can you believe this?"

"They are amazing," Major said. "So are you; I love you."

She kissed him. "I love you too, Major." Her mouth lingered on his, and she kissed him again with more passion.

"You know, we're married. You don't have to call me *Major* anymore."

"Okay, *Major Honey*." Vanessa giggled.

He frowned. "I'll call you *Counselor*."

"You'll forget, Major," Vanessa said.

"Eh, you're right." He laughed.

The sheriff sat next to Major. "Well, this marriage is starting off right."

After more songs and lots of laughter, Brad said, "Wally and I need to take our tired families home. It's been a wonderful party."

"Sara," Heather said, "you're a natural with the tambourine. You can keep it, if you like."

Sara's eyes widened, and her face broke into a grin. "Mommy, is it okay?"

"Yes, if you'll take good care of it."

"I will, I promise. Thank you, Aunt Heather." She tapped her tambourine and danced in the grass.

"Stuart and I will head out," Jim said. "We want to get to the house before the families, so we can do a security check."."

Holding hands, Major and Vanessa strolled outside and checked the animals for the night, and Shadow trotted after them. When they stopped at the fence around the garden and listened to the crickets and tree frogs, Major put his arm around Vanessa, and she turned to hug him and bury her face in his chest.

Vanessa lifted her head and gazed at his face. "Something's on your mind, Major."

"No. Well, yes. I'm worried about Aimee Louise. She sees things, and not only clouds. She puts pieces together before the rest of us even realize the pieces exist. I think there's more to come, and it's not good. What bothers me is that I don't know if I'll see it in time to keep her safe."

## CHAPTER TWENTY-EIGHT

"Isn't June early for it to be this hot and humid in the morning?" Aimee Louise said while she and Rosalie hung the day's laundry on the clothesline. Aimee Louise reached down for a wet towel and brushed her damp hair away from her face. "I'm surprised the clothes dry at all."

"And afternoon showers only add to the sticky." Rosalie breathed in the clean smell of the basket of laundry. "I guess growing season is over for our lettuce, broccoli, and brussels sprouts. All wilted. And I droop like the flowers." She leaned over like an overcooked strand of spaghetti.

"Good droop," Aimee Louise said.

In the afternoon, Major and Aimee Louise stretched the shade cloth over the garden to save the peppers and tomatoes from the relentless sun, humidity, and heat.

"I want to read about shade cloth and spring and summer growing seasons. And Florida fall crops," Aimee Louise said as they headed to the barn.

"Look in Gram's gardening books. See what you can find."

Sara and Brett raced to the barn, arriving there red-faced and out of breath.

"Joanna's broody," Sara said. Her blond curls stuck to her sweaty forehead.

"Did you say we could give her eggs to hatch when she went broody? We have fifteen eggs from yesterday," Brett said.

Major climbed down from fixing the roof and folded the ladder, ready to carry it to the shed. "We need to set up our maternity ward. Annie made a large box for us."

Major put the maternity box in the small spare coop. Sara ran to the barn for straw, and Brett found water and food containers for Joanna. While Sara filled the containers, Brett placed the eggs on the straw inside the box.

"All ready for Joanna?" Major said. He lifted Joanna out of her favorite nest box and moved her to the maternity box. Joanna flattened out, rearranged the eggs, and swooped each one underneath her warm body with her wings.

Brett's eyes were wide. "Wow. I can't see any eggs. All of them are under Joanna."

Major smiled. "We'll candle the eggs in a week. Check her water in the mornings and evenings. We don't want her water to run low."

After a week, Major showed them how to candle the eggs and what to look for. They removed the three eggs with no baby chicks inside.

"Now what?" Brett asked while Sara jumped up and down.

"We leave Joanna alone except to check her food and water and clean up any poop in the coop. She won't poop in the maternity suite. In two weeks, we'll be close to time for the baby chicks to hatch."

* * *

"This has been the longest two weeks of my entire life," Sara said at breakfast. "I'm too excited to sleep. I think I have insomnia."

"I'm egg-cited too," Brett said.

Sara groaned and rolled her eyes.

Major discovered that they had spent the rest of the morning at the maternity coop and were peeking in at Joanna every few minutes. "You need to give Joanna some privacy so she can focus on her babies."

Right before supper, Major said, "Okay, you can go check on Joanna."

Sara danced, leaped, and twirled when she returned. "Joanna has babies under her. We heard peeps."

"Little heads peeked out. I think I saw three," Brett said.

"Great news," Major said. "You can check again after breakfast."

* * *

The next morning, Sara and Brett scarfed down their breakfast and raced out to Joanna's coop then returned with news.

"There are babies all over the place. Joanna taught them where the food and water are," Sara said.

"I saw one baby chick on Joanna's back," Brett said.

"Can we go see too?" Annie asked.

"Sure," said Major, even though all the children, Molly, and Vanessa were already out the back door.

"I'll supervise," Mr. Young said as he headed out.

On the third day, Sara reported that Joanna had taken the babies outside in the run.

"Mommy, Brett and I will be at the chicken coop," Sara said. "We'll watch the baby chicks today."

"Chores first," Molly said.

"Really?" asked Brett.

"Yes, really."

* * *

A week later, Sara and Brett peeked into the barn and spotted Major. Brett said, "Pops, we looked for you everywhere. We need to talk to you about the chickens."

"We're worried they're sick," Sara said. "Yesterday they laid only half as many eggs as they have been, and they've lost feathers. Lucy looks like somebody stripped all the feathers off her neck."

Brett frowned. "We know it's hot and humid, but should they go through all their water by lunchtime? They never did that before. Did we do something wrong?"

"You two do a great job with the chickens. The heat's got them down," Major said. "It's not a surprise you've gathered fewer eggs, and it's good they're drinking so much. Don't worry about Lucy. She's molting. Chickens lose their feathers once a year or so and grow new feathers. She looks a little strange, but she's fine."

Sara nodded. "Thanks, Pops. Something else. What do you think about the chickens free-ranging longer, like maybe all day? We've noticed when they free-range all morning, we refill the feeders with much less food the next day. We told Aimee Louise, and she said we should ask you."

Major sat on a hay bale. "It's a risk because of predators, but Shadow and Penny guard the chickens and farm animals. Great way to stretch the feed. Only the larger chickens, though, right? The little ones are too vulnerable to hawks."

"Right, Pops. Thanks," Brett said. The two children ran to the house.

Major chuckled as he stood to go inside too. *How did I ever run the farm without these kids in charge?*

* * *

Later that afternoon, Josh sat on the back porch with his sketchbook. Molly sat next to him and peered over his shoulder.

"Why, Josh," she said, "that's Joanna and the babies."

"Yep. I thought I'd surprise Brett and Sara, but I need to sign it. What's the date?" he asked, his pencil raised.

"I'm not sure. Rosalie knows. She keeps track of the date for her wildlife database. Your drawing is outstanding, Josh."

Josh jumped up. "Thanks, I'll check with her."

Molly walked into the kitchen, where Mr. Young steamed eggs. "Mr. Young, Josh showed me a drawing he did of Joanna and her chicks. It was great, but he asked me what today's date is, and I didn't know."

"Rosalie would know," he said.

Molly laughed. "That's what I told him, then I remembered how much I love to celebrate birthdays. We need to know everybody's birthday."

"Rosalie would track birthdays if we asked her," Mr. Young said.

"That's what I thought. Thank you, Mr. Young; you are brilliant."

Molly hurried out of the room to find Rosalie.

"I could have told you that," Mr. Young said with a chuckle.

Molly returned. "Mr. Young, I forgot to ask: when's your birthday?"

"March," he said.

"Good news. We didn't miss anyone's birthday. Josh's birthday is later this month. He'll be nine."

* * *

A few days later, Aimee Louise and Rosalie stepped out to the front porch and joined the adults as they drank their morning coffee. The sun peeked over the horizon and brightened the clear sky, and a slight breeze and dew on the grass hinted of cooler weather.

Rosalie sat on the steps. "Interesting news on the radio today. There are rumors of electricity. My favorite rumor is that one of the larger electrical companies was offline when the grand outage occurred. The company was testing an upgrade to their computer system and installed the upgrade onto their production system by mistake. They took their production system offline for their test, and their customers experienced an accidental outage a few minutes before the real outage, but everyone assumed they were part of the big outage."

Major laughed. "I love it. A serious mistake brings a ray of hope."

Rosalie continued. "What happened next is the most interesting part, especially if it's true. Can you imagine the surprise of the customers when this company's electricity abruptly came on? An engineer who was involved in the test brought the production system back online just to see if it worked. Anyway, that's the rumor. Hams will check with their contacts to find somebody whose electricity suddenly came on."

Mr. Young laughed. "Gotta wonder if the engineer was fired or promoted."

"I vote promoted," Vanessa said, "or if fired, maybe he or she would like to tinker with our electricity."

Rosalie snickered. "A second rumor is that some of the smaller regional companies took down or isolated their systems before everything else collapsed. They joined together to see how to bypass the sections no longer operational to provide a minimal level of electricity in a rotation. People get an allotment of electricity in the mornings three days a week, for example."

"Only rumors, but good news for a change," Aimee Louise said. "We can expect only occasional power when we do get electricity."

"Well, you're right. Definitely interesting," Major said. "It doesn't change our farm operations yet, but it's nice to hear good news."

* * *

At breakfast, Molly said, "Josh, did you know it's your birthday tomorrow? This is your last day of being eight."

Josh blinked. "My birthday is tomorrow?"

"What should we do for your birthday?" the sheriff asked. "What can a nine-year-old do an eight-year-old can't do?"

Josh pushed his eyebrows together and pursed his lips. "I need a pocketknife."

"Okay," the sheriff said, "I think you are right. A nine-year-old should have a pocketknife. And a sharpening stone so you can be responsible for your knife."

"True. The only knife that will cut you is a dull one," added Mr. Young.

"I don't have a knife, and I'm ten," Annie said.

"Well, Annie," Molly said, "you can ask for a knife for your birthday in August if it's what you want."

"Oh."

"Next question, Josh," said Molly. "What do you want for your birthday dinner?"

"I want—" Josh took a big breath. "Pizza."

"Pizza? Okay, Josh. Pizza it is."

After the younger kids went outside, the adults and the older girls remained at the table and sat in silence.

Molly narrowed her eyes at the sheriff. "Where are you going to get a pocketknife?"

"Where are you going to get pizza?" the sheriff asked.

Vanessa raised her eyebrows. "Need a little magic here."

"I can help with the sharpening stone," Mr. Young said.

"I'm sure I have a spare pocketknife somewhere," Major said.

"Pizza," Aimee Louise said.

"Seriously?" Rosalie bit her lip. "Okay, Aimee Louise and I can help with pizza."

"I'll help however I can. Tell me what to do," Vanessa said.

"Thanks, Aunt Vanessa," Rosalie said. "We might need some help."

"Let's plan," said Aunt Molly. "I'll make a pizza crust. It might be an extra-large tortilla."

"We've got home-canned tomato sauce, spices, and herbs," said Vanessa. "I can pull together pizza sauce."

"I'll cut thin slices of Spam and crisp it up like bacon," Mr. Young said.

"We can make cheese," Aimee Louise said.

All heads turned to Aimee Louise.

"Pastor John," Aimee Louise said.

"I'll go with you to see Pastor John," said the sheriff. "Then what?"

"Goat milk," Rosalie said. "Aimee Louise, you are so smart. We can make goat cheese; Aimee Louise and I read about it. Do we have something we could trade for goat milk? We read people traded goods as currency in the old days."

"I have some strawberry jam I canned last fall. Take them a couple of jars," Molly said.

The sheriff added, "Let's go first thing in the morning, right after breakfast. We'll take Number 48. It would be faster than running to Mr. Young's farm, and we have a lot to do tomorrow."

"Yes," Aimee Louise agreed.

The sheriff sighed. "Perfect. I knew if I didn't have a good reason to take the wheels, I'd be running over twenty miles tomorrow."

Major nodded and smiled.

* * *

A little before daylight the next morning, Josh slipped downstairs and joined the adults on the back porch.

"Now that I'm nine, can I have some coffee?"

The sheriff poured him a quarter of a cup before Molly could say no.

Josh lifted his cup, blew into it, and set it on the porch. He gazed at the dark sky and picked up his cup with one hand and fanned it with the other. He held the cup with two hands, took a tiny sip, set his cup down, and leaned back against the step with one foot flat and his knee bent. Josh raised an arm and rested it across his knee. "This is how the sophisticated nine-year-old looks."

Mr. Young choked on his coffee. After he cleared his throat, he said, "Josh, I whittled and carved wood quite a bit in my younger years. Let me know if you're interested, and we can carve an animal, maybe a bear, when you get your pocketknife."

"Gosh, yes. Thank you. I like to draw. Carving is like drawing in 3-D, right?"

He blew on his coffee.

"You know," said Vanessa, "it's a tradition in my family that when someone turns nine, they have nine sips of coffee on their birthday to celebrate not being eight anymore."

"That's what our family did too. How many sips of coffee so far, Josh?" Mr. Young asked.

"Well, I'm not sure—"

"I counted," Vanessa said. "You just took sip number nine."

"Really? Then I'm done with my coffee?"

"You are officially nine years old. Congratulations, young man." Mr. Young stood up and pumped Josh's hand.

Josh beamed while everyone else either smiled or wiped away a tear then Molly said, "Breakfast won't cook itself."

"Lead the way, Chef," Mr. Young said. After breakfast, Aimee Louise, Rosalie, and the sheriff grabbed their backpacks and water.

"Aunt Molly gave me two jars of strawberry jam to trade." Rosalie climbed into the bed of Number 48.

"Aimee Louise, would you like to drive Number 48?" The sheriff asked.

She ran to the house and returned with her Laplander hat. "Thank you."

The sheriff directed Aimee Louise to Mr. Young's farm.

"Stop here. We're about half a mile or so from the state road. Listen for my whistle, and then join me," he said.

He crouched near the road, waiting in the brush for a few minutes before whistling. The girls slipped in behind him.

"We'll run together across the highway," the sheriff whispered.

On the other side, they crouched in the bushes and listened.

"Single file," he spoke in a soft voice.

When they arrived at Mr. Young's farm, the girls hid in the brush while the sheriff approached the house.

He whistled, clapped his hands, and shouted. "Halloo, the house. Sheriff here."

Chuck stepped out from behind the back of the house, Pastor John came up from the barn, and the sheriff saw a face in a window. After the sheriff established the area was safe, he called for the girls to join them.

"It's nice to see you all," Chuck said.

"What's the occasion? You look like you are on a mission," Pastor John said.

Rosalie addressed them. "We need some goat milk to make cheese. Aunt Molly sent strawberry jam to trade."

"You don't need to trade anything for goat milk," Pastor John said. "We'd be happy to give you some."

"Speak for yourself, preacher-man," Vicki said as she joined them. "It's rude to turn down a gift, especially Molly's strawberry jam. Thank you, girls. Let's get you some goat milk."

Aimee Louise and Rosalie returned with a pint jar of goat's milk. Vicki walked with them.

"Are you sure you have enough?" Vicki said. "It doesn't seem to be much."

"Oh yes," Rosalie said. "We don't need much. We're making cheese. It's Josh's birthday today, and he asked for pizza."

"Please tell Molly thank you for the jam. And tell Josh happy birthday," Vicki said with a smile.

Chuck said, "I like the idea of pizza for a birthday dinner. That Josh is a smart guy."

The sheriff and girls returned to the state road, ran to Number 48, and headed home. When they got back to the farm, Molly and Vanessa waved from the porch.

"Pops found a perfect pocketknife for Josh, and Mr. Young found his spare sharpening stone. I discovered manly wrapping paper in the storage closet," Molly said.

"Good; you got the goat milk. I've got the cheesecloth ready; let the cheese-making begin," Vanessa said. "Good thing we're making mozzarella not some fancy cheese; it takes only an hour or so."

"Did you know a cheese maker is called a fromager?" Mr. Young asked.

"La-dee-dah. Let the fromager magic begin," Molly said.

"Mommy sent us on a secret mission, and it's a secret," Brett said at lunch, and Sara beamed.

Molly sighed, Sheriff and Major laughed, and Vanessa covered her mouth.

"Did I miss something?" Mr. Young asked as he took his seat at the dining table.

"It's a secret." Sara put her finger to her lips.

Mr. Young nodded. "Understood."

The younger children gathered on the porch after lunch, and the two older girls helped Vanessa with laundry.

"In honor of today being your birthday, Josh," Annie said, "we decided to play Chutes and Ladders for our relaxation time."

The younger children set up the board on the porch to play. Josh won most of the games, but Sara won one, and Brett won two games.

"Happy birthday, Josh. You are definitely the undefeated Chutes and Ladders champion," Annie said as the four of them raced to do their afternoon chores. The aroma of pizza greeted them when they returned to the house.

Mr. Young said, "Nothing like garlic, onion, oregano, and basil to set the tone for a pizza party."

"I thought I heard a pizza-delivery guy. Looks like I was right," the sheriff said as he walked in.

Molly cut and served slices of pizza, the first one going to Josh.

Everyone waited for Josh. He took a big bite and grinned with a mouth full of pizza and a dab of sauce on his chin.

Josh attempted to switch to a serious face. "It's not good. I'll have to eat the entire pizza."

Mr. Young took a bite, closed his eyes, chewed, and swallowed. He looked at his plate. "Unbelievable. The acidy-sweet tomato sauce, the crunchy thin crust, the aromatic, sweet ribbons of fresh basil, topped off by the creamy, earthy goat cheese—party in my mouth."

"Gourmet pizza," Vanessa said. "Except Mr. Young said it better."

Everyone agreed with nods and grunts. After everyone ate his or her fill, only one large piece was left.

"I could save the last piece for Josh's breakfast if it's okay to use a little propane for the trailer refrigerator," Mr. Young said.

"Outstanding idea," Major said.

"Wow. Thank you. A two-day birthday," Josh said.

"Now we can have our Farm Cupcakes," Molly said. "We have biscuits with honey and berries Brett and Sara collected this morning."

"Awww, Mommy," Sara said. "It was a secret."

"It's okay, honey. You kept the secret like you were supposed to. Now you and your brother can take credit for the sweet berries."

Molly brought out the Farm Cupcakes with a bright green candle on top of one. She lit the candle and set the cupcake in front of Josh. Josh looked around, and his eyes glistened. After the family sang "Happy Birthday," Josh blew out the candle to cheers and whistles.

While everyone ate a cupcake, the sheriff gave Josh his present.

Josh ripped away the paper and grinned at his pocketknife and his sharpening stone. He jumped up from the table, waved his arms, and danced. "This is my happy dance for my pocketknife."

A tear escaped down Molly's check as she led the applause.

After Josh finished his cake, he and Mr. Young went out back to sharpen his knife and find wood to carve.

At bedtime, Josh hugged Molly and the sheriff.

"Thank you. Being nine is sick."

He looked at their blank faces. "You know, the bee's knees."

Molly laughed. "You are too funny. I love you, Josh."

"I love you."

The sheriff said, "I love you, buddy."

"I love you too." A tear slipped down his cheek. "But I miss Mom and Dad." He broke down into sobs.

"I know you do, and I am so sorry." The sheriff hugged Josh and held him until Josh's tears subsided.

"Let's go check the goats," the sheriff said.

On their way to the goat shed, the sheriff said, "Your dad would have loved the goats. He'd be proud of how you take care of them."

"I don't care. I just want him here." Josh ran for the house.

"Are you okay?" Brett asked when Josh threw himself on his cot.

"No. Leave me alone." Josh covered his face with his pillow.

The sheriff motioned to Brett, and the two of them walked to the back porch.

"What's wrong with Josh? Is he okay?" Brett asked.

"He's sad. He misses his mom and dad."

Brett nodded. "And it's his birthday."

The next morning, Josh shared his breakfast pizza with the twins and Annie. Molly cooked scrambled eggs as a side.

"Happy second-day birthday," Molly said.

* * *

The following week, after the sheriff returned from his town patrol early one morning, Molly brought him a cup of coffee while he joined the adults on the front porch.

He dropped into a chair. "There have been more deaths among those with long-term illnesses whose prescription medications ran out, and more people left town for homes of relatives. Most of them left on foot, and I'm afraid they're not prepared for the walk ahead of them. Occasionally, there's a rough element on the streets despite the blockades, but people are staying close to home or only go out in groups."

"Sounds grim," Vanessa said.

"It does, but on the flip side, there's a real sense of community alive in town like Pete and his buddies at the diner. There's a well behind the diner from way back; when the city water dried up, Pete put the well back in service with a little help from some neighbors. They ran the water until it was clear, then six of them drank two big glasses of water every day for three days. When none of them got sick, they declared the well safe."

Molly broke in. "Can I say something? That's the craziest idea I ever heard. Where did Pete find six…oh, never mind."

The sheriff chuckled. "Pete told people they could help themselves to drinking water, but to take only what they needed for that day. Everyone respects the rule. The diner is still the best place for news and to trade items. A couple of the doctors and a dentist who own small farms nearby come to the diner once a week or so to see people."

Rosalie and Aimee Louse stepped onto the porch, and Rosalie gave the morning report.

After Rosalie finished, Aimee Louise said, "Sara's cloud; it's different."

"Different? How? Is she sick?" Molly asked.

After a few minutes, Aimee Louise said, "Not sick; sad, but not sad. Different sad."

Everyone remained quiet to give Aimee Louise time to work through her thoughts.

Mr. Young pulled off his glasses to wipe them off. He looked up at Aimee Louise, who stared at him.

"Mr. Young's cloud. Sara's cloud."

Molly said, "That doesn't make—"

Rosalie jumped in. "Mr. Young, please put your glasses back on."

Mr. Young nodded and complied.

"Aimee Louise?"

"Yes."

"Sara might have trouble with her eyesight," Rosalie said.

Vanessa groaned. "Molly, I meant to say something earlier but forgot. Sara's reading has dropped off. She insists Brett reads first, and she wants him to read out loud, then she reads. It's almost like she memorizes what he says. I put it down to a twin thing or a phase, but now, when I think about it, she never reads on her own anymore, and she loves to read."

"What do we do?" Molly asked.

"Let me talk to Sara," Vanessa answered. "I can check her vision in a relaxed way. I'm a lawyer, remember? We are compassionate souls."

Everyone laughed except Aimee Louise; Major continued laughing after everyone quit.

Vanessa frowned and spoke in a stern voice, "Major, I tried to break the tension. You can stop laughing."

Rosalie said in a soft voice, "Aunt Vanessa and Pops made a joke."

Aimee Louise said, "Oh."

At the evening meal, Vanessa said, "Sara and I think it would be okay for her to get her eyes checked because she might need glasses."

"I can see fine, but Aunt Vanessa says maybe it would be good for me to see finer."

"Sounds good to me," Molly said.

"Sara can go with me into town in the morning," the sheriff said. "We'll see if Doc can check her. We'll figure out what we do from there."

The next morning after breakfast, the sheriff and Sara prepared to leave. "We'll run to the deputy house, take a break, then run into town from there. It looks like today will be another cloudy day," the sheriff said. "Our run will be a little easier without the sun beating down on us."

"Me too," Aimee Louise said.

The sheriff was silent for a few minutes. "Major, what do you think?"

"No one else has Aimee Louise's perspective. She's a good backup. Of course, it's safer here."

"Right." After a few more minutes of thought, the sheriff asked, "Why, Aimee Louise?"

"Sara."

"I'm not sure why, but okay. Let's go."

The three of them grabbed their backpacks and ran to the deputy house.

"I'd like to go into town too," Stuart said. "I won't be too far behind you. I'm smart enough to let you all run on ahead."

When they reached town, the sheriff stopped and scanned the streets.

Aimee Louise said, "Worried cloud."

The sheriff nodded. "Not many children, and no girls. Only a few boys."

Aimee Louise pulled two ball caps out of her backpack. One of them was Brett's. Sara put it on and pushed her curls under the cap.

The sheriff said, "You could be Brett's twin."

Sara giggled. "Oh, Daddy."

Aimee Louise pulled her long hair under the other cap.

When they got to the diner parking lot, the doc was there. He waved them toward the diner, went inside, and led them to the kitchen. Pete stood in the kitchen behind a table, his hands hidden.

When Pete saw the sheriff, he set a shotgun on the table and walked over to shake hands. "Town's a little rough right now. I didn't recognize you right off. Haven't seen you in a while."

The sheriff said, "I'm glad to see you are cautious." He pointed to Sara. "Doc, we need her eyes checked."

"Read this for me." The doc handed Sara a newspaper.

Sara read the headline of an article, moved the newspaper to four inches from her face, and read the first two lines of the article.

"Nearsighted," the doc said. "Not unusual around this age. We need to find somebody who wore glasses at the age of six to eight. We need their old glasses."

"The library collected old prescription glasses," the sheriff said. "We can see if they still have any."

"I suggest you leave town and send somebody," Pete said. "I'm not sure how safe the town is for young'uns, especially girls."

"Thanks, Doc. Thanks, Pete. We'll leave town immediately."

Stuart walked into the diner. "Leave immediately?"

"Yep. Meet us at the stand of trees where we found the bear bait last year."

When they left the diner, the sheriff turned away from the road leading to the farm.

"We'll go this way for now."

They jogged down the road and diverted into a stand of trees. The sheriff crouched in the brush, and the two girls crouched behind him. Three men walked briskly down the road from town.

The sheriff asked Aimee Louise, "Uncle Dan?"

She nodded, so they waited. Stuart showed up in the brush behind them.

"Doc says Sara is nearsighted and needs glasses," the sheriff said. "The library used to collect glasses. Could you check?"

"Sure. I'll see what I can find and come to the farm."

Stuart headed back to town, and the sheriff, Sara, and Aimee Louise ran toward the farm. When Sara stopped, Aimee Louise declared a water break. When they arrived at the farm, everyone gathered for the sheriff's report.

"We saw the doctor, and he said Sara's nearsighted. We planned to check the library for glasses, but Pete told us we shouldn't be in town. In fact, when we first got to town, I noticed there were only a few children out, and they were all older boys."

He stopped and frowned. "Aimee Louise, you pulled those ball caps out of your backpack. How did you know to have them?"

"Rosalie," she said.

Rosalie tilted her head. "I don't get it. Wait…we talked about disguises one time. I said people could disguise themselves with a hat. Is that why you took the ball caps? In case you and Sara needed a disguise?"

"Yes."

"It threw everyone off," the sheriff said. "Not even the doc knew these two were girls until he got close up. Smart move, but when we headed out of town away from the farm, we were followed."

He looked at Molly. "We lost them; Stuart went the library to check for glasses. He'll come to the farm with any he can find."

"It worries me when you all have scary adventures, but I'm glad you're back and okay," Molly said. "Let's eat; lunch is ready."

As they walked to the table, Sara pulled on Aimee Louise's shirt. "Thank you, brave, smart Aimee Louise." She curtsied.

Aimee Louise said, "You're welcome, bright, shiny Sara."

Molly smiled. "Sara will have her bright, shiny cloud again when we get her some glasses."

Later in the day, Stuart showed up at the farm with a dozen pairs of glasses.

"I went to the head librarian's house; she was excited someone could use the glasses they've been saving. She and I went to the library, and she sent all the glasses that might fit a child."

"I'll take back the glasses we don't need," the sheriff said. "Thanks again for all your help."

"Sure. I better get back."

"Water?" Aimee Louise asked.

"That would be great, Aimee Louise. Thanks."

Aimee Louise returned from the kitchen with a glass of water. Stuart sipped his water and watched Sara's process of selecting a pair of glasses.

Sara lined the glasses up by the color of the frames. She tried on shiny silver frames first and looked at a page with different sizes of print. She pointed with a big smile to the fine print at the bottom of the page.

"Shiny, bright cloud," Aimee Louise said.

"Sara will only need the glasses for reading," Vanessa said.

"I want to wear them forever," Sara said. "I can see finer. I love them."

Molly said, "I may understand clouds a little better. Before Sara tried on those glasses, she wasn't herself. She looked, I don't know, not like Sara. When she tried on those glasses, her whole face lit up. Bright, shiny Sara. That must be the way clouds work."

"Maybe similar," Rosalie said. "We don't have anyone who can see both faces and clouds, so we can only surmise."

Major smiled. "My scientist."

"Yes, she is," Molly said, "and a good one too."

Stuart peered into his empty glass. "Guess I better get back. Thanks again for the water, Aimee Louise."

Aimee Louise cocked her head. "You're welcome."

Stuart handed his glass to Aimee Louise, grinned, and left.

Major scowled. Molly raised her eyebrows at the sheriff, and he shrugged.

## CHAPTER TWENTY-NINE

The week after Sara got her glasses, Aimee Louise and Rosalie sat at the radio, waiting for the hams to sign on.

"I think Stuart likes you," Rosalie said. "He's really cute, doncha think?"

"What?" Aimee Louise asked.

"Sorry. I just realized how dumb I sounded." Rosalie chuckled. "I do think he likes you."

"I like the deputies too," Aimee Louise said.

"It's not what I meant, but sometimes I forget we don't always see things the same."

The first ham signed on, and Rosalie grabbed her notebook.

The girls joined the adults during the morning coffee time. "We have a lot of news and rumors," Rosalie said. "One rumor says a hostile country or international terrorist group took down the electricity to blackmail the federal government for weapons. Another says the bad guys wanted their people in key government positions, or else they'd take down the rest of the grid."

Mr. Young shook his head. "Sometimes rumors have a basis of fact."

"The big news is there might be a major weather system headed our way," Rosalie said. "A strong hurricane went through Puerto Rico, the Dominican Republic, and Cuba. It brushed the Florida Keys, and the Gulf might be next. There's a lot of guesswork about where it will go and when, or if it will turn into a big rainstorm. The people who live near the Gulf talked about their seven-day plans."

"The first step of the seven-day plan is prepare," Major said. "It's that time of year. We need to look at our plans for a big storm."

"And the interesting news is that the rumor about the company that took its system offline for testing might have been true. There are reports about power being back on in a wide area. Statewide, one ham said, but he didn't name the state. Not us, obviously."

"My shift in town is today, but I'll visit Pastor John before I head in to be sure they know about the storm," the sheriff said. "I'll take Number 48."

"Can I go along?" Molly asked. "I'd like to get away for a bit. And not run."

The sheriff put his arm around Molly. "I'd love your company."

Vanessa rose from her chair. "You certainly deserve a little time off. Let us know what you planned for this morning, and we'll divide and conquer."

Molly and the sheriff left together on Number 48.

On his way to the barn, Major stopped by the garden to chat with Vanessa. "Mr. Young is busy with lunch, and Aimee Louise and Rosalie are in the middle of laundry. I'll be in the barn. I want to inventory my plywood and organize my tools for storm preparations."

"I checked on the young ones. Annie's with her rabbits, and the other three are at the chicken coops. All safe and accounted for."

Major and Vanessa heard Aimee Louise shout, "Inside!"

Everyone ran into the house.

Major heard a car coming toward the farmhouse. "Vanessa, take the children and Penny upstairs to the back bedroom, stay low, and take the shotgun and one of the farm radios with you. Mr. Young, get one of the farm radios and stand inside near a front window, but out of sight. Keep Vanessa informed about what you see. Aimee Louise and Rosalie, keep Shadow with you and stay with the third farm radio in the kitchen. Watch the back. Everyone, stay quiet and stay out of sight. No one's here but me. Got it?"

Everyone nodded and hurried to their assigned positions.

Major ran to the barn and drove the tractor to the front of the house. The racing dust plume careened down the road toward the farm. The driver stopped at the gate, stepped out and inspected the lock then climbed the gate.

After the man walked a few yards, Major shouted from behind the tractor. "That's far enough."

The man stopped. "Major, it's me; I came to see Rosie. I heard in town you had food."

Major didn't move. "Marty, are you alone?"

Marty glanced back at the car. "I've got some friends with me."

Major frowned. "What do you need?"

Marty shuffled his feet and scratched and picked at his face. "Some food and to see Jolene's daughter. Maybe take her with me; I'm sure she misses me. Maybe her friend, Amber, I think that's her name, would like to come too."

Major's jaw tightened. He took in a breath and blew out slowly. "I'm almost out of food. Drought hit, then raiders came through here. I have enough for today, and that's it. I was about to leave to go hunting. Do you hunt, Marty?" He raised the deer rifle he'd held low.

Marty's eyes widened. "No."

Major nodded and kept the deer rifle in position. "Rosalie's not here. She and my granddaughter have gone to a farm north of here."

Marty glanced back at the car and shook his head. "No girls? Did Rosalie leave her stuff here? Did she leave anything for me?"

His eyes narrowed, but Major kept his voice even. "No, no girls. She took all her things with her; nothing for you."

"You sure none of Rosalie's things are here? Maybe I should look. She has something of mine." Marty pointed. "Hey, there's a chicken."

"That's Buttercup. She's my favorite. I've had her for three years. A good layer. You know how to butcher a chicken, Marty?"

Marty looked down and took a few steps toward the farmhouse. "Me? No."

Major raised his rifle, sighted it off in the distance toward the car, moved it in Marty's direction, and swung it back to the car. "Well, if there's nothing else. Nice to see you. Sorry it's under these circumstances. I need to get ready to go hunting. It might be good if you take your friends back to the city before it gets dark. This area has gotten a little rough, especially at night. I've got nothing."

Marty stopped, stood for a few minutes, and squinted at the chicken. "Well, maybe I could take that chicken."

Major held back a snort. "Have you ever caught a chicken?"

Marty's head jerked. "Me? No."

"You have to be careful. They peck your eyes."

Marty picked at his face, looked at the sky, and glanced back at the car. "Well, I guess I need to head back. Not easy driving here. Lots of roadblocks. I need to get back before dark, like you said."

Major kept his rifle trained on the car.

Marty turned and hurried down the driveway. He climbed the gate, got into the car, and had an animated conversation with his companions. He started the car, made a U-turn, and drove back the way he came.

Major pointed his deer rifle in the direction of the car until it was out of view. After he was sure the car wasn't returning, he took a deep breath and strode back to the house.

When he got inside, Major heard sobs from the back of the house.

He hurried to the kitchen. "What's wrong?"

Mr. Young stood near Rosalie. He turned and exhaled when he saw Major. "Rosalie heard Marty's voice when he got close to the house. She started toward the front door. Aimee Louise was behind her, but Aimee Louise saw Marty first. She grabbed Rosalie's shirt and said, 'Uncle Dan.'"

Rosalie hiccupped and sniffed back tears. "I was really mad. It was my dad."

"Danger," Aimee Louise said.

"Rosalie continued to the door," Mr. Young said. "Aimee Louise pulled her back to the family room. I told her to return to her post."

Rosalie nodded.

"I'm sorry, Rosalie. These are hard times, and your dad needs to straighten out his life," Major said. "You kept all the children safe because you stayed quiet and out of sight. You showed amazing strength and loyalty to your family."

"Thank you, Pops. I'm better now," Rosalie said. "I'm still mad at you, Aimee Louise."

Aimee Louise said, "No, you aren't."

Rosalie rolled her eyes. "It's not fair to check my cloud. I might still be mad. You don't know."

Aimee Louise said, "Okay. You're mad."

"No, I'm not."

"Is that what's called contrary?" Aimee Louise asked.

Rosalie giggled, Mr. Young chuckled, and Major exhaled.

Aimee Louise said, "Good joke."

"Agreed," Mr. Young said.

*I guess the joke's on me. I don't get it.* Major stepped to the bottom of the stairs. "You all can come down now."

After the children thundered downstairs and Vanessa followed a little more slowly, Sheriff and Molly walked into the house.

The sheriff said, "Pastor John and his family will take storm precautions. I'm glad we—"

Molly interrupted. "What happened here?"

"Let's finish up our chores," Vanessa said. She, Mr. Young, and all the children hurried out.

"Marty showed up with companions," Major said. "If I give him the benefit of the doubt, I'd assume Marty's original intention was food, but his companions entertained other ideas. He was really focused on something Rosalie might have, but if he'd come any closer, I would have punched him in the face and probably wouldn't have stopped there. I know how terrible it sounds."

Molly nodded. "I'm not sure I could have held back. How awful. Do you think Rosalie heard what he said?"

"I don't think so, but I plan to talk to her later. It was bad."

The sheriff growled. "I'll cancel my trip to town."

"I understand," Major said, "but we need to let the deputies know about the approaching storm."

"You're right," the sheriff said. "I'll stop there first, then go to the diner and talk to Pete. He'll put a note up on the board. I won't be gone long, though; we have work to do."

The next few days, Sheriff and Major boarded up the ground-level windows, leaving one window on each side of the house to allow for air circulation and a little light then moved the generators and tractor into the barn. Aimee Louise, Rosalie, and the rest of the children moved loose outdoor items into the barn while Mr. Young and Vanessa made the trailer as stormproof as possible.

On the evening of the fifth day, Rosalie said, "Do you smell it?"

"Smell what?" Vanessa asked.

"Tropical. It smells tropical."

Major said, "We may get bands of rain tonight."

"Birds," said Aimee Louise.

"You're right," Annie said. "The birds stopped singing. I didn't hear any birds today."

"They've gone farther inland or north," Mr. Young said.

The sheriff rubbed his chin. "Is there anything we need to do tonight in case the storm hits sooner than we expected?"

Josh said, "Recheck the goats."

Annie nodded. "Move the rabbits into the hutches in the barn."

"Move the chickens into the house," Sara said.

"No," Molly said.

Brett laughed. "Good one, Sara. We do want to double up the chickens' feed and water."

Molly mumbled, "This wild crowd is a bad influence. Making jokes; laughing."

"Let's go, Ts before we all get a timeout," Vanessa said, and they giggled and scurried out.

Mr. Young said, "Let's move the spare mattress from my trailer into the family room, in case I have to move inside quicker than planned."

The sheriff tapped his forehead with his fingertips. "Mattress. I almost forgot. Brad said they had a spare bed we could use. I'll go pick it up first thing tomorrow. Unless I should get it tonight. Major?"

"I think get it now," Major said. "Number 48 has headlights, but don't use them if you don't need them."

"I'll help Josh get the goats settled and take him along."

The sheriff and Josh moved the goats into their large shed, filled their water, and secured the door. They carried a large tarp and straps to Number 48, in case of rain, and hooked up the small trailer.

Sheriff and Josh were back within thirty minutes. They carried the twin mattress, box springs, and bed frame into the family room and placed them against the wall.

"Josh, your face is grimy and sweaty," the sheriff grinned.

"Moving a bed is hard work, but we did it together, didn't we?" Josh beamed.

* * *

When the children were asleep in their beds, the adults gathered on the back porch.

"The sky has the looming-storm look to me," Major said.

"I think we'll be fine if the storm shows up tomorrow," Mr. Young said. "This crew is a machine."

Molly stopped rocking and frowned. "If we get strong winds, I want the children to sleep downstairs."

"It'll be easy to move the cots, rollaway, and twin mattresses downstairs," Major said. "Just give the word."

"Thank you."

By early morning, the bands of rain started. Rosalie said that a few hams near the Gulf coast reported bands of heavy rain and wind gusts.

After lunch, Molly said, "Let's move the upstairs beds down here and set up Mr. Young's bed."

"Will do. Okay, team. Let's get busy," Major said. "It's the all-hands-on-deck move-and- make-beds project."

Molly directed. "Girls' beds in the master bedroom, boys' cots in the computer room, and the twin bed for Mr. Young in the family room."

After the girls' beds were set up, Molly brought in sheets for Mr. Young's bed, and Vanessa helped make it.

"We've boarded up most of the downstairs windows. We need to do something about this dreariness." Vanessa turned on the battery-powered lanterns in the family room.

"You're right. We need light in here." Molly lit an oil lantern and placed it on the stove.

Major strolled into the family room after he helped the boys move their cots.

"Did you see what we did?" Vanessa said. "The lights chased away the gloom."

He strode to the stove and moved the oil lantern to the dining table. "Not a good idea."

Vanessa frowned. "What are you talking about? It does a better job of lighting up the whole space sitting over there." She glared and reached for the lantern.

"The gas stove has a pilot light. If there a spill of oil into the stove, we'll have a fire."

Vanessa's face turned red, and she stomped to the bathroom and slammed the door.

*I won one.* Major frowned so he wouldn't laugh.

The family spent the afternoon reading and playing board games. Josh sharpened a pencil with his pocketknife and sketched farm animals. Vanessa sat with him. "Josh, your pencil drawings are excellent. That's Joanna and the stinky boy goat, isn't it? Well done. If you like, we can add art to our class time. I saw some books around here somewhere."

"I have the books," Josh grinned. "I'm most of the way through them. I like to draw. Mom said I got it natural. Dad sketched all the time. He was really good at drawing people."

By late afternoon, Major noticed that the sound of the rising wind bothered Aimee Louise despite the earflaps on her Laplander hat. She read, but she covered her ears with her hands and held her book open with her elbows. He brought out two battery-powered CD players and a collection of books and stories on audio CDs. He gave Aimee Louise a headset and a CD player. Her hands relaxed while she listened to the stories.

Molly and Annie made tortillas for the evening meal.

"My tortillas are tiny." Annie complained. "They shrink before I can get them to the stove."

"Takes practice. That's what mine looked like for a long time. They'll still be tasty."

Molly heated pork stew, and Annie opened the canned peaches Molly had put up in the spring. Annie set the honey on the table for the tortillas.

"This is my favorite meal," Josh said.

"No argument here," Mr. Young agreed. "Well done, Annie."

Annie beamed.

After they ate, Aimee Louise and Rosalie went to the computer room to listen to the ham radio. Aimee Louise held her hands over her ears.

Major and the sheriff threw on rain slickers and ran outside to check the house and the animals. They soon ran back in.

Major leaned against the doorjamb to catch his breath. "The wind. It's difficult to walk. Hard to see with the driving rain."

The sheriff dropped into a chair. "Five or six large branches on the ground, but no damage to any structures, so far."

"The hams say the storm is a hurricane. Nobody has any data about wind speed or size, but everybody agrees it's big," Rosalie said. "Most of the Florida west coast got hit, but it sounds like the worst of it is headed toward north Florida and south Georgia."

Sara's eyes widened. "That's us, Mommy. Right?"

Molly bit her lip, and Mr. Young jumped in. "Yep, that's us. But we're the readiest of the ready. We've got books."

The wind rose and howled, and the sound of the bands of rain hurled against the house was unnerving. Major brought out a box of earplugs and hearing-protection earmuffs. Aimee Louise put on a pair of earmuffs so she could read. Sara requested earmuffs and read too. Rosalie listened to an audio CD. The rest of the children played Monopoly with Molly, Vanessa, and Mr. Young.

"I love a good cutthroat game of Monopoly," said Mr. Young, "and this crew would make any cutthroat pirate proud."

Molly laughed. "You're right."

"Aarrrgh," Vanessa said as she took money from Annie for landing on her property. "Almost wiped you out, my sweetie."

Annie growled and wiggled her eyebrows. "I'll get you, Aunt Vanessa."

"Need to check upstairs for leaks. Need anything?" Major asked.

"I'll write up a quick list. Just a sec," Molly said. She handed her list to Major.

Major and Sheriff went upstairs to check for any signs of damage or leaks. Major checked the attic. *Good. Dry.*

"Here's our list. I'll grab the girls' things," Major said.

Sheriff glanced at the paper. "I can get the boys' things before I get what's in the bathroom."

Molly organized the washing up for bedtime, and soon all the children were in bed. Aimee Louise and Sara wore their hearing protection.

Molly checked all the children. "I was worried the kids wouldn't be able to sleep, but they're out. I guess all of us are exhausted by the hurricane."

Major inclined his head toward Mr. Young, who was asleep in the recliner. "The low-pressure system impacts us more than we realize. The animals acted skittish and nervous earlier, but they've settled down. Hunkered down, like we have."

"How long do you think this will last?" asked Vanessa, her anxiety apparent in her tight face.

"It's hard to say," the sheriff said, "but it might move faster than expected since it got here a day early. Then again, we don't know how big it is or whether it will stall. We'll have to see."

"I vote move fast," Molly said. "I'm ready for bed too. I am whipped."

"Major and I are going to take turns standing watch," the sheriff added.

"Mr. Young," Vanessa said in a loud voice, "Molly and I are on our way to bed. Good night."

Mr. Young woke up. After Molly and Vanessa left the family room, he climbed into his bed.

Major took the first watch. The wind sounded like waves of revving jet engines. He couldn't tell whether wind or rain slammed into the house. The relentless storm battered the farmhouse like an animal trying to claw its way in, and the monster storm continued its out-of-control rampage all through the night.

Major paced. *Hardest part is I can't do anything to stop the storm.*

* * *

The next morning, Mr. Young was awake and dressed when Molly came into the family room.

He poured her a cup of fresh coffee. "I woke up a couple hours ago and took over watch from Major." They drank coffee and listened to the howl of the wind and the onslaught of rain. It wasn't long before the rest of the household was up too.

During breakfast, Josh said, "Do you hear that?"

"What?" Molly asked.

"Nothing. The wind and the rain stopped."

Brett jumped up and ran to the back door. "Can I look? Can I go out?"

The sheriff opened the back door. He and the two boys went outside to welcome the sunshine that replaced the rain and wind.

Vanessa stepped outside and looked at the sky. "It's a long time since we've had a big hurricane here. This is almost eerie."

Aimee Louise and Rosalie rushed to the computer room, and Annie followed them. The rest of the family hurried outside to check for damage. After a few minutes, the three girls ran out.

Rosalie shouted, "Inside!" Everyone ran to the house.

"This is most likely the eye of the hurricane," Rosalie said. "The storm has started back up on the west coast."

"We can check the animals and give them food and water, but we probably have less than an hour. Maybe only thirty minutes," Major said. "Annie, after you feed the rabbits, come find me with your hammer. I saw some urgent repairs if the storm's going to hit us again."

"Brett and Sara, I'll help you with the chickens if you help me get some things out of the trailer," Mr. Young said.

Vanessa said, "I want to check the garden."

"I'll come with you then I'll help the Chicken Gang," Molly said.

Mr. Young, Sara, and Brett laughed.

"Watch out for the Chicken Gang," Brett said.

Mr. Young smiled. "We need to ask Rosalie for a Chicken Gang song."

"Be careful and stay away from trees," the sheriff said. "We don't know if we have branches ready to fall. I'll help with the goats, Josh."

"Annie, go help Pops. Aimee Louise and I will take care of the rabbits," Rosalie said.

* * *

Major and Annie repaired loose boards on one side of the barn and the fence around the goat shed, where a limb had fallen. "The wind's pulled the equipment shed door off its hinges," Major said. "I'll hold it in place, if you can nail it shut, Annie."

Rosalie ran to Pops. "The rabbits are taken care of. I can help you now."

After the goats were settled, the sheriff said, "Josh, help me drag limbs away from the house."

Aimee Louise fired up the tractor and pulled the larger branches away.

"We can drain these dammed-up pools of water around the chicken coops. Just pull the debris away," Molly said. Vanessa grabbed a shovel, and Brett and Sara used garden hoes to clear leaves and sticks. Mr. Young cleared a path with a rake to direct the water away from the coops.

The rain started, the wind picked up, and everyone ran inside.

"I thought the storm was over. I'm not sure I'm ready for more wind and rain so soon," Molly said.

"Let's play Sorry," Mr. Young said.

Molly smiled. "Sounds perfect."

"I'll get the board. Who wants to play?" Brett said.

"How about another game of Monopoly?" Vanessa asked. "I went out first yesterday. I need to redeem myself."

"I'd like to play Sorry," Annie said.

Josh, Rosalie, Sara, and Major joined Vanessa at the Monopoly board, while Mr. Young, Brett, Molly, and Annie played Sorry. Aimee Louise put on her headset and listened to a CD. The sheriff picked up the book on goats. Everyone found a morning activity.

The wind picked up even more. Soon the too-familiar, unabated roar of wind and the clamor of rain pounded the house, except the winds and rain came from the opposite direction.

The sheriff replaced Molly at the Sorry board while she made cornbread for lunch. She opened home-canned pinto beans and canned pears. By the time food was on the table, everyone was ready to eat.

"This is my favorite meal," Josh said.

Molly laughed. "I love how easy you are to feed, Josh."

"Somehow a hurricane stimulates the appetite. Wonder if it's the sudden drop in atmospheric pressure? Okay if I finish off the pears?" Mr. Young reached for the bowl.

After lunch, Major said, "I need to go upstairs to inspect for leaks."

"I'll check the attic," the sheriff said. After he climbed up and inspected the rafters, he called down to Major. "I thought the wind and rain were loud, but it's deafening up here. The attic's still dry."

Major relaxed his tensed shoulders. "No signs of water intrusion around the windows. I'll gather clothes for the kids."

When they came downstairs, they found Brett and Sara snuggled with Molly on the sofa while she read a C. S. Lewis Narnia book to them. Both Molly and Sara wore "ears," as Sara called the hearing-protection earmuffs. Mr. Young napped in the recliner. Annie, Josh, and Vanessa played Chutes and Ladders. Aimee Louise and Rosalie sprawled on the floor and listened to audio CDs with headsets on. Shadow and Penny wedged themselves between the two girls.

Everyone jumped at the deafening sound of a crash on the south side of the house as the house shook. Annie and Sara screamed, Shadow growled, and Penny barked. The sheriff dashed upstairs two steps at a time. Major hurried to the computer room to see if anything had crashed into the south wall.

The sheriff called downstairs, "Major, I think a large limb hit the house."

Another crash shook the house. The sheriff said, "It's another limb. The wind picked up."

Major rushed upstairs. The sheriff climbed up to inspect the attic. "I can't tell if there's any damage to the house, but the attic looks okay." As he climbed down, the house shook again with another crash. The sound of glass shattering and even louder roar of wind and rain rolled from the other end of the hall.

Major hurried to the boys' bedroom. The force of the wind blew sheets of rain through the broken south window. A large tree limb, angled toward the ceiling, rested on the windowsill.

Major yelled over the wind to the sheriff. "Get the shower curtain. And grab some towels." He pushed the tree limb out and away from the window and shouted downstairs. "Annie, bring me a hammer, nails, wood, and duct tape."

Annie dashed upstairs, carrying the tools, supplies, and wood scraps they had for the fireplace.

"Good thinking, Annie. I'll tape the shower curtain over the window, then secure it with the wood scraps."

The sheriff held the shower curtain while Major taped the top. Annie held onto the curtain with both hands. The strong wind whipped a corner of the curtain out of Annie's hands. She closed her eyes and put her head down to protect her face from the driving rain.

"We need a large board to hold the shower curtain," Major said. "It's ready to rip."

The sheriff grabbed a flathead screwdriver and the hammer, took the closet door off its hinges, and carried the door to the window. "Large board."

They secured the sides of the shower curtain, nailed the door over the window, and mopped up the water on the floor with towels. Annie ran for more towels. The sheriff took the towels to the bathroom and squeezed them into the tub. Major pulled the linens off the bed and discovered both the bottom sheet and the mattress were dry. After they got the floor as dry as they could, and all the towels and wet bed coverings hung up in the bathroom, they took their tools downstairs.

"You are all soaked," Vanessa said. "What happened?"

"A limb crashed through the boys' bedroom window," Major said. "We covered it to keep the rain out."

Vanessa put her hands on her hips. "Why didn't you call me to help?"

"Because I needed Annie. She knows where all the tools are and understands construction. She knew what to grab when I asked for wood."

"I'm not admitting you're right," Vanessa said. "But I wouldn't have known where to find anything and didn't understand why Annie ran to the fireplace. I couldn't imagine what you needed wood for. By the way, you three are dripping all over the floor."

They changed into dry clothes, and Molly hung their wet clothes in the downstairs bathroom. The wind continued to howl, and the rain hammered the house.

Brett said, "We got angry giants who pitch buckets of water at the house."

Annie curled up to Vanessa and shuddered. "This is a terrible nightmare surrounded by out-of-control trains headed toward you and not being able to wake up."

Sara looked up from her book. "It's a contest where gusts of wind try to outdo each other."

"Mr. Young, do you suppose we could warm up some hot chocolate?" Major asked. "I think we could use some comfort food."

"Sure can."

The twins clung to their mother, who sat on the floor and held them. Even though she wore hearing protection, Aimee Louise wrapped a pillow around her ears to block the sound. She and Rosalie sat on either side of Major.

Vanessa was on the sofa sandwiched between Annie and Josh. "I'm glad Annie and Josh keep me safe. I feel much better."

She returned Major's smile with a weak smile of her own.

The sheriff helped Mr. Young serve the hot chocolate and replaced Molly so she could begin cooking. When the sheriff hugged the twins, they relaxed.

Vanessa said, "Rosalie, would you please play your guitar and sing?"

Rosalie picked up her guitar and strummed. Annie moved next to Aimee Louise.

Molly opened jars of fruit and mixed dough for a cobbler topping. "Why don't you sing 'She'll Be Coming 'Round the Mountain'?"

Rosalie played her guitar and sang. The other kids joined in, and Aimee Louise hummed. They sang all the verses they knew, then Rosalie taught them a new one.

"Oh, the wind will blow my troubles all away. Whoosh! Whoosh!"

Everyone joined in, even the adults. The younger children and Vanessa waved their arms in the air with every "Whoosh."

The children and Vanessa sang while Molly and Mr. Young cooked. Major and Sheriff slipped out of the room to check other parts of the house for water intrusion.

When he returned, Major said, "Everything's okay."

Molly made a peach-pear cobbler then heated canned sweet potatoes and green beans. Mr. Young fried Spam because the crew agreed nobody fried it like Mr. Young.

Between forkfuls, Mr. Young said, "I love this cobbler. Do we have any ice cream left?"

Molly laughed and flipped her napkin at him.

After everyone finished dessert, Brett said, "This is Josh's favorite meal."

Josh patted Brett on the back and laughed. "Good one."

"You get the award for best joke of the day, Brett," the sheriff said.

"What's my award?"

"What would you like?" The sheriff looked at Molly and waggled his eyebrows. She snickered.

Brett replied without hesitation. "Pizza."

Molly laughed. "Okay, Brett. First chance we get, we'll have award pizza."

Everyone congratulated Brett on the exceptional award.

Mr. Young tapped his chest with his thumbs and rolled his eyes toward Sara. "Don't forget. Chicken Gang." Sara nodded in agreement.

Josh leaned over and rested his elbow on Brett's shoulder. "Brett, pizza is my favorite meal."

"Let's get cleaned up and ready for bed," Molly said. "Be nice to have time to read before bedtime."

"Mr. Young, do we have hot tea?" Vanessa asked.

Mr. Young opened his box of teas. "Your choice."

Vanessa relaxed with her cup. "Take that, Monster Storm. Green tea wins."

Major and Sheriff went upstairs to check the broken window and the attic.

"The floor is still dry in the boys' bedroom," Major said. "No signs of leaks around the windows. "All I can see is hard-driving, sideways waves of rain."

"Attic is still dry." Sheriff met him in the hallway.

When they came downstairs, everyone was waiting.

"Still dry inside. Raining outside," Major said.

Vanessa laughed. "I think you should leave the weather to Rosalie. Rosalie, is it raining?"

"There's a song for that." Rosalie giggled as she sang, "It's raining, it's pouring. The old man is snoring."

"I'm awake. I'm awake," Mr. Young said.

"Good one, Mr. Young. You can share in my award. First pick," Brett said.

Aimee Louise and Rosalie left to listen to the ham radio.

Major pointed at the Ts, as Vanessa called them, who were nodding off. "Molly."

"Bedtime," Molly said. The four younger children lumbered off to bed. All of them wore their "ears" to bed. Mr. Young took off his shoes, laid down on his bed, and pulled the sheet up.

"Good night," Molly said. "I'm going to bed too, and I'm taking my ears."

Aimee Louise and Rosalie returned to the family room.

"The Gulf Coast hams think their winds and rain have lessened," Rosalie said. "Everyone is worn out by the storm. Aimee Louise asked about damage, and some reported damage to windows, like ours. There were rumors of demolished mobile homes, ripped-off roofs, and overturned tractor trailers. Rumors for now."

"Thanks," Major said. "How are you two?"

"We're fine," Rosalie said. "Really."

"Family makes a difference," Aimee Louise said.

"We feel safe," Rosalie said.

"Safe," Vanessa repeated. "That's what I feel here too."

After the girls left for bed, Vanessa said, "I have learned so much from all of these children. They are amazing: strong, brave, funny, and brilliant. I want to be like them when I grow up."

Major nodded. "I understand; we are truly blessed to be in their lives. Shall I take first watch, Sheriff?"

"No, you go to bed. I'm not quite ready yet. I'm still a little wound up."

A few hours later, Major went to the family room, where the sheriff sat with the soft light of a small candle on the kitchen stove.

"No change; it's still loud. Good night, Major."

Major sat in the flickering light of the candle.

*I can't help but wonder about the Gastons and Russell's stepbrother, Lee. What did Lee say to make Russell change his mind? Why did Russell send his children away alone? Russell was always so cautious and wouldn't have allowed his children to cross a road by themselves, much less leave them on the side of a highway. He must have had a damn good reason. Margo was always protective of her children; overprotective. Margo wouldn't have agreed if she hadn't been desperate too.*

He flashed on the image of people on a train headed to a death camp, people who handed their children to strangers on the side of the tracks. He couldn't shake the suffocating feeling of desperate parents doing anything to save their children, even if it meant sending or giving them away.

*I wonder what their clouds would look like. Desperation? Anguish? I hope Aimee Louise never sees those kinds of clouds.*

"You okay, Major?" Mr. Young said. "Something on your mind?"

Major hadn't heard Mr. Young get up. He had trouble shaking off the feeling of parents' pain. "Yes. Just thinking about the Gastons and Russell's stepbrother."

"There were stories about Lee," Mr. Young said. "He'd gotten in with a bad crowd. Did you know him? He and Russell were stepbrothers, but they didn't grow up together. Russell's parents were African-American. I didn't know his mother. She died young. Russell was ten or so years younger than Lee. Lee's father was white, his mother was Hispanic, maybe Mexican. I'm not sure. Lee's mother divorced his father after he went to prison, and later married Russell's father."

Major nodded.

"I guess you know all the history," Mr. Young said. "Russell loved his stepmother and grew up in a loving household. I don't know about Lee. I did hear he was married with a couple of kids and then divorced. Those kids would be grown. I also heard he married again, but it's hearsay."

"I don't know why this was so heavy on my mind. You okay to take over watch?"

"Yep. I nap during the day. I'm good to go."

After Major left, Mr. Young started a pot of coffee then hid in the dark while he dressed.

While Molly and Mr. Young relaxed with their early-morning coffee, she breathed in the fresh aroma. "I enjoy our coffee and adult conversation before the onslaught of unlimited energy called *The Family* surges through the house."

She heard the sheriff and the two older girls stir. Molly poured the sheriff's coffee. The boys charged into the family room, and Vanessa and the girls followed.

"Morning has officially arrived, Mr. Young," Molly said.

While Aimee Louise and Rosalie listened to the ham radio in the computer room, Sara shared the details of her convoluted dream. "And then the fairy came and chased away the bad monster."

The two older girls joined the family for breakfast.

"The coast is storm-free," Rosalie said. "People have already assessed the damage. One ham said his trees were stripped bare—like toothpicks. Except most of his palm trees are fine. Others reported a lot of damage to vehicles and outside equipment. And, of course, trees and power poles. A few old barns down. This is the early assessment. And like one ham said, these are the people who were ready for the storm."

"Well, I'm ready for Sara's fairy to chase away our wind. Poof," said Vanessa.

"Poof," said Sara.

All at once, everyone came to the same realization: No wind, and no rain.

Molly laughed. "It's about time, Fairy."

They all ran to the door. The sheriff was the first one out.

"Sun," Aimee Louise said.

"This is beautiful," Vanessa said. "The weather has always been nice after a storm, but this is wonderful. Look at the clear sky. And no humidity. Amazing."

Sheriff and Major headed toward the barn and coops, and Vanessa and the children followed them.

Molly turned to Mr. Young. "Their breakfast is getting cold."

He laughed. "Ours too."

She took his arm, and the two of them stepped around debris to check the trailer.

When Major and Sheriff came inside, everyone else had returned to the table.

Major said, "We checked around the house. There's damage to the side of the house, but it doesn't appear to be structural. We've got quite a bit of work with the chainsaw to clean up those limbs and branches. We'll need to spend today, though, on a more permanent repair for the upstairs window."

"A large limb is across the top of the trailer," Mr. Young said. "Molly climbed up and inspected the roof, and it's dented, but we hope it's still intact. No water damage or leaks inside the trailer, but we don't know about inside the walls. We should move the limb and patch the roof."

"That's a priority for today," Major said. "Barns were fine. Equipment's good. Yard's a mess with debris, mostly trees and limbs."

"Chickens are fine. They were ready to be out of their coops, and they told me the storm was my fault," Vanessa said. "The coops are fine. A few limbs down, but no damage. The garden took a beating, but I think most of it will come back. We might want to put our shade cloth back up in the next few days. Our fruit trees may be done for the season. We'll see how they do."

"Goats and rabbits were ready to be out too," the sheriff said. "Only minimal damage to the farm structures from what I saw. We can complete the repairs in a day or so. I want to check on the deputies."

"We want to run," Rosalie said.

"Okay," the sheriff agreed. "We won't be gone long. We can get to work when we get back."

Mr. Young said, "I'd like to check on my house and Pastor John."

"We could take Number 48, and you can ride shotgun, literally," Vanessa said.

Major frowned. "I'm not crazy about the idea, but no argument from me. Makes sense; take a farm radio and a whistle. The radio range is only a mile or so. We won't hear you unless you are close, but at least it's something."

The sheriff, Aimee Louise, and Rosalie picked up their backpacks. Aimee Louise grabbed water, and Rosalie added dried fruit. Shadow positioned himself to run with them.

Vanessa slung her backpack over her shoulder, and Mr. Young put a few things in his pack. Rosalie gave them water and dried fruit.

After they left, Molly sent Annie, Josh, Brad, and Sara to feed the animals and clean the animal pens and chicken coops.

She said, "Stay together." Penny stood guard.

Molly found Major removing boards from the windows. "I think we'll hear chainsaws over the next few days, don't you?"

"Well, yes, I think you're right."

"So, a little more engine noise might be okay, right?"

"What are you thinking, Molly?"

"I'd like to run the generators. I want to do laundry with the washing machine and dryer. It will get everything caught up and won't be labor-intensive. While the machines do the laundry, we can get a lot of other things done."

"Good idea. Let me come with you to be sure there's enough gas in the generators, and I'll get them started for you."

They started up the generators for the well and washer, and Major made sure the generator for the dryer was ready.

"It'd be a real treat if we run a generator this evening for the water heater for showers in the house," Molly said.

"Good idea. It'd be a great surprise for everyone."

Molly stripped all the beds, gathered up all the towels to wash, and swept and mopped floors as she went from room to room. When the washer finished, she started up the generator for the dryer and tossed the next load into the machine.

After Mr. Young and Vanessa returned, Vanessa hurried to the kitchen while Mr. Young stopped to talk to Molly who had come outside to greet them.

"Vanessa has the jar of goat milk that Vicki gave us; we'll make pizza as a surprise."

"How did your house fare?" she asked.

"I'm pleased my house protected the families; the only damage was to a fence, and it was relatively minor."

What about the ride?" Molly peered at Mr. Young.

Mr. Young rolled his eyes. "Definitely room for improvement."

Molly chuckled. "Let me know if you need any help with that pizza."

The sheriff and the girls returned in time for lunch. "The house is fine, but the wind tossed the fifth-wheel," he said. "No one hurt. Stuart and Jim moved into the house before the storm. They'll need help righting the trailer to inspect for damage. I told them I'd be there tomorrow."

"I'll go too. We can take the tractor if it would help," Major said.

"Good idea. We could return the twin bed at the same time if Mr. Young's trailer is okay."

"I think it will be after we move the tree," Mr. Young said.

"Let's get organized," Molly said. "I'll move the beds back."

"We'll help," Rosalie said.

Annie added, "I want to help Pops repair the window."

"I can help the sheriff remove the limb from the trailer. I'd like to inspect the trailer and clean it," Vanessa said.

"I want to help patch the trailer roof," Josh said.

. "Me and Sara can fold laundry," Brett said.

"I'll take care of the evening meal," Mr. Young volunteered.

## CHAPTER THIRTY

The Board contacted The Boss through a neighbor. "I got a letter for you. Some guy appeared while I was fixing a fence. He said the letter was for my neighbor's son-in-law. That's you."

The Boss strode to a nearby shade tree, perched on an old log, and opened the envelope. The letter said that after Howie disappeared, the Board assigned an escort to go with the doctor to retrieve the missing information, but they failed; it was up to The Boss; he sighed. All his resources from back in the day were gone. "Back in the day," he said with a cynical chuckle. "Only a few months ago."

The Boss knew how damning the information was. Gaston wiped his laptop before he sold it, but Howie bought it, and The Boss recovered the documentation about the Board's partners and plans. *The Board doesn't know about the laptop copy or Gaston.* The Boss was certain the doctor asked Gaston to keep the copy on his laptop. If the information became public, everyone connected with the Board would be exposed.

*I'd give the Board what I got from Gaston and be done. But if it's incomplete, the Board would think I double-crossed them. Best to get what they want and keep quiet about what I have.*

The Boss watched the doctor's predictable downward spiral into drugs: first as a user, then as an addict, and finally as a small-time dealer and one of The Boss's best customers. The Boss was his primary supplier.

The doctor would have trusted Gaston because he was someone outside his day-to-day contacts of users and suppliers. Gaston was a do-gooder from way back. The Boss was lucky the doctor didn't know about his connection with Gaston. *Almost a direct line. Only a step away.*

The Boss didn't know where the doctor hid the information, but he did know where the doctor was. *Unless some incompetent, freelancing thug took out the one person who has what the Board wants.*

The Boss's old truck looked like it was on its last legs, but it was reliable and fuel-efficient. The hidden compartments were perfect spots to stash fuel, water, food, and ammunition. The sides, windshield, and windows were bulletproof. He looked like a bum while he traveled like a king.

*I'll stick to state highways and county roads. My old pals will steer me to safe travel routes.*

His wife fixed him a breakfast sandwich, and he left before daybreak. He popped his clutch to sputter and backfire when he thought someone might be close. Even with stops and detours, he expected to talk to the doctor by nightfall.

The Boss came across only one unplanned stop—a thrown-together roadblock of traffic barrels. He stopped and let them walk to him. He planned to wait until they got closer before he fired, but he recognized the leader.

He yelled out the window. "You sorry sack of redneck peanuts. Does your mama know you're off the porch?"

"Loser, is that you?"

The Boss stepped out of his truck. "The one and only."

His old pal Peanut walked to the vehicle, and his companions trailed along behind him.

"Guys, this is my old buddy, Loser. You must be on a job to travel through here."

"Yep. I've got a message to deliver."

Peanut nodded. "About two miles up, take the county road to the left. Some crazy vigilantes in the next town think everybody they see is the James gang."

"I should come back through here in the next couple of days. Will you guys be around? Anything you want me to try to bring back?"

Peanut rubbed his chin and spit on the road. "We could use vegetable seeds, if you can find any. We've got families, and we're okay for now, but the future's grim."

"I'll keep my eyes open."

"Thanks, Loser. Much appreciated."

The Boss took the recommended turnoff and continued to his destination with no further interruption. He drove to a small town outside of Mickleton and turned down a residential street, where the houses looked deserted. The Boss stopped at a modest-sized home at the end of the road and sat in his truck for a few minutes to give the occupants time to see him. He stepped out and strolled to the door with his hands low, but away from his body. He tried to look as nonthreatening as possible.

He waited a few minutes and knocked. The cheap paint was peeled and cracked on the side of the house. The downspout was separated from the gutter. *Typical druggie slob.* He snorted. No one had mowed the tall grass in several months. There were papers, cans, and other trash in the front and side yards. He tapped on the door and maintained his relaxed, casual posture.

Marty opened the door. His face was marred with dark purple and yellowish bruises and an open cut on his chin. His left eye was swollen. "You alone?"

"Yes."

"Come on in."

The Boss wrinkled his nose. The house reeked of old garbage, and the living room was cluttered with trash and discarded clothes. Dirty cups and plates contributed to the place's sour smell.

Marty limped to clear a chair. He dropped onto the stained sofa and talked about his troubles. The Boss listened and nodded at appropriate times.

"So what's your plan?" The Boss asked. "What do they want?"

"I should have asked you first—why are you here? What do you want?"

"I need some product. You must not have any, or you would have already told me. So I'm just here."

Marty nodded. "They want some information, but I don't have it anymore. It wasn't mine in the first place. I don't know what I was thinking. I thought it was insurance, but I was wrong. It'll kill me."

"Do you want me to get it for you? Where is it?"

Marty rubbed his face. "I don't know. If I give them the information, I'm dead. If I don't, I'm dead. But it doesn't matter, because I don't know where it is."

The Boss stared at the floor and waited.

"Here's the thing. I got this information. My insurance, you know. On a thumb drive. I hid it in a good place. Safe. My wife went to the hospital, and I couldn't find it. It wasn't where I hid it. My wife died. I practically tore the house apart. Still couldn't find it. I checked everything my daughter took from the house."

"Could your wife have put it somewhere?"

Marty scratched at his face and picked at a scab on his arm. "No. She was too weak to move off the sofa, and when she died, I searched her stuff at the hospital. Nothing. I went to see the girl, my daughter. I wanted to ask her if she knew anything about it, but the old man sent her somewhere else. I don't know where. I don't see how she could have it. She wasn't at the house at all. But, I thought—I don't know. She has this friend. I think she sees things. Maybe she can tell me. I don't know."

The Boss asked a few more questions. "I'll see what I can do." He heard a noise from the back of the house. "Who's here?"

"It's my girlfriend. She's helped me with my problem."

"Nobody else?"

"No. Only her and me."

"Okay."

The Boss rose and shot Marty in the head before he moved to the hallway. The girlfriend stood frozen in the bedroom doorway, her eyes wide with terror. He shot her. *Two down.*

He put on latex gloves before he went into the bedroom. He stepped over the girl's body and around the clothes tossed on the floor.

*Well, Marty, let's see how predictable you are. I'm allowing myself five minutes, and then I'm outta here.*

He found the drugs he expected on the cluttered bedside table. He chuckled and dumped out a black duffel bag he spotted on the floor.

*Medical stuff. Exactly what I'd expect a doctor to have thrown into a bag. Nothing useful.*

He put the packet of drugs into the duffel bag.

*Now for the toilet and the medicine cabinet. Marty did a good job with his clean, respectable façade for the outside world—I'll give him that. But he was a sloppy druggie when it came to his life.*

He removed the top of the toilet tank and pulled off the drug packet taped underneath it. He checked in the medicine cabinet and found prescription narcotics. He threw the pills and all the over-the-counter medicines into the duffel bag. *I'm sure he has more drugs in the kitchen. Freezer, oven, coffee can. But I've got other things to do, and my five minutes are up.*

He locked the front door behind him and strolled to his truck.

*Good choice of neighbors, Marty. They mind their own business.*

He knew where to find Marty's daughter. But first, Plainview. He parked behind a vacant building and walked to Marty's house. He picked the lock and let himself in the back door.

He searched each room, bedrooms first. He found more drugs and several pistols, but no ammunition.

The Boss snorted. *What was your plan, Marty? To scare people to death when you waved your gun?*

He searched the kitchen—drugs in the freezer and behind the refrigerator. He put everything he'd found into a recycling bag.

*I'm bored with this, Marty. Drugs everywhere, but no reason to leave all this product for some petty thief.*

The Boss dropped the cash from a computer desk drawer into the computer bag. He flipped through the printer paper and searched the trash. He unlocked the file cabinet and discovered partial printouts of Marty's information.

*This must have been what you showed to the Board. Big mistake. You can't be small time and take on big time.*

He stuffed the papers into the computer bag and completed his search. He didn't find any kid's toy on a thumb drive like Marty described. A unicorn. The Boss locked the door when he left.

Dusk rolled in, and The Boss drove his truck out of town and into a ditch. He got out and walked the road.

*Can't see the truck from the road from either direction, even if I walk with a flashlight and shine it toward the ditch. I can sleep tonight. So tired.*

He returned to the truck, unwrapped a sandwich, and gulped down a bottle of water. After he ate, he went for a short walk in the woods. He scanned the area, climbed into his truck, and fell asleep.

When he woke at dawn, he stepped out of the truck and rubbed his arms against the morning chill. The early morning fog lingered low to the ground.

*I need a short walk to work out this stiffness. I'm too old to sleep in a truck.*

After his walk, he returned to the truck for an energy bar and water.

*Being known around here might work in my favor. I need to grab the unicorn and get out. Easy in. Fast out. Kids are the answer. Kids are smart. They know stuff.*

The Boss walked into town to the diner. He didn't see anyone he knew. He looked at the lists on the board and walked to the tables strewn with barter items. Something caught his eye.

"Would you take a bottle of allergy meds for the seed packets?"

"Three packets? You can pick which three."

And the trade was completed. He wandered from table to table and listened to the talk, most of it about the hurricane and how much damage the town had suffered.

An old man at a table with hand tools turned to the man at the next table, which was loaded up with old camping equipment. "Did ya hear about Mr. Young's old wood and steel trailer, stood rock-solid in the hurricane at Major's farm, while the almost new fifth-wheel at the Gaston house flipped?"

"They just don't build stuff like they used to. Gimme an old truck or an old trailer every time. Were the deputies hurt?"

"Naw. They'd moved into the house with the rest of the deputies before the storm hit."

*Thanks for the information. Now I know where I can find the law if I need them. I'll bypass the Gaston property.*

He walked away from town and away from the road to the Gaston home and Major's farm. On the outskirts of town, he went into the woods and followed the power lines south. He knew the lines led to Major's farm. When he got close, he changed direction and headed toward the dirt road near the farm. He wanted to be where he could watch the house and the garden and chicken coops. He knew the farm.

*I haven't thought about Dad in a long time. My old man always said Major was a sucker for a kid. He said I got him out of a situation more than once, but when Major looked at me, his eyes seemed to see into my soul. He knew why Dad brought me.*

The Boss shook off the creeping feeling of doubt.

He found a comfortable spot with a clear view of the farm in the brush close to the gate, but not too close. After The Boss settled in and drank some water and ate another energy bar, he dozed, but prison had taught him to nap yet stay alert for sounds. When kids' voices woke him, he looked through the brush toward the chicken coops and spotted them—young girl and a younger boy. They were a lot taller than the last time he saw them, but he knew who they were. *Russell's kids.* There were several adults around; he recognized Mr. Young and the sheriff's wife, but he couldn't place the other woman.

Then he saw her. *Jolene. No, it's a young Jolene.*

Everybody knew Jolene. She was the town beauty even when she was a little girl.

*I never knew Marty married Jolene. There's Jolene Junior. That taller girl must be Ted's kid. Too bad it's Jolene's kid who has the unicorn.*

He took in their routine. The dogs were on guard and stayed close to the children. The border collie circled the children and reminded him of a shepherd's dog. The other dog, a German shepherd, maintained an alert stance. The Boss was a dog charmer and a master at exuding calmness. Dogs loved him. *Only two dogs. Good.*

When it was close to dark, everyone went into the farmhouse. The Boss stood up, walked to the road, fast-walked for the exercise, and returned to his spot. He had enough moon to see, but it wasn't a bright full moon. The Boss set up his one-man tent and zipped up. It was snug, which meant restricted movement once again, but at least he was safe from the onslaught of mosquitos. Later, The Boss heard someone walk around the house, chicken coops, and barn with a dog he assumed was the German shepherd. He heard them go back to the house, step up on the porch, and go inside.

*Late night check. I'll bet they keep a night watch, though.*

The Boss woke up at first light and groaned.

*Oh, man. I feel like I slept in a gravel pit on top of small boulders. It might be sand, but I swear I could feel each grain like it was razor blades.*

He unzipped his tent and crawled out. His back ached, and his legs were stiff. He went through the few yoga stretches he knew. He moved to a position where he could see the farmhouse without discovery and settled in for the day, drinking water and eating an energy bar.

While it was still early morning, he watched Major hook up a trailer to the tractor. Major and Russell's boy loaded up field fence boards and wire. The sheriff went to the barn. He drove a UTV to the house, and his wife joined him. Major went toward the Gaston house. The sheriff and his wife headed south, maybe toward Mr. Young's farm.

The Gaston kids and a couple of younger kids were all in the barnyard. *They must take care of the animals. Looks like my opportunity is now.*

He climbed the gate and headed toward the chicken coop.

The Boss was about halfway to the coop when the German shepherd rushed him. He stopped, offered his hand for the dog to smell, and spoke in his calm dog voice. "Good boy." The Boss expected the dog to be more docile, but all his limbs were still intact, so he was happy.

He took his time as he drifted toward the house. The dog stayed with him and eyed him warily.

*Smart dog.*

The Boss strolled to the barnyard. "Let's go see the kids, boy." Shadow stayed close.

Annie said in surprise, "Uncle Lee."

When Josh looked up and saw the man near Annie, he ran to join them. The three of them talked while Uncle Lee eased closer to Annie and Josh.

"Are you sure you don't know?" Uncle Lee said.

"Positive. We were supposed to come see you. Did you know that?" Annie asked.

"What was Dad like? Was he your best friend?" Josh asked.

"Inside!"

Annie, Josh, and all the children ran to the house without a word.

"What the hell?" Lee said to the dog.

The dog ran to the house. For the first time in a long time, Lee was confused. He didn't know whether to run to the house or run for the gate. In his indecision, he froze.

A man's voice came from the house. "What do you want?"

Lee lifted his arm to shade his eyes. "Who's that? That you, Mr. Young?"

"You can leave. Now."

A double-barrel shotgun pointed at him from the first-floor window.

"Okay. I'll leave. Tell me. Is everything okay here?"

"Go," said a woman's voice.

He trotted to the gate, turned, and waved. "Sorry for the inconvenience. Bye, kids."

Lee climbed the gate and walked north on the road. He continued until he was no longer in sight. He stepped into the woods and walked to town.

He shook his head. *How did I lose the element of surprise?* He never lost the element of surprise.

*I was close. It was crazy. Like a lion ready to leap into a herd of gazelles, but they all ran off at once. I did confirm the kids don't know anything about a unicorn. The Board's safe. I'm safe. Time to head home.*

Lee retraced his steps and stopped at the diner to refill his water containers. He looked at the tables again and saw someone had left a few sweet potato slips. They were small and dried out, and after he glanced around, he put them in his backpack.

When he returned to his truck, he ate and wrapped a blanket around his shoulders to sleep. He dreamed about a unicorn that laughed and chased him, and he woke in a sweat.

*I'm done with this. I need to be home.*

He headed home the way he came. He slowed as he neared Peanut's location. After he popped his clutch, his truck backfired and three men stepped onto the road ahead of him. He slowed down even more and stopped.

"Hey, peanut shell. Got your crackerjacks with you?"

"Ha. Ya always was good with the words, Loser."

Lee smiled as he pulled the items he'd brought out of his backpack and stepped out.

He strolled toward Peanut with the seed packets and sweet potato slips in his hand.

"Brought you something," he said.

"Got the unicorn?"

Lee turned cold inside. *How fast could he take down all three of them?*

He sighed. *Peanut first.*

Lee was lightning fast. They didn't see his gun when he fired until Peanut went down then the second guy went down. The third guy swayed as Lee dropped to the pavement.

The third guy's wound was on the right side of his upper abdomen, below his ribcage. He clutched his wound as it bled through his fingers and soaked his shirt and pants.

He staggered over to Lee to see what Lee still grasped in his dead hand. The man pried open Lee's fingers then snatched away the seeds and sweet potato slips.

"Thank ya, Loser," he said as he collapsed.

## CHAPTER THIRTY-ONE

Josh's face was red as he stomped his feet. "Aimee Louise, why did you call us in? You ruined it. Uncle Lee wanted to talk to us."

Annie glared and crossed her arms. "That was our one chance to talk to Uncle Lee. Now he's gone. It's not fair."

Aimee Louise sobbed as she shook. "Uncle Dan. Danger." Rosalie helped her to the sofa and sat next to her.

Rosalie said, "Three-banded, take a breath, Aimee Louise; everyone is safe. Annie, would you sit with Aimee Louise, please?"

"Okay, but I don't understand." Annie scooted next to Aimee Louise. "Sorry, Aimee Louise."

Rosalie moved to the back door to stand guard.

While Vanessa stayed at the window, Mr. Young remained at the front door. When Lee left the yard, Mr. Young headed out the front door with his hunting rifle. Vanessa kept the shotgun trained on Lee's path. Shadow ran in front of Mr. Young. Penny stayed at the front door to guard the children.

Mr. Young walked to the front gate and headed to a small hill for a better view of the road. Vanessa stayed back. When Mr. Young was satisfied Lee hadn't doubled back, he walked cautiously back to the house.

When Sheriff, Molly, and Major returned to the farmhouse, their eyes widened as they walked inside—the kids sat at the dining table with candy in front of them and empty candy wrappers on the table.

"What on earth? Where'd you get candy?" Major said.

"What's going on?" Molly asked. "What now?"

The replies tumbled over each other, "Uncle Lee." "Inside." "Unicorn." "Aunt Vanessa." "Shotgun." "Mr. Young." "Awesome." "Aimee Louise."

Major held up his hands. "Whoa, whoa. One at a time. Vanessa? Mr. Young?"

Vanessa sat at the table next to Aimee Louise. "Aimee Louise called *Inside*. Of course, we all ran in. Aimee Louise's reaction to the man in the yard was quite severe. I don't know how he got as far as he did without the dogs raising a fuss. He suddenly appeared and was talking to Annie and Josh."

"It was Uncle Lee," Annie said. "He acted strange, and he asked us about a unicorn. He walked to us with Shadow super close. I thought Shadow might attack him."

Josh added, "He said Mom's favorite toy was a unicorn, and he wanted to know if we knew anything about it. Like who had it. Totally bogus. Mom's favorite toy was the fluffy dog she slept with when she was little. I have Mom's fluffy dog."

"We told him we didn't know about any unicorn," continued Annie, "and Josh asked him what Dad was like when he was a little boy, but Uncle Lee said first we needed to tell him about the unicorn and who had it. I told him again we didn't know anything about a unicorn. Then Aimee Louise called *Inside*, and we ran. I wanted to talk to him some more. I wanted to hear about Dad and what he was like as a little boy too."

Josh mumbled, his head down. "Yeah. I was mad at Aimee Louise. Sorry."

"Rosalie was cool," Brett said. "She was the sentry at the back door."

"I didn't know that. Thank you, Rosalie," Vanessa said. "Mr. Young told Lee to go away."

"And Vanessa backed me up," Mr. Young continued. "We made sure he was gone and not coming back, at least not right away."

Sara put her hand up to hide her mouth filled with candy. "Then Mr. Young told us to sit at the dining table. Brett said it wasn't time to eat, but he didn't say anything else after Mr. Young dropped candy on the table."

"Hey, it's always time to eat candy," Brett said.

Major looked at the children. "So, does anyone know anything about a unicorn?"

Annie and Josh shook their heads. Major noticed that Rosalie stared at him. She picked up a pair of sewing scissors before she left the room then returned a few minutes later with a small rubber unicorn in her hand.

"When Mom was sick in the hospital. That last time I went to see her—" Rosalie choked then cleared her throat.

She took two breaths before she continued. "Mom told me she sewed a small unicorn into my winter jacket lining. I wasn't to tell anyone about it, especially Dad. She said Dad was sick and in a bad place, and I shouldn't trust him. She said I could trust Pops and Aimee Louise, and I would know the right time to talk about the unicorn and who to tell. She said it was a thumb drive Dad called his 'insurance.' She sewed it into my jacket the day she went to the hospital."

She handed the unicorn to Major.

Vanessa wiped away a tear. "Your mom was brave. And strong."

Major looked at Sheriff. "Let's fire up a generator and hook up a computer. I want to see what's on this thumb drive."

After Rosalie started the generator, Aimee Louise turned on the computer and inserted the thumb drive. Major and the sheriff sat on either side of her while she scrolled through document after document.

"Look at this," Major said as Aimee Louise displayed page after page of the files. "We have indisputable evidence on why the grid was taken down—and by whom."

Sheriff shook his head. "It's a study in reprehensible criminal activity and treason. Russell put a lot of time and research into this. These are prominent people, and the details are incriminating."

Major held his breath while he read. He breathed out with a loud sigh. "This little unicorn is a fire-breathing dragon."

The sheriff scooted his chair back. "We need to get this to someone we trust right away."

"What do you think about the special agent in charge of the state field office, Charles McNeil?" Major asked.

"He has a good reputation from an investigations standpoint, but I don't know him personally. The county sheriffs who know him speak highly of him."

"I knew Charlie years ago. He and I worked together a couple of times back in the day," Major said. "Sometimes people go sour over time. Great to know his reputation's still good."

"You know the state field office is over one hundred miles away. How do you plan to get the unicorn there?"

Major laughed. "I have no idea. Let's take it to the troops for a brainstorm. After all, we've got the best brains in the state in this house."

Aimee Louise copied the documents to her thumb drives.

Major gave Mr. Young and Vanessa each a thumb drive and called a family meeting.

"There is critical information on the unicorn. Remember Rosalie's mom said not to tell anyone until it was the right time?" Major asked. "Rosalie knew now was the right time. It's important we all remember Rosalie's mom said not to tell anyone about it. We won't talk about it among ourselves, and we won't ever talk about a unicorn with anyone else. Everybody clear? Everybody okay?"

Everyone nodded.

"Good," Major said. "Sheriff and I need to get this information to the right people, so we don't ever have to think about it anymore. We want to take it to an office almost one hundred miles away from here. We need some ideas on how to get there and back."

"You could use my old truck to drive there," Mr. Young said. "It has a full tank of gas."

"You could take Number 48," Molly said. "It's a little slower, but it might use less gas. It could go off-road if that's safer."

"My turn," Brett said. "You could ride bicycles. They don't need gas."

Josh stood and raised his arms. "My answer to any problem is pizza. In this case, you could have a relay of pizza-delivery drivers take it a hundred miles. But, oh, never mind. The tip would be ginormous." He frowned and sat down.

"You could ride horses," Annie said. "They are quieter than a truck or Number 48 and would go almost as fast. I'd go along and take care of the horses."

Sara patted Annie's shoulder. "Brett and I will take care of your rabbits for you while you're gone, Annie."

Molly opened her mouth to speak, but then saw the sheriff raise an eyebrow.

Major nodded. "We're tossing around ideas here. Every viewpoint gives a new perspective on the problem."

Molly closed her mouth and glared at the sheriff.

"You could run," Rosalie said. "Or walk and run."

Brett nodded. "I'd run with you. Maybe Sara too. We'd stash food and water along the way for the run back, like Hansel and Gretel. I think they were twins."

Molly put her hand on her chest and bit her lip.

"What about radios?" Major asked. "Seems like there would be a possibility there somehow."

"All the good ideas are already taken. What about a boat?" Vanessa said. "Are there any connecting rivers you could take?"

"For north and south, yes, but not west to east," Mr. Young said.

"Anybody know how to fly a plane? Maybe an ultralight?" Sara asked. "Can an ultralight go a hundred miles?"

"I know the answer," said Josh. "An ultralight is limited to five gallons of fuel. At the average fuel consumption of five and a half to six gallons an hour, an ultralight can go about sixty miles. With a tailwind, it might go up to eighty miles. With a headwind, maybe only thirty miles."

When Josh looked around and saw all the dropped jaws and incredulous looks, he said, "What? I want to fly an ultralight someday."

"Motorcycles," said the sheriff. "They'd take less of our gas to make the trip and back."

"Want a list of all the ideas?" Rosalie asked. "I wrote them all down."

"Sure," Major said.

"Okay. Here ya go. One, Truck. Two, Number 48. Three, Bicycles. Four, Pizza Delivery Relay. Five, Horses. Six, Run and Walk. Seven, Radios. Eight, Boat. Nine, Ultralight. Ten, Motorcycles."

"Eleven, Everything," Aimee Louise added.

At first, no one said anything.

Major scratched his head. "Everything?"

"Yes, of course. Everything, or at least the best from each," Rosalie said. "Aimee Louise, you are brilliant; I see it. We need to get it all on paper."

"I'm confused," Vanessa said. "I can't put the pieces together. How can everything be the answer?"

"Mr. Young, will you come too?" Aimee Louise asked while she and Rosalie left the room, and Mr. Young beamed as he rose and followed the girls.

"Let's finish up the morning chores, and I'll pull together lunch. We've got lots to do today," Molly said.

After Aimee Louise, Rosalie, and Mr. Young joined everyone else at the table for lunch, Mr. Young said, "We reviewed everyone's ideas, and we think we may have something later. Maybe later today. We do think any solution will depend on communication with the special agent. We're worried about the chores, though. Do we need to pitch in this afternoon?"

Molly said, "We've got it covered for today. Don't worry. We're fine. You work on the plan, and we'll take care of chores."

"I'll get in touch with Special Agent McNeil to let him know we'll pay him a visit," Major said. "He's a ham operator. I've heard him on the radio. I suspect he listens in every day like we do."

"Let's check the animals' and chickens' water and food," Molly said. "I think everything else can wait until morning, when it's cooler."

At supper, Mr. Young said, "After we eat, we'll explain our findings."

It didn't take long for everyone to eat, clear the table, and gather on the porch to listen. The adults occupied the rockers, and the children sat on the porch.

Mr. Young said, "We won't walk you through our entire findings. We have a lot of technical detail, but for now, we'll go through the highlights. We thought it would be good to give you till morning to think things over."

Rosalie raised her hand. "For the record, I was outvoted. I wanted to go through all the details."

Mr. Young smiled. "True. We did agree our goal is to deliver the data to the field office, and our priorities are speed and safety. We listed all the ideas and advantages and disadvantages of each."

"We saw two ways to travel. On the road and off-road," Rosalie said. "Because roads have a mapped travel route, we went with roads."

Penny flopped down between Josh and Brett on the porch. Sara and Annie moved to sit on the steps together.

"We saw two basic modes of travel—noisy and quiet," Aimee Louise said. "Because noisy or engine-driven transportation is faster and requires less physical stamina, we settled on noisy, which would not have been my first choice."

Major chuckled and nodded.

Mr. Young continued. "We compared the truck, Number 48, and a motorcycle by looking at the capacity of their fuel tanks, the expected range of travel on one tank of fuel, and the additional fuel required for the two-hundred-mile round-trip. By the way, this was my only contribution. The girls came up with everything else. Anyway, our assessment shows travel by truck would be safer and the most cost-effective, and the truck has the best capacity to carry the supplies needed for the trip."

Rosalie said, "Here's Aimee Louise's twist on the pizza-delivery and relay part—use radio communication with the four county sheriffs' departments between us and the field office. At a minimum, the sheriffs could direct the truck to safe roads and be available for help."

Brett pushed Josh and said, "Pizza delivery."

Josh reached to put Brett in a headlock, noticed Molly's glare, and put his hands in his lap. The sheriff and Major smiled.

Aimee Louise added, "But we recommend asking each county sheriff to provide an escort for the truck from one county line to the next, like a relay pizza delivery."

Everyone was quiet for a few minutes while they processed all the information.

Major cleared his throat. "I'm impressed. I never would have thought of half the things you mentioned. Sounds great; I contacted Special Agent McNeil, and he'll wait for us to let him know when we'll be at his office."

"I'll contact the other sheriffs to see if they can help us out, and I'll let our deputies know what the plan is," the sheriff said. "Major and I can talk about when we want to leave and what we want to take."

Mr. Young smiled. "We happen to have a list of supplies for the trip, if you are interested."

Major chuckled. "Of course, you do."

* * *

Early the next morning, Major talked to the special agent, and the sheriff spoke to the four county sheriffs and explained the pizza-delivery plan. All the sheriffs committed to at least one escort across their counties. The family loaded supplies, finished the day's chores, and planned the next day's workload.

At day's end, Major and Sheriff loaded the remaining supplies. Aimee Louise and Rosalie finished kitchen cleanup before it was time to listen to the radio. Molly, Vanessa, and Mr. Young rocked on the back porch while the children and dogs ran.

Molly sighed. "You know part of me wants to go with them to be sure they are safe."

Mr. Young laughed. "Yes, and the other part of you wants to stay here because you know how much trouble we get into when you're gone."

"Good point. I'll stay here."

* * *

When Major and Sheriff rose early the next morning, Molly had their coffee ready.

"Do you think we could have an in-hand breakfast?" Major asked. "I want to get on the road as early as we can."

Molly and Mr. Young made tortilla wraps of scrambled eggs and Spam.

Before Major and Sheriff left, Aimee Louise gave Major a small paper sack. "For Deputy Stuart and the other sheriffs."

Deputies Brad and Stuart waited for them at the road. Stuart said, "Hey, Sheriff. We didn't want you to leave town without a parade. We'll escort you to the county line."

Major talked to Stuart before they headed out. The four of them were happy to see the next county's sheriff and deputies waiting at the county line.

"Sheriff Starr, you know we expect a nice tip for this delivery, right?" one of the deputies snickered.

"No," another deputy said, "we need pizza."

"Got a question—does every deputy in the state know about Josh's pizza delivery?" the sheriff asked.

"Oh, no," said the first deputy.

The second deputy laughed. "Only the ones who read the email."

One or two deputies, a sheriff, and pizza comments met Mr. Young's old truck at each county line. Major chatted with each county sheriff, and Sheriff Starr thanked the deputies.

On the road before the last county line, the sheriff snapped his fingers. "Major, I remembered something. Remember Aimee Louise asked about a security camera for the storage place behind Jennifer's store? I contacted them the Monday before the outage. I heard back from them the next day. Their security camera saved the pictures to their hard drive, and they made a copy for me. As far as I know, my copy is still at the office for the storage place. Maybe we can find some time to get my copy."

"Too bad it's not on the way back from the field office," Major said.

The sheriff grinned. "I know, but we can ask our travel experts to plan another excursion for us."

They reached the field office close to noon. Special Agent Charlie McNeil and two other agents waited for them in the parking lot. The two agents wore jeans and T-shirts with their government IDs hanging from lanyards. McNeil wore jeans and an open collar white shirt.

McNeil said, "You made good time, Major. These guys will sit with your truck while we go inside."

The three men went into the building. "My office is on the fourth floor, but we've relocated on the first floor and kept the laptops charged. Let's see what you've got."

Special Agent McNeil inserted the thumb drive and reviewed the information. To give the agents a break, Major and Sheriff ate their lunch at the truck.

After almost three hours, Charlie walked out to the old truck and said, "We have a secure data line between field offices. I'll send this to all the field offices. This is the original, right? No other copies floating around?"

"That's the original. No floaters," Major said.

"Good to know there's no chance of any security breaches," Charlie said. "Each field office has an area of specialization. I think our best approach is to attack from every side. Thanks to you, we've got this."

The men shook hands, and Charlie said, "Thank you again. And safe travels. My guys will stay with you until your county escorts arrive."

Ten minutes later, Sheriff and Major were on the road with their county escorts.

"I'll breathe when we get home," Major said.

"No floaters, huh?" Sheriff asked.

"Not a one; not one dead body floating face down anywhere, and I don't want anyone to think there might be. I followed Jolene's instructions."

The sheriff laughed. "I thought it was brilliant. You've obviously been around Aimee Louise; you went literal. Well done, Major."

"I can't explain it, but something's off. Aimee Louise's influence, again. Don't tell her or Vanessa, but I wish she'd been here. Meanwhile, mission accomplished. We delivered pizza to the right people."

When they got to the second county line, no one from the third county was waiting for them.

"You don't have to stay," the sheriff told their escorts. "We'll be okay. I'm sure they'll be along soon."

"No, sir," the youngest deputy said. "We're staying. In fact, if they aren't here when you are ready to go, we'll go with you to meet up with your deputies. We'll expect their share of that pizza and a big tip."

The wait was short. The next group of deputies soon appeared and took a lot of good-natured ribbing about their lost tip. The caravan continued. They arrived at their county line in the late afternoon. Wally and Jim were waiting for them.

When they pulled into the farm, the dogs and Mr. Young waited at the gate, and the family was on the porch. As they drove down the driveway, the children jumped up and down then mobbed them with hugs when they got out of the truck. Sheriff and Major made their way into the house with difficulty.

Molly shooed the kids off the men. "Give them some space."

When everyone settled down, Major said, "What happened while we were gone?"

"Only chores. Everything is okay," Vanessa said. "I know it sounds incredible given our history, but it's true. How was the trip?"

Aimee Louise and Rosalie brought the travelers some water and sat on the floor along with the rest of the children.

Major gulped down his glass of water. "We didn't have any problems at all. The idea for road escorts was brilliant. We delivered the flash drive, and the information's in the right hands."

"I was glad it was a one-day trip," Sheriff added. "A little nerve-racking, but the road escorts made us feel like we were the Pony Express delivering the mail."

"Pizza Express," Josh said.

"You're right about that," Major said. "The famous Pizza Express."

## CHAPTER THIRTY-TWO

Early in September, Rosalie summarized the morning's radio traffic at breakfast. "There's a lot of talk about a big shake-up at the federal and state government levels. The hams concluded the rumors about a foreign government with plans to disrupt or take over the US were rumors. They said the big shake-up is because of the electrical outage."

A week later, Rosalie said, "The news this morning centered on weather, as usual. It's been dry everywhere too long, and everybody needs rain for crops and gardens. Weather and electricity. Rolling electricity showed up in more areas—the power goes on for a few hours every day or every other day."

Toward the end of the month, Rosalie said, "There are fewer and fewer hams on the regular daily updates. One of the regulars said everybody wanted to forget about the hard times and move on. When Aimee Louise asked what they changed, they said there was nothing to change. Everything's back to normal."

"Debrief," Aimee Louise said.

The sheriff raised his eyebrows and exhaled. "Aimee Louise is right. 'There's nothing to change. Everything is back to normal.'

Very haunting—gives me the chills. Those are the same words the city council said after the explosion. We always come out ahead when we plan for the worst and hope for the best."

"Why don't we relax after lunch and talk about what we did well and what we'd change," Molly said. "I'll bake killer brownies. After all, brownies are brain food."

The children erupted in excited cheers.

Mr. Young chuckled. "Well done, Molly. This crew is a well-oiled machine, and I think you found the magic oil."

## CHAPTER THIRTY-THREE

Special Agent Charles McNeil notified Sheriff and Major that they were recipients of recognition awards for their service during the National Emergency, as it was called. The two men were invited to the state capital to receive their much-deserved awards.

After a short discussion with Major, the sheriff called the agent, "We appreciate the honor, sir, but neither of us is prepared to leave our families quite yet."

"That's okay, Sheriff. I'll come to you."

* * *

Aimee Louise and Rosalie stood together near the side exit in the church hall, the largest meeting room in town. Aimee Louise counted the rows of gray-metal folding chairs as people chose their seats. The front and back rows filled up first. Uniformed men and women clustered in the back of the room and talked with Major and the sheriff. Major put his hand on Stuart's shoulder, and the two men stepped aside and chatted.

"I didn't know there were this many people left in our area," Aimee Louise said.

"You okay?" Rosalie asked.

Aimee Louise watched Rosalie's soft, upward-spiraling worried cloud.

She squeezed Rosalie's hand. "Lots of people, but I'm good here. I have space and a way to get out."

Rosalie left to find Annie and the others. A man walked in with several other men.

Aimee Louise's eyes widened, and she gasped. Her hands trembled, and her face grew hot. She was almost overcome by the urge to escape.

*That is the most massive danger cloud I have ever seen. Almost looks like a bubbling cloud of magma on the verge of eruption— impressive, in a terrible sort of way.*

She stiffened and lifted her chin.

Stuart appeared next to her. "Shall I stand with you?"

She glanced at him. *Protective cloud.*

Aimee Louise nodded and narrowed her eyes while the man shook hands with Pops and the sheriff. The three of them walked to the front together. Aimee Louise took in a big breath and exhaled; Stuart moved a little closer to her.

Rosalie waved to Aimee Louise to sit with her and Annie near the front. Aimee Louise shook her head and kept her position next to Stuart at the exit.

The room quieted, and the mayor spoke, and while he spoke, six Florida state troopers came inside and stood at the back. Aimee Louise didn't hear what the mayor said. All her senses focused on the man with the danger cloud.

Stuart leaned in so only Aimee Louise could hear. "Let me know what you need me to do."

Aimee Louise nodded.

The mayor said, "It is my honor to introduce Special Agent Charles McNeil."

The local newspaper editor, who was also the photographer and journalist, stepped up and took pictures of the mayor and the lava man, who shook hands while everyone applauded.

Aimee Louise swayed and said under her breath, "Whoa."

Stuart grabbed her right elbow and steadied her. "What is it?"

"Great Uncle Dan, cloud of magma."

Stuart held onto her elbow, then Aimee Louise watched as he motioned a signal to Brad. Brad stepped to the back of the hall and whispered to a state trooper.

Lava man spoke and presented Sheriff and Major with impressive plaques. More applause, then Sheriff spoke, Major waved, and it was over. Lava man, Sheriff, and Major stood at the back of the hall and shook hands with people.

Lava man walked toward Aimee Louise, and she tensed. Stuart rested his right palm on his belt, near his holster.

Lava man stopped in front of Aimee Louise. "I understand you are the one responsible for the unicorn and success of the Pizza Express, young lady. All our investigations are resolved and closed, thanks to you."

Aimee Louise swallowed and said, "Thank you." And she did her best to look into the boiling cloud.

After lava man walked away, Brad whispered to the sheriff, and the two of them joined Aimee Louise and Stuart. Major frowned and sauntered over.

"Major, why did McNeil say Aimee Louise was responsible for a unicorn?" Stuart asked.

Major growled. "He said what?" He clenched his fists and stepped toward the door but stopped when Stuart touched his elbow.

The sheriff narrowed his eyes. "We removed the unicorn from the thumb drive before we gave it to him. No one outside the farm family knew about the unicorn except for the thugs who tried to find it."

"Time for pizza slices," Aimee Louise said.

"Pizza Express—pizza slices. I think I understand," Stuart said. "Aimee Louise, you mean the thumb drives the county sheriffs and I got from Major, right?"

The sheriff frowned. "Major, is this what you meant when you said we delivered pizza to the right people?"

"It was a good way to get the drives to all the sheriffs without looking like that's what we were doing, and Aimee Louise's twist gave me the idea. Best I could come up with on short notice, but I didn't expect McNeil to be involved."

"The Board that Mr. Gaston talked about in his documents is headed by lava man, Great Uncle Dan," Aimee Louise said.

"Lava man is Special Agent McNeil, right?" Stuart asked.

Aimee Louise nodded.

Stuart continued. "He must have deleted the incriminating files before he sent the files out, but the county sheriffs have copies of the originals, and so do we."

The sheriff shook his head. "Hard to hear, but it makes sense. I was surprised when Charlie declared the case closed. Aimee Louise, you are brilliant, and Major, I see where she gets it from. Pizza slices. I'll call the other sheriffs together for a pizza party."

Aimee Louise said, "The details about the Board are on page 317 in Mr. Russell's document."

Major strolled to the back to join Brad and the state troopers.

* * *

Special Agent Charles McNeil stopped at the door. He turned to look at Aimee Louise. His eyes narrowed. *Strange girl. Doesn't look people in the eyes, but she seems to see something. Could she be a threat?*

The state troopers approached McNeil, and McNeil smiled. *More admirers. Probably want autographs.*

"Charles McNeil?" one of the troopers asked.

McNeil chuckled. *Star stuck fan.* "You can call me Charles."

"You're under arrest."

Two of the troopers stepped behind McNeil while the uniformed men surrounded him. After the troopers handcuffed McNeil, the group led him away.

Sheriff strolled to Major. "Are those troopers old friends of yours?"

"Yep. I could never shake the feeling I had when we saw McNeil and how much I regretted we didn't take Aimee Louise with us. On our way home, I asked one of the sheriffs to share his thumb drive with the right people, and when I heard McNeil was coming here, Mr. Young and I invited my friends."

## EPILOGUE—Jennie, Pedro, and Gordo

A week after the explosion at the substation, Alejandro's wife, Jennie, stiffened when he slammed the door and came into the kitchen after work.

Alejandro wrapped his arms around her familiar, ample waist while she stood at the sink. "Something wrong?"

"A loud man knocked on the door this afternoon. He said he needed to talk to Pedro. I told him there was no Pedro here, but he said to tell Pedro that Gordo would be back this evening to talk. He sounded positive this was the right house. Do you know a Pedro? Or Gordo?"

Alejandro stepped back. "What? He said what?"

There was a knock at the door, loud and insistent. Alejandro opened the door.

"Pedro," Gordo roared with a big grin. "I knew I'd find you. I need Team Three. I need my partner."

Alejandro sighed. "Come inside. We can talk."

Alejandro led Gordo to the room Jennie called the parlor. Jennie stayed in the kitchen to put on a pot of coffee and to finish her meal preparations. Alejandro knew that as far as she was concerned, anyone who entered her home was company, and she expected Gordo to sit down and eat with them. Gordo wiped the seat of his pants before he sat on the sofa.

*Gordo? How could Gordo find him, and why? And if Gordo could walk up to his door, so could anyone else. Time to move on. Fast.*

"It's like this. I have some property in the country, a farm in Kansas I bought years ago," Gordo said. "A couple rented it for a long time, but they retired. I'd like to go there and live. Grow a garden. Raise some goats, maybe cattle. I have some money set aside for the operation, but I need a partner to help me do the work. It's a large farm, and I can't run it by myself."

Gordo frowned and raised each foot to sneak a peek at the soles of his shoes.

Alejandro smiled. "You're fine, Gordo. You didn't track in any dirt."

*Gordo's still* un perro grande peludo*, a big shaggy dog, trying to stay out of trouble.*

"Thanks. I tried to wipe my feet good before I came in. My farm has a house and a guest house. I'd be happy in the guest house, and you and your wife could live in the big house. What do you think? We'd be our own bosses and live off the land. One thing I learned from our hiking is I like the country. Except for bobcats. I don't like bobcats."

Alejandro leaned forward. "I tell you—this is a surprise, Gordo."

"I think the little explosion was only a start. I think something big is on the way, and Kansas will be a good place to be. On a farm. Where no one knows us, and we can't be found."

Alejandro shook his head. "I don't know, Gordo."

"Let's ask your wife."

Alejandro laughed. "Well, that's the smartest thing you've said so far. If we are Team Three, then she's the brains of the operation."

Jennie called them to the dining room. When Alejandro saw each plate piled high with beans, salad, rice, and chicken, with sides of salsa and tortillas, he knew she'd spent the day preparing for Gordo's return. The coffee pot sat on the table.

When the men sat, Jennie bowed her head. Gordo dropped his chin to his chest.

Alejandro smiled and closed his eyes. "*Bendícenos Señor, bendice estos alimentos y bendice las manos que los prepararon. Amén.*"

Gordo said, "Amen."

Alejandro poured coffee into their cups. "We blessed the Lord and asked his blessing for the food and the hands that prepared it. Eat, Gordo."

Alejandro and Gordo grabbed their forks and dug in.

Alejandro knew Jennie approved of Gordo when she said, "Dessert is in the refrigerator."

Alejandro returned from the kitchen with three plates of *tres leches.*

After they ate, Gordo leaned back and patted his middle. "Thank you, Miz Jennie. That's the best meal I've eaten in a long time. Me and Pedro been talking. We'd like to know if you'd like to live and work on a farm."

"Gordo and I worked together on a project," Alejandro said. "We were a good team. Some said the best. He's always called me Pedro. I've always called him Gordo. He's a good man. A hard worker."

*Her mamá told me Jennie can see into a man's soul. Wonder what she'll see in Gordo?*

"He has a large farm, a house for us to live in, and a house for himself," Alejandro said. "Farm work is hard work, but Gordo and I would be the bosses. It's in Kansas, and Gordo thinks we should leave right away. I think I agree with him, but we wanted to know what you think."

She sat with her head down and her arms on the table. Alejandro held his breath, and so did Gordo.

"Gordo, I don't see with my eyes like other people do," she said. "It's a blessing to be blind, because I see more than sighted people do. I see you've had a rough life, but you're a hard worker and a good man. I grew up on a farm, and I like the work. My man deserves to be his own boss. We will be your partners. What do you want from us?"

"I want us to leave for Kansas tonight. Can you be ready to go in three hours? You can follow me. We'll drive most of the night, and we'll be halfway there sometime tomorrow. We'll take a break, then see how far we can go before we need another break. What do you think?"

"If my man wants to do this, we will do this. I will be ready in three hours."

Gordo grinned. "Okay, Miz Jennie."

Jennie smiled. "Okay, Gordo. Okay, Pedro. Let's do this."

ACKNOWLEDGMENTS

Huge thanks to my husband for his patience, support, technical expertise, and guidance. Every day is adventure and finds a spot in a novel, doesn't it?

Thanks to my faithful family and friends whose willingness to read, encourage, critique, and promote gave me strength when the shivery doubts crept in.

*Thank you for reading. You keep reading; I'll keep writing!*

Tell a friend how much you loved Major and Aimee Louise and leave a short review with your favorite bookseller. Authors can always use a few sparkles to brighten the gloomiest days.

PRO TIP: Post a five-star rating or recommend a book: both count the same as reviews!

Ready for news about what's next?

Subscribe to my not-your-typical newsletter via my website: https://judithabarrett.com

## ABOUT THE AUTHOR

Judith A. Barrett, award-winning author, lives on a farm in Georgia with her husband, two dogs, and chickens. She writes series for her readers:, post-apocalyptic science fiction, thrillers and cozy mystery novels. Stories with a twist: not your typical characters from not your typical author!

Her motto: *You keep reading; I'll keep writing!*

When she isn't writing, Judith is working on farm chores, hiking or camping with her husband and dogs, or rocking on her front porch while she watches the sunset.

Not into emails, even though Judith's story-focused newsletters are interesting Not Your Typical newsletters? Follow Judith on Bookbub or your favorite bookseller for news of her latest release!

Let's keep in touch!

Made in United States
Orlando, FL
19 March 2023